The Waymhete Trilogy

VOLUME 1

The Achilles Gene

N.E. Miller

Published by Clink Street Publishing 2021

Copyright © 2021

First edition.

ISBN:
978-1-913340-21-6- paperback
978-1-913340-22-3 - ebook

Acknowledgements

Nothing about computer viruses or spyware could have been built into this story without the help of Ed Skoudis, author of "Malware: Fighting Malicious Code" and "Counter Hack Reloaded" (Prentice Hall). The map of Jordan showing the location of Wadi Rum was prepared by Alexandra Miller.

My thanks are also due to Paul Manson BA for editorial advice, and to Irina Miller MD PhD for valuable suggestions.

The author

Norman Miller is a doctor and medical scientist. In the 1970s, he and his brother discovered the link between 'good' cholesterol and protection against heart disease, their paper on which became the most cited ever published in The Lancet. This important discovery was to form the bedrock of a distinguished research career in the UK, USA, and Australia.

He was the scientific adviser and presenter for two award-winning documentaries on the prevention of heart disease, and was an expert consultant to the biotechnology company that developed the first gene therapy to be approved for human use in Europe.

He turned to writing fiction when a Visiting Fellow and Waynflete Lecturer at Oxford University's Magdalen College.

He is a Fellow of the Royal Society of Medicine and Royal Society of Arts.

Chapter One

Giles Butterfield was not a man from whom other dons in Oxford University's Magdalen College had come to expect surprises or heroic exploits. As the Marchese di San Marzano Professor of Genetics for longer than he cared to remember, the maverick ways of his former years in Liverpool University had long since waned. In the great maritime city that had grown so close to his heart his adventurous spirit and disregard for convention had led friends and students alike always to expect the unexpected from their favourite boffin. But to the disappointment of those who had kept in touch, all that had seemed to have been left on Lime Street Station's platform one wet and windy October morning.

His move south had also affected him in other ways. In Flanagan's Apple or Kelly's Dispensary, his regular haunts of a Saturday evening, the sight of his stocky figure in the doorway, tossing his battered Barmah onto the coat stand or propping his umbrella against the wall, had always been a cause for celebration by those already on their first. But in Oxford's smart bars and bistros the banter and yarns that had been so in tune with the Merseyside character were now rarely heard. Only during his increasingly frequent trips to congresses would they return for the benefit of overseas colleagues and new acquaintances.

"You mightn't believe me," he would often quip after a glass or two in the hotel bar, "but inside Bishop Waynflete's crumbling walls, I'm like a re-corked bottle of bubbly, long abandoned in a fridge door. They all think I've gone flat, lost my fizz. But I haven't, you know. One day someone will leave that bloody door open…and pop…you won't be able to see me for froth. I don't know when, and I don't know why. But mark my words, happen it will."

He had never understood Magdalen's effect upon him. Perhaps the move south had been too late in life, or too soon after the death of Hillary, his beloved wife of more than twenty years. But he did know it had started the first time he'd crossed St John's Quad from the Porters' Lodge to knock uneasily on the door of the President's Lodgings. He would never forget that moment, as he waited in the now-familiar Oxfordshire drizzle, listening to Sir Quentin Philpot's heavy footsteps on the lobby's cold stone floor. It was as if all the magnificent old buildings around him—the Great Tower behind, the Founder's on his right, the Grammar Hall to his left—were peering down in toffee-nosed indignation, wondering what on earth he was doing there.

His adjustment had been made all the more difficult by his disenchantment with so many of his new colleagues. This was particularly true of three elderly emeritus fellows, who would occasionally turn up for no apparent reason other than to chat on the lawns with Sir Quentin, shaking his hand graciously and patting him on the back like good old chums. He had never got to know them properly, always instinctively steering clear and viewing them with curiosity from a distance, as if repelled like opposite poles of a magnet. Having looked them up in the College's website, he knew their academic records were no less than one would expect. But why be so pompous about it, so irritatingly self-satisfied?

"How could such great minds", he would ask in moments of jaded cynicism, "once such rich loam for germinating forests of new ideas, now serve only as clay for cultivating laurels?"

They couldn't always have been like that…could they? By nature, academics are not in that mould. Perhaps Magdalen does that to you, he feared, and sooner or later he would join them. Heaven forbid!

Although conscious his attitude was irrational, and likely down to prejudice after so many years in the Northwest, he'd never been able to shake it off. Unreasonable it might be, foolish even, it nevertheless had become immutably ingrained in his psyche. And that troubled him. It also strained his relationships with other members of the College, unencumbered as they were by the same bigotry.

How often had he bemoaned not having heeded the advice of his brother, Conrad, now enjoying life as an executive of a computer security firm in Cape Town.

"For all your intellect and erudition, Giles," he'd exhorted during one of their tramps among the Drakensbergs, "you're not the Oxbridge type. Liverpool changed you. Deep down, you're a scouser at heart now, and you know it. For God's sake, man, stay put!"

But he couldn't stay put. He'd had itchy feet ever since spending his boyhood with their diplomat parents, as they toured the Middle East from one embassy to another, while Conrad stayed in his West Sussex boarding school with his rugby pals. If it had been any other college, he might have turned a deaf ear to Sir Quentin's overtures. But the lure of a life among Magdalen's manicured gardens, its quiet quadrangles and wisteria-clad cloisters, had been too strong to resist. And what dyed-in-the-wool academic would not have chosen to be a part of that peerless history of scholarship?

Even now, after so many years, he would gaze through the New Library's windows of a winter's eve, and picture the spirits of the College's greatest gathering on the moonlit lawn below. The scene was always pretty much the same. Ahead of the rest would be Erwin Schrödinger, the atomic physicist whose famous equation, framed in gold, hung over Giles's bedhead as a constant reminder of his own brain's limitations. Howard Florey, Australia's "lord of penicillin", would arrive next, chatting to his compatriot John Eccles, while that other great neurophysiologist Charles Sherrington listened attentively from behind. Peter Medawar, the immunologist whose work had paved the way to organ transplantation, would emerge from Longwall Street with Robert Robinson, the wizard of molecular puzzle-solving at a time when chemistry had been as much an art as a science. Alfred Denning, "the greatest judge that ever lived," would appear from the library itself in the company of Edward Gibbon, hugging a volume of his "Decline and Fall of the Roman Empire". Oscar Wilde and John Betjeman might squeeze through the High Street door in animated jocularity after a night in the Eagle and Child, followed at a studied distance by C.S. Lewis. And so it went on. But he needed more than spirits. He needed spirit itself.

It had not all been pain. Indeed, there were many things about the place that he cherished. His cosy office and adjoining reading room in St. Swithun's, entered from the wide archway that divides the building, were Sir Quentin's reward for a large donation Giles had secured from an Italian aristocrat. With windows on both sides ensuring the benefit of any sunshine on offer, and oak doors and walls of Headington stone uninterrupted quiet, they were a haven where he could work from dawn until dusk. A second bequest from a wealthy Russian, whose son he had diagnosed with a rare inherited disease, had given him the unique privilege of a small laboratory in the New Building, overlooking the Deer Park. Though cramped and rather poorly designed, it was adequate for his purpose and wonderfully convenient. These boons, along with his neat terraced house in Holywell Street, just a stroll from the College's gates, had kept him there in spite of everything. Like the old tweed jacket he was inclined to wear this time of the year, although it ill-suited him in many ways, Magdalen had been too comfortable to discard.

Though still cited in the top journals, his celebrated work on poxviruses was now behind him. At the behest of the Marchese, whose sister had died of leukaemia, he had switched his research to cancer genes. Although this had been less successful, he and his young Scottish assistant, Fiona Cameron, were satisfied with their achievements nevertheless. Lately, with his retirement in Italy on the horizon, he had been leaving the practical work to her, devoting himself to teaching the students, his autobiography, and his sideline of medical journalism.

He had been a regular contributor to The Oxford Times ever since impressing the editor, a distant relative, with a short article on stem cells. His latest piece was about the recent announcement in Stockholm that the next Nobel Prize in Physiology or Medicine was to be awarded to Dr Stephen Salomon, Director of the US National Cancer Institute in Bethesda, near Washington, DC. Having covered all the Nobel Prizes for the past eight years, he knew exactly what to do. An anecdote to stimulate the reader's curiosity would be followed by an outline of the subject matter in question. After that would come a biographical sketch of the Laureate, and finally a description of the breakthrough for which the great honour was to be conferred, usually with an illustration or two prepared by Fiona.

To date all his Nobel pieces had been about a field of medicine of which he was not an expert. Indeed, this was one of the things he liked about the job. For there was nothing he enjoyed more than a few days alone in the libraries, delving into the origin of an important medical advance. With the help of the Internet, he could have done most of it without leaving his desk. But writing about a Nobel Prize was something special. He wanted to go back in time, get close to the people involved, sense the thrill of discovery they had experienced as one stepping stone had led to the next. And the only way of doing that was to feel the print in his hands. Seeing a breakthrough paper for the first time in a long-neglected issue of a journal, dog-eared and dust-covered, in a dimly lit basement, its pages yellowing and musty, was always a moment of great emotion.

But this year it had been different. There had been no bespectacled ladies to harass at their desks, no stacks of creaking shelves to climb, no dust to sweep away with his handkerchief. For the field the Nobel Committee had chosen this time was his very own: the business of what goes wrong inside a cell to make it cancerous, senselessly multiplying out of control until it kills the entire organism of which it was once just a tiny part. On top of that, the winner was an old friend with whom he had spent a year of sabbatical leave. He had worked beside him at the laboratory bench, shared his coffee and doughnuts while debating politics in his office, even suffered a ball game or two. They had not seen each other for quite a while, but Stephen Salomon had remained a part of his life ever since.

As the article that had so impressed the Nobel Assembly had reported the creation of an artificial piece of DNA that promised to revolutionise the treatment of cancer, he had picked up his pen (for on these occasions he always reverted to handwriting) with a buzz of excitement. But as time went on, his mood had slowly changed. With great reluctance, he had started to suspect there was something irregular about his friend's widely acclaimed scientific paper. In fact, if his fears were right, it would be more than irregular; it would be the biggest case of scientific fraud since the Piltdown Man. After much anguish and soul-searching, he had come to the unwelcome conclusion that he would have to do something about it. And with Stockholm's big day now only five weeks away, there was no time to waste. But what should he do?

It had become obvious to all in the College, from the President to the gardeners, that something was bothering the old boy. By day sitting alone on a bench in the Fellows' Garden or University Parks, by night brooding in his office or aimlessly perusing shelves in one of the libraries, his mood had become a recurring topic of conversation. On his rare visits to the Senior Common Room, he would be disinclined to talk, eating little more than an apple and a piece of cheese, or a roll with a bowl of soup, before excusing himself with his customary courtesy. Later, in the Smoking Room, if he went there at all, he would sink into a chair with a magazine, picked up at random from the many on offer, and suck on a long-abandoned briar he had resurrected from his cottage, all the noisier for being empty.

"Giles is definitely up to something," the others would whisper over their cups. "Better leave him to it. No doubt we'll know sooner or later."

And how right they were! For on that bright and blustery

November morning, as he scurried from his office to catch the coach to Heathrow, his briefcase bulging and his crumpled trousers betraying a sleepless night, it would not be long before they, and the entire world, would learn the unimaginable story he was about to expose.

Chapter Two

By the time he had reached Gloucester Green bus station, panting and perspiring from the unaccustomed effort, the next coach to Heathrow was ready to leave. After struggling onboard apologetically and paying the driver, he made himself comfortable by a window and tried to relax while regaining his breath. But it was impossible. He was shaking from head to foot in a way he'd not experienced since a bout of dengue fever in Cairo many years ago. Perhaps he was about to have a stroke or a coronary, he feared. What with the unremitting stress of the past few days, hardly any sleep last night, and that final desperate dash, anything was possible.

After checking his pulse a couple of times, he turned his unshaven face toward the window to avoid the inquisitive stare of an elderly lady across the aisle. As the bus made its way down High Street, he scanned the familiar scene in the hope of taking his mind off the daunting task that lay ahead. But it did nothing of the sort. Instead, he found himself fixing every detail in his mind—a postman delivering letters to McDonald's, two students' bicycles propped against St. Mary's, a Yorkshire terrier cocking his leg on the steps of The Queen's College. It's as if he was creating a photographic record of a great historic event. And then it dawned upon him that that's exactly what it might be. After all, if he found that his suspicions were justified, he would have made history, wouldn't he? There would never have been anything like it in the history of the Nobel Prize. Over the years, a few winners had been found to have made major blunders, or to have been less than virtuous in one way or another, but what he had in mind was a very different matter.

On the other hand, if it turned out that Steve had done nothing wrong after all, the news of his own impending crime, which would inevitably leak out sooner or later, would be such an embarrassment to the College that Sir Quentin would surely have no alternative but to let him go. How many Magdalen dons had suffered that humiliation down the centuries?

As the College's tower disappeared from sight, he wondered what would be waiting for him when it next came into view. A line of cheering secretaries, gardeners, bursars, clerks, and maids to greet their returning hero, while the cooks made preparations for a banquet in his honour? Or only silent glances from those who had witnessed Sir Quentin's outrage at his sudden unexplained absence, and suffered the disastrous publicity that had followed?

Perhaps he should keep his nose out of it after all, he wondered. It was not too late to get off the coach and forget about it. The driver was bound to stop if he invented some kind of personal crisis at the approaching roundabout—the realisation he had left a suitcase on the pavement, for example, or that he'd locked his cat in the garage. But he'd been through everything a thousand times, hadn't he? For days he had agonised over the facts, the possibilities, the options, and the ethics, as objectively as he could manage and with a scientist's attention to detail. And he had made the only decision he could live with, hadn't he? That he owed it to medicine and to scientists everywhere to do something, anything, to get at the truth. That's what he had decided, and that's what he should stick to. And if he made a fool of himself or upset a few people in powerful places, so what?

Fortified with renewed resolve, he opened his briefcase and withdrew the students' essays on their latest laboratory class. Always conscious of her responsibilities, Fiona had been pressing him for his report for several days. If he didn't get it done before arriving at Heathrow, it would be too late. He was going to have plenty of other things to think about during the long flight ahead.

On this occasion, Fiona had taught them about DNA fingerprinting, the test used in forensic laboratories to trace the origins of blood and other bodily fluids through the uniqueness of each person's genetic code, the precise order in which four simple chemicals run the length of every strand of DNA. She had shown the students how DNA can be extracted from blood and then broken down into many tiny fragments by heating it in a test tube with enzymes from bacteria. After separating the fragments according to size by filtering them through a gel with the aid of an electric current, she had placed the gel under an ultraviolet light to reveal a pattern of bands resembling a supermarket bar code, the person's DNA fingerprint—each the only one like it in the world, unless they had an identical twin. Finally, she had given the students a problem to solve based on a collection of different DNA fingerprints, the topic of their essays.

Fiona excelled at that sort of thing. Her preparations were always thorough, with painstaking attention to detail. And Giles had never known anyone who could lecture with such clarity and captivating style. As he flicked through the pages, he pictured how impressive she would have been, standing at the head of the lab in her crisp white coat, her red hair held in a French plait to look "less glamorous", while she explained the complexities of molecular genetics in her mellifluous Western Isles brogue. If anyone could seduce a reluctant rugby player or varsity politician into the world of forensic science, it was she.

Marking essays had never been something Giles enjoyed. Examining the students in person was a different matter. Then there was the opportunity for discussion, for probing, for enlightenment, even humour. Quite often he would learn a thing or two himself, so well informed were some of them in the latest progress reported in the journals. It was a two-way process, which both sides enjoyed. But marking essays was a job he would invariably put off until the last minute, much to Fiona's exasperation.

By the time the ordeal was over and his report was completed, the coach was well on its way down the M40 motorway. At last he could close his eyes and let the gentle jogging of the vehicle and the warmth of the sun through the windows nurse him to sleep.

Awakening with a start as they came to a halt at Terminal 5, he hurriedly gathered his papers from his lap. After scribbling a note to Fiona, he slipped everything into a large stamped envelope brought along for the purpose, which he would drop into a letterbox in the departure lounge.

"Thank God for that!" he muttered to himself. "I'll give Fiona a call when I get there. Tell her what a splendid job she did. Now for a cuppa, and a bloody strong one at that!"

As he waited for the waitress, relaxing for the first time in more than twenty-four hours, he gazed at his boarding pass. A first-class long-haul ticket was a luxury he had never previously entertained. But he had convinced himself that on this occasion, it would be essential. He was going to need space to go through his cuttings, photocopies, diaries, and notes, while he recounted the facts of the case one more time. For he would need to be absolutely certain he had not overlooked or misunderstood a single detail before throwing himself into the perilous task he had in mind. A first-class seat was also the only way to guarantee he wouldn't be lumbered with intrusive or disagreeable neighbours. The agony of his last long-haul flight to Chicago, trapped between a talkative Texan on one side and an overambitious Mormon on the other, had left him with wounds that would never heal.

As soon as the 747 was above the clouds, he went to the washroom to shave and freshen up. Back in his seat, smelling of the airline's cologne, splashed liberally in the hope of disguising all evidence of his night in the office, his thick grey hair swept back and his moustache neatly trimmed, he loosened his collar and prepared himself to revisit the long days of suspicion, confusion, doubt, and anguish that had brought him to this point.

The events that would eventually make him a household name had started two and a half years ago with an announcement in The Times of the first of April. He opened his briefcase and rummaged through his cuttings to dig it out.

World class medical research centre opens in Jordan
James Wallis, Science Correspondent

In a crowded press conference in the Burj al Arab Hotel in Dubai yesterday, Professor Rashid Yamani, Director of Jordan's new Middle East Centre for Cancer and AIDS Research (MECCAR), which opened last week, predicted that his hand-picked team of scientists would return the Islamic world to the Golden Age of the Abbasids by winning the twin races to a cure for cancer and a vaccine against AIDS. He claimed that his research centre, the first of several to be funded by an anonymous Saudi prince, is the most advanced in the world. After showing a video of its lavish facilities, he......

Putting the crumpled scrap of newsprint to one side, Giles reflected on how upon first seeing the article he had assumed it was an April Fool's Day prank of the type sometimes played by British newspapers. But a visit to the official MECCAR website had soon made it clear this definitely was not a joke. The home page had included a relief map pinpointing MECCAR's remote location, alongside a photograph of a rocky mountainous desert. Close to the border between Jordan and Saudi Arabia, about fifty kilometres east of the Gulf of Aqaba, it was an extraordinary place in which to build a medical research centre.

Even without the map, Giles would have recognised the spectacular landscape from a trekking holiday he had enjoyed in his youth, shortly after his parents had been posted to Amman. Wadi Rum, the "Valley of the Moon" so familiar to Lawrence of Arabia, wild and desolate yet supremely beautiful, was unmistakable.

The next page had shown a satellite photograph of a group of low sandstone-coloured buildings encircled by a high wall in the Wadi Saabit valley, between the mountains of Jebel

Khasch and Jebel um Adaami. A newly constructed supply road could be seen stretching north, joining the campus to the tiny Bedouin village of Rum.

It was clear from the description that followed that this was indeed a remarkable research centre. To the envy of every Western medical scientist, photographs had shown vast laboratories with the very latest equipment, banks of supercomputers, luxurious offices, and lavish facilities for cell culture, genetic engineering, mass spectroscopy, and every other conceivable modern technology. The Bayt al-Hikmah Library, named after ancient Baghdad's famed "House of Wisdom", to which thousands of Greek texts in medicine, mathematics, and science had been transported from Constantinople for translation before its destruction by the Mongols in 1258, was a stunning piece of architecture. The Al-Andalus Residential Centre, celebrating eight centuries of scholarship in Moorish Spain, provided sumptuous apartments for the senior scientists so they would always be available for consultation by laboratory staff. The problem of an electricity supply had been solved by the construction of a concentrated solar power plant in the neighbouring valley. The entire complex was surrounded by gardens of Babylonian splendour, irrigated by fresh water from a purpose-built seawater greenhouse in the Gulf of Aqaba. It was astounding.

Middle Eastern scientists, mostly trained in the West, had been lured from far and wide by facilities that gave credibility to the centre's mission of returning Islam to the pinnacle of science. Unlike their opposite numbers in the USA and Europe, perpetually competing for grants to fund their work, they would have virtually unlimited funding on tap, enabling them to devote every minute to their research. The laboratories would function twenty-four hours a day, 365 days a year, with eight-hour shifts of technicians to ensure unbroken continuity around the clock.

The website had named Professor Rashid Yamani as MECCAR's Director. Born in 1953 in Zahleh on the banks of the Bardawni River in Lebanon's Bekaa Valley, where his family had an alfresco restaurant, he had moved to California after his father had won a green card in a lottery. After gaining a PhD in biochemistry at Stanford University, he had moved to Harvard as a research fellow, where he had shown himself to be a highly talented geneticist, soon becoming the country's youngest full professor of molecular biology. He had been persuaded to return to his homeland only when Beirut Arab University needed a new dean for its faculty of science. Under his skilful management, the faculty had gone from strength to strength, and it was from there that he had been recruited by MECCAR's search committee.

The website had also announced a sensational programme of travelling research fellowships. "With the objective of promoting cooperation in science between Islam and the West," it had declared, "one thousand Alhazen International Research Fellowships will be created to enable young Muslim graduates to study and work in the world's top research centres for cancer, AIDS, and genetics. Each fellow will spend five years in a carefully selected host laboratory, which will also be given a generous grant for the purchase of equipment and running expenses."

It was appropriate that such a prestigious and ambitious programme should be named after the man acknowledged as Islam's greatest scientist and polymath. Born in Basra in present-day Iraq in AD 965, Abu Ali al-Hassan Ibn al-Haytham had devoted his life to the study of optics, visual perception, mathematics, physics, and astronomy, in the process writing more than two hundred books and laying the foundations of the scientific method of enquiry. European scientists who were destined many years later to be profoundly influenced by his work included Leonardo da Vinci, Francis Bacon, Johannes Kepler, René Descartes, and Isaac Newton. During the two thousand years from Aristotle to Newton, there had been nobody to match him anywhere.

The twin announcements had stunned the medical world. There had never been anything like it. As no university or research institute in the West, increasingly dependent as they were on extramural funding, could afford to ignore the Alhazen fellowship programme, its website had been inundated with expressions of interest. Very soon a host of young scientists had been on their way to further their education and acquire the new skills that would eventually enrich Middle Eastern universities upon their return.

In a celebrated letter to The Times, a group of retired Oxbridge professors had expressed the hope that "the creation of MECCAR heralds the recovery by Islam of the spirit of the Caliphate of al-Mamun, when Madinat as-Salam (modern-day Baghdad) had been the most literate and enlightened city on the face of earth, and of Moorish Spain, whose scholars in Cordoba and Toledo saved Christian Europe from centuries of ignorance."

But such enthusiasm had not been universal among Western scientists, most of whom were in one or other of two extreme camps: those who ridiculed MECCAR as doomed to failure, and those who took it so seriously they feared it might diminish the standing of their own universities. To the former, the idea that "a bunch of upstart Arab rookies in the back of beyond," as one published letter had scoffed, "could compete with the know-how of US researchers and beat them to the breakthroughs was absurd." The other camp had disagreed and stressed the impact that massive funding could have on research. Success in the increasingly competitive world of academia requires more than know-how and experience, they had argued. It also needs the best equipment, the space to accommodate it, and the staff to operate and maintain it. It was no use having brilliant ideas if you did not have the wherewithal to go after them. MECCAR's staff would also have that most precious commodity of all: time—to read, think, experiment, and discuss. Western scientists had become bogged down in a quagmire of paperwork for advisory boards, panels, and regulatory bodies. Whichever way they looked, they were faced with guidelines, rules and red tape, forms to complete, committees to satisfy. Every cent of research funding had to be competed for through grant applications, whose failure rates were absurdly high. MECCAR's staff would have none of that, and their laboratories would never sleep. Rashid Yamani's predictions about his new centre had to be taken seriously.

When it had been announced that the construction of a second centre would soon get under way in an undisclosed location, politicians on both sides of the Atlantic had become concerned. Success in science and technology was an invaluable asset at election time. It was evidence of sound investment in education, the right policy decisions, prudent prioritising. If the Middle East were to have a renaissance in medicine and science, and MECCAR achieve its objectives, the impact on the prestige of their own research institutes and universities would be massive.

The pressure on the politicians had increased when The Lancet published a frank letter from Rashid Yamani. As the aircraft approached its cruising altitude, Giles took another cutting from his briefcase to remind him of its message.

"Sir,

Having received a great number of requests to visit MECCAR, I am writing to explain why this will not be possible in the foreseeable future. First, it would create a security problem. Our mission is of such importance that we cannot take risks with our intellectual property. It was for this reason that MECCAR was built in such a remote location. Second, its construction would not have been possible without the cooperation of both Jordan's Royal Society for the Conservation of Nature, and the local Howeitat, Zilabia, and Zuweida Bedouin tribes, who had expressed concern about the effects of excessive traffic on the local ecosystem. Wadi Rum is a protected area with many rare species: the black iris, red anemones, camel spider, and the Arabian sand cat, to name but a few.

I will take this opportunity to explain also our policy on the publication of our research, which is that no external communications will be released until we are confident of having made a major breakthrough. We believe that the traditional approach of publishing one small step at a time, each the subject of a single article in a peer-reviewed journal, is wasteful of time and resources. Our breakthroughs will be announced on dedicated websites. As details of our experimental procedures will be provided, universities everywhere will be able to confirm the accuracy of our findings.

I realise that these policies may be controversial, but we have considered them carefully and believe they are in the best interests of our institute, our research, and medical progress.

Professor Rashid Yamani MD, DSc
Middle East Centre for Cancer and AIDS
Research, Wadi Rum, Jordan"

To hide medical research behind closed doors was the antithesis of centuries of practice in academic life, traditions that Islam itself had fostered in Spain at a time when the rest of Europe was an intellectual wasteland. But it was the policy of posting research discoveries on a website, instead of the time-honoured procedure of publication in a journal after approval by independent referees, that had attracted more criticism. Rashid Yamani had later defended this decision by asserting that the traditional way of publishing research findings was flawed. In what had become a famous interview on CNN, he had declared: "The process is far too slow, and furthermore is vulnerable to bias, gamesmanship, time wasting, and intellectual property theft on the part of the referees, who are invariably among the authors' competitors. This would be particularly so in our case, as undoubtedly most Western scientists want us to fail. Furthermore, in spite of all the peer reviewing you do, all the criticisms and feedback, the nit-picking, the multiple revisions, the demands for more data, which can delay publication by several years, studies have shown that up to ninety per cent of scientific papers are never cited by other authors, and that about half are probably never even read by anyone. On top of which, Juan Miguel Campanario, writing in the American Journal of Information Science a few years ago, revealed that no less than twelve scientific papers that went on to win the Nobel Prize for their authors had been rejected by the editors of top journals before eventually finding a home. When MECCAR has a breakthrough to share with the world, it will happen promptly and without hindrance. I am sure that all our website reports will be highly cited in years to come. Indeed, they will become classics. About that I have no doubt."

Giles had watched the CNN interview while vacationing in Provence. Although he had conceded that many of the points Rashid Yamani had made were true, he had felt instinctively that his philosophy might be a recipe for disaster. Without peer review by experts in the same field, MECCAR's published work might be so flawed and contain so many errors that it would create only confusion. This had worried him, for he believed Islam had the potential to make a contribution to science equal to that of bygone years, and dearly wanted MECCAR to succeed.

"If they could do it centuries ago," he had said to his new friends as they toured the streets of Avignon, "with a library of thousands of books in Toledo alone, while the popes here were living in their ignorance, why not again? But I think they need to go about it in the right way."

The same evening, while the others tasted local wines in the hotel lobby, he had written a letter to Rashid Yamani. Making good use of the Arabic he had learnt in his youth, he had expressed his concern about MECCAR's policies but given his good wishes for the success of the venture. Not expecting a reply, he had been delighted three weeks later to spot a letter from Jordan among the mail that Mavis, his daily, had collected during his absence. To his delight, it had borne the news that, as a gesture of appreciation of his goodwill, Rashid Yamani had personally authorised one of the best Alhazen fellows to work his laboratory.

Unfortunately, Aram Abd al-Jabbaar had not been to Fiona's liking. From his very first day she had complained to Giles that she found him odd, not at all like any other scientist with whom she had shared a lab during her long and varied career. He was too quiet for her liking, too distant in his manner. On most occasions his only response to her attempts to chat over the bench, whether of a personal nature or about their work, would be little more than a gesture, his eyes remaining fixed on his glassware or notebook, or at the most flicking momentarily in her direction with a nod, a shrug of the shoulders, or a strange smile. So unfamiliar was his body language that at times she was at a loss to know how to respond. In most labs, everything from frivolous rumour mongering about the latest student-staff affair to heated debates about politics played their part in keeping the wheels turning. But Aram's presence had had a stultifying effect. Since his arrival, she and Francesca, the lab tech from Vigevano, had never listened to the radio so much.

And yet in other ways, he seemed eager to please—in fact, too eager. It was irritating. She didn't need him to open the door when her hands were wet, or to enter her office to steady the stool she was standing on to reach the top shelf. Nor was it necessary to remain in the lab most evenings to wash the day's glassware, wipe the equipment down, and generally tidy up. The university employed cleaners for that sort of thing. It was as if he desperately wanted to impress her, to keep her sweet. But why? He didn't really need her. His work was under Giles's supervision, not hers. And it certainly wasn't sex. She had wondered if he was trying to get her to trust him for some reason, without actually earning that trust. Was he preparing the ground for something, a big favour perhaps, or her support if he happened to get into trouble? And yet his seeming kindness and generosity had ring fences. His computer in particular was always out of bounds, no matter how urgently she needed to consult a website. Was he up to something? And if so, what could it be?

Giles had teased her about Aram many times. She was "too suspicious", "getting paranoid." But that was only on the surface. Deep down, he knew she was a better judge of character than he. She had shown that many times. And that *was* a little worrying.

***

Up to this point, the flight to Washington's Dulles airport had been blissfully smooth. After such a difficult night and hectic morning, he was wallowing in the unaccustomed comfort of his plush seat. He had never understood why so many of his colleagues disliked flying. For him it was therapeutic. For a few blissful hours, there could be no unexpected problems in the lab, no rejection letters from editors, no last-minute jobs dropped on him by Sir Quentin—and best of all, no tearful calls from his daughter in Sydney after yet another row with her brute of a husband. Every time the wheels left the runway, he could feel his muscles relaxing, his pulse slowing. It had been so even on this occasion, despite the risky job that lay ahead. Now that he was really on his way, the uneasiness and uncertainty he had suffered as the coach made its way down High Street had been replaced by excitement and enthusiasm. Even if his suspicions were to prove groundless, at the very least the episode would make a good chapter for his autobiography. And with that in mind, he decided there and then to keep a daily record, starting that evening in the hotel.

The Jefferson had been his favourite lodging in Washington ever since he had met Stephen Salomon there at the start of his sabbatical in the National Cancer Institute seven years ago. He looked forward to entering the lounge from the lobby, taking a table near the massive stone fireplace, ordering a cup of coffee and a few biscuits, and starting to work on his notes. With any luck a fire would be crackling and someone playing the grand piano. As he lowered the back of his seat and prepared to return to the job in hand, he wondered if Virgil, the tall, ever-happy African American bell captain, would be there to greet him with his broad grin, flashing eyes, and courteous manner. He hoped so.

***

The next episode of the story had taken place during the previous year's Pacific Congress of Clinical Oncology, held as always in the Hawaii Convention Center, at which he had been invited to chair one of the sessions. As it had been his first visit to the Pacific for many years, he had taken the opportunity to spend a few days before the congress relaxing on the beautiful island of Moloka'i. While sunning himself on Pap'po'haku Beach, he had tried to picture the paradise it must have been when Captain Cook had first sighted it, and how his crew, hungry, dirty, and weary after so many weeks at sea, must have felt as HMS Resolution, battered and burdened with barnacles, made her cautious approach. If he could go back in time and change places with another person, he had decided, it would be Joseph Banks, Cook's botanist—

adventure, companionship, the discovery of new worlds, new plants, new birds, new people. What an experience!

After the tranquillity of Moloka'i, the bustle of Oahu and the pressures of the congress had been difficult to take. By the time the final evening had arrived, he had been so overloaded with information from lectures, seminars, symposia, updates, and workshops that he had decided to forego the banquet in the ballroom and instead go for some fresh air on the rooftop garden, taking a glass and a bottle of wine with him from the bar.

He had been enjoying the fresh ocean breeze and the unfamiliar sounds of local birds and insects for almost an hour before deciding it was time to return to the Hawaii Prince Hotel, about a mile away, where he was staying. After offering the half-empty bottle to an elderly couple playing chess at a nearby table, he had made his way down to the lobby. Upon entering, he had been surprised to see what looked like preparations for a press conference. Curious to learn more, he had stopped to chat with the gathering journalists, but none had had any information. It was not in the programme, they had said, and there had been no announcement. It was all a bit of a mystery.

Within a few minutes, a black stretch limousine with darkened windows had arrived in the forecourt. A short, olive-skinned man with a heavy moustache struggled out, smartly dressed in a grey suit, pocket handkerchief, and matching tie. Without saying a word or acknowledging anyone, he had crossed the floor purposefully to adjust two projectors and a laptop computer that were waiting for him on a glass table. After taking a gyroscopic computer mouse from his pocket, he had waved it around to check it was working.

Assuming they must be in for something important, Giles had switched on the audio recorder of his smartphone, and propped it against the base of one of the indoor palms.

***

There was no way in which Giles could reach this point in the story without reliving every second of the stunning presentation that had followed. Struggling up from the comfortable position he had made for himself in the aircraft's reclining seat, he dropped his phone onto his lap and replaced the aircraft's earphones with his own.

"Ladies and gentlemen," the visitor had boomed with a confident smile, "good evening. I am the Communications Director of MECCAR in Jordan and am here on behalf of our Director Professor Yashid Ramani and Professor Ahmad Sharif, the chief scientist of our Laboratory of Molecular Oncology, to give you some wonderful news: the news that MECCAR has kept its promise, and already has a major breakthrough to announce.

"Just a few minutes ago, an account of this wonderful achievement was posted on a dedicated website: www.Achilles-Gene.net. I have come here from Jordan to give you some details of the great discovery."

Onto the large wall that separated the lobby from the exhibition hall, he had projected a video clip of hundreds of cancer cells rapidly multiplying out of control. Leaving it running, he had proceeded to give a brief account for the journalists' benefit of what had gone wrong with a single cell's chemistry to produce that situation.

"I'm sure all of you know that cancer is as much a disease of our genes as the blood-clotting disorder haemophilia, for example. But it differs from inherited conditions in two ways. First of all, it starts inside the nucleus of a single normal cell, any cell. Second, it is always the consequence of damage not just to one type of gene, but to several types. One is always of a type whose normal function is to make cells multiply during the growth and repair of tissues, such as after an injury. A second is of a type whose normal function is to do exactly the opposite, namely to hold cell division in check. In healthy cells, these two types work in unison, like the accelerator and brake pedals of a car. A cell starts dividing out of control when damage to the first type of gene makes it too active, and damage to the second makes it underactive. The accelerator pedal is now flat on the floor, and the brake fluid has leaked away.

"This would not be a problem, if there was a limit to the number of times the cell's descendants could go on dividing. But this is not the case. When healthy cells divide repeatedly, the tips of their chromosomes, the strands of DNA that carry the genes, get a bit shorter each time, until eventually they're too short for the cell to divide any more. It's as if the cells have run out of gas. But cancer cells never run out of gas. Why? Because they keep topping up those chromosomes, the consequence of damage to a third type of gene.

"The sort of damage I'm talking about is not unique to the genes I've referred to. It's happening to all our genes every minute of every day owing to the effects of molecules called free radicals. And the numbers are staggering.

"Let's work them out. How many cells are there in the human body? About 40 trillion. How many genes in each of them? According to the Human Genome Project, about 25 thousand. There are two copies of each gene, and each gets damaged on average about twice a day. So…how many times per day does one or another take a hit? Let me see."

Taking a calculator from where he had placed it by the projector, he polished its screen with his pocket handkerchief, and tapped in the numbers.

"That comes to four million trillion times a day. That's a lot of cuts and bruises! I'll leave it to you to work out what it comes to in a lifetime. Fortunately, our cells have ways of detecting when a gene has been hit, and of summoning special molecules that rush to heal them, like teams of car mechanics on call twenty-four hours a day. So, what's the problem then? Well, unfortunately as we get older, those mechanics get tired and sloppy, and more and more of the damage doesn't get fixed. As a result, by the time we are my age, every cell contains more than a million unrepaired injuries in its genes. That's the reason why I look like this, and not like I did when I was at university. Fortunately, most are in places that don't matter. But it's only a question of time, and chance, before one cell has accumulated enough damage in the wrong places of the wrong genes for it to start dividing out of control, in other words to become cancerous."

Replacing his handkerchief in his top pocket, he adjusted his glasses, and rubbed his chin pensively.

"If only our cells had a mechanism that would kick in at this point and save the day before it gets out of control. What a dream!"

He had broken off at this point to pace up and down, his hands clasped behind his back as if in deep thought, before stopping to turn towards the audience with a twinkle in his eye.

"Well, my friends," he had smiled, "in fact, it is not a dream. You see, the good news is that it is already a reality…or at least it will be very soon. For what Professor Sharif and his team in MECCAR have discovered is that all our cells contain a gene that *could* do exactly that."

As he had spoken, the first page of the website to which he had referred earlier had appeared on the wall.

**A GENE WITH THE POTENTIAL TO
KILL ALL CANCER CELLS**

THE ACHILLES GENE

Ahmad Sharif, MECCAR, Jordan

"MECCAR has discovered that each and every one of our cells contains a previously unknown gene with an extraordinary property — the ability to promptly kill the very cell of which it is a part should it ever change into a cancer cell. In other words, the potential to rid humankind of the scourge of the disease…forever."

He had then paused again to allow the muffled chatter among the audience to settle, before resuming in a more measured and sombre tone.

"Unfortunately, however, it does not do the life-saving job of which it is capable. For whenever a cell does become cancerous, instead of killing it, the gene does nothing… absolutely nothing. It remains inactive, a 'sleeping dragon' as Dr Sharif has called it — except, as you will soon learn, in a small number of extremely fortunate people who live in the desert some distance north of MECCAR.

"We have called this gene *Achilles*, and as I'm sure you will be intrigued by this choice of name, I will explain."

With a wave of his mouse, the slide had been replaced by one of Abraham Bloemaert's painting, "The Feast of the Gods at the Wedding of Peleus and Thetis."

"Most of you will know the story of Achilles, the son of the couple tying the knot in this famous painting that hangs in the Mauritshuis gallery in The Hague. One day his mother, Thetis, dipped him into the River Styx, knowing that every part that touched the water would be protected henceforth from injury. But the heel by which she held him did not get wet, and many years later, when Achilles was a young man, this led to his death in the Trojan War when Paris's arrow entered that heel. Achilles' entire body was vulnerable because a very small part of it had a fatal flaw. Well, unfortunately the gene that Dr Sharif and his team have discovered also has a flaw, one that leaves us vulnerable to cancer. If it were not for that flaw, we would never be afflicted by the disease. And that is why MECCAR has called it *Achilles*.

"So, what sort of a gene is it? And in what way is it flawed?"

***

At this point during the playback of the recording, the Boeing 747 hit a pocket of turbulence, dislodging his earphones onto the cabin floor. After picking them up, he thought he would remind himself of Bloemaert's masterpiece, and reached into the pocket of his briefcase for the copy he had printed from the website. As he admired its luminous oils, the First Class stewardess surprised him by arriving at his shoulder.

"Mmm! I must say, I like that picture *very* much," she oozed softly, her long hair brushing against his face. "You can almost feel that flesh, can't you?"

"Oh, hello!" Giles gasped, taken aback. "Er…yes…I suppose you can."

"Van Gogh?"

"Sorry?"

"I said is it by Van Gogh?"

"Ah…Van Gogh! Never did get used to how you Americans say it."

She smiled at him sweetly.

"Canadian actually, sir."

"Sorry. Never could tell the difference. Like Aussies and New Zealanders. No, it was by a Dutchman, who was…"

"I thought Van Gogh *was* Dutch."

"He was, yes, you're quite right. Sorry, I didn't mean that he wasn't. But he didn't paint this one here."

"He gave up after that, did he?"

"What do you mean? Why should he have given up after creating such a wonderful work of art?"

"I thought you said he didn't paint with one ear. I knew he'd cut one off."

Giles scratched his own, confusion written across his face, before realising what was going on.

"Ah, I see! Obviously, with all this engine noise I need to enunciate more clearly."

"You need to what?"

"I need to pronounce my words more clearly. What I actually saidwasthatVanGoghdidnotpaint…this…one…h…h…here."

Rocking with laughter, she dropped onto the arm of the seat on the other side of the aisle.

"Silly me! I thought he might have had nowhere to put his brushes after that, half of them anyway."

"Ha! I must remember that one. But now you've raised the subject, I can tell you that his self-mutilation didn't reduce his output at all."

"No?"

"No. In fact, between then and his suicide less than two years later, he rattled off more than two hundred paintings, including 'Sunflowers' and 'Irises.'"

"Wow! That's amazing! That's...er...about two a week."

"Quite. But what you're looking at was by Abraham Bloemaert, born about three hundred years earlier."

"Very interesting, isn't it? Was it common to get married naked in ancient Rome?"

"They weren't in Rome. They were in…"

"Very sensual too, isn't it?"

"You go for muscular types like Peleus, do you?"

"*Him*? No thanks! When it comes to men, it's brains, not brawn, that turn me on.

She's the one I fancy. Can I get you anything?"

"Cappuccino, please."

"No problem. The name's Vicky by the way. Ciao!"

As she continued on her way towards the galley, Giles replaced his earphones, closed his eyes, and returned to Oahu.

Chapter Three

The next page of MECCAR's website projected onto the lobby's wall had shown two satellite photographs of buildings in a desert. But this time they were not MECCAR, and the desert was not in Jordan.

"The picture on the left shows Israel's Dimona nuclear reactor in the Negev," the speaker had snarled, making no attempt to hide his disdain. "This monstrosity pollutes the air and the earth around it with uranium and plutonium. Condemned by Jane's Intelligence Review, experts predict it will eventually cause a catastrophe greater even than Chernobyl. But the Israelis have refused to close it down. Why? I'm biased, of course, but in my opinion it's because the only people living nearby are Arabs, the El-Ezazme Bedouins to be precise. These poor people are also perpetually exposed to what you see in the other picture: Israel's Ramat Hovav industrial complex, with its toxic incinerator and chemicals dump.

"Not surprisingly, the Bedouins in this region have very high rates of several types of cancer. This shameful situation gave Dr Sharif the idea that new insights into our natural defence mechanisms against cancer might be discovered, if a family could be found with no recorded case of the disease over several generations in spite of all that radiation. So MECCAR sent a team of field workers into the Negev to see if such people exist.

"They went to a village called Wadi al-Na'am. You won't find it on any map, as the Israelis don't recognise such Bedouin villages. But I can assure you it exists. And what's more, its name will soon be famous. Why? Because it was there that Dr Sharif found exactly what he was looking for. And here they are."

The next slide had shown a photograph of a group of Bedouins in traditional dress, some of them very old, standing in front of a large tent with a few goats.

"Here you see no less than six generations, the youngest being the baby in her mother's arms, and the oldest the lady next to them, reputed to be one hundred and eight, the child's great-great-great-grandmother. In spite of living close to the reactor since it was commissioned in 1963, not a single member of this family, living or dead, has ever been known to develop cancer.

"Suspecting they might have a unique cancer-fighting gene, Dr Sharif grew cells from biopsies of skin taken from several members and transformed them into cancer cells by exposing them to a papilloma virus and carcinogenic chemicals. To his amazement, he found that within a few hours every single cell had died. Furthermore, he found this was because they had started to produce a protein that had disabled their mitochondria, the 'batteries' in all our cells that provide energy from glucose. Dr Sharif never found this protein in cells from any other Bedouin tribe or people living in Amman. Only in cells from this special family...and only after they'd become cancerous, never before.

"At this stage, I think I should pause to take any questions."

The audience had been awestruck. It had been clear to all the researchers who had joined the event that this had been a brilliant piece of research of huge importance in the fight against cancer. For a minute or so, there had been only muffled conversations and expressions of amazement, until eventually an elderly Chinese professor had raised his hand.

"Perhaps I can ask the first question?"

"Please."

"What else can you tell us about the protein? What exactly does it do?"

"I can't give you all the details, but it has two parts. One part acts an enzyme that digests a hole in the walls of mitochondria, while the other part is similar to molecules you've probably never heard of called efrapeptins, which…"

"Efrapeptins? How fascinating! I'm a pharmacologist. They're found in a type of fungus. They're inhibitors of the enzyme ATPase in mitochondria."

"Precisely. That's how it exerts the killer blow. It starves the cell of energy."

"And the gene that produces it is your *Achilles* gene?"

"Yes."

"So, if we all have this wonderful gene, why doesn't it work properly in all of us, not just in those Bedouins?"

"Presumably they've got something extra the rest of us don't," an American journalist had shouted from the back row, "something that gives *Achilles* a kick in the butt at the right time. Right?"

"Correct."

"Do you know what it is?"

"We do indeed. As you may know, genes are not self-sufficient. They need other pieces of DNA to help them function. One type is known as an enhancer, but I'll call it a gene switch, because basically that's what it is. They turn genes on and off in response to chemical messages arriving from other parts of the cell. When *Achilles* evolved millions of years ago, nature didn't finish the job. It didn't give it a switch. And that's the way it has remained ever since…except in that Bedouin family. At some time in the past, a germ cell in one of their ancestors developed a mutation that created a small length of DNA, which by chance functioned as a switch for *Achilles*. Under normal circumstances, such a precious mutation would have slowly spread throughout humankind. But in this case, it didn't happen because the family has never inter-married with other Bedouin families. Their marriages have always been between cousins, a habit that is very common in Bedouins. And that's why nobody else has the switch. Unknowingly, they kept it to themselves."

"What else can you tell us about this switch?" the American had interrupted excitedly.

"It's a DNA insertion, in other words a small extra piece of DNA that became added to the chromosome, probably due to an error when a reproductive cell was dividing. It's well known that this sort of thing happens every now and then. In this case, purely by chance, it created the switch that *Achilles* had been waiting for."

The questioner had now stood up, waving his notebook in the air.

"I'm a correspondent for Hawaii News, and I'm trying to think of a way of explaining all this stuff to my readers. Do you think it would work to say something like this?

"As an analogy, imagine that the *Achilles* gene is a car engine. To start a car's engine, you need two things: an ignition switch, and a key that fits it. The extra piece of DNA is like the ignition switch; and a chemical that cells produce when they go cancerous is like the key. All human cells have the engine. And they all produce the key when they become cancer cells. But only those Bedouins have got the switch.

"Would that be okay?"

"I would say that's an excellent analogy."

"Thanks."

A tall lady with a French accent had asked if the protein had been given a name.

"Yes. We have called it *achillicidin*."

"What else can you tell us?" the Chinese professor had resumed. "What do you know about the structure of *Achilles* and its switch? And where is the switch located in the chromosome? We're going to need all that information when we get back to our labs."

With a click of his mouse, the speaker had projected a chain of small letters, snaking backwards and forwards across the wall.

"This is the entire sequence of nucleotide bases in *Achilles*—in other words, its genetic code. You can study it more closely on our website."

"And what about the switch? Do you have its base sequence too?"

"Yes, but I'm afraid I can't show it to you."

"Why not?"

"I am not allowed to. In order to persuade the Bedouin family to participate in this research, our Director had to pledge to the elders that we would never disclose the details of any unique length of DNA we might find in their cells. There is a legally binding contract about this, which if broken could result in the closure of our institute."

"Why?"

"As simple, poorly educated people, they didn't like the idea of revealing something so personal in newspapers around the world. After Dr Sharif had explained what his work might lead to, they were also anxious that copies of parts of their DNA might be put into animals for experiments, and eventually end up in other people. To them the mere possibility was horrifying. So, MECCAR gave them a promise of absolute secrecy."

"Forever?"

"Yes."

"But can't you get out of it somehow," an Australian had asked, "buy them new tents or a few goats?"

"I am afraid there is no possibility of that, sir. MECCAR is an exclusively Muslim institution. Sura sixteen of the Qur'an says we are forbidden to break promises. All promises have Allah as their witness and guarantor.

"And there is another reason. One day copies of their switch will almost certainly end up in gene therapies for cancer, developed for profit by multinational companies. That's little different from trading in human body parts, which is also forbidden in Islam."

"But genes aren't body parts!"

By now the speaker, not accustomed to such question-and-answer sessions, had been showing signs of irritation. He had looked at his watch, as if to send a message, before responding.

"No? Well, if they're not body parts, what are they? That's all I can say on that score, I'm afraid. I have no doubt many scientists around the world will now devote themselves to inventing an artificial switch for *Achilles* that does the job just as well, perhaps even better, than the Bedouin family's natural one. It may take them many years, but eventually somebody will get there."

"But surely you can give us a clue!" an irate German had shouted.

"I'm sorry. I can take no more questions. My aircraft is waiting, and I have a long journey ahead of me."

While the speaker had been waiting for a technician to collect his equipment, Giles had seized his opportunity.

"Before you rush off, sir, I'd like to comment, if I may. Butterfield's the name. It's well known that Bedouins are prone to developing inherited diseases on account of all those consanguineous marriages—rare forms of kidney disease and deafness, for example— but as far as I know, this is the first time it's done them any good. Fascinating!

"As you say, your great discovery opens up an unexpected route to a gene therapy for cancer. This is extremely exciting. But I'm puzzled as to why you didn't mention that some cancer cells are already known to commit suicide by a different process."

"You're referring to what's known as apoptosis?"

"Exactly."

"I didn't mention it because it's not relevant, sir. Obviously, it's not very reliable, is it? Otherwise we would not need congresses, like this one!"

"But why is *Achilles* much more reliable?"

"As I'm sure you know, apoptosis depends on several genes. When one of the them is knocked out, the whole system fails. *Achilles* is different. It's a single gene. We feel that's the likely explanation. But there may be other reasons. It's too soon to be sure."

Looking unconvinced, Giles continued.

"Er...I see. Okay, thank you. My second question concerns a practical matter. How did MECCAR, a Muslim centre in Jordan, get access to Bedouins living in an Israeli desert? Did Ben-Gurion University help you out?"

"No."

"But you took skin samples from the Bedouins to grow those cells. You needed permission to do that, and it must have taken a lot of organising, what with surgical instruments, sterile dressings, and so on."

"Bedouins have a special ceremony," the speaker replied, dropping his voice. "It's called *es-selkh*."

"Ah, yes, of course…when young boys have their … mmm… right! Well, the last thing I have for you is not a question, but a comment. As an Englishman, I'm sorry to have to say that I don't think *achillicidin* is a very appropriate name for the killer protein. You see, there's a convention for such words. In 'homicide,' for example, the first part comes from the Latin for 'man,' and the second part from the Latin for 'to slay.' In 'genocide,' the first part is from the ancient Greek for 'race.' See the pattern? What or who is being killed goes first. So, you'd expect *achillicidin* to be a person or a thing that kills people called Achilles…such as Paris or his arrow."

Giles had then proceeded to twist the sword.

"And I'm sorry, but I don't like the gene's name either. The expression 'Achilles heel' was coined by Coleridge to mean a weakness in defences. Your *Achilles* gene isn't exactly that, is it? It's something with a potential that cannot be realised. If you were so attached to Greek mythology, it might have been better to name it after an impotent chap, like Attis or Iphiklos."

Amid whoops from a group of American students who had just arrived, the speaker's patience had been exhausted.

"Thank you so much, sir, for the lesson in entomology. Now I really must go."

Giles had chuckled as he whispered in the ear of the pretty hostess at his side.

"I think he meant *etymology*, dear."

"No, sir!" the speaker had thundered from the door. "I meant *exactly* what I said."

***

Giles chortled as he switched off the recording and removed his earphones, dropping them into the pocket on the rear of the seat in front of him.

"Cheeky little bugger! Exercise in entomology indeed! What sort of bug was he likening me to, I wonder—a scarab beetle, regurgitating crap? Couldn't have been a stick insect, that's for sure!"

As he collected his fallen napkin from the floor, he spotted Vicky's black tights approaching. But it was too late to pretend he was asleep.

"Whatever that was all about, it must have been very funny," she said, smiling. "I've been watching you from the galley, peeking between the curtains. Here's your cappuccino. Sorry it took so long. The machine's faulty. But at least it's a nice big one in one of our special china mugs. After all, one is in First Class, isn't one?"

"Thank you, Vicky, very kind. While you're here, I'll let you into a secret."

He beckoned her to lend him an ear.

"There's really no such thing as a big cappuccino."

"What is it then?"

"You see, in Italian 'ino' at the end of a word means 'small.' So, a cappuccino is actually a small cappuccio."

"So what I've brought you is a cappuccio?"

"That's right."

"So that means a 'beautiful big baby' in Italian must be a 'bello bambo.' I must remember that next time I go to Milan."

"Er, well not…"

"Biscotti?"

"Thank you, but one will do."

"That's all there is. See, it says on the packet 'one biscotti.' They're from Naples."

"Naples, Florida, presumably! You see, my dear, plural words in Italian…oh never mind. Sorry, I have this tendency to nit-pick about words. They've always fascinated me, you see. It's one of the reasons I've always had a passion for poetry. My assistant in Oxford complains about it bitterly. She says it sounds patronising. My wife used to say the same, bless her. What do you think? Do I sound patronising?"

"You could say that, just a bit. Well, more than a bit, really! But it didn't upset me, don't worry. I like to learn new things. But I think it could annoy some people."

"Must do something about it. I've been saying that for years. Anyhow, now I should get back to work, I'm afraid. Might lose the thread otherwise. So, if you'll excuse me, Vicky, I'll pop these on again."

"Here, let me do it for you."

***

By the time the speaker in Oahu had disappeared behind the dark windows of his limousine, the journalists had scampered in all directions, leaving Giles alone with a handful of stunned academics. After collecting his smartphone, he moved to the glass doors to gaze across Kapi'olani Boulevard, while he considered the implications of the extraordinary presentation he had just witnessed. For the first time in many years, he had felt that the entire field of cancer research had reached a genuine turning point, one that would go into the history books. It was as if he and the rest had been struggling in a traffic jam along a country lane for hours, and then quite unexpectedly had come upon the entrance to a motorway. There would be no stopping them now.

He had been pondering how many of the pedestrians outside would one day have their lives saved as a consequence of MECCAR's great achievement, when an excited group of men and women in evening suits and gowns had come charging down the staircase towards him. Somebody had gate-crashed the banquet to announce the great news.

Press-ganged by a frenzied group of Australians, he had soon found himself in a bedroom of the nearby Pagoda Hotel, dishevelled and sweating, as one of them scrolled through the *Achilles* website on his laptop. By the time they had reached the last page, everyone had agreed that no breakthrough in cancer research had been more important. The race to an artificial switch for the gene was going to test the best brains in the field for as long as it took.

And what a contest it was going to be! Two things would be needed for success: the right sequence of nucleotide bases, the building blocks that make up the genetic code of every piece of DNA; and the best place to put it in the chromosome. It might take years to get it right, but the rewards would be enormous. Patients might then be cured by gene therapy—viruses hijacked to deliver *Achilles* and its new switch straight into the cancer cells. Once inside, *Achilles* would wake up, cause the cells to manufacture the killer protein, and within days the patient would be on the road to recovery.

The group had closed the meeting in unanimous agreement that MECCAR would soon be celebrating its first Nobel Prize. As it was then the middle of July, and the annual call for nominations always closes at the end of January, Ahmad Sharif would not be shaking the king of Sweden's hand in the coming December's ceremony. But there had been no doubt in anyone's mind that he would be doing so very soon.

Giles had reflected on the mixed reactions the Australians had shown. While some had been only thrilled by what it would mean for patients, others had been more concerned with the impact it might have on their careers. New budgets would soon be allocated to *Achilles* research by governments, charities, and universities. That would be good news for geneticists, for whom more laboratory space, equipment, and staff would lead to more publications. But what about research fields outside genetics, like diet, carcinogens, new ways of detecting the disease, and how antibodies can slow it down? If a simple cure were developed, none of that might be of such great interest anymore.

Even with their extra funding, one of the Australians had pointed out, geneticists in the West would still be at a disadvantage, as they would still need to waste precious time writing grant applications for a share of the pot, whereas MECCAR's team would have none of that to do. Ahmad Sharif was probably already well into the next stage of his research. If he played his cards right, he could keep his nose in front for many years. The only woman in the room had gone further.

"I bet all that stuff about a pledge of secrecy is a load of possum crap," she had exclaimed, wringing her hands. "I'm sure those bastards are keeping the details of that switch to themselves. Their next breakthrough's probably just around the corner. Blokes like us will be playing catch-up for ever."

"You couldn't blame 'em, Julie," a man named Wayne had groaned from under a pillow. "We all do it, don't we? If you've got something really hot, better keep it under your hat—if not that, throw a red herring to send the rest up a gum tree. Anything to keep ahead of the pack than let the cat out of the bag by putting your cards on the table. It's the only way to keep your head above water in this bloody rat race. Let's be honest."

***

Breaking off his train of thought to admire the clouds below the aircraft, Giles smiled at the thought of Wayne's master class in mixed metaphors. But there was certainly some truth in what he had said. Even some of his own colleagues in Oxford were known to have delayed publication of important findings, or drop a misleading comment or two during a congress, with the purpose of gaining an advantage over their competitors. If you were the only one who knew something important, especially if it was unexpected, or had information that suggested conventional thinking or a popular laboratory procedure was flawed, you could do yourself a big favour by delaying publication. And by doing it time and again, you could gradually extend your lead until a field was virtually yours. The information withheld might have been obtained at great cost and be potentially lifesaving, but it was undeniable that on occasions such considerations could take second place to personal ambition.

***

When the Australians had made a move for the bar, they had found Stephen Salomon slouched against the wall in the hallway. After following them to the hotel and up the staircase at a safe distance, he had remained outside the bedroom for fear of the reception he might receive upon entering. Nevertheless, through the half-open door he had seen the computer screen and heard everything. As they had passed by, giving him little more than a glance, it had been obvious that he was now a very different man from the one who had given such sparkling lectures during the congress. Drawn and pale, his hair untidy and his loosened tie knot skewed to one side, he had been staring ahead like a blind man waiting to be helped across the road.

Giles had been only too aware that his friend would take the news badly. For Steve, the urge to beat the next man was not something thrust upon him by his vocation; it was the only way he knew how to live. During his sabbatical in the National Cancer Institute, Giles had seen first-hand how badly Steve could be affected by this obsession. The news that another team had beaten his own to a discovery, or that the editor of a journal had been critical of his latest work, had invariably been greeted with anger, paranoia, or depression. On those occasions, the only option had been to leave him alone until he had recovered. But would he ever recover from this blow? This was not just a disappointment. There was also the humiliation of having been beaten by a fledgling institute that he had so often publicly derided.

As the last one to leave the room, Giles had stopped to put a sympathetic hand on Steve's shoulder.

"Hi, Giles," Steve had muttered in his soft Texan drawl. "I saw y'all, and just followed like a sheep. This is mind-boggling. I can't take it in. It's a nightmare. I'm the chief of the most important cancer research centre in the world, and I've been beaten to this thing by a bunch of Arab rookies in a desert."

"Don't forget they had the advantage of those Bedouins, Steve. In a sense, they were lucky."

"Nice try, Giles. But they won't see it that way back home. 'MECCAR found that tribe because they looked for it,' they'll say. 'That gene's been sitting in all of us, asleep, while millions of Americans have been dying of cancer. All you had to do, Salomon, was find it and turn it on.'"

"Tell them you didn't have MECCAR's money."

"You bet I will! I've been telling Congress for years we need more bucks; that money gets results; that it's not all about brains. But that's not the way the public sees it. Americans think people like me get enough of their tax dollars, and they expect results. So far, I've kept 'em happy. But now they'll turn on me like a pack of wolves. You'll see. And so will those stupid politicians. 'The whole world is laughing at the United States,' they'll shriek. 'What are you going to do about it, Salomon?'

"Go and have a drink with the others, Giles. You can't help me."

Giles had been almost lost for words. A few minutes ago, as he had studied the picture of the gene on MECCAR's website, he had reflected on how the letters zigzagging across the screen were as stepping stones towards the conquest of a terrible disease. But to Steve they were a serpent, writhing and spitting at him in mockery. It was a catastrophe—for his reputation, for his career, for his entire future. Americans had got used to their National Institutes of Health being world leaders in their respective fields. To learn that their dollar-consuming NCI had been eclipsed by an unknown team in Jordan would be crushing.

"It's important not to take it too badly, Steve," Giles had resumed as they slowly descended the staircase. "Many of us have been through things like this. Focus on what it will mean for millions of people. That's pretty important, isn't it?"

"But that's precisely the problem, Giles," Steve had retorted. "It's because it's so important that it's so important, if you see what I mean. This is not humiliating just for me. It makes the NIH and the entire United States look stupid. It'll take years for us to recover."

"Perhaps you can turn it to your advantage, Steve. It wouldn't be the first time a personal crisis had proved to be a godsend. Maybe the politicians will start giving the NCI more money, and before you know where you are, you'll be back in front again, where you belong."

"Yeah, that's a thought. In an hour from now there'll be the daily press conference. I'll tell 'em the only thing this business proves is that the NCI needs more bucks. It's not enough to have the best brains. You need the best equipment, and you need time— to think, read, be at the bench, analyse the data. You know, Giles, studies have shown that faculty in our universities spend literally half their time on paperwork— reports, grants, proposals, you name it. Ain't that stupid? If it wasn't for all that shit, they could get twice the amount of research done. That's two things the Arabs got right— money and time. That's how they got to *Achilles*, simple as that. I gotta get that message out, Giles. But first let's have a beer."

Giles had found a table in the bar overlooking the Japanese Garden, hoping the tranquillity of the view would calm his friend down. But it had had no such effect. Fidgeting and sweating, Steve had drummed the table with his fingers, his eyes fixed on the marble floor. He had looked as if he was heading for a breakdown.

"Perhaps this wasn't such a good idea, Steve," Giles had suggested, gently prising the bottle of Asahi from his hand. "You'll need to have a clear head for the rat pack, won't you?"

Steve had offered no resistance.

"I think you're right, Giles. Thanks. What I really need is a pee, and a few minutes on my own, while I get my thoughts together. Get myself psyched up. I don't want to make a hash of it. This is gonna be on front pages from LA to the Big Apple in the morning. God, think of it!"

Giles leant across to offer a comforting hand.

"Keep it in perspective, Steve. Give it to them straight. Refuse to take questions. And then for the next few days just tough it out like an errant politician. The spotlight won't be on you for long. Eventually, everything will get back to normal. Keep that prospect in sight. And remember, you've got nothing to be ashamed of. Nobody has done more for cancer research than you. They did it because they have the best facilities, the most money, those Bedouins, and a large helping of good luck."

Steve nodded as he struggled to get on top of the situation.

"Thanks, Giles. That helps. You're a great guy. And then when the ordeal's over, I'll round up my team. We need to have a plan in place before we get back to Bethesda."

"That's the spirit. If you don't mind, Steve, I'd like to be there…in the press conference, I mean. Is that OK?"

"Of course. You're welcome."

When he had entered the press room twenty minutes later, Giles had found it packed with journalists. Standing behind the back row, he had soon spotted Steve making his way to the platform, acknowledging nobody as he pushed through the throng.

"Hi folks," he had barked on reaching the rostrum. "Steve Salomon, Director of the NCI. I'm going to make a brief statement about the *Achilles* gene you've been hearing about and then go. As I've many important things to do, there'll be no questions. I'll keep it short and to the point."

Steve had gripped the sides of the rostrum, as he paused to scan the audience from left to right. He was looking better now, more composed, more confident. Giles had been pleased.

"Well, folks, today seems to have been a good one for medicine. If MECCAR's right, and of course we'll have to check it out, they've made a real breakthrough. I'm sure the big question you guys are asking is, 'How did they manage to do it? How come they beat not just the NCI, but the entire world?' There are three reasons. First, they had the money. Second, they had the time. Third, they had that Bedouin tribe. If the US had built a leaking nuclear reactor outside the Navajo Indian Reservation in the sixties and then given the NCI unlimited funding to study the consequences, I've no doubt we'd have gotten to *Achilles* first. But life's not like that."

After waiting for the laughter to settle, he had continued in the same theme.

"In fact, when you think about it, the Knesset should be given some of the credit."

As some of the journalists hooted and stamped, Giles had been amazed by Steve's transformation. It was almost too much, too soon.

Like a rock star acknowledging his fans, Steve had raised his hands to quieten the room.

"But joking aside, folks, there's an important lesson here. Great breakthroughs are rarely the result of genius. Sometimes it's an accident that does the trick; sometimes it's serendipity; sometimes it's just damn hard work. But there's no substitute for money. As the wealthiest medical research centre in the universe, MECCAR had a massive advantage. If the discovery of *Achilles* proves anything, it's that size matters—the size of your budget. At the NCI, we've got the best people in the world. My colleagues and I have made many, many important discoveries. Our record speaks for itself. But we would have achieved even more if our political masters had not ignored my pleas over the years. Some of you will know how often I've lobbied for more federal funding. But it always fell on deaf ears. I didn't discover *Achilles*, but I did learn something else about the natural world: when it comes to deafness and stupidity, there's nothing to choose between donkeys and elephants!"

He raised his hands again to quieten the laughter.

"Today's news from Jordan proves I was right. If my pleas had been heard, *Achilles* would be old news by now. And that's the message I'll be taking from this congress to that other one in DC. Thank you, good night, and God bless America."

By the time Giles had caught up with him in the corridor, Steve had been busy sending a text message to his team: "room 315, Ala Halawai Concourse, 30 min, everyone!"

"Can't stop, Giles," he had gasped. "See you later."

Steve had never told Giles what he had said to his team on that occasion. During breakfast the following morning, the rumours were of a heated exchange with a highly contentious outcome.

"If I know Steve, he'll do whatever he wants," one of them had remarked, anticipating the worst. "He's desperate, and with that guy, anything's possible."

The only thing on which everyone had agreed was that the Nobel Prize would soon be on display in Ahmad Sharif's office. Trying to improve the atmosphere, a girl from Yale had pointed out it was still possible for someone in the United States to share it. After all, it was common for two or three scientists to be honoured in the same year for work in the same field.

"I said to Steve in the powder room—he'd wandered in by mistake before meeting the press—that if he could do something spectacular with *Achilles* and get it published real quick, who knows what might happen?"

After a strong coffee and a muffin, Giles had returned to his room to collect his laptop. As he had been passing through the lobby en route to the terrace, a New Zealander struggling with a heavy suitcase had dropped it to the floor and offered his hand.

"Bill Burke…University of Otago. You're Giles Butterfield, aren't you?"

"That's right."

"Don't remember me, I suppose; crossed paths in Christchurch a few years back. Quite something this *Achilles* business, eh? There's a rumour that Steve Salomon's off to the White House. Left first thing, I was told."

"He's seeing President Crabb?"

"So they say…goodness knows why. Well, I'd better keep moving. I see my cab's just arrived. When do you leave?"

"Tomorrow, to London via San Francisco. Bon voyage!"

"You too."

***

Giles was still brooding about Steve, when Vicky emerged from the nearby washroom, dusting herself down and straightening her skirt.

"What a painful experience that was!" he muttered.

"You can say that again!" she exclaimed. "Sorry about that but even Captain Wilson can't do anything about clear air turbulence. At least you were safe. I nearly got sucked

55

down the loo! Toilet, I mean, sorry. Got that from my English girlfriend…along with a lot of other bad words."

"Oh, it wasn't that, Vicky. I was referring to a rather unpleasant experience during a congress I'd been reliving. Talking to myself is another one of my bad habits. Part of the mad professor syndrome, I suppose."

"Do you talk in your sleep too?"

"Not that I'm aware of."

"My ex-husband did," she confided in his ear. "That's why he's *ex*. One night, about four in the morning, fast asleep, he came out with what he'd been up to with the tart next door. Lots of really juicy bits! Went on and on about them. So I recorded what I could on my smartphone, which I use as an alarm clock. Next day I took it to an attorney. And that was that. End of marriage!"

"I'm sorry. It must have been very painful."

"It was for *him*," she winked, "when he woke to find his nuts in my hair tongs!"

"Ouch!"

Chapter Four

While waiting for his connecting flight in San Francisco International Airport, Giles had bought as many newspapers as he could find, and upon his arrival in Oxford cut out the relevant articles and stapled them together. After checking that Vicky was not on her way back, he took them from his briefcase to remind himself of how the discovery of *Achilles* had been announced to the world.

The San Francisco Examiner had done its best to rub salt into Steve's wounds with the headline "Saladdin's Revenge! Islam routs Western science." The Washington Post had carried a photograph of the two of them in the bar of the Pagoda before Steve had left for the press conference, above an equally derisive caption: "Not-so-happy-hour for NCI Director." Under the heading "Scoffin' boffin swallows his pride", the New York Times had shown a picture of Steve pausing for a drink of water during the press conference, followed by a lengthy column:

> "The Director of the US National Cancer Institute, Dr Stephen Salomon, is today coming to terms with the fact that the MECCAR research institute in Jordan, opened only fifteen months ago, has already discovered what may be the most important anticancer gene yet. The *Achilles* gene has the potential to kill all cancer cells but is missing a small piece of DNA without which it cannot do its job. Although it is probably some years away, researchers believe it can be fixed and then used for gene therapy.

The announcement, made during a cancer congress in Oahu, came only a few weeks after Dr Salomon had ridiculed MECCAR by telling Fox News, 'It's a great pity, but there's really no chance that MECCAR will achieve anything. The entire venture is a rather foolish enterprise. It's not possible that those guys have got what it takes to do world-class science without collaborating with world class teams like mine.'

It seems likely that Salomon will lose his job over what is widely regarded as a humiliation not just for the National Institutes of Health, but also for the United States, and indeed Western medical science in general. President Ted Crabb is said to be furious, but the White House has declined to comment until they have more information.

The discoverer of the gene, Dr Ahmad Sharif, is widely......"

Seeing the headlines once again reminded Giles of how anxious he had been about their effect on Steve's state of mind. It had occurred to him during the flight to London that his near-manic performance during the press conference might not have been such a good development after all. Perhaps it was the forerunner to a deep depression. And if so, what might come next?

Unable to put the worst-case scenario out of his mind, he had telephoned Steve's wife as soon as he was back in Oxford.

"Marie-Claire, this is Giles Butterfield," he had announced apprehensively.

"Giles, what a surprise! How are you?"

"Well, thanks. And you?"

"As good as can be expected, I guess. What brings you to the phone?"

"I'm calling to check that Steve's okay. I was in Oahu when the news broke. He took it so badly I've been worrying about him."

"What a sweet man you are, Giles. But I already knew that, didn't I? Steve has taken it badly, very. He feels humiliated. And of course, so he should. I've been telling him for years he doesn't go about his work the right way. He doesn't have the right priorities. But it's too late now. And it's not just him who's suffering. It's all of us, the whole family. The neighbours are ignoring us. Mom is livid, says she'll never talk to him again. And as for the local shopkeepers, they don't seem to know where to look. I've told him he's got to get us out of this mess. He must do something and do it quick! Otherwise I'll be on a flight to San Diego to move in with the girls."

"Hold on, Marie-Claire. Science isn't like that. You should know that by now. All he can do is get his head down, carry on, and hope for the best. What do you expect him to do, wave a magic wand?"

"I don't care what he does, Giles. The newspapers are printing such awful things.

I can hardly bear to read them."

"Ignore them. As I told Steve in Oahu, he should tough it out. It's only a matter of time before the press gets bored. They'll need another story soon."

"But I can't ignore it, Giles. People believe all that garbage. It will leave scars. Our journalists are not like your Oxford ones, Giles. They're incredibly ignorant. Did you see the San Francisco Examiner? Saladin's revenge indeed! Revenge for what? Obviously, that reporter hasn't heard of the Treaty of Ramla. And he couldn't even spell the man's name correctly!"

"I agree about the name, but the rest is a bit much to expect, Marie-Claire. Not everyone's an ex-professor of history like you, you know."

"But if he doesn't know the subject, he shouldn't pretend he does, should he?"

"Fair enough. To get back to Steve, I've heard he's off to the White House. Is that true?"

"He's on his way there this very minute. He's going to ask Ted Crabb for emergency funding for the NCI. He says the next challenge will be to create an artificial enhancer, or something like that, to get that gene to work. He reckons he could do it with enough money."

"But that's a long-term job. Several years, I'd say."

"*Several years?* Oh no, he *must* do it faster than that, Giles!"

"Does he think Ted Crabb will give him the money?"

"He's not sure. He's going to tell him to stop wasting money training scientists from backward countries, like all those Alhazen Fellows who seem to be everywhere."

"But MECCAR's paying for those fellowships, not the United States. I think you need to soft pedal a little, Marie-Claire. Show Steve he's got your support; give him some encouragement; remind him of his many great achievements, that sort of thing. We don't want him to hit the bottle, do we?"

"If he doesn't do something soon, Giles, it'll be the other way around. The bottle will be hitting *him*, and yours truly will be on the other end of it. Anyhow, I must go, sorry. I've a dental appointment in half an hour. Thanks for your call."

For the next few days, Giles had kept a close eye on the American press in the hope of learning something about Steve's visit, but the White House had made no statements. Then a cover article had caught his eye. A secretary who had been in the Oval Office throughout the meeting had secretly recorded every word and sold the transcript to the highest bidder, *Newsweek*.

After introductory paragraphs about MECCAR and the press conference in Oahu, the article had reproduced the secretary's statement verbatim:

> "Dr Salomon entered the Oval Office to find President Crabb slouched behind his desk. The Director of the National Institutes of Health, Dr Henry Weinberg, was reclining on one of the sofas, his head in his hands, his tie undone, his shoes scattered on the floor. Neither looked up until the door closed again. The President acknowledged Dr Salomon with a gesture of the

hand, but Dr Weinberg remained motionless. There was no hand-shaking, in fact no real greeting at all. The atmosphere was very cold. Then Mr Crabb jumped up and thumped his fist on the stack of newspapers on his desk.

"'Salmon!' he blurted. 'What the hell's going on? This is the blackest day for American science since the Soviets put that hamster into orbit years ago. You've made the NIH a laughing stock. You let a bunch of Arabs beat us to the biggest breakthrough in cancer for years, and it was sitting there in our chromostones all the time. And just to rub it in, they announce it just before I'm off to see Sheikh God-awful in…er…where is he?'

"'Sorry sir, who?' Dr Salomon stuttered.

"'Ted's pet name for Colonel Gaddafi, Steve,' Dr Weinberg explained from the couch, his eyes remaining closed. "He's in Libya, Ted."

"'What the hell's he doing there? Never mind…! It's a disaster! What do you have to say for yourself, Salmon?'

"'The name's Salomon, sir. I'll get straight to the point. It's all a question of dollars. I've been saying for years the NCI needs more. We've got the best brains, but it's not enough. MECCAR beat us because they were able to pour money into the project, period. This gave them all the manpower they needed: field workers, cell biologists, geneticists, biochemists, statisticians…'

"'Okay, okay, okay! I get the point.'

"'They also have all the latest equipment, sir. Their labs function twenty-four hours a day, seven days a week, fifty-two weeks a year. They don't have to order chemicals when they're needed, then wait for them, like we do. They have them stockpiled in a refrigerated warehouse. And their staff don't need to waste time on paperwork, justifying everything they do, getting permission for this and for that.'

"'Money, paperwork? Don't try to pull that crap on me, Salmon. That institute of yours is one of the best funded anywhere. And *you* don't have to write grant applications like university people do.'

"'That's true, sir, but I do have to write reports and plans justifying our expenditure, submit budgets for approval, and so on. It all takes time. If MECCAR's people want to do something, they just do it. They've got the money, and they've got the time. They had a good idea, but instead of sitting on it like I have to so often, they were able to go after it. And when they did, they got lucky and found that Bedouin tribe. Without that tribe, they couldn't have done it. Ask Hank over there.'

"President Crabb walked over to Dr Weinberg.

"'Is he right, Hank?'

"'Mmm…?'

"'Never mind! Okay, Salmon, I believe you. But I also believed Hank when he told me you'd let him down, and that your performance hasn't been up to scratch lately.'

"Dr Salomon glared at Dr Weinberg, whose eyes remained closed.

"'However, Hank's a reasonable guy. He's agreed to give you a chance to redeem yourself. You've got one year, just one year, no more, Salmon, to pull your act together. So how much money do you need to get your nose in front again?'

"'For the next twelve months?'

"'As I said, that's all you've got.'

"'A million would make a difference.'

"'Okay, I'll double it. I don't want any excuses. Don't ask me where it's coming from either. That's my business. And don't tell a soul about it, d'you hear? If the press gets onto this, we'll both be in deep water. You came here to brief me, that's all. Okay?'

"At this point, Dr Weinberg got up and walked over to Dr Salomon. He took his hand and spoke quietly but firmly.

"'I'm sorry Steve, but a year is all I can give you. Pull out all the stops. We need something really big. You need it. I need it. The NIH needs it. America needs it. Ted here needs it. If you come up with the goods, Ted will get your paper into Science quicker than a blink, and your problems will be over. On the other hand, if you—'

"'Hank said the Nobel can be shared by up to three of you guys,' the President interrupted, 'often whoever made the big breakthrough plus one or two others who did something with it. The MECCAR report about that gene had only one author. You discover something new about it, Salmon, and I'll be on the phone to Stockholm in a flash. Sven Larsen owes me a favour.'

"Dr Salomon smiled nervously.

"'Well, thanks for the money, sir. All I can say is I'll do my best.'

"'Let's hope your best is good enough. Okay, now I'm out of here. Hank, keep me informed.'

"Upon reaching the door, the President stopped and turned.

"'By the way, Salmon, who was the guy you were chatting to in that 'not-so-happy-hour' picture in the Washington Post?'

"'Giles Butterfield, sir, from Oxford. Did a sabbatical with me a few years back. He was good in those days. Bit of a fuddy-duddy now. Why?'

"'No reason. Bye!'

"He was halfway out, when he stopped and turned again.

"'Ha! It's just occurred to me…what I said before about you and me…a Salmon and a Crabb in deep water…ha…ha…ha!'"

Predictably, the news of Ted Crabb's generosity towards the NCI had leaked out, provoking outrage among less privileged researchers struggling for funds in university departments. But he had refused to reverse his decision, claiming it was in the national interest.

In the weeks that followed the *Newsweek* article, Marie-Claire had telephoned Giles several times for sympathy and moral support. During these lengthy and difficult calls, she had described how Steve had arrived home from the White House in a state of near-suicidal depression. With the deadline for the nominations for the next Nobel Prize little more than six months away, he had known that his chances of discovering something sufficiently important about *Achilles* to share the podium in Stockholm had been remote in the extreme. To make matters worse, in ten days' time he had been due to attend the next get-together of the New York Cancer Club, and five weeks after that be the chairperson of the annual symposium of the International Oncology Society in Sorrento, a responsibility that would consume much of his precious time and dwindling reserves of energy. Although he had believed all he had said to Ted Crabb about the importance of money, he'd also known it could not make miracles.

Stretched out on the sofa after his return from the White House, while Marie-Claire was making coffee, Steve had pondered on how he would cope with the loss of all he had created over the years—his highly skilled team selected from some of the country's brightest, his postdocs whose future careers were so dependent on his guidance, and most of all his cherished research. For him, nothing in life ever approached the thrill of being the first person on the face of the earth to learn something new about the natural world. To every successful scientist, a novel experimental observation is a fairly common occurrence, and for most just part of the job. But for Steve each discovery had always been a very special occasion. It might be how a gene controls a tiny aspect of its cell's chemistry; how a molecule sitting on the surface of a cell sends messages to the interior about what's going on outside; or how a protein ushers chemicals from the bloodstream through the cell's wall, like a sheepdog herding lambs into a pen. Ever since cycling to work each morning as a young postdoc, he had relished the prospect of finding the overnight printouts that might provide the first glimmer of such wonders. How would he live without them? His work was not just part of his life. It *was* his life.

And then there were the familiar faces and voices that would disappear. His social life was almost entirely related to his work. He had never spent much time with neighbours or relatives. Virtually all his friends were colleagues. He was aware that many of the friendships were probably superficial, and even the genuine ones often tainted with jealousy, prejudice, or mistrust. Cancer research was a fiercely competitive business that could bring out the worst in people. Nevertheless, it was always good to see their smiles and waves, feel their handshakes, and hear their greetings upon arriving at a hotel, congress centre, or lecture hall after a long and tiring journey. It made him feel a member of a worldwide family, one that would suddenly vanish if he lost his job.

To lose so much so suddenly would cause unimaginable pain. But as Marie-Claire had poured the coffee, what had terrified him more than what he would lose was what he would *not* lose, what would *remain* with him for the rest of his life: the ideas already conceived but not yet born, the hypotheses not yet tested, the questions only others would someday answer, each preserved inside his head. A research scientist lives with such thoughts. They are his constant companions day and night, as much a part of his brain as its neurones, noradrenaline, and neuroglia. They cannot be shredded and tossed aside like unwanted documents.

And to top it all, there would be such a massive loss of status. With the turn of a door handle, the journey from one world to another would be complete—one moment a respected, successful man strolling through life, the next a failure with no walk of life. It had been this aspect that had worried Giles most of all. Would Steve be able to handle it?

Chapter Five

The LCD screen overhead showed that the aircraft was now approaching the coast of Newfoundland. Much as Giles enjoyed flying, at this stage of a long journey his back would usually be telling him it was time to get out. But not on this occasion. After the pressure and stresses of the past few weeks, the process of going through the story from beginning to end, his big decision behind him, was only energising.

***

He had not met Steve again until the following September, when he had attended the symposium of the International Oncology Society in Sorrento. Although he could little afford to be away from Magdalen at the time, his recent election as the Society's next Honorary Secretary had given him the perfect excuse to spend a few days in his favourite country. Furthermore, knowing that Steve was to be the chairperson, and therefore responsible for putting the programme together, he had been confident the meeting would be of the highest standard.

He recalled arriving at the Albergo e Centro dei Congressi Splendido Palace, perched on a cliff top overlooking the town. The view of the Bay of Naples and Mount Vesuvius in the setting sun, as he signed in at the Welcome Desk in the garden, would have made the journey worthwhile on its own.

On entering the vast marble lobby, Steve had been the first person he had set eyes on, chatting to one of the staff outside the business centre. Anxious to see how he was standing up to the strain, Giles had gone over to greet him.

"Hello, Steve. How are things?"

"Giles, great see you! So far, so good, thanks. Pretty hectic just now, of course, being chairperson and all that."

"It's certainly an all-star cast, Steve. You've done an excellent job with the programme."

"Thanks, but you don't know the best part. There's a last-minute special guest.

Thought I'd give y'all a big surprise. If you look inside that bag of commercial junk they've just given you outside, you'll find a yellow flier with the news."

Steve had propped himself against the wall with an air of self-satisfaction while Giles found the sheet of paper.

"What! Ahmad Sharif, discoverer of *Achilles*? You got the great man himself to come here? Steve, I could kiss you."

"Ha! I'll take a rain check on that one, thanks."

"How did you do it? Bribe him with some of Ted Crabb's cash? Sorry! Poor taste."

"Don't worry, I've gotten used to those sort of gibes. Water off a duck's butt. I called him ten days ago and asked if he'd give our special lecture. He was in Indonesia at the time, something to do with another MECCAR-type research centre. He jumped at it. Said as long as he got the go-ahead from his boss, he would fly here from Jakarta, collecting his wife and kids en route. It meant Pierre Dupont stepping down from the lectureship at short notice, but I knew he wouldn't mind. We'll give it to him next year."

"Just as well it was him and not one of our prima donnas, Steve. But you must have offered Ahmad something, surely? That's a horrendous journey just to give a lecture at a fairly small symposium. A fat honorarium?"

"Not a cent."

"I'm astounded. He must have received hundreds of invitations to give lectures around the world since *Achilles* was announced. I'm not aware he's given any, are you?"

"No, in fact I know he hasn't. But I can assure you I haven't been dreaming, Giles. It's actually going to happen. The only bait I offered was the hotel's Presidential Suite. As chairperson, it had been reserved for me, of course, but I took a standard room instead. Not even a sea view!"

"You're a hero, Steve. I'm sure everyone will agree with that. But even so, all the way from Indonesia just to stay in a plush suite? Can't believe that did the trick. From what I've seen on MECCAR's website, he already lives like a pharaoh in their residential building. There must be another reason: the opportunity to visit a close friend or relative perhaps, the museum in Naples, a trip to Paestum, something. He can't be planning to show off some new data on *Achilles*, as that would go against MECCAR's publication policy."

"Afraid so. He stressed that on the phone more than once."

"So at a few days' notice, he downed tools and travelled through seven or eight time zones to give a lecture about old data in a small symposium without an honorarium?"

"That's about it."

"Seems odd to me, Steve, very odd."

Steve had smiled smugly

"Perhaps I was the attraction?"

"Ah yes, never thought of that. I guess that must be it...you arrogant bastard!

Anyhow, the important thing is he's here. And we're all indebted to you for making this symposium so special, Steve. I noticed at the reception desk, by the way, that the Presidential Suite's terrace has just been given its own swimming pool."

"Yeah. Actually, I didn't know that before I offered to switch. What a sacrifice!One thing I really enjoy is a splash before breakfast."

"You used to play water polo, right?"

"Sure did. Those were the days! So, remember what a martyr I've been, please, when you're casting your vote for the Society's next president."

"You can count on that."

"Now, if you'll excuse me, Giles, Marie-Claire's expecting a call."

"Of course. Send her my love. See you around."

As soon as Giles was in his room and had unpacked his suitcase, he had sat on the bed to read the flier again.

> "Hi everyone
>
> ### Change of program
>
> It's my great pleasure to announce that our coveted Peyton Rous Lecture will be given this year by Dr Ahmad Sharif of the MECCAR institute in Jordan. The great event will take place in the Sala Morgagni, the Congress Center's main auditorium, at 1:30 pm on the second day of the symposium. The title will be "The *Achilles* gene". What else!
>
> Enjoy the meeting
> Steve Salomon
> Symposium Chairperson"

Two days later an enthralled audience had been treated to a flawless lecture. As the applause had subsided, Giles had been slow to rise, taking time to run through some photographs he had taken for his autobiography. After filing out of the auditorium with the last few, he had spotted Steve in the company of two girls in their twenties, and made his way through the crowd to greet him.

"Well, Steve, we were right: very nice lecture by Ahmad, but nothing new."

"Hi, Giles. Yeah, he's so secretive. Over breakfast, I tried to squeeze him into giving something away, but he wouldn't budge."

"Never mind, that's life. Unfortunately, too many of us are tempted to keep our most recent findings close to our chests. MECCAR cost such a huge sum of money, it's not surprising they want to protect their investment."

Giles had sensed a tenseness in the atmosphere, as though his arrival had been unwelcome. Glancing nervously in Steve's direction, one of the girls was about to speak when Giles took the initiative.

"Shall I introduce myself, Steve?"

"Oh, sorry, Giles, yes, let me do that. Two of my next bunch of research fellows. Carina Taricani from Milan, Italy, and Amandine Coupe from Bordeaux, France. Invited them along at the last minute."

"Milan, *Italy*, and Bordeaux, *France*, eh?" he had chuckled, giving the girls a wink. "So that's where those cities are? Always wondered. You Americans make me laugh, Steve. Have you ever heard we Brits talk about 'Chicago, USA,' or 'New York, America'? We don't need the geography lessons."

Sensing his good-humoured gibe had fallen on deaf ears, he had tried to break the ice with Amandine, taking the opportunity to advertise his French.

"Enchanté, mademoiselle. Je suis très heureux de faire votre connaissance."

When this had prompted nothing more than a rather stern "Bonjour, monsieur", he had turned to Carina in the hope of greater success.

"Buongiorno, signorina. Spero che il congresso lei piace. La conferenza del professore arabo era molto interessante, si?"

But she had only nodded politely before Steve intervened, clearly irritated by Giles's behaviour.

"Very impressive, Giles! I knew you were multilingual, but you can't practise on the girls, I'm afraid. Since they joined the NCI, they've had strict instructions to speak only the Queen's English from now on. That's the only language permitted in my lab these days."

"The *Queen's* English in *your* lab, Steve? You're referring to the rock group, I assume?"

At that moment, Steve had spotted Ahmad Sharif emerging from the crowd and waved him over.

"Ahmad, great lecture! I'm sure everyone enjoyed it."

"Thank you, Dr Salomon, but I must apologise for having arrived at the lectern a little late. One minute past one o'clock was the time for my Dhuhr prayers, you see. And so it was all a bit of a rush."

"No problem, Ahmad. We respect everyone's customs around here. Let me introduce you to an old friend of mine from Oxford, England...Giles Butterfield."

Giles had bowed respectfully.

"As-salaam alaykum, Dr Sharif."

Beaming with pleasure, Ahmad had grasped his hand.

"Wa alaykum as-salaam, Professor. Kayf haalak. Al-humdoolillah bikhair.

"But how come you speak Arabic?"

"Spent my youth in the Middle East. My parents were diplomats there."

"Ah, I see. Then you must be the Giles Butterfield who's going to be the Society's next Secretary?"

"Spot on. But how did you know that?"

"I read your biography in the programme. You have done some excellent work over the years. Congratulations!"

"Thank you. You're very kind, but it's been a long time since I did anything very exciting in the field…in any field for that matter…and you can take that any way you like…ha!"

"You are too modest, Professor," Ahmad replied, seemingly oblivious to Giles's frivolity. "I read your recent paper in Nature last night. It was most interesting."

"Thank you, but it was mostly the work of my co-author, Dr Fiona Cameron, my lab assistant from Scotland. She was the brains. Anything I've ever done pales by comparison with your latest achievement."

"The *Achilles* gene is but one accomplishment, Professor. You have a lifetime of success behind you. And from what I have seen, a most interesting life too."

"Yes, I've been very fortunate, it's true. In fact, I've been working on my autobiography. When it's published…I should say if it's published…I'll send you a copy. You might be interested in my experiences as a young man in your neck of the woods, at least the ones that are fit to air in public!"

"Please do. I enjoy biographies enormously. That's virtually all I read when I'm not working, them and history."

"What about poetry? That's my real passion."

"Poetry? No, not at all, I'm afraid."

"That surprises me. I thought it was in your lot's genes, what with all those illustrious bards down the centuries: Ibn Hazm, Abu Nuwas, al-Farazdaq, Abu —"

"Like every schoolboy where I come from, I used to know all those names. But I just cannot get on with poetry, I'm sorry. That's just the way I am."

"No reason to apologise. Many people can't appreciate it. My wife was one, in fact. listen to this. A few years before she died, we were strolling on Hampstead Heath in London. As we reached the top of Parliament Hill, I stopped in wonderment at the almost pastoral scene that lay before us, and quoted a few lines from William Henry Davies.

> 'What is life if, full of care,
> We have no time to stand and stare.
> No time to stand beneath the boughs,
> And stare as long as sheep and cows.'

"After which there was nothing but silence. You could hear the worms breathing. 'Well go on, Giles!' she said eventually, giving me a prod. 'Aren't you going to finish?' 'I *have* finished,' I said. 'No you haven't,' she insisted, 'as long as sheep and cows do what?' See what I mean? Ha…ha!"

With Ahmad again looking only confused, Steve had grasped his opportunity.

"I hope he does, Giles, because I certainly don't. Now, I'm sorry to break up the party, but Ahmad's kindly agreed to talk to the girls about their projects."

Seeing they had retreated into a corner, Steve had summoned them to return.

"Ahmad, let me introduce you to Amandine and Carina. You know all about them from my emails."

"Delighted to meet you, ladies," Ahmad had oozed. "Dr Salomon has indeed told me all about you and your most interesting projects."

As the girls shook his hand, again saying nothing, Steve had turned to Giles.

"I've booked one of the small meeting rooms for them, Giles. Thought this was a golden opportunity the girls shouldn't miss.

"Good, well everyone, now the formalities are over, there's just enough time for a quick drink. Follow me. The bar's this way."

Upon entering the crowded bar, Giles had shepherded Ahmad to the counter, leaving Steve with the girls to find a table.

"I think that Col Vetoraz Prosecco would do nicely," he had proposed, beckoning the barman to take a bottle from a glass-fronted cabinet. "Let me see what it says on the label: 'light bodied, fruity floral notes, and a clean delicate finish.' Sounds perfect. But what will you have, Ahmad? You probably don't touch alcohol, do you?"

"Oh, no, of course not. As you know, my faith does not permit it. I'll have a bottle of Chinotto, please."

"You like that stuff, do you?"

"It's my favourite beverage. Do you know it?"

"Only by sight. Seen it in very bar from Pavia to Palermo, but never tried the stuff."

"You should. It's delicious, absolutely unique. I highly recommend it to you."

"Well one day, I certainly will. And I'll be thinking of you as I slurp it down. Now, why don't you join the others, and I'll bring it over in a few minutes?"

Arriving with everything on a silver tray, Giles had found them all standing on ceremony at two small tables drawn together in a poorly lit corner.

"Here we are! I hope you like my choice of wine. Sorry, Ahmad, they only have cans of Chinotto, no bottles. I hope that's okay?"

After Giles had poured the drinks, Steve had picked up the open can and given it a sniff.

"Hmm…smells like a poor Italian imitation of Coke or Pepsi."

"Oh no, not at all!" Ahmad had protested. "It's made from a Chinese sour orange and specially selected herbs. I used to visit Milan a lot and developed a taste for it there. I was telling Professor Butterfield, it's my favourite drink. I was disappointed to see there's none in my suite's frigobar, in spite of its great size. Plenty of champagne, brandy, liqueurs, and other fancy drinks, but nothing so humble as Chinotto. I suppose it's not the sort of thing the hotel expects its rich guests to drink."

After carefully arranging the glasses and napkins, Giles had chided Steve over his choice of tables.

"Rather gloomy and out of the way here, isn't it, Steve? Afraid of being snapped with this old fuddy-duddy again?"

For a moment Steve had looked only perplexed.

"Ah, of course, the famous Newsweek article, or should I say infamous! Sorry about that, Giles. Just a little joke for Ted Crabb's benefit. Not offended, I hope?"

"As you'd say, Steve, water off a duck's butt."

Steve had promptly sat down, and then, realising the girls were still on their feet, jumped up, catching the table with his knee and knocking over a small bowl of orchids. Giles had never seen him so jittery.

As a distraction while the waiter was clearing up the mess, Giles had told Ahmad of his lifelong interest in ancient Mesopotamia.

"Well, well, what a coincidence!" Ahmad had exclaimed, his eyes sparkling with pleasant surprise, "My wife is quite an authority on the subject. She has published a book on the Bisistun Inscriptions. Let me give you the title and so on. It's bound to be available in England. What a pity you cannot meet her. She is in Lugano at present with our two children."

As he was writing the book's details on a scrap of paper, a flash of light had appeared from the bar's glass doors.

"Damn!" Steve had bellowed, stamping his foot. "Another paparazzo, and this time with me squeezed between a blonde and a brunette. No doubt I'll be on the front pages again tomorrow with more stupid headlines."

"Calm down, Steve," Giles had urged. "It's only the symposium photographer doing his rounds. You're one of the stars, remember? You seem rather nervous today. Is everything okay?"

"Yes thanks, perfect. Now, I hate to break up the party, but Ahmad and the girls have a lot to talk about. We'll have to drink up, I'm afraid."

"If you insist, but we've hardly started."

"Sorry, Giles. But they have important things to discuss."

"As you wish, Steve. Are you going with them?"

"Yeah, I wasn't planning to originally. I'd invited a very smart guy from Munich to join them, a biochemist who was in my lab for a while and who's been working on something similar. So I thought he'd be useful. But he got ill after getting here, and went straight back to Germany. Sent me a text. That's all I know. So, I'll join them until I have to go and talk to the sponsors. After that, I'll be chairing the session on radiation biology."

"No problem, Steve. Before I disappear, let me give everyone my phone number."

After he had scribbled it onto three beer mats, Ahmad had passed him a flashy business card with an embossed gold border and a hologram of MECCAR.

"From one extreme to other, I'm afraid," he had joked. "MECCAR does everything in style. I've written the Presidential Suite's number on the back. It's a direct line, so you can also use it from outside the hotel."

"We're in the same boat as you, Professor," Amandine had giggled, clearly relieved the ordeal was coming to an end. "I'll write ours on this paper napkin."

Giles had passed her an envelope from his jacket pocket.

"Pop it in there, dear. It'll make sure I don't blow my nose on it, and toss it down the loo. Wouldn't be the first time.

"Judging from your accent, at some stage in your life you've spent a few years in the USA, have you, Amandine? Where was…?"

"No time for pleasantries, I'm afraid," Steve interrupted brusquely.

"Yes, of course. I'll leave you all now. Delighted to have met you, Ahmad. Not the last time, I hope. Laila tiaba."

After accompanying them to a small room adjacent to the bar, Giles had made his way to the terrace for some fresh air and another drink. A couple of hours and a much-needed nap later, he had spotted Steve on the far side, and got up to work his way through the crowd to greet him.

"Sorry I didn't get to your session, Steve. Radiation biology never was my forte. How did the girls get on with Ahmad?"

"Pretty good. He's a not a bad guy actually. Agreed to send us some stuff — monoclonal antibodies, cell lines, and DNA probes. It'll make a huge difference in the lab, jump start several *Achilles* projects. I'll also use them as bribes to get access to some equipment from colleagues here and there. First stop will be Herb Wilkins at MIT."

Steve gave a smirk of self-satisfaction.

"Quite a lucky break then, Steve?"

"Some would say lucky. Personally, I put it down to a talent for getting the most out of people. I've always said that when you've lost some ground, the key thing is to get on the right side of whoever's in the lead, then get their confidence and cooperation. And before you know where you are, you're snapping at their heels."

"I have to admit, it makes good sense."

"As you know, I'm usually the one leading the pack, but I have to be realistic, swallow my pride. That's what Marie-Claire said. 'Don't try to compete with them,' she said. 'Even with Ted's extra cash, you can't be sure you'll succeed, because you don't know what they're up to. And you're still a much bigger fish. You've got history. Soon, they'll be falling over themselves to join forces.'"

"Well, this is a good development, Steve. Did Ahmad give anything away about what he's up to in Wadi Rum?"

"Nope, he didn't. But I didn't expect him to, did I? MECCAR has a certain way of doing things, and I have to respect that. No problem."

"Good for you. Is that it then?"

"No, we didn't finish with the girls' projects. He was a bit subdued actually. Not much experience with Western women perhaps. Also, he was struggling with jet lag. He's in his suite now having a sleep. But he's agreed to see the girls again this evening. I've booked them a table in the restaurant. Hopefully he'll be a bit more forthcoming, when they've warmed him up."

"Better tell them not to overdo it!"

"Giles, get serious."

"I am. Don't forget she's in Switzerland. By the way, talking about corkers, did you notice the raven-haired beauty in the bar? She was by the counter, wearing a red dress and fishnet stockings."

"Yeah, I did, actually. Don't know how whores get in here with all the security. Bribed the concierge, I imagine."

"Sorry to disappoint you, Steve, but she's not a whore. She had a symposium identity card dangling between her cleavage. I was hoping you knew her, being the chairperson. She had a newspaper I like to read when I get the chance. Wondering where she got it from locally. One of the best ways to keep up with a language, I find."

"Yeah?"

"Yes. You should try The Times every now and then. Ha… only joking! Now I must be off. Why don't I wine and dine you this evening? Not often I get the chance."

"Thanks."

"I'll book a table in Pesce Spada, off the lobby."

"Does it have to be there?"

"No, but I happen to like it. And it looks like rain anyway. So, if it's OK with you…"

"Er…okay."

"Eight?"

"Fine."

"I'll bore you with the latest about my autobiography. Thought of a great title, by the way, 'Memoirs of a Pox-Hunting Man.' A reference to my early work on poxviruses, I hasten to add, not my wasted youth. Don't think Siegfried Sassoon would object, do you?"

"I'm sure he wouldn't, whoever he is."

"Not *is*, old boy…*was*. He was a Great War poet, and a very brave soldier to boot."

"Sorry, I know nothing about German poets."

"He wasn't German. He was English. His mother called him Siegfried because she loved Wagner. Isn't that a howl?"

"Sorry, I've never heard of him either."

"You've never heard of Wagner?"

"Not Siegfried Wagner."

"Steve, Siegfried is the title of…oh never mind. See you later."

Leaving Steve on the terrace, he had gone directly to his room to finish a handwritten letter to his brother, something he had done religiously every month since his time in the Middle East. That done, he had nodded off once again, until the alarm clock had told him it was time to prepare himself for dinner.

On entering the Pesce Spada a few minutes early, Giles had been surprised to see Steve was already seated, studying the menu as he stirred ice cubes in a glass tumbler. Quietly arriving at his shoulder unannounced, he had slapped him on the back.

"What's this? Kentucky corn juice before fish? Steve, *really*!"

"Giles, don't do that! You gave me one hell of a shock. I happen to like bourbon before fish, before everything, in fact. I'm sorry if it upsets you. I suppose you'll be having one of those fancy Italian cocktails, made out of rhubarb or artichokes?"

"They're not cocktails, Steve. They're *aperitivi*. Sorry…I didn't say that…I'm trying to…never mind. Anyhow, the answer to your question is 'no.' A dry sherry will suit me fine. My tastes are very simple. You should know that by now. So, what'll you have to eat?"

"I'm thinking of trying the 'sogg-lee-ola', if that's how you say it. What sort of fish is it? Do you know?"

"It's pronounced 'sol-yo-la', Steve, sole to the likes of you, the only fish to which Queen Victoria's favourite poet paid homage."

"Here we go again!"

"I promise you. It was Tennyson, her Poet Laureate."

"Tennyson paid homage to a *fish*? Pull the other leg, Giles."

"If you don't believe me, listen to this."

Rising to his feet, Giles had cleared his throat, and posed as if about to deliver a great piece of oratory.

> "'For tho' the Giant Ages heave the hill
> And break the shore and evermore
> Make and break, and work their will;
> Tho' world on world in myriad myriads roll
> Round us, each with different powers
> And other forms of life than ours,
> What know we greater than...*the soul*?'

"There you are. What did I say? Can I sit down now?"

"Please do...before the waiter asks us to leave."

"Of course, being a lord, our Alfred would have had his sole deep fried in batter with mushy peas and chunky chips, all wrapped in yesterday's newspaper. I don't suppose you've ever had fish that way. Used to be a great British tradition. And I can tell you it's absolutely scrumptious. But I'm sure your—let me see, where is it? — ah yes, your 'filetto di sogliola al forno con salsa di gamberetti' will be almost as good."

"Huh! You know, Giles, Dick Tobias told me that when he saw you a few months ago, you were a mere ghost of your former self. He was even worried about you. When I get back to the NCI, I'll tell him I saw no ghost, just the same old Giles Butterfield."

"Ah, well, he met me in Magdalen, didn't he? I'm a different man when I've escaped into the real world.

"So where were we? Ah yes, the menu. I'll take the 'baccala alla vicentina con fagioli al fiasco', as near as you'll get around here to one of my North of England favourites—salt cod and butter beans, served with mashed spuds and a knob of salty Irish butter...lovely!"

Once their orders had been placed, Steve had been keen to resume.

"I see your food preferences haven't changed, Giles. You know that's one thing that's always struck me as a bit peculiar about you, if you don't mind me saying. You're a pretty cultured guy. You speak four languages. You can spout poetry. You live in Oxford, with its gourmet restaurants and villages with Michelin-starred gastropubs. And yet you have this love affair with the simplest of English food. I don't get it. What do you see in that stuff?"

"What do I see in it? That's easy, Steve. I see ingredients, not a *mélange* of their pulverised remains. I can taste those ingredients individually. I can smell them. I can feel their textures on my tongue. I used to be like you once. With my parents waltzing off to diplomatic banquets and buffet receptions every other night, for a meal to be worthy of my attention it had to have a recipe as long as your arm, be smothered in sauces, and infiltrated with a plethora of herbs and spices. But when I went 'up north', I realised what real food should be like."

"Yes, but…"

"Hold on, I haven't finished. I have a theory we believe complicated dishes are best because we've been bred to think that way, and that's because society's conditioned to think that way about *everything*, because human progress has been linked to increasing complexity: engineering, architecture, electronics, manufacturing, medicine, you name it. It's around us all the time. The best is always the most complicated. So our brains extend the same attitude to food. If a dish is complicated, and you can't imagine how it was put together, like the latest laptop, your brain believes it must taste better and interprets the signals from your taste buds and nose accordingly."

"But you know, Giles…"

"I still haven't finished, Steve. Tell me how many of these you have ever tasted: potted shrimps from Morecambe Bay, black pudding cooked in malt vinegar, butter pie with beetroot, Lancashire hotpot, Cumberland sausage? They're simple, they're delicious, and there all from Merseyside—or within spitting distance. You know some time ago…"

"Okay, okay, Giles! I don't need yet another lecture, thanks. I've already had an overdose today. And since you asked, I've never heard of any of them. But presumably that's because…"

"Most people don't care for them. Isn't that what you were about to say?"

"Yeah, it has to be, otherwise…"

"Well you're wrong. It's because in the posh South they haven't tried them. If you stayed with me for a week, I'd prove it to you. Mavis, my housekeeper from Keswick in the Lake District, is a wonderful cook."

"I may take you up on that."

"Good. By the time you're packing, you'll be wondering why all the restaurants in DC don't offer Lancashire and Cheshire cheese, instead of that perpetual Roquefort and Camembert, not to mention Manchester tart and Eccles cakes. I tell you, you're in for a life-changing experience."

Giles had stopped to taste the wine before filling Steve's glass.

"Thanks, Giles. Does this mean it's over?"

Giles had leant forward and lowered his voice.

"Yes, it does. So, to change the subject…tell me what you're up to, you old scoundrel."

"What the hell d'you mean?" Steve had snapped. "I knew you'd be suspicious about the girls. They're damn good scientists. Brains and beauty can go together, you know."

"Jesus, Steve, what's got into you? You're so touchy today. I wasn't suggesting anything improper. Good heavens, of course not! I was asking about your work, that's all. What you're up to in the lab."

"Why the old scoundrel bit then?"

"Take it as a term of endearment."

"Gee, thanks."

"Talking about the girls, they might be bright, but they wouldn't win any medals for conversation skills, would they? Are they always so reticent?"

"They were nervous, that's all. Don't forget they're just at the start of their careers, and today they found themselves between a couple of big shots in front of their new boss. That kind of situation can be very intimidating."

"Fair enough. And thanks for the compliment. I've never been called a big *shot* before—something sounding rather similar, many times, but not quite that! But to be fair, when they did open their pretty little mouths, their English was very good. Pity about the accents though. How did that come about?"

"Amandine lived in New York as a child, and Carina did her PhD in Seattle. But why is it a pity? We don't all have to sound like Sir Laurel Oliver, do we?"

"Who? Oh, yes. Quite!"

"So let's get back to you, Steve. How's the research going?"

"Don't be offended, Giles, but I'm going to take a leaf out of MECCAR's book and keep it to myself. I know I can trust you, don't misunderstand. But you know how it is. You could get talking to someone after one glass too many, and before you know where we are, it would be all over the symposium. Can't take any chances, sorry. But it's going very well, thanks. I'm very happy."

"Fair enough, perfectly reasonable under the circumstances. It prompts me to invent a new word. How about this for a future entry in Webster's Dictionary? 'Meccar-nization: the practice of nondisclosure of the results of academic research for personal advantage.'"

"I like that. It's neat."

It had not been until they were well into their desserts that Giles had spotted Ahmad, Carina and Amandine, preparing to leave the restaurant.

"Well, blow me down! They've been over there all the time, Steve—Ahmad and the girls. Their table must have been behind those prickly pears. Whoops! I wish you'd seen that."

"Seen what?"

"I knew Arabs liked a bit of bottom, but that was…"

"Whose?"

"Both…at once, must be ambidextrous."

Steve had refrained from turning his head, seemingly intent upon showing no interest.

"The girls are collecting their raincoats, Steve. Aren't they staying here?"

"No, they're in the *Cesare Augusto* down the road. This one's fully booked."

"Well they're certainly not going there yet, because they're not putting them on. Wonder where there off to. Seeing them reminds me of your two girls, Steve. Unfortunately, I never got to know them on that sabbatical. They must be about the same age, are they?"

"Yeah, you're right."

"How are they getting on?"

"Pretty well, thanks. Tried to persuade them to come here for a vacation actually, but couldn't drag them away from their boyfriends in San Diego. They both think they're in love… whatever that is."

"Now there's an interesting question. Why don't we move into the lounge and talk about it? I'll treat you to a glass my favourite drink before we retire."

"What's that?"

"Dark 'n' Stormy, more commonly just D 'n' S, Bermuda's greatest contribution to civilisation. Grew on me during a golfing holiday there. It's one part Gosling's Black Seal rum, two parts ginger beer, some ice, and a slice or two of lime. Delicious!"

"I'll stay with bourbon, thanks. But it'll have to be quick. I have to pack. Early flight from Rome tomorrow. You'll fly from Naples, I suppose?"

"In a few days, yes. But I'm having some 'R and R' first. Okay, let's go.

"And oh yes, by the way, I think the Englishman you had in mind earlier, like whom we don't all have to speak in your opinion, is Sir Lawrence *Olivier*. You were probably mixing him up with a couple of silent movie comedians, Stan Laurel and Oliver Hardy!"

"Sorry."

Chapter Six

It had been several years since Giles had started the habit of extending his trips to scientific meetings for one reason or another. Sometimes he would arrive a few days early to have a rest before the demands of a large congress were upon him. On other occasions, he would wait until the event was over, and then delay his departure to visit a local university or merely reflect on what he had seen and heard. He might also take the opportunity to make some progress with his autobiography or his next piece for The Oxford Times, alternating such sessions with walks or trips to sites of historical interest. Unhindered by responsibilities and interruptions, he could be enormously productive on such occasions.

The Bay of Naples had fascinated him ever since his father had given him a copy of Goethe's Italian Journey as a teenager. Although he had stayed in the city on several occasions in the past, he had always been too busy for any relaxation, rushing from one university department, lecture, or meeting room to another. But this time he had been determined to take full advantage of what was on offer by spending his first day of freedom in Ercolano, the lesser known victim of Vesuvius' eruption.

The ruins had more than lived up to his expectations, so much more atmospheric, he thought, than those of Pompeii. Wandering alone among the silent empty streets and roofless homes, he had tried to picture the terrible scene that the stones had witnessed—the children screaming, the terrified mothers running with their babies, the occasional old man motionless amid the mayhem, mystified by the sight, sounds, and smells, as the great cloud of dust descended on their erstwhile earthly paradise. Never had he so vividly sensed the ghosts of so many. After several hours of exploration, he had rounded off a near perfect day in a small trattoria with a bowl of fish stew and a bottle of ice-cold Taurasi, before making his way back to Sorrento on the Circumvesuviana, the train that skirts the coast overlooking the Bay of Naples.

Upon arriving at the hotel, he had been alarmed by the sight of two glum-looking Carabinieri whispering to each other by the small elevator that was the exclusive preserve of the Presidential Suite. He had been about to ask Marco, the concierge, what was going on, when a display of the symposium's official photographs, pinned to a corkboard propped against the staircase, had caught his eye. As they included the one of him, Steve, Ahmad, and the girls in the bar, he had stopped to jot down its number and the photographer's email address. By the time he had finished, the two men were in such deep conversation with Marco that he had been disinclined to interrupt.

The following morning, he had taken breakfast on the patio overlooking the hotel's small citrus orchard, enjoying the aroma and the prospect of another interesting day, this time visiting the Greek temples of Paestum. But his plans had been dashed when he unrolled his complimentary copy of Il Mattino and saw the shocking headline.

"Arab scientist drowns in hotel swimming pool
Luigi Mancia, Sorrento

Dr Ahmad Sharif of Jordan's Middle East Centre for Cancer and Aids Research (MECCAR), expected to win the Nobel Prize for discovering a gene that will revolutionise the treatment of cancer, drowned yesterday in the swimming pool of his suite in Sorrento's Splendido Palace Hotel. His maid entered the suite at around 9.00 a.m.

to find him lying at the bottom of the pool, fully clothed apart from his jacket and tie.

His wife, who was on vacation in Lugano but had been in contact with her husband regularly by phone, said he had not known that the suite had a pool until checking in. As he was a non-swimmer and disliked the smell of chlorine, he had asked the receptionist if he could change to an alternative suite. She had contacted the occupant of the only other one, the Capo di Monte, which does not have a pool, but had been told it would not be convenient.

Captain Francesco Cortese of the local Carabinieri said that the door to the terrace had been wide open. The suite was tidy and there were no signs of a struggle. Dr Sharif's jacket and tie were in the bedroom. The table was bare apart from an almost-empty bottle of Svaneke Session pilsner.

A pathologist had put the time of death at around 3.00 a.m. and said there were no injuries. A blood sample was found to contain alcohol and although the concentration was quite low it could have been sufficient to impair his judgment.

As he had recently flown to Italy from Indonesia and had been complaining of jet-lag and difficulty sleeping, Captain Cortese believes he probably went onto the terrace for some fresh air in the early hours. As the pool has bright underwater lighting and raised terra cotta tiles around its perimeter, he was likely dazzled by the glare and tripped.

As there were no suspicious circumstances, there are no plans for a criminal enquiry. Nevertheless, Mrs. Sharif intends to sue the hotel over the fact that the Carabinieri found that a bulb was missing from one of the lights above the terrace. When the manager, Signor Rodolfo Patrono, was asked to comment on this, he said that all bulbs and electrical equipment are checked every week."

Thunderstruck, Giles had flapped the newspaper in the direction of a priest who was sitting at a nearby table.

"Carpe diem, Padre. Ho appena letto che un amico…"

"Bishop, actually," he replied congenially over his demi-lunettes. "I don't speak a word of Italian, sorry. Lovely day, isn't it?"

"Apologies…Your Excellency. A lovely day it is indeed for you and me. But alas not for a colleague of mine. I've just read here that he was found dead in this very hotel yesterday. Can you believe it? He was staying in the best suite in Sorrento, possibly the best this side of Rome, and what happens? He trips into the pool on his terrace and drowns. Just like that. I ask you! You never know when you're going to kick…I mean when the good Lord in his infinite wisdom is going to take you. Do you?"

"Indeed not."

"He was doing brilliant work too, destined to save the lives of millions of people from cancer. Why should God drag him off before it's finished, I wonder?"

The bishop had smiled benignly, assuming the question had been asked without any expectation of an answer. But Giles had persisted.

"Any ideas?"

"Oh…er…no…not really. These things do seem strange, I know. But so often He works in mysterious ways."

"Doesn't he just? Of course, we have to remember he's the one who invented cancer in the first place. Perhaps he's attached to it. It's certainly a masterpiece, all those mutations, overactive and underactive genes, and so on. Even the best brains in the world haven't cracked all its secrets yet."

"Are you a scientist?"

"Yes, that's right."

"I thought you must be!"

"Well, in case God decides to let his masterpiece loose on me, I'm off for another slice of that apricot tart, this time with two dollops of mascarpone."

While waiting in line at the buffet table, Giles had reflected on the circumstances of the tragedy. It had certainly sounded like an accident, hadn't it? And anyhow, people don't get murdered during medical congresses, do they? Who could possibly have wanted to kill Ahmad? But there was one thing about the newspaper's report that had surprised him—the fact that he had been drinking beer. As a young man, Giles had seen Muslims drinking alcohol in the privacy of his parents' home many times. It was common knowledge that it happened behind closed doors, especially among the diplomatic set. But Ahmad hadn't seemed to be that type. After all, his prayers had made him late for his lecture, hadn't they? And in the bar afterwards his adherence to Islamic law had been strict.

No longer having any stomach for Paestum, he had spent the rest of the day aimlessly wandering around Sorrento's streets: a cup of coffee here, a glass of wine there, a chat with a shopkeeper, a few minutes stroking a one-eyed cat. Newsagents were completely out of bounds. No matter what he did or where he went, he had been unable to rid his mind of the picture of Ahmad's motionless body in the pool. There had been no choice but to cancel the next day's trip to Capri and head back to Oxford.

As always during Michelmas term, the next few weeks in the College had been busy with tutorials and lectures for the students. There had also been a rush of manuscripts from editors to review before the festive season, several committee meetings to sleep through, and his daily sessions with Fiona.

Once the pressure was off, he had set off for a break in his 1960s Austin Healey 3000, leaving Fiona with a few experiments to get on with. He had learnt to enjoy the occasional motoring vacation since Hillary's passing, something they had never done together owing to her hip problem. His main purpose this time had been to look at cottages around Albi with retirement in mind, an idea Fiona had suggested after attending a congress in Toulouse. But he had seen nothing that appealed. Tuscany had remained unchallenged, and he had little doubt that that's how it would stay until the big day arrived.

As soon as he was back in his office, he had returned to his autobiography. In spite of Jane's bothersome habits, he preferred to work on it there rather than at home, as all the diaries, notes, old photographs, and other paraphernalia that he needed were to hand. Equally important was the view of the Longwall Quad over his desk. He never tired of the soft-textured, honey-coloured stones of Scott's masterpiece, draped in their mantle of honeysuckle and ivy, the expertly pruned bushes that fringed the lawn, the two silver birches in the centre, their slender branches forever swaying in the breeze — so much more conducive to nostalgic reflection than the ugliness of the slate tiles, brick chimneys, and scruffy pigeons through his windows in Holywell Street.

Always well organised, albeit in his own unconventional way, his office and adjacent reading room were so comfortable that their only downside was that colleagues and visitors were inclined to overstay their welcome. Like everything he did, the two rooms had been planned with great care. The door from the passageway, of solid oak with a small leaded window and fleur-de-lis handle, was at his left shoulder as he worked, enabling him to see at once who was ringing the brass ship's bell that hung outside. To the door's right a Bentwood coat stand stood before a tall framed mirror, propped against the wall at just the right angle to see Jane entering from the reading room, which doubled up as her office. The wall between the rooms was mostly occupied by a heavy rosewood bookcase with exceptionally deep shelves. On first seeing it in a Mossley Hill junk shop one summer, he had reckoned its proportions would be ideal for storing his papers, avoiding the need for filing cabinets, such ugly noisy contraptions in his opinion. Each stack was held in place by an improvised paperweight connected with a place, person, or event of significance in his life. For his letters, it was a copper bowl from Pondicherry on India's east coast, his father's birthplace, which Hillary had been in the habit of using for her everyday jewellery; for his manuscripts, an Edwardian magnifying glass they had bought during their first holiday together in Keswick; for his grant applications, a chunk of red and orange conglomerate rock, collected during a visit to the Olgas of central Australia. And so it went on. He loved to chat about their origins and histories. The only exception was an ivory-handled dagger with a curved blade engraved in Arabic, whose significance remained a mystery even to Fiona. All that anyone knew was it had something to do with a girl in Cairo many years ago. But he had resolutely refused to say any more than that.

"Why a dagger of all things?" Fiona had ventured one winter afternoon after too many mugs of mulled wine, as she moved to pick it up for close examination. "Who was that girl anyhow?" But all she had got in return was a deep sadness in his eyes before dropping them to the floor. Whatever the significance of the weapon, Giles had no intention of revealing it to anyone.

On another occasion, when he seemed to be going through a bit of a depression, she had tried to persuade him to put every one of his paperweights out of sight, bringing a large cardboard box along for the purpose.

"I don't think they're good for you, Giles," she had explained. "At times like this they make you think too much about the past. Don't be upset with me, but I've watched you through the window, gazing at one, then stroking another, then picking up the next one and talking to it. If they were merely ornaments lined up on the top shelf, it would be different. Then they would just be part of the room, most of the time unnoticed. But as it is, you have to keep picking them up every damn time you need something. And then you start thinking. Here, let me…"

"Fiona, stop!" he had snapped with rare assertiveness. "You don't understand. Yes, they can make me a little melancholy at times. You're right. But that's okay. There are different types of sadness. Which is better, to be sad that certain happy days are no more and can never return, or to be happy that sad days are behind you? I know which I prefer. All those objects are important to me, and the only emotions they evoke are positive ones. That doesn't necessarily mean they're joyous, just positive. That's what matters. So let's leave it at that, shall we…dear?"

She had never forgotten that brief exchange. In all their years together, it was the first time he had addressed her in that way. Until then it had been only "Fiona," or "lass," or "lassie," or occasionally "m'dear" when he had wanted to get a message across strongly—but never "dear" on its own, as if he really meant it. She had agonised about its sincerity for days. Had he paused before saying it to make sure she noticed, or because he'd been uncertain about the wisdom of going that far? Or had he used the word merely to show he was not cross with her? Of course, it might have had no significance at all, just a habit he'd picked up in Merseyside, where she knew it was common for men and women to address each other casually in that way without any implied affection or even interest. To try and settle the matter, during the following week she had attempted to prompt a repetition with a series of furtive experiments that gave him reason to be annoyed or frustrated, or sympathetic on account of a contrived minor injury. After several such provocations had failed, she had taken the step of touching his hand as they both reached for the magnifying glass to examine one of Jane's potted plants. His failure to recoil as if threatened by a snake, his regular response in such situations, had been the clearest signal of which he was capable — and the catalyst for which she had been longing.

On the wall facing the rosewood shelves were a couple of mahogany bookcases he had bought in Woodstock soon after arriving in Oxford. Of more traditional proportions, these had retained their original purpose. He had a very practical approach to arranging his many books: they were simply kept in alphabetical order of the author's surname, or the first author's if there was more than one. Fiona thought this was "so brilliantly simple, it was simply brilliant" but had conceded it would not work for her, as she would never have the patience to put each book back where it belonged.

As with most things, Giles's niece, Charlotte, did not share Fiona's view on the matter.

"They look so horrible, Uncle Giles, all higgledy-piggledy like that," she would reiterate during every business trip from her home in Durban. "They ruin everything."

"I'm puzzled as to why the very few women in my life expend so much energy telling me how to arrange my office," he had once responded.

"You should be pleased!" she had retorted. "I think about you a lot now you're alone, and I want to picture you just as I'd like you to be."

"That's very touching, Charlotte, thank you," he had answered. "I'm sorry you don't like picturing me just as I am. But you see, I'm not one of those paperweights over there, or that bowl of hyacinths on the windowsill. I like my books arranged like that. I'm very happy, deliriously happy even, to see them all higgledy-piggledy. There's something about higgledy-piggledy-ness that for me is an art form. Obviously, you don't have that sort of artistic appreciation. Apart from which, it works. You won't catch me looking for a book for so long that by the time I've found it I've forgotten where my glasses are, or why I wanted it in the first place."

The only exception was on the top shelves, where his many diaries, dating from his youth, were arranged in chronological order.

In the corner next to the books was a mock Tudor fireplace bearing the College's crest. On its hearth a stained-glass screen fabricated from a discarded church window concealed several logs of seasoned oak on the grate. On the mantelpiece, two brass candlesticks framed an agrarian oil by Georgina Lara, his only inheritance from an aunt in Suffolk.

His idea of sharing his adjoining reading room with Jane had worked out better than he had feared. The master stroke had been to put her walnut Milton desk and Tiffany lamp under the window overlooking the St. Swithun's Quad, so often frequented by students that there was usually plenty to occupy her old maid's curiosity. The fact that she was part-time also helped, and he did most of his reading during her afternoons off.

To the right as one entered from his office hung a large and rather overpowering portrait of the Marchese whose generosity had made it all possible. Immediately below its heavy gold frame, more suited to a castle's entrance hall than an academic's retreat, an electric kettle, an antique copper teapot, and four chipped Denbigh mugs occupied the top of a Chinese lacquered chest. Centre stage was shared by a Burmese teak coffee table and a battered leather-upholstered Chesterfield. Behind the door as one entered, a rattan chair draped in a Mojave blanket stood under a tall brass floor lamp with a deep orange satin shade.

The windows of both rooms had dark green silk curtains, rarely drawn except on the windiest of winter nights. The stone floors were partly covered by two matching Tabriz rugs. From each of the low ceilings hung a three-armed iron lamp with parchment shades.

It was an eclectic mixture, but one that he loved. And so did Jane, who insisted on cleaning both rooms every Monday morning, arriving early for the purpose. Once the dusting and polishing was finished, she would arrange some cut flowers from her cottage garden. A lively spinster in her fifties, she had taken a sisterly interest in her boss from her first day at work. Since then, her attentiveness had grown to the point of polishing his shoes or popping a flower in his lapel before permitting him to leave for a lecture or meet a visitor at the railway station. Her interest in his welfare was too much for his liking, but he tolerated it as long as it didn't impinge on his personal life.

It had not been with any enthusiasm that he had returned to writing his book after his motoring holiday. For more than a few weeks before setting off, he had been finding the task a bit of a chore, and the return journey from Albi had brought this to a head. As one day on the road followed another, he had realised how his journey through the French countryside, at first so varied and full of interest in the Massif Central, later far less exciting and more predictable as he made his way through the Loire, mimicked his personal journey through life.

"All those ups and downs," he had mused over a glass of Bordeaux one evening, "the forks in the road, the twists and turns, slowly giving way to roads that were pleasant enough but nothing to get excited about. And in a few days' time, I'll be in the College's parking lot…exactly where my life has got to, a sort of parking lot while waiting for a journey into the unknown. It's all there in that blasted autobiography!"

Before arriving at the ferry in Calais, he had decided that come hell or high water he would get the thing off his back by the end of the month.

***

After a week of little sleep and countless cups of coffee, he had typed the last letter of the last word of the last sentence at exactly 8:32 p.m. on the last day of November.

"Well, that's that, and thank God!" he had said with a sigh, scrolling through the pages. "Now, to celebrate…and there's only one place to do that. Harry Barnes should be there by now. His daughter's a bit of a writer. She might give me a few tips on publishers, if she's there."

As expected, he had found the Turf Tavern packed with regulars. Harry was in his usual spot, on his own, his head buried in yesterday's Sunday Times, seemingly oblivious to all around him.

"A large Shiraz for my friend please, Mabel," he had asked the barmaid, "and you know what I want."

"Hello, Professor. Nice to see your face again. It's been quite a while."

"Burning the midnight oil, Mabel. See these bags?"

"What's it this time?"

"My autobiography, can you believe?"

"Ooh, that should be interesting! What with all the things you've done, and places you've been to. I hope I get a mention."

"As a matter of fact, you do, Mabel — the fact that you make the best Dark 'n' Stormy this side of Hamilton."

"Thanks, but where's that?"

"The one I'm referring to is in Bermuda, where it was invented."

"Bermuda? Fancy that! There you are. Didn't take long, did it? Shall I put them on a tray?"

"Not necessary, thanks. Keep the change."

After negotiating the crowd, acknowledging a few familiar faces on the way, he had placed the glass of wine at a safe distance from Harry's elbow before patting him lightly on the head.

"Harry! How are you doing?"

"Good heavens, it's you! Take a seat, Giles…here."

"Thanks."

"How are you? Saw you at your desk a few times lately through your window. Didn't ring that bell of yours though. You looked too engrossed. What's it this time, another column for the local rag?"

"Not what *is* it, Harry, what *was* it, thank God. My autobiography. Got the brute finished at last. What a struggle. Cheers!"

"Down the hatch… and thanks for this. Your autobiography? That was a well-kept secret. Well, you know, Giles, I'll tell you something. I haven't met a man or woman yet who'd actually finished one of those things when they thought they had. Now that you think it's behind you, you can bet your bottom dollar something really special's about to happen to you. It always does. Could be anything—a discovery in the lab, unexpected money, romance…you name it. But it's coming, I can guarantee. And what's more, it's just around the corner."

"I doubt it, Harry. It won't be long before I'll be pruning the roses in bella Italia."

"Perhaps that's it? A new life, a new life with the bella Fiona perhaps?"

"Come off it, Harry. Fiona and I are just colleagues. We get on well together, yes, but that's all there is to it."

"Yes, of course you are, just *colleagues*. That's why I spotted the two of you cuddling on the sofa in that reading room of yours on my way through Magdalen the other evening. Good colleagues are always doing that sort of thing. Builds team spirit they say."

"What! You were snooping through my window?"

"Not at all. Wouldn't have noticed, if it hadn't been for a bunch of students on the lawn, sharing a take-away and a bottle of wine…and a pair of horse-racing binoculars, you know those big things."

"Binoculars?"

"That's right…Sir Quentin's."

"Sir Quentin's?"

"Yes, he was with them. You should keep those curtains drawn, Giles."

Harry smirked as he swirled his glass, and sniffed the wine appreciatively.

"We were *not* cuddling, Harry! We were just sitting together, discussing her latest lab results actually. If you'd used the binoculars properly, you'd have seen there were books and papers scattered all over the sofa. There was hardly room for the two of us. *Cuddling?* What nonsense!"

"Ha, ha, ha…! You can calm down, Giles. In truth, I was on my own. But you *were* rather, shall we say, intimately juxtaposed?"

"Rubbish!"

"Nothing to be embarrassed about. Wish it had been me, I can tell you. She's a lovely girl, and I mean that in every way. You really should—"

"Can we change the subject, Harry?"

"By all means. Where were we? Are yes, I was saying that I'm pretty damn sure something important's about to happen in your life. I've seen it so many times, I've a theory it's cause and effect."

"How come?"

"The idea is that the very act of finishing your life's story up to now puts you in the frame of mind to do something you wouldn't otherwise have contemplated—simply because none of us likes to think it's all over bar the slippers and the rose-pruning. This doesn't actually make things happen. It just gives you a push to pick something up when it lands on your doorstep, instead of stepping over it and going on your way… to the garden shed for the secateurs."

"Interesting theory, I must admit. Makes sense, I suppose."

"Of course it does. You mark my words. But to get back to the nitty-gritty, sooner or later you're going to need a publisher. I'll ask Denise to give you a call."

"Thanks."

"But whatever you do, for God's sake don't sign a contract. Burn your book onto a CD tonight, then lock it away, and forget about it. After all, there's no hurry, is there?"

"Not really."

Harry had raised his glass.

"Good man. Now, let me treat you to a celebratory meal at the Old Parsonage. I'm famished. It'll be on me."

"Very kind, but I've a better idea. Let's have some real grub at my place instead. Mavis cooked a cowheel pie and some Lancashire hotpot last night. We can warm them up and have them with what's left of last week's pickled cabbage."

"Er…you sure you want to go to all that trouble?"

"Of course."

"Perhaps they're for a special occasion?"

"We never have any."

"Not ever?"

"No, so come on. Empty your glass, and let's go."

"If you insist!"

Chapter Seven

After an uneventful December, Giles had spent Christmas and New Year as the guest of an old student chum, Bill Eccles, now enjoying retirement in a finca near Valldemossa in Majorca. A trip to the island this time of the year had been a regular event ever since Hillary had fallen in love with the Tramuntana Mountains during a wedding anniversary there. Bill Eccles was always good fun, and two weeks or so without newspapers or television, just plenty of long walks, Bill's regional cuisine from his rustic kitchen, and lazy afternoons with jugs of tinto de Verano had been just what he needed to prepare himself for the next semester.

He had returned to Oxford on the third of January, a Sunday, and gone straight into his normal routine first thing the following morning. Mavis had prepared his usual breakfast: a large bowl of thick porridge, Scottish style with a pinch of salt, two soft-boiled Old Cotswold Legbars, three slices of toast hand cut from a local granary loaf, and a jar of thick-cut Scottish marmalade, all washed down with a steaming pot of Taylor's of Harrogate tea. After that would come a brisk walk to the College, picking up The Guardian from the floor of the entrance hall on his way out.

Seeing nothing of interest on the front page, he had dropped into Magdalen's library to catch up on his usual journals: Nature, Science, New England Journal of Medicine, and anything on genetics. He had just finished perusing their pages and was marking some articles for Jane to photocopy, when Fiona had come running through the door, her long red curls in disarray.

"There you are!" she had gasped with a warm smile. "Saw you coming through the gate. It's so nice to have you home again, Giles. This place is not the same without you around. I really missed you."

She had dropped her eyes with a faint blush, before promptly raising them to catch his response.

"For some reason, it wasn't the same for me either this year," he had sighed, "perhaps my priorities are changing."

As she had ventured a little closer, he had noticed she was wearing more makeup and perfume than usual.

"You know, Fiona, your eyes get prettier and prettier—as green as the fields of Connemara, as my aunt Cathleen used to say, as bright as…"

Nudging his shoe with hers, Fiona had fixed her gaze over his shoulder in the direction of the librarian, who had unexpectedly appeared from behind the counter.

"Have you read the recent article by James Watson, Professor Butterfield," she had asked, hastily raising her voice, "the one on DNA methylation in replicating viral vectors?"

"What are you talking…? Oh…no, not yet, Dr Cameron. But I shall do, of course."

Fiona had acknowledged the librarian's thin smile, as she passed with a stack of books in her arms. After waiting until the old lady had struggled up the wooden staircase near the entrance, she had resumed in a whisper.

"I've seen they're looking for a new lecturer at Green Templeton College. Do you think I should apply?"

Learning to her relief that the question had caused only alarm, she had promptly returned to the purpose of her journey from the laboratory.

"Don't worry, not serious! The real reason I came rushing over was to tell you about a paper Steve Salomon has just published."

"Steve? Where?"

"In Science."

"What's it about?"

"Wait till you see! You've got to read it for yourself. I want to see the look on your face. It's in the lab. Let's go. And by the way...Happy New Year! I've a feeling it's going to be a good one."

Grasping his hand, she had hastened to the laboratory as quickly as Giles could manage. By the time they were there, he was gasping like a fish out of water.

"My God, Fiona, you're fit!"

"Why don't you come with me to the gym every now and then? You'd feel the benefit, I assure you."

"Good idea. But right now, what I need is a breather and a cup of char, if you don't mind. While you're brewing it, I'll read Steve's article. Where is it?"

As she was placing a beaker of water on a Bunsen burner, she had nodded towards a stack of articles on her desk. The latest copy of Science was on the top, already open at the right page.

The article's title had left no doubt about the reason for her excitement.

A DNA INSERTION THAT FUNCTIONALIZES
THE ACHILLES GENE
A. S. Salomon, National Cancer Institute
Bethesda, MD, USA

"Ugh!" he had bellowed, dropping the journal onto his knee. "Isn't that bloody typical! Is there really such a word as 'functionalizes'? I don't think so, is there? Not on this side of the pond anyhow. The way the Yanks mutilate our language infuriates me. What's wrong with 'gives function to' or 'activates'?"

Fiona placed her hands on her hips.

"Here we go again! Professor Giles 'The walking-talking Oxford English Dictionary' Butterfield. Does it really matter? We all know what he means, don't we?"

"You know what a stickler..."

"Yes, I do know what a stickler...now, are you going to read the rest?"

"Sorry!"

Giles had worked his way through the article with his customary attention to detail. As in all papers reporting original research, it had opened with a summary of the background to the work and its objectives. This was followed by a description of the laboratory procedures, an account of the results, a discussion of their significance, and finally a list of published papers that had been cited for one reason or another.

Fiona had kept her eyes trained on Giles's face throughout. Over the years, she had come to know the meaning of every expression at moments like this: the almost imperceptible raising of an eyebrow, the chewing of his lower lip, the long inhalation through his nose with tight lips, the stroking of his chin, and, if all was looking good, the occasional nodding of the head.

Conscious that so often in the past, when she'd excitedly drawn his attention to a recent article, he had spotted something that undermined its value, her fingers had been tightly crossed inside the pockets of her lab coat. Sometimes the problem had been a weakness in the study's design, on other occasions an error in the way the data had been analysed, or a flaw in the author's interpretation of the findings. The ability to critically assess a complex paper was one of Giles's greatest strengths, a talent that made him popular with editorial boards and grant review panels. Fiona's forte was very different, but no less important for their work. It came earlier in the research process: integrating other people's data from publications to develop new ideas, and the practicalities of setting up the best experiments to test them. Their skills were complementary, and they liked it that way.

After she had placed a mug of tea beside him, his eyes had remained fixed on the page during a long and noisy slurp. Other than that, he had made no sound or meaningful movement. He had seemed transfixed, mesmerised by what was before him. Fiona relaxed her fingers confident that on this occasion her enthusiasm had been justified.

"You were right, Fiona!" he had pronounced, as he prepared to photograph the paper's only figure. I must make a slide out of this picture for the students' next seminar. Its legend says it all, doesn't it: 'Base sequence of the DNA fragment and its optimum position in the chromosome to activate the *Achilles* gene." This is fantastic stuff. There must be countless teams all over the world trying to find a way of getting *Achilles* to work. And Steve of all people has beaten them to it. Isn't that amazing? Of course, he's had the advantage of Crabb's extra funding. But money doesn't do the job by itself. Crabb could have given the same cash to a hundred labs, and they wouldn't have achieved this much so quickly. I have to take my hat off to him. It's brilliant work. I must give him a call this evening."

Leaning across to turn the page, Fiona had pointed to a line of small print.

"It says here, Giles, that the editorial office received the manuscript on 13 November. That's only four months after *Achilles* was announced in Oahu. That's incredible— well, not *really* incredible. You know what I mean. In that short space of time, he did the work, wrote the paper, and got it into print. And as there are no co-authors, he must have done it all himself, which in turn means he must have already made good progress by the time you were together in Sorrento. He didn't mention it to you?"

"No."

"Strange."

"Not really. When I asked him how his work was going, he said he was pleased, but he wasn't prepared to give anything away. Fair enough. I think you and I would have kept this one under our hats too, wouldn't we? After all, this is the stuff of Nobel Prizes."

"That's true. I bet Ted Crabb's already on the phone to Sweden."

"I hope not, but unfortunately I suspect you're right. I hope they tell him to bugger off. Lobbying for Nobel Prizes may be common, but it's shameful in my opinion."

At that moment, the telephone on Fiona's desk had rung. It had been Jane to say that a journalist was on the line seeking their opinion on the article. Fiona had promptly handed the receiver to Giles, silently mouthing "journalist" seconds before the call was transferred.

"Hello, Professor Butterfield here. Your name…and the magazine?… I see, well I gather you want an explanation of the Salomon paper that's just come out. As it happens, by an extraordinary coincidence, I've got it in front of me this very minute. So, are you ready?

"You probably know that when the *Achilles* gene was announced last summer, the MECCAR institute explained that although it has the *potential* to kill its own cell should it ever become cancerous, unfortunately it doesn't do so. And that's because something is missing, something without which the gene cannot function. It's always been like that, ever since it first evolved many years ago.

"Let me backpedal a bit. Every one of our genes, which I'm sure you know are made of DNA, contains the blueprint, a kind of recipe if you like, that tells the cell how to manufacture just one particular protein. This recipe is what we call its genetic code. In the case of *Achilles*, the recipe is for a protein that would immediately kill the very cell of which it is a part by knocking out its batteries, little metabolic factories called mitochondria. It's like a cyanide capsule waiting to be bitten when the time is right. But it never happens, because another piece of DNA of a type that all genes need to switch them on when needed, is missing. It's as if the cyanide capsule can't be bitten because the cell has no teeth. It's edentulous.

"Pardon? I said edentulous. You know…toothless."

Giles had turned towards Fiona, shaking his head in disbelief.

"Without that switch, every *Achilles* gene is the genetic equivalent of a couch potato. If its cell turns into a cancer cell, it just carries on staring at the ceiling, instead of jumping up and throttling it. In the process, of course, it would also destroy itself, because a gene cannot survive without its cell. But the organism, that's you and me, is saved.

"Hold on a tick, I need some tea. My throat's dry…

"Now, where was I? Ah, yes… the only exception to this situation is in a unique tribe of Bedouin Arabs, the only people in the world, as far as we know, whose *Achilles* genes *do* have a switch. As a result, when any one of *their* cells becomes cancerous, its *Achilles* gene wakes up, and zap…end of cell. What did you say…?

"You've heard that some of our cells do have a type of suicide mechanism? Yes, that's true actually. Full marks! It's very different from *Achilles*, and the problem is it's very unreliable, which is why so many of us end up getting cancer. In contrast, when *Achilles* has the switch it needs, as it does in those Bedouins, it seems to be failsafe. We know that's the case because over many generations those lucky Bedouins have never been known to die from cancer, and that's in spite of living in an area where there's lots of radiation and contamination with toxic chemicals.

"Sorry? You asked why don't all Bedouins have the switch and not just that particular tribe? I was about to come to that. You see, Bedouin tribes are like one big inbreeding family. Most of them never marry members of other tribes. And in this tribe's case, they'd taken it to an extreme. Their marriages have *always* been between cousins. So once one of their ancestors had the gene, it was passed down from one generation to the next until it was present in every member of the family. A that's the way it's remained. And because they've never married into any other tribes, they've kept it to themselves. They're unique.

"'So how did one of their ancestors come to have it in the first place?' I can hear you thinking. Well, many years ago a germ cell in one of them acquired a…. What did you say? What kind of germs? I didn't mean germs as in bacteria or viruses. Germ *cells*, you know…sex cells…sperms and ova."

Giles had rolled his eyes at Fiona, prompting her to place a sympathetic hand on his arm, only for him to raise it to scratch his head.

"What I was going to say is that the DNA of the chromosomes inside a sperm or an egg cell in one of their ancestors must have acquired a mutation when it was being formed. Without going into the technical details, it's well known that this sort of thing can happen. In this case, an extra length of genetic code was created that purely by chance was able to act as a switch for *Achilles*. There's nothing extraordinary about this. Evolution depends on the formation of chance mutations during the formation of germ cells.

"Now, what Dr Salomon has done is to manufacture a short artificial piece of DNA, which when put into just the right place in the same chromosome as *Achilles* works just like the Bedouins' natural switch. It's a giant leap, because it means we may soon be able to cure people by treating them with viruses that have been engineered to infect cancer cells and give them packages of *Achilles* genes attached to Dr Salomon's switch.

"Hold on…more tea needed.

"Pardon? You ask why it was necessary for someone to invent an artificial switch, when presumably copies of the Bedouins' would have worked? I thought you might ask that one too. It's because before MECCAR did its research, it pledged never to disclose anything unique about their DNA. They're a superstitious lot, you see, and they didn't like the idea that one day doctors might put their genes into other people— rather like some Christian sects won't accept blood transfusions from other people. And to its great credit, the Islamic faith takes promises very seriously. In fact, the Qur'an says that God forbids them to break a promise. So we've had to wait for somebody smart enough to invent an artificial switch. Enter Dr Salomon.

"What? You'd like me to say something about the structure of genes in general to introduce your readers to the subject? Who's writing this article by the way, you or me? Sorry, only joking!

"Er… okay… right. I don't think you need to say much. I've already said they're made of DNA. If you could see a DNA molecule under a microscope, it would look a bit like a spiral staircase. Each of the two railings on either side is made up of a chain of sugar molecules, a special sugar known as deoxyribose, and each step of the staircase is composed of two molecules of a type of chemical called a nucleotide base, or just base for short. Four different bases are found in DNA, and the order in which they occur as you go up the staircase is the gene's genetic code. Simple as that.

"I think that's all you need to say actually So, there you are. That'll have to do anyhow, I'm afraid. Must go now, cheerio."

After he had replaced the receiver, Fiona had burst into applause.

"Bravissimo! Sono molto colpito."

"Thanks. I don't find it easy talking to journalists, I must say. But hold on! Since when have you been learning Italian?"

"I thought that would surprise you. I started taking classes a couple of months ago."

"Why?"

"Well, I've always felt a bit inadequate speaking only one language."

"But you speak Gaelic."

"That doesn't count."

"Why not?"

"Do you know anyone else who speaks it apart from me?"

"No, but why Italian in particular? You must know a little French from your schooldays. Why not improve on that?"

"Well, I thought Italian might come in useful in the future."

Receiving no response, Fiona had turned to the nearest bench, where she started to sort some glassware while Giles quietly moved to the window, taking his empty mug with him. After he'd gazed vacantly at the branches of a nearby sycamore for a minute or so, she returned to place a hand lightly on his shoulder.

"Interesting that tree, is it?"

"Er…in a way. Even this time of the year, it looks so graceful."

"But you can't see much of it from here, can you?"

"No, not a lot…that's true. See that nest up there? We might see some chicks in the spring."

"That would be nice. Young animals are so cute. I love babies too, don't you?'"

"Damn, look at those clouds! I think it's going to pour down any minute. The weather in England gets me down—that, dog poop in parks and dirty tables in restaurants. Which reminds me, did you know it's not just unhygienic to brew tea in the lab, I think it's actually illegal?"

Taking his eyes off the window for the first time, he peered into his mug.

"Goodness knows how many microbes, radioactive isotopes, and chemicals are lurking in there. Or I should say, *were* in there, but are now in my stomach."

"Giles! I seem to recall it was *you* who asked me to make the tea, wasn't it? And anyhow, according to the Health and Safety regulations, it's also forbidden to *drink* tea in here. But that didn't stop you, did it? We've been doing it for years. So does everyone, even Sir Quentin."

Perching himself on the tall trash can they kept under the window, Giles had started to fiddle with his watch. The uncomfortable silence that followed as he polished it with his handkerchief and then wound it up, while she stared at the ceiling her arms crossed, had said more about their feelings for each other than a thousand words.

It would not be long before Giles was mocking the stupidity of his behaviour on that occasion. All that complaining about the journalist, dog poop and the dirty tables had been typical. Why had he always been so inept with women? He would never have got anywhere with Hillary, if she hadn't dragged him onto the dance floor during a varsity ball, after he'd been watching her all evening.

He had been about to invent a reason to run back to his office, when Aram had walked in. Sensing the atmosphere, he had gone directly to the small kitchen table that served as his desk, before asking Fiona if he could borrow her laptop.

"Aram, this the third time in as many weeks you've asked me that!"

"Yes, I know. Sorry Miss Cameron, but…"

"*Doctor* Cameron please!"

"Yes, sorry. The thing is I've left mine at home and need one rather urgently."

"Aram, this is getting ridiculous!" she blurted, slamming a cupboard door closed with her foot. "On the first occasion, you said yours had got a virus, because you hadn't kept your antivirus up to date. On the second, your charger wasn't working and you'd forgotten to buy a new one. And now you've left it at home. Brilliant! Are you like this with everything?"

Aram had glanced at Giles, looking for support, but none had been forthcoming.

"Don't you think you've got a bit of a nerve?" she'd continued. "On the only occasion I've ever asked to borrow yours, you refused point blank, didn't you? Conveniently, you were just about to leave."

"As I said, I'm really sorry, Dr Cameron, but I need to look up a few websites before my next meeting with Professor Butterfield."

He had glanced at Giles again, only to find him preoccupied with his cufflinks.

"If I let you, where will you use it, Aram?"

"Can I use the Internet cable in your office?"

"No, I'm about to work in there. What's wrong with the lab's wi-fi?"

"Sometimes the signal's very weak. Can I take it to Henry's lab across the corridor?"

"Okay, if he's agreeable. But don't let your memory stick anywhere near it! I don't want it getting infected."

Aram had shrugged his shoulders, as if there was nothing to get fussed about.

"And bring it straight back when you're done, please."

"Of course. Thank you."

"And please close the lab door after you."

After he'd done so, Fiona had made eye contact with Giles for the first time since they'd left her office.

"As I've said before, Giles, I really don't like him using it. With anyone else, it wouldn't matter. But I think he's dishonest. I know you think I'm being paranoid, but there's something shifty about him. I'm with him more than you, don't forget.

"Anyhow, to get back to where we were. Are you feeling all right?"

"Yes, thanks," he sighed.

"Are you sure?"

"Yes. If Hillary were here, she'd explain."

"Hillary?"

"Yes."

"Well, unfortunately she isn't, is she, Giles? So I suppose you'll have to instead…if it's important enough?"

"It is important, Fiona, *very*. I think we both know what's going on, don't we?"

"I think I'm starting to. I hope so anyhow. But I want to hear it from you, Giles…please."

That was all he'd needed.

***

"Excuse me, sir," a familiar voice whispered in Giles's ear above the whir of the engines. "Captain Wilson said we need to buckle up. Apparently, the jet stream will give us a bumpy ride for the next few minutes."

After helping him with his belt, Vicky departed to leave him with his thoughts, having sensed it was not the right time to talk.

As he watched her talking to another passenger, Giles reflected on the contrast between her outgoing frivolous nature and Fiona's very different approach to life. Getting to know each other after her arrival from Aberdeen had been a slow process. From very different worlds, she born into a family of modest means near Oban on Scotland's west coast, he into more privileged circumstances in the south of England, their relationship had been strictly professional for a couple of years. The ice had not been broken until Giles had stood in for a boyfriend who had pulled out of a date at the last minute. The following day they had started going for walks together, first at lunchtime, then at weekends. On a Friday they would drop into a pub after work, avoiding any they knew were popular with colleagues.

Although she'd had her fair share of boyfriends in Scotland, and had continued to be popular after crossing the border, Fiona had avoided getting emotionally involved with any of them. There had been too many divorces among relatives and friends to rush into a relationship. Nevertheless, in Giles's case she would probably have moved more quickly, if it had it not been for Aram and the unseen eyes behind the College's many leaded windows overlooking every path and quadrangle. And Jane's combination of inquisitiveness and maternal attitude towards Giles, always keen to protect him from his perceived weaknesses as much as other people's ambitions, had added to the difficulty. Romantic as Magdalen might appear to the casual visitor, it was certainly not an ideal place in which to have an affair.

It had been just before his trip to Majorca that Giles had come to accept the reality that he had been smitten. But had Fiona reached the same point? Would she ever? He'd seen no alternative but to wait and see, and the few days with Bill Eccles had been the perfect salve to soothe his torment. For Fiona's part, it had given her an opportunity to come to terms with her feelings, and the appearance of Steve's paper during their separation the catalyst to express them.

Chapter Eight

Giles and Fiona had left the College early that afternoon to spend a few hours in her flat together. During his short journey home afterwards, it had occurred that Steve might have organised a press conference to get some much needed good publicity from his success. Even if he had not taken the initiative, there was a good chance the NIH would have done so. By the time he was putting the key into his front door, he'd decided to waste no time searching online for a press release. Hearing him enter, Mavis had run to help him with his clothes.

"Just in time before I'm about to leave, Professor! I've been waiting to get my hands on this jacket. I noticed before you took it to Spain it's about time it went to the cleaners. Do I have permission?"

"Of course, Mavis. You're quite right."

"Mmm! Smells better than it did, I must say. I think you've been shopping for perfume this afternoon, haven't you, Professor?"

"Er...yes, that's right."

"Jane's birthday, is it?"

"No...my...niece's actually. Those shop assistants in Cornmarket Street spray the stuff everywhere."

"Don't they just? Clumsy too. Somehow, one of them got lipstick on you."

"Where?"

"On your shirt collar, just here."

Giles had looked at himself in the Victorian mirror that hung by the door.

"So she did! I remember she was holding several lipsticks in one hand for another customer, while juggling with the perfume testers in the other one."

"Never mind, it'll come off in the wash. I hope nobody in the university spotted it when you were on the way here. Wouldn't like them to think you'd been up to something, would we?"

"Ha...no we certainly wouldn't!"

While Giles was taking off his shoes, Mavis folded his jacket and dropped it into a plastic bag ready for collection.

"Which perfume did you decide to buy, Professor?"

"None. Couldn't decide. I'll try again tomorrow. Must go to my computer now, Mavis. Thanks for your help."

Once at his desk, Giles had gone to The Guardian website. After scanning the pages for 19 December, he had found what he was hoping for.

Scientist reveals secret of cancer gene breakthrough

"At a press conference in Washington, DC yesterday, Dr Stephen Salomon, Director of the US National Cancer Institute, explained how he had managed to create an artificial strand of DNA that can function as a switch for the *Achilles* gene in such a short space of time, an achievement he has just reported in the journal Science. Copies of the *Achilles* gene, discovered by the MECCAR institute in Jordan, are present in all our cells. Each has the ability to kill its cell should it ever change into a cancer cell. But it does not do so, because it is missing a crucial DNA switch that is required to activate it when needed. The only exception is in a tribe of Bedouins, who have such a switch and have never been known to develop any kind of cancer. As MECCAR had pledged to the tribe it would never go public with anything unique about their genes, researchers everywhere have been racing to invent a piece of DNA that would act as an artificial switch. Two pieces of information were required: the right sequence of nucleotide bases, commonly known as its genetic code, and the position in the chromosome where it would need to be inserted by molecular surgery for it to work.

Dr Salomon said he had managed to beat everyone else to the solution because he had already developed a revolutionary computer programme that can predict the properties of any DNA insertion, as such extra pieces of DNA are called, for whatever function is required. He declined to give any details of his software, as it had taken him several years to develop as a private venture. He was in the process of filing a patent application for it, and when that was awarded he would sell or licence the programme to biotechnology companies and universities. When it was put to him that, given its potential value to medical science, it might be unethical to deny other researchers access to the software until then, he said any short-term negative impact on progress would be more than offset in the long-term by the fact that all money from its sale or licensing will go to a new cancer research charity that he plans to create."

***

Giles was perusing a printout of the article, when the familiar rattle of Vicky's trolley approached. Hoping to avoid another chat, he grabbed his copy of the Science article, and pretended to be engrossed in a figure of the *Achilles* gene with Steve's

DNA insertion shown next to it. But to his disappointment the ploy backfired.

"I recognise that!" she squealed. "It's DNA, what genes are made of. Let me have a closer look. Believe it or not, I know a bit about that. Each gene is like a long ladder that's twisted into a spiral, isn't it? That's why it's called a double helix."

She pointed to one of the white ceramic bowls on the trolley, containing fusilli pasta with pesto sauce.

"It's a bit like those twisted pastas here."

Using a fork from the trolley as a pointer, she continued enthusiastically.

"Each of those bits here going across, joining the two sides, is made up of a couple of chemicals called nucleoside...no, hold on... nucleotide bases. There are just four different types of those, and their order as you go round and round the spiral is a set of instructions that tells the rest of the cell how to make one single protein."

She stood up to put her hands in her hips, and gave him a smug grin.

"Surprised?"

"Just a bit!" he spluttered. "How come...?"

"I used to be a lab tech with a small biotech company in Iowa. Bio-Iowa-Ceuticals they were called. But I left it to take this job."

"Why was that? Too much of a mouthful?"

"Ha! No, I got the wanderlust. Iowa's very small, very provincial, and exceptionally boring, unless you happen to like endless flat fields of corn, or when there's no corn, endless flat fields of nothingness."

He placed his hand over the page to conceal the picture.

"I bet you can't remember the names of those four bases that make up the gene's alphabet."

"Er...let me think. There's adenine...cytosine...er... thiamine, no that's a vitamin, isn't it? I mean thymine...and finally...garnine. No, that doesn't sound right...you tell me."

"Guanine. My, I'm impressed."

She lifted his hand to look at the page again.

"What's an *Achilles* gene?"

"It's a very important gene indeed."

"In what way?"

"They're present in all our cells, and each one has the ability to kill its own cell should it ever turn into a cancer cell."

"How?"

"By producing a protein that starves the cell of energy."

"Wow, that's clever!"

"It would be if it worked. But it doesn't."

"Why not?"

"There's a bit of DNA missing. It's always been like that."

She pointed the fork at a short series of letters above the gene.

"Is that it?"

"Not exactly. It's represents a manmade piece of DNA that can substitute for the piece that's missing. If it's put into the chromosome in just the right place, *Achilles* works a treat from then on."

"What straight away, and kills the cell?"

"Only if it's a cancer cell, or becomes one later."

"You mean that extra little piece functionalizes the gene?"

"Er…yes…you could say that. In fact, that very word appears in article's title. Look."

He turned the copy over to let her see the first page.

"It was invented by a friend of mine. He's going to get the Nobel Prize for it in a few weeks' time."

"My, how exciting! Are you on your way to see him?"

"No, he's on a lecture tour before going to Sweden for the ceremony."

Vicky took the article out of his hand to look at the figure again.

"The bit he invented is quite short, isn't it? Only seven bases long."

"That's right."

She pointed to a number printed above *Achilles*.

"What's this?"

"It's the position in the chromosome where the extra piece of DNA needs to go. Closer to *Achilles* or farther away, and it doesn't work."

She screwed up her eyes to read some of the small print.

"It says here that the article was published just before last Christmas. And you said he's getting the Nobel Prize next month. Gosh, that's one year almost to the day! Most people have to wait much longer, don't they?"

"Yes, they do. In fact, one man had to wait fifty years, by which time he was almost ninety. I've never heard of a Nobel being awarded as quickly as this one. But it was an extraordinary achievement, acknowledged everywhere as a huge breakthrough the day it was published. He must have been put up for it in January, just before the deadline."

"Smells of politics, if you ask me. When's the big day?"

"Tenth of December, same day every year."

"Why's that?"

"It's the day in 1886 when Alfred Nobel went to the big ammunition dump in the sky."

"Sorry?"

"The day he died. He made his money by inventing dynamite."

"Ah, I see. How did your friend manage to do it before anyone else? There must have been lots of people trying."

"He said he'd developed a computer programme for this sort of thing, which nobody else has got. But that's all we know. He's keeping it under wraps until he can commercialise it."

"Almost makes me want to go back to the lab. Almost, but not quite. Well, must go, otherwise your meal will get even colder. If you'd like me to give it another blast in the microwave, just press the button."

As Vicky wandered off with her customary little wave, Giles cast his mind back to a conversation he had had with Fiona.

***

They had been taking a stroll along Addison's Walk behind the College, speculating about what sort of software could have guided Steve so swiftly to the answer, and neither had come up with any good ideas.

"I'm not surprised Steve's keeping it to himself until he's got a patent," Giles had remarked as he'd stopped to admire a couple of mallards in Holywell Stream. "It must be worth a gold mine. That's the way it is these days. Years ago, academics never thought of patenting anything. It was unheard of, contrary to the spirit of science and all that. You'd be ostracised just for thinking about it. But then universities started to behave like private companies under pressure from politicians. Very sad!"

On reaching Holywell Ford, Fiona had sat down on one of the wooden benches and raised the hood of her anorak to shelter from the wind.

"You know, Giles, what sort of software Steve claims to have invented is not the only puzzle. I've been thinking about what you said over brunch about Steve patenting it. I don't understand that either."

"Why? It's common sense, isn't it, if he plans to market it?"

"Well, the thing is I'm pretty sure software's automatically protected by copyright, like books and music are, and usually is not patentable unless there's something really special about the programming."

"Are you sure?"

"I think so. You see, most software doesn't have anything that's novel to programming itself. Most programmes are just sets of instructions written in a language that computers understand. It's a bit like you writing a piece of poetry in Arabic. You couldn't patent that, and what's more you don't need to. It's protected by copyright. Most computer software is the same. When you go back to your office, take a look at PowerPoint or Word. I'm sure it'll say somewhere that it's protected by copyright."

By now, the two mallards had gone on their way. After dropping a few pebbles in the water and waiting for the ripples to reach the far bank, Giles had also sat down.

"If you're right, I agree that's also rather odd. Talking of patents, I heard on the radio last night he's also planning to patent a viral vector he's engineered for gene therapy."

"You mean a modified virus that contains both *Achilles* and its switch packaged together?"

"Yes."

"That's a different matter, of course. That *would* be patentable."

"Apparently, the big pharma companies are already lining up to buy the rights. The BBC said he's decided to call the switch *Deidamia*, and the cancer-killing virus containing the two of them *Neoptolemus*."

"I wonder where got those names from."

"Probably his brother. He's a professor of Classical literature. I don't think Steve could have thought it up. In Greek mythology, Deidamia was Achilles' lover. She had a child by him called Neoptolemus. So, in the same way that he was created by the union of the Deidamia and Achilles, Steve's engineered virus will be created by the of the union of his *Deidamia* and MECCAR's *Achilles*. On top of which Neoptolemus, grew up to slay lots of Trojans, just like…"

"Steve's virus will one day slay armies of cancer cells. Very clever!

"Well, I must get moving before this wind freezes my bum. By the way, I hope you haven't forgotten it's my birthday tomorrow. I'm off to the Sales now to treat myself to a new dress. But before I go, there's something I haven't told you. When Aram returned my laptop the other day, I discovered two things. You remember I instructed him not to use a memory stick? Well, he did. My antivirus software says that about ten minutes after he left the lab it automatically scanned a piece of hardware with only one item in it. I don't know about you, but to me that sounds very much like a memory stick. What else could it be? So the next thing I did was to take a look at my 'Recently Changed' folder, which revealed that he'd opened several of my folders and files soon after that. The big question is, 'Why?'"

"Have you spoken to him?"

"No."

"Okay, I'll have a strong word with him. Leave it with me."

"I'd rather you didn't."

"Don't worry about upsetting him."

"It's not that. It's just that I don't want him to know that I know what he's been up to. As I've said before, I don't trust him. He might be up to something. I'd like to keep an eye on him."

"All right, have it your way. But I think you're overreacting, you know. He probably just wanted to see how you do things; how you present your data and so on. He's on a learning curve."

"You may be right, Giles. But you may also be wrong. And when you take into account his other oddities, I wouldn't put my money on the first one."

After walking together as far as the Porter's Lodge, Giles had gone to his office to see if Fiona had been right about Microsoft Office being protected by copyright. When he found that she had, and there was no mention of a patent, he had dropped into his chair as he tried to take it in. If it was true that Steve's programme was of a type that could be patented, what could it be? Or had he been misleading everyone? If so, why should he have invented such a story?

After several minutes without any ideas, he had decided his next step should be to consult a few colleagues. Taking a pencil and a sheet of paper from his desk, he had jotted down a few names: Pete Strange in Boston, Tom Ballantyne in Edinburgh, Pierre Fruchart in Paris, Vladimir Kapralov in Moscow, and Ernst Pijpers in Leiden. They were the best minds in the business as far as he was concerned. If they couldn't come up with any brainwaves, nobody could.

"Jane," he had called through the half-open door. "Could you come through, please?"

She had appeared holding a mug of coffee in her hand.

"I was just about to bring you this, Professor. You and Fiona looked chilled to the bone when you passed my window a few minutes ago. No wonder you were huddled so close together. I thought you were cuddling her at first. Wasn't that silly of me?"

"Ha! Anyone can make a mistake, Jane. Thanks for the coffee. I'd like you to set up a conference call, please, for seven o'clock this evening. I'm too busy between now and then. Here's the list of names. I think you have their numbers. I'll take it at home. Presumably they'll do likewise given the time of day, apart from Dr Strange."

The call that evening had produced a lively debate with plenty of suggestions about the possible nature of Steve's computer programme. But after lengthy discussion none had stood up to scrutiny. The general consensus had been that whatever it was, it must have been a stroke of genius on Steve's part. But that's as far as it went. The details were a complete mystery.

Giles had always recognised Steve's great ability as a researcher. That's why he had spent his sabbatical year at the NCI. But he had difficulty accepting the notion he was a genius. His talent was for solid work along conventional lines—rigorously testing other people's ideas experimentally, and then moving on to the next logical step. He was a good organiser and an extremely hard worker, but definitely not a great original thinker.

First thing next morning, he had donned his duffel coat and gone for a walk on Christ Church Meadow, just across the road from Magdalen. Troubled throughout the night by the confusion over Steve's programme, he had been hoping the cold air and the quiet solitude would stimulate some new ideas. To his great disappointment it had had no such effect, but the occasion was one he would long remember nevertheless. For as he had stood by the bank of the River Cherwell, he had become strangely drawn to the sight of the moon over the silhouettes of the distant trees. As it had disappeared and reappeared with each passing cloud, it had seemed to glow ever brighter. He had soon become mesmerised by it in a way he found quite disturbing. During his youth in the Middle East, the full moon had often fascinated him, with its valleys, mountains and craters so sharply visible in the clear desert air. But this had been a very different experience. And it had not been a full moon. For on that twelfth day of January, it had been little more than a sliver of a waning crescent.

When it had eventually disappeared behind a mass of dark storm clouds, he had headed pensively into the wind down Broad Walk towards St Aldates. By the time he had reached the steps opposite Christ Church, the likeness of the moon's crescent to the symbol of Islam had taken root in his mind. Was he receiving a message that something to do with the Middle East was not right in his world? And those storm clouds, had they been a portent of disaster? Startled by these questions, he had tried to put them out of his mind. Leaving the path to shelter under one of the conifer trees when it had started to rain, he had dropped onto his haunches to mull it over, raising his hood to hide his face from the students' windows opposite.

"A message?" he had whispered to himself. "Is that possible? Could it *really* have been a message? No, come on, Giles! Don't be ridiculous. You're a scientist, remember. It must have been an optical effect of some sort—the cold air, high-altitude ice particles, thin clouds, something like that playing tricks. Nothing more than that."

Chapter Nine

Come the following July, after an uneventful spring, Giles had felt the need to do some maintenance on his cottage in Little Compton, the small village tucked between Chipping Norton and Moreton-in-Marsh among the woodlands and farmlands of the Cotswolds, less than an hour's drive from Oxford. At around six o'clock on a Friday evening he would set off with the trunk of his Austin Healey packed with any tools he might need. Once he had brushed the cobwebs from the beams, washed the windows, cleared the leaves from the gutters, oiled the hinges of the gates, and creosoted the fence that enclosed the small front garden, he had started on the two big jobs that were essential before the autumn— grouting the stonework and painting the window frames.

Each Saturday had followed the same routine. First thing after a mug of tea, he would be off for a brisk walk through the local lanes and footpaths. If the skies were clear, he would usually make his way past Hawton Farm to Barton-on-the-Heath before heading south to Long Compton, where he would stop for breakfast in the Red Lion—usually a plate of hand-carved ham and a basket of freshly baked Cotswold Crunch, washed down with a pint of Benson's cider. Then after reading one of the newspapers on offer, he would be on his way to the ancient stones of Rollright before completing a full circle back to his village.

He loved to feel the country wind on his face, relishing the myriad of aromas it carried from grasses, flowers, and leaves. If something of interest caught his eye, an unfamiliar moss on a stone perhaps or a hapless egg between the roots of a tree, he would stop to remove his glasses and study it, sometimes taking a photograph or two to show Albert, the College's head gardener.

If he had the time, he might drop into one of the small churches to soak up the atmosphere and admire the craftsmanship. His favourites were St. Denys in Little Compton, where on a good day he would enjoy the sun on his face through the Edward the Confessor window, and St. Philips in Little Rollright to admire its celebrated wall tombs. Seated in the back pew of any church, he would picture the baptisms, marriages, and funerals the damp musty walls must have witnessed over the centuries. Afterwards, he might pick his way among the weathered headstones of the churchyard and peer at their inscriptions between moss, lichen, and liverwort. Before departing, he would pause to stroke the gnarled branches of an ancient yew tree, their bark and sap reincarnations of the flesh and blood of villagers of centuries past.

Back in the cottage, the hard work would start at around one o'clock. To break the tedium, he was inclined to alternate painting and grouting at hourly intervals. When too bored with both, he would break off to put some finishing touches to the hard work that Benjamin, his gardener, had done during the week. The afternoon would end with a shower and a change of clothes before going to Little Compton's own Red Lion for dinner and a chat with the locals. The rest of the evening would usually be spent sorting through his vast collection of unread books. If the weather was fine, he would do this on the patio until the sun had set behind his neighbour's oak trees.

The only downside to these rural breaks, and it was a big one, was Fiona's absence. Having taken her Italian lessons very seriously, she had arranged to spend every Saturday and Sunday in conversation with a drama student from Pozzuoli, near Naples. Although Giles had tried to convince her he could do a better job, she had not been persuaded.

"Mille grazie," she had replied with a cheeky grin, "but I'd rather end up with a Neapolitan accent than a 'Liverpolitan' one."

"If I don't have one, why should you?" he had retorted.

"Only teasing."

"The fact that he's a native doesn't mean he's necessarily a good teacher, you know, Fiona."

"But he is that too. He did a great job teaching me to roll my Rs the other day! Went home very pleased with my performance."

When he was not working, relaxing, or thinking about Fiona, his mind would sometimes drift to Steve and his DNA switch. The silence from the NCI had been deafening since his Science article had appeared. What was he up to? Of the many rumours, the most plausible had been that he was testing *Neoptolemus* in mice to see if it could cure them of cancer. And what had happened to that mysterious computer programme?

His lonely weekends had continued until the start of the Michelmas term. The first few weeks had been like any other. Then on the fifth of October, while he was waiting for Mavis to serve breakfast, The Guardian newspaper had dropped through the letterbox. Normally he would have left it in the hallway to collect on his way out, his normal routine over breakfast being to prepare for the day ahead. But this time he had gone to pick it up, knowing that the Nobel Prize in Physiology or Medicine would have been announced in Stockholm the previous day, always the first Monday of October.

What he'd been looking for was on page five:

"Nobel Prize for US cancer researcher

It was announced yesterday in Stockholm that this year's Nobel Prize in Physiology or Medicine will be awarded to Dr Stephen Salomon of the US National Cancer Institute for inventing the *Deidamia* insertion, a short length of DNA that is able to activate the *Achilles* gene, a potential killer of cancer cells. To exert its life-saving effect, this piece of DNA needs to be inserted at just the right position in the same chromosome that *Achilles* occupies. Hitting on the right combination of genetic code and position so quickly was heralded as almost miraculous when Dr Salomon reported his success in Science. The key to his success was a new computer programme he had developed, details of which he has not yet released. The achievement has opened the door to new forms of cancer treatment. Dr Salomon will receive his award during the annual ceremony in Stockholm Concert Hall on 10 December.

The *Achilles* gene was originally discovered by Jordan's MECCAR institute, which opened only…"

While he had been working his way down the column, Mavis had brought his porridge and topped his eggs, before going to the windows to draw back the curtains.

"Beautiful sky today, Professor," she had said with her broad Lancastrian smile. "I love October. And doesn't the moon look wonderful this morning? Reminds me of the flag of Turkey that was on a form my George was filling in the other day. He's going to import figs from there…or is it dates? I'm not sure."

She had tied back the curtains and opened the window a little, before taking a deep breath.

"Ah, smell that air from the countryside! Does you a power of good, doesn't it? Did you see that programme on TV last night about the terrible pollution in London? Said it kills thousands every year. Hope you don't end up there. Do you think you'll ever leave Oxford?"

Not receiving a reply, she had turned to find him staring out of the window, the newspaper at his feet.

"Oh dear, I can see you're lost in your work again! You professors are all the same. I can see you don't want to listen to all my chitchat. So I'll be off to the kitchen to iron those shirts.

Would you like less starch this time? You said the collars were too stiff last week."

"Er…what was that, Mavis?"

"I said shall I make it less starch today, Professor?"

"Good idea. Fiona's been saying I'm putting on weight. A salad would do nicely this evening."

Giles had now moved to the window.

"Didn't hear a word I said, did you?" she had giggled. "Dr Hickson down the road was just as bad. I was talking about your *shirts*, Professor, not your *dinner*."

"Sorry, Mavis! I was miles away, about a quarter of a million actually. Yes, yes, that would be better, thank you."

"Are you all right? You look a bit strange."

"No, er, I mean yes, I'm fine, thanks. It's just the moon. Unusually bright, isn't it? Almost dazzling. Hard to take my eyes off it."

Mavis had joined him to take another look.

"No more than usual, I'd say. Are you sure you're okay?"

Mavis had stood on her toes to feel his forehead.

"Your head's gone all sweaty."

"Has it? Better get on with my porridge then. Low blood sugar perhaps."

Making his way back to the table, he had recalled the occasion on Christ Church Meadow nine months ago, when he had been similarly spellbound by the moon's waning crescent. He recalled how that had occurred after he'd been pondering Steve's computer programme during a restless night. How odd it should have happened again at the very moment he was reading about Steve's Nobel Prize.

Arriving at his office, he had found Jane already at her desk, smartly dressed in a red tweed suit. She had got up to move into his office and greet him cheerfully.

"Good morning, Professor. That was good timing. This year's invitation to write your regular piece about the Nobel Prize for The Oxford Times arrived a few minutes ago. They don't waste time, do they? I heard on the radio that Dr Salomon's been selected. Isn't that nice? And there's something else for you. Fiona asked me to give you her latest grant application to read through. It's there on your desk."

"Thank you, Jane. You're looking very colourful today. Brightens the place up, I must say."

"Thank you. It's a Christmas present from my sister in Gloucester."

After dictating a short letter of acceptance to the newspaper, he had spent the rest of the day working on Fiona's draft. As there had been much rewriting to do, it had not been until the evening that he had left for the Turf Tavern.

Upon entering, he had heard Fiona's unmistakable laughter in the far corner, as a couple of girlfriends were bidding their farewells. She had spotted him at once and waved him over.

"Giles! Haven't seen you all day. Have you heard who the Nobel Prize has gone to?"

After glancing left and right, he had leaned forward to touch her hand.

"Yes, I have, dear. And in asking that question, you've illustrated perfectly why you haven't seen me all day. Let me explain."

"Oh, God, spare me," she had gasped, rolling her eyes. "Here we go again, I suppose. Another sermon on the virtues of perfect English?"

"I'm afraid so. First, there's the grammar. What you meant to say is, 'Have you heard *to whom* the Nobel Prize has gone?' Second...vocabulary...it could not have '*gone*' to anyone. While certain prizes may have legs, those awarded by the Karolinska Institute definitely do not. What you meant is, 'To whom the Nobel Prize has been *awarded*.' And finally, there's the small matter of accuracy. It has not *yet* been awarded to anyone. Steve will become a Nobel Laureate on December the tenth. Between now and then, he has been *selected* to receive it. That's all. Got it...grammar...vocabulary...accuracy?"

By now Fiona was propped against the wall pretending to snore.

"Sorry, Fiona. I know you've told me many times I'm a patronising, sanctimonious, nit-picking bore. I've promised to get rid of the habit, and I shall one day. But this is a special case. Unfortunately, many reviewers of grant applications are irritated by sloppy English. And when they're in a bad mood, it's not good for you, no matter how good the science, which, by the way, I thought was pretty good. When they're in a bad frame of mind, they start to get picky. It's important to keep the bastards happy. You should know that by now."

"I do, but the problem is I've been so tired lately. And that's partly your fault!"

"But grantsmanship is very important. It's an essential survival mechanism."

"Yes, I know that all too well. And…er…by the way, Giles, I looked up the word grantsmanship in a dictionary once. And guess what? It don't exist. It ain't there. There's no such word. Sorry!"

She had pulled her tongue at him playfully.

"Well, I'm sure it will one day. I'm just ahead of my time, that's all. So to get back to where we were. What do you think about the big news?"

"First, don't you want a drink?"

"Yes, thanks, almost forgot. I'll have my usual."

Fiona had caught the attention of the barmaid behind the counter, and drawn the letters DS in the air with her hand.

"What do I think about it? Far too soon, Giles, in my humble opinion. They should have waited a few years to see how it works out. There could be a problem that hasn't surfaced yet."

"Possible, I agree—but unlikely. Don't forget, several labs have already confirmed that *Deidamia* does what Steve said it does."

"But why should he get it so soon, when others have had to wait half their entire lives? I think it's an American conspiracy. First, the NCI gets special funding. Then his paper gets fast-tracked into one of the very best journals. And to top it all, the Nobel lot elect him in record time. I can see Crabb's grubby fingerprints everywhere."

"You may be right. But that's the way of the world, I'm afraid. Unfortunately, it doesn't pay to play by the rules all the time.

Machiavelli was right. 'A virtuous man will always come to grief among so many who are not virtuous.' I don't like it any more than you, but alas it's as true today as it was five hundred years ago. If Steve had said no to Crabb's money and influence, he'd be out of a job by now, and probably divorced too. But instead, he grabbed the opportunity with both hands, and is now a national hero."

"It's also unfair that Ahmad Sharif can't share it. It's ridiculous that Nobels can't be awarded posthumously."

"Doesn't make sense, I agree. But you have to remember that the Nobel Prize is very important for Sweden's image. It gives the Swedes kudos with a capital K. Puts them on a pedestal from which they, and only they, can proclaim who are the world's very best scientists. And to make the most of it, they need a big event: an impressive ceremony, a sumptuous banquet, speeches, a ball, royalty. It would all be a bit flat if the winners were six feet under."

"Alfred Nobel would certainly agree. Nobody liked a big bang more than him...sorry, more than he."

"Ha, ha...well said. Although to be fair, he didn't make that rule. It was someone else's idea. Here comes my D 'n' S, thanks. You read my mind."

"I wish I could do that more often! To change the subject, Giles, you haven't mentioned Steve's computer programme for a long time. Did you ever hear any more about it?"

"No, I didn't. Pity, because you could certainly make good use of it. That grant application's solid, but something extra to make it sparkle wouldn't be bad thing. You know what I mean?"

Fiona had nodded pensively.

"If you were to add some fancy genetic engineering, it could very well make the difference between success and failure. They award only about one in ten, don't forget."

"Don't remind me! It's depressing. I don't know what I'll do if it's turned down. Where would my salary come from next year?"

She had been waiting for his answer, when she'd spotted another of her girlfriends entering.

"Oh, look who's here. It's Ros. She'll cheer me up."

A tall brunette, smartly dressed in a black woollen overcoat and gold silk scarf, approached them cheerfully.

"Giles, let me introduce you to Ros Hitchcock. We met in Scissors a few weeks ago. She's the one who showed me how to do this French herringbone. She used to be a model."

"Delighted to meet you, Ros. Here, have my chair. I'll fetch another while you take off your coat. There's a peg on the wall behind you."

"Ros got fed up modelling, Giles. Now she's studying art in evening classes, and earns her bread and butter as a typist with Hamilton Reeves, the law firm in Rose Lane opposite the College. Which reminds me—I haven't told you yet, have I? Excuse me a tick, Ros, but this is really important. Ivor, my lawyer cousin in Inverness, dropped in to see me the other night. Do you remember my telling you—notice the my, not a me in sight—that software is automatically protected by copyright?"

"Yes."

"Well, not only is that true, but according to him, software cannot be patented in either the UK or Europe. In the States, it can be under some circumstances, but even there it's unusual. He also said a patent application in the States could easily take five years to process, and cost tens of thousands of dollars.

Forgive me, Ros, but I had to get that out. Now, I'll go and fetch another bottle of wine and an extra glass, while the two of you get to know each other."

Fiona had returned to find Ros giggling.

"Oops! Sorry, am I interrupting something intimate?"

"Giles is so funny, Fiona. He said I shouldn't complain about being a legal secretary because it could be worse, I could..."

"Stop! Let me guess...er...I know...because you could be an *illegal* one. Yes? Ha, ha...yawn...yawn. Giles, if you really want to impress one of my gorgeous friends behind my back, you'll have to do much better than that."

After taking the bottle and filling the glasses, Giles had returned to the subject of Steve's software.

"I think I should give him a call tonight, Fiona."

"Ivor?"

"No, Steve. Sorry to be talking shop, Ros. It'll end soon. I'll congratulate him on the news, then ask him if his software is on the market yet. If it isn't, which I assume is the case, I'll tell him about your grant application—how important it is, how hard you've worked on it, and how it would stand a much better chance if he would lend you a copy."

Fiona had raised her glass and winked at Ros.

"Isn't he wonderful? Giles is a chum of this year's Nobel Prize winner in medicine, no less. Now you know why I put up with his flirting. Cheers!"

When Giles had got out of bed to call Steve from his study that evening, it was just after 7:00 p.m. in Chevy Chase. He could still recall every word of the conversation.

"Hi Steve, it's Giles Butterfield in Oxford."

"Giles, this is a nice surprise!"

"I'm calling to offer my congratulations."

"Gee, thanks. Still haven't gotten used to the idea. Seems too good to be true."

"I can imagine. I'm sure Hank's over the moon too."

"You bet! He'll be partying all week. Ted Crabb too. He's organising a special reception in my honour at the White House."

"I hope you're ready for all those after-dinner speeches."

"I'm not actually, or for the rest. The phone hasn't stopped: interviews, chat shows, documentaries, you name it. I've decided to escape on a lecture tour at the end of the month, ending up in Stockholm for the ceremony."

"With the family?"

"Not for the lectures. Marie-Claire will join me in Europe when they're over, and then we'll fly to Sweden together."

"I won't ask what you've been doing in the lab lately. I'm sure that's under wraps."

"Afraid so, Giles. All I can say is I've gotten some exciting results in animals. But I'm not publishing until we've got a patent for *Neoptolemus*. You know how it is. NIH policy—patents first, papers second."

"Do you have one for your software yet?"

"Not yet."

"You still reckon a patent's necessary?"

"So my attorney says."

"Copyright protection's not enough?"

"Apparently not, unfortunately."

"Have you filed the application?"

"Ages ago."

"Still waiting?"

"Yeah. He says it will be months, years even."

"And he thinks you'll get it?"

"Certain."

"Will it be yours or the NIH's?"

"Mine. It's different than *Neoptolemus*. Did it on my own. Paid a freelance guy to help me with the programming."

"We're all longing to know how it works, Steve. Is there nothing you can tell us? No details, just a few clues."

"All I can say, Giles, is that I pulled together lots of different types of data from hundreds of publications, crunched the numbers, and worked out an algorithm that describes a previously unknown law of nature that governs the regulation of genes by DNA enhancers. The programme's basically a very complex formula. I enter the values of several variables, the programme does the calculations, and it points me in the right direction."

"That's mind-blowing, Steve. I'd never have dreamt it possible."

"Ah, well, there you are…I did. I'd been thinking about it for years. It was a gut feeling."

"You've clearly got very clever guts, Steve. Anyhow, to change the subject, do you remember my assistant, Fiona? You've met her at a few congresses."

"You bet, charming girl, lovely Scotch accent."

"Yes, very nice Scottish accent. I'm afraid she's in a bit of a spot, and I've been wondering if you could do her a favour."

"Fire away, Giles, anything to help a young and up-and-coming geneticist."

"The problem's this, Steve. Her contract runs out soon, and she desperately needs another grant. Otherwise she'll be out of a job. She's written a good application, but it might not be quite good enough. You know how it is. It could do with something extra, something state of the art. If you could lend her a copy of your amazing software for a couple of weeks, she could…"

"Hold it there, cowboy! Giles, my attorney would *kill* me. The programme would then be in the public domain, giving it no chance of a patent. It could have been copied, hacked, infected with a virus, anything. Sorry, no possibility—much as I'd like to help. Anything else but that, sorry."

"Well, it wouldn't really be in the public domain, would it, Steve? After all, you wouldn't be giving us the source code or details of the formula. I presume all she'd have to do is plug in some numbers, and get the answer. Yes?"

"Well, yes, that's true. But unfortunately attorneys in the US don't look at things that way, Giles. As far as they're concerned, giving you a CD of the programme is a security risk. They don't know what you're going to do with it. Don't forget, it could be worth millions, and they don't know you."

"We wouldn't lend it to anyone, I promise. We'd keep it under lock and key, and return it to you the minute she's finished."

"Nope, sorry, Giles, can't take the risk. Not even for you."

"What a pity. She'll be devastated."

"Sorry."

"Well, it was worth a try. If you change your mind, let me know. I'd better be off now. Past my bedtime. Enjoy the lecture tour, and your big day, of course. I'll be thinking of you. Bye for now."

Chapter Ten

"The bastard! The selfish effing bastard," Fiona had screamed as she kicked the trash can across the lab. "I never did like him. How could he be so mean? Surely, he knows he can trust you of all people?"

Giles had broken the bad news first thing the following morning.

"What am I going to do now? I suppose I'll have to submit the application as it stands."

"It's not the end of the world, Fiona. We'll just have to prepare another one to keep in reserve, that's all. Then if your present one is rejected we follow up with that one."

"Which will take me at least six weeks, *and* mean postponing the next series of experiments we've been planning. Brilliant!"

"Have I let you down?"

"Of course not. It's him. I was convinced he'd do you a favour."

"He's done me many in the past. But not this time, I'm afraid. He wouldn't budge."

"Did he tell you anything about the programme?"

"Only that it's an algorithm that describes a natural law governing the regulation of genes. Said he'd discovered it by analysing data from hundreds of published studies."

Fiona had looked at him in amazement.

"An *algorithm*? You mean like a mathematical formula?"

"I suppose so. Something like that anyway."

"Now I *am* confused. Do you remember last night I mentioned that Ivor had told me that in the States software can be patented under some circumstances, but not others?"

"Yes."

"Well, what I didn't tell you is that he gave me Albert Einstein's famous equation E = mc2 as an example of something that definitely could not have been patented even in the States, because…wait for it…it's an *algorithm* describing a law of nature. His very words."

"He said that?"

"Yes. You don't think it could all be a fairy tale, do you? That the truth is the programme doesn't actually exist? That he made it up for some reason?"

***

Even now, so many months later, as Giles watched another aircraft skimming above the clouds, its four vapour trails glistening in the sunshine, the thought of Fiona's question sent a chill down his spine. Up to that point, there had been only confusion about the nature of Steve's programme. The numerous emails Giles had received from colleagues around the world had expressed bewilderment about what Steve could have learnt about the regulation of genes that the rest of them did not already know, but none had gone as far as doubting the programme's existence. If Fiona was right and it was all a fabrication, what possible reason could Steve have had for committing such a deception? Could it be he had come across the formula for *Deidamia* purely by chance, as sometimes happens in science, and he didn't want to admit it to the world, and especially to Ted Crabb? Or was there something more sinister behind it?

***

After Fiona had collected the trash can and returned it to its place next to the fume cupboard, she had gone to collect the brush and dustpan. Half-regretting she had questioned Steve's honesty, she had set about sweeping up the paper tissues and plastic pipette tips she had spilled in her tantrum.

"Sorry about this mess," she sighed, her eyes fixed on the floor shamefully. "Do you think I shouldn't have said those things about Steve, especially the last bit? He's a good friend of yours, isn't he?"

Moving to take the brush from her, Giles had given her hand a reassuring squeeze.

"Here, let me help. You were quite right to raise the issue. The fact he's a friend is irrelevant. Perhaps you've hit the bull's-eye, Fiona. But if so, what could it mean? What could he have been up to?"

"I tell you what, before we jump to any conclusions we might live to regret, why don't we check that Ivor's got his facts right. After all, intellectual property isn't his specialty. He's mostly into real estate. Ros mentioned the other day that one of Hamilton Reeves's partners is a big name in IP. Why don't you go and see him?"

"Good idea! I think you're right. That's exactly what we should do. I'll ask Jane to set up an appointment this afternoon. It'll mean you'll have to take the students, I'm afraid. Is that okay?"

"On one condition."

"What's that?"

"No gawping at Ros's legs this time."

By a quarter to five the same afternoon, Giles had explained everything in Hamilton Reeves's comfortable offices behind Merton College.

"It's quite simple, Professor," Richard Hamilton had explained, pacing the room with an aristocratic air. "Your colleague's cousin was absolutely correct. Your American friend's software will be protected by copyright law. He's as safe as houses. On top of which, there's no possibility of his getting a patent for something like that, none at all.

"Countries differ in their attitudes towards the patenting of software. In the EU it's out of the question. In the United States, the situation has changed over the years. Once upon a time, their approach was like ours. Software is just a series of operations, they used to say. As such it doesn't manipulate subject matter in any way. Therefore, it's not patentable. However, about thirty years ago all this was challenged in a famous case about software used for controlling the heating cycle during the vulcanisation of rubber. When to everyone's surprise a patent was granted, it set off a series of court cases, the consequence of which was to make the patentability of software in the States progressively easier and easier— all designed, of course, to benefit their economy. Nowadays, they grant patents to about five hundred pieces of software every week. Pretty ridiculous in my opinion. Nevertheless, even over there, some types of software are still not patentable. Let me show you."

After moving to his desk, he had worked on his keyboard for a couple of minutes before swivelling the computer's monitor towards Giles.

"What you see here is the US Patent and Trademark Office website. Because the courts' attitudes have changed so much over the years, they use what's happened in the past as a guide to the future—what's called case law.

"As you may not be able to see it clearly from where you are, I'll read it to you, leaving out the bits that don't matter. It says here: '2106.02 Mathematical Algorithms'…er…okay…'Patentability. Mathematical algorithms have been held to be nonstatutory'— that's legal jargon for nonpatentable—'because they represent a mathematical definition of a natural phenomenon.' Blah, blah… 'A mathematical algorithm representing…a law of nature… defines a fundamental scientific truth…In such a case, a claimed process which consists solely of the steps that one must follow to solve the mathematical representation…is indistinguishable from the law of nature…A patent cannot be granted on such a process.'

"So there you are, that's pretty clear, isn't it? Even in the good old USA you cannot patent a formula that describes a natural phenomenon, even if the formula is newly discovered and very complicated.

"Now let's go to BitLaw.com. This is a site that interprets things like USPTO statements, case law decisions, and so on. Very useful for people like me."

After a few mouse clicks, he had turned the screen towards Giles again.

"Here we are. Now let me see. Listen to this: 'Claims to computer-related inventions that are clearly nonstatutory fall into the same general categories as nonstatutory claims in other arts, namely natural phenomena…and…laws of nature which constitute descriptive material.'

"So, there you have it, Professor. It's pretty straightforward. If Dr Salomon's software is nothing more than a formula, in other words a way of doing a calculation that describes how genes work, it's definitely not patentable. It doesn't matter that it's very useful and very sophisticated, or that he had to read hundreds of scientific papers and analyse thousands of numbers to discover it. All of that's irrelevant. The point is he didn't create the relationship the formula describes. It already existed in nature. It's just that neither he nor anyone else knew about it."

Grabbing a marble paperweight from his desk, he had tossed it in Giles's direction.

"Well held! A geologist can't patent a previously unknown type of rock that he finds in Patagonia, any more than Newton could have patented his law of gravity when an apple dropped on his head, or a nuclear physicist a new type of squawk or fartino or whatever they call those particles. Why? Because they're natural phenomena in the same way Dr Salomon's formula is a natural phenomenon.

"So that's that. Now, what is very difficult for me to understand is why Dr Salomon's attorneys appear to have given him a very different story. To sort that one out, we need to return to the USPTO website and see what his application actually says… because if he has already filed it, it will be there for the world to see.

"OK, so here we go back to www.uspto.gov, click on 'patents,' then on 'search patents,' and finally 'quick search.' Now all we have to do is to enter a couple of search terms and their fields. Well, we've got his name, so I'll put that in for starters. Now, Professor, do you know its title or the date of the application?"

Giles had shaken his head glumly.

"Neither, I'm afraid. But I suppose the title must contain one or more of '*Achilles,*' 'insert' or alternatively 'insertion.' Probably also 'gene.' Perhaps 'enhancer.'"

"That's plenty. Jot them down on my notepad there, and I'll give them a try."

Giles had waited, quietly sipping his coffee, until Richard Hamilton had finished.

"Nothing, absolutely nothing, Professor. Which can only mean one thing: they haven't received such an application, which in turn means he hasn't filed one. Because if he had, it would *definitely* be there. Is it possible it was filed under someone else's name, his employer perhaps?"

"He said not, but you could check. He's the Director of the National Cancer Institute, which is part of the National Institutes of Health."

A minute later, Richard Hamilton had drawn another blank.

"Zilch. Sorry, Professor, it simply isn't there."

"Could he have filed it somewhere else, Richard, like the EU?"

"Not at this stage. It would have to be the USPTO for starters. So that's as far I can take it, I'm afraid. Unless you have any more questions, I'll see my next client now, if you don't mind. I think I heard Sir Anthony chatting to Miss Hitchcock a few minutes ago."

When Giles had arrived back at the College, Fiona was busy in the cell culture room with the 'no entry' sign switched on.

"Your Ivor was right, Fiona," he had shouted through the window. "The programme Steve described definitely would not be patentable. And what's more, he hasn't filed for one."

"Steve's done what? I didn't catch the last bit."

"I said he hasn't filed a patent application. There's no trace of one."

"How do you know?"

"Richard Hamilton did a search."

"Hold on."

After discarding her disposable gloves, taking off her protective glasses, and hanging up her white coat, Fiona had joined him in the corridor.

"Phew, it's so cold out here! Is he certain?"

"Absolutely. He showed me everything on his computer, all the rules and regulations about software, and then the result of his search with all the right key words"

"Including *Achilles*?"

"Of course."

"And he spelled it correctly?

"Yes. A, K, I, L, L, E, E, S. The system's phonetic."

"You're not serious?"

"No, I'm not. But ask a silly question, and..."

Fiona had poked him in the ribs.

"Ouch!"

"So, it's all a hoax? There is no programme?"

"Well, we can't be completely sure of that. All I know is what I've told you. It could be a hoax, yes, but I've thought of another possibility. Perhaps he's just stalling. He has a programme, yes. That part is true. But all his talk about a patent is a hoax to extend the time during which he has an advantage over the rest of us. As long as he has the programme to himself, he can do experiments to test ideas the rest of us can't. Unless he has an attorney who is a complete charlatan, he must know he can't get a patent, but as long as we and the rest think he has that intention, he has the perfect excuse for keeping it under wraps."

"Never thought of that one. And I'm his first victim?"

"Possibly."

"Let's talk about it over a meal."

"Where would you like to go?"

"How about Wagamama? I could do with something hot and spicy."

"Which reminds me…"

"What?"

"Ros sent her best regards."

Chapter Eleven

"Sorry, you didn't like the kedgeree, sir?" a familiar voice whispered in his ear. "You should have had the stroganoff instead."

Giles raised an eyelid to see Vicky collecting his tray.

"The soccer player over there said it was scrumptious."

"Never mind, I'll soon be dining in The Jefferson."

"Ooh, that'll be nice! Lovely hotel, I've heard. And very comfy beds, one of my friends told me. As usual, they've put me in the Holiday Inn on the Hill. It's a world apart from The Jefferson, even though it's only a stone's throw away, just a short walk in fact."

She gave him a cheeky smile and a wink.

"Anything I can do for you?"

"Er…no thank you."

"Later on perhaps?"

"If I do need anything, thank you, I'll press the button."

"I'll leave you with your thoughts then. Bye."

***

As they made their way towards the restaurant, Fiona had been in a world of her own, almost knocking a child over as she turned to enter. Although Giles had been itching to know what was on her mind, he had known from past experience that when she was lost in thought, it was better not to disturb her. Whatever it was, he would know pretty soon.

Once their orders had been placed, she had returned to the puzzle of Steve's software.

"Giles, on the way I was wondering why Steve might want the rest of us to think he has a programme when in fact he hasn't."

"And…?"

"How about this? He didn't create *Deidamia* at all. It was not his invention. It's nothing more than the Bedouins' natural switch. Somehow, he got his hands on the details. Then he came up with the idea of a fancy computer programme so that his claim to have created the piece of DNA so quickly would be credible."

"But where could he have got the information from?"

"Perhaps a rogue lab tech in MECCAR, one who felt very strongly that the information should be made public?"

While Giles had been chewing it over, she had gone a step further.

"Or how about the great man himself?"

"Ahmad?"

"Yes. After all, don't forget it was Steve who invited him to Sorrento and gave him the five-star treatment—a prestigious lectureship, the Presidential Suite to which Steve himself was entitled."

"Come off it, Fiona! I can't believe a man like Ahmad would be so easily bribed. A lectureship and a comfy bed in Sorrento? Not possible!"

"I agree it would have to have been much more than that, but we don't know what might have gone on behind the scenes, do we?"

"But whether it was a lab tech, Ahmad, or anyone else in MECCAR, Rashid Yamani would have recognised *Deidamia* as the Bedouins' switch as soon as he set eyes on the Science paper. He would have blown the whistle, wouldn't he?"

"He would have recognised it, yes. But he couldn't have blown any whistles on account of his promise to the Bedouins. If he'd gone public that *Deidamia* was nothing but their DNA switch, he would have broken his pledge. MECCAR would have been in the dog house, and there would have been no chance of further help from the Bedouins, or anyone else for that matter. And all for what? Nothing would have been gained. Steve could have claimed it was just a coincidence. Many coincidences have happened in science. I could give you plenty of examples. Take Darwin for starters. Although he gets all the kudos for evolution, he wasn't the only one to come up with the idea, was he? Alfred Russell Wallace did so at the same time thousands of miles away. In chemistry, the anaesthetic chloroform was synthesised by the same process simultaneously in France, Germany and America. In physics, Michael Faraday wasn't the only one who discovered electromagnetic induction, a guy called Henry also did in America. I know these things because I wrote an essay on the subject as a student. It won a prize."

"Congratulations! I knew about Darwin, of course, but not the other two. So, let me get this right. Are you suggesting Ahmad *gave* Steve the secret?"

"That's one possibility."

"But What could Ahmad have possibly accepted that would have been worth the risk?"

"How about money and sex, good old 'bucks and fucks'? It wouldn't have been the first time a good man has been led astray by that combination. You don't know for sure the girls in Sorrento were Steve's research fellows, do you? Perhaps they were there for another reason."

"Are you *serious*? "

"I think so. You said they were good looking; that they crawled into a corner when you arrived; that Steve panicked when he was photographed with them in the bar. It could all fit, couldn't it?"

"I suppose so. But it's not much to go on, is it?"

"It wouldn't be, I agree, if that's all there was. But there's more."

"What?"

"Their names."

"Their *names*? What about them?"

"Carina Taricani and Amandine Coupe, right?"

"Yes."

"I know 'carina' means 'pretty' in Italian, because my tutor…never mind."

"Your tutor? That long-haired scruff bag from Pozzuoli said you were pretty?"

"Yes."

"What was he up to?"

"He wasn't up to anything! Don't *you* think I'm pretty?"

"Yes, of course. But if he was handing out compliments, he was probably after something."

"Don't be ridiculous!"

"I'm not being ridiculous."

"Yes, you are."

"Fiona, Neapolitans are notorious. Remember Casanova?"

"Giles, you're being ridiculous! Even if they are notorious, and I don't know if that's true, and even if he was 'after something' as you put it, what makes you think I can't look after myself? Am I supposed to be some delicate rose, helplessly waiting to be plucked by the first male who happens to fancy me? Don't be such a chauvinist."

"Sorry…you're right."

"And anyway, Casanova was Venetian."

"My apologies to Naples."

"So, can we get back to where we were?"

"Let's."

"Okay, we've done 'carina'. Now for 'amandine.' That's a French name that means 'much-loved.'"

"How come you know that?"

"I learnt it in drama school. We did one of George Sand's plays, translated of course. Amandine was her real first name."

"You went to drama school?"

"Well, sort of, evening classes, before I moved to Oxford."

"Ha! That could explain a lot."

Fiona kicked him under the table.

"And what is that supposed to mean?"

"Nothing really."

Dropping her chopsticks into her bowl, she rested her chin on her hands and glared at him across the table.

"You must have meant *something*, Giles. What were you getting at?"

"Nothing, dear, I promise. Just a rather silly flippant remark. Trying to be funny, that's all."

"And failing miserably. You're not doing very well today, Giles, are you?"

"No, I'm not. Apologies. Carry on."

"Now, let's move onto surnames. What does 'coupe' mean in French?"

"Cup. Not the type you drink tea out of. A prize or reward, a trophy."

"Just as I thought. So, there you are! It fits. We've got 'pretty'. We've got 'much-loved.' And we've got 'trophy.' Perfect names for a certain type of professional lady."

"Ha…ha! Oh, come off it, Fiona! Now you are stretching it. There must be thousands of girls with those names. And why would Steve want to have left clues lying around by making up sexy names?"

"I'm not suggesting it was Steve who made them up. Does he speak French or Italian?"

"Not that I know of. Some German."

"So? If he hired the girls from an agency, they could have had those names. Escorts sometimes adopt sexy names."

"How do you know?"

Fiona pursed her lips and blew him a kiss.

"Are you serious?"

"*Giles!* I can't believe this is happening today. Did Richard Hamilton give you a drink? Ros told me he's a bit of a boozer."

"No, he didn't, more's the pity. He had a very appealing bottle of Finlaggan on his desk."

"Okay, let's get back to where we were…again. My point is that if the girls already had those names, they wouldn't have meant anything to Steve, or presumably to Ahmad. So, all we're left with is Taricani. Does that mean anything to you?"

"No, although I must say the word does have a familiar ring for some reason. But this theory can't be right, Fiona, because

Steve said he'd invited another scientist to their meeting with Ahmad, a German. He would hardly have done that if they were high class whores, would he?"

Fiona had shrugged her shoulders.

"Did you see this German?"

"No. Steve said he'd been taken ill after arriving, and had gone home. Steve took his place instead."

"I'll have to think about that one. Okay, that was sex. Let's move onto money. Mrs Sharif was on holiday in Lugano at the time, correct?"

"Yes."

"That was a strange choice for a woman with a passion for archaeology. What a missed opportunity after travelling all that way from Jordan. The only old relics she would have seen in Lugano would have been draped in diamonds and mink. On the other hand, if she'd stayed with Ahmad in Sorrento, she would have had a plethora of museums and archaeological sites on her doorstep. Lugano was a very poor choice for history… but a very good one for banks. Perhaps she was looking for somewhere to hide a pile of cash."

"But where would Steve have got that sort of money from?"

"He might not have had to. That could have been the CIA's job."

"The CIA? Where did they come from?"

"They take their orders directly from the White House, don't forget. Ted Crabb was as desperate to salvage his country's reputation as Steve was to save his neck. He'd already given the National Cancer Institute a couple of million. The same again for the Bedouins' secret would have been money well spent."

Suddenly, Fiona had buried her head in her hands.

"Oh God, and now I've had another thought, a dreadful one. Maybe Ahmad's accident wasn't. Perhaps once they knew Steve had got what they wanted the CIA bumped him off."

"Hold on a minute, Fiona! From out of nothing, you've created an international conspiracy involving the White House, the CIA, two agents provocateurs, a secret payoff in

Switzerland, and now a murder. Perhaps it wasn't Steve in Sorrento at all. It was James Bond in disguise."

"Such things can seem incredible to people like us, I know, but that's because we live in the cosy world of Oxbridge academia. There's a very nasty other world out there. It wouldn't be the first time the CIA had eliminated a partner in crime simply because he or she was the only witness. Killing means nothing to them. If it's good for America, it's good for the world. That's what they think. What's one life when it's for the benefit of many? Don't forget the CIA tried to assassinate Castro…and Tito…and there was an African guy…."

"Lumumba?"

"Yes, him. Ahmad would have been a pushover…*literally*."

"But it's all wild speculation, Fiona. You don't have a shred of evidence, do you?"

"Not really. But it would fit."

"Let's finish this meal. If there's one thing I can't stand, it's cold noodles."

Chapter Twelve

Giles would never forget the dark days that had followed his chat with Fiona in Wagamama, now four weeks ago to the day. Jane had seen him for only half an hour each morning, as he had read the mail before dictating a few brief replies for her to sign on his behalf. As soon as that was out of the way, he would don his Alpaca coat and disappear to be alone with his thoughts. More often than not it would be to the Fellows' Garden, or if farther afield the University Parks. Then there would be a long walk, in which direction it didn't matter, until he found a bench or wall upon which to rest, while he continued to brood over his next move. When his bones were chilled, he would go for a cup of tea or a bowl of soup somewhere, anywhere. On a couple of fine days he had wandered out of town as far as Wytham Woods and Woodstock, in the latter case dropping into The Bear for a ploughman's lunch, before catching the number 20 bus back to Oxford. His evenings in the Turf Tavern had ceased completely.

Having reluctantly come to the conclusion that Fiona's theory was not so fanciful after all, he had considered the likely course of events once Steve had got his hands on the details of the Bedouins' switch. As the Editor of Science had received his manuscript in the middle of November, Steve would have had just ten weeks after returning from Sorrento to do everything. Not a lot of time, but perhaps just enough to synthesise the short length of DNA, and check that it worked when put into cancer cells growing in a tissue culture bottle. That sort of experiment was bread and butter to him, and all the equipment and chemicals he needed would have already been in the lab. He could have dropped everything, worked flat out, written the paper over a weekend, taken it personally to the Editor, and alerted Ted Crabb to the fact. Yes, it was feasible all right, if only just.

During one of his longer walks, Giles's thoughts had wandered to Fiona's speculation about the girls' names. It was certainly a bit odd that three of them were so suggestive. And they *were* very good looking. Quite a coincidence that both of Steve's new research fellows should be so pretty. But what if the name Taricani didn't fit? That would blow the theory to smithereens, wouldn't it?

The more he had walked in the wind and rain, the more had he become obsessed with what 'taricani' might mean. Seated in a bus stop while sheltering from a heavy downpour, it had jumped into his head that it might be derived from the Arabic word *tariq*. After all, the Arabs had been in Sicily for more than two hundred years before the Normans arrived, hadn't they? But no matter how hard he had tried, he had not been able to recall what it meant. After renewing his journey during a break in the clouds, the minutes had seemed like hours before Magdalen's tower had come into view, bringing with it the prospect of the elusive answer.

As soon as he was through the office door, he had consulted a website on Italian surnames. And what he had found provided no comfort: "Taricani, Tariccone, Tarricane: Probably from the Arabic root *tariq,* meaning "who arrives in the night" or "evening caller."

"Oh my God! Wait till Fiona hears about this."

His feet wet and sore after the long march, he had moved into the reading room to drop onto the sofa and remove his shoes and socks. As he did so, he'd looked towards the portrait of his aristocratic benefactor.

"Oh, Alfredo, how you envied my supposed 'gradevole vita di considerazione e pace.' If only you knew the half of it! Is it possible there's a simple explanation to this business that we've all overlooked? If so, give us a sign, please, there's a good chap. If not, guide me to what I should do next. Go and talk to

Hank Weinberg at the NIH? Telephone the Nobel people in Stockholm? Contact Rashid Yamani in Jordan? Or perhaps climb to the top of that tower over there, and add a touch of tragedy to its long history?"

Some hours later, awoken by the barking of a fox on Christ Church Meadow, he had raised himself from the sofa, brewed a pot of tea in the semidarkness, and taken it to Jane's desk. Her calendar, propped against the Tiffany lamp, had reminded him that Stockholm's big day was now only five weeks away. He had tried to imagine how he would feel when it arrived, and indeed on the same date each year for the rest of his life, if he were to turn a blind eye to all he knew.

Hoping that more fresh air off the Deer Park would help him reach the right decision, he had opened Jane's window as wide as its rusting hinges would allow. How peaceful it looked he had thought: the lonely holly tree in the centre of the lawn, its branches swaying in the breeze; the timeless silhouette of the Grammar Hall beyond; the soft light filtering through the curtains of the odd student's room; the clouds floating behind the Great Tower. It was as if there wasn't a problem in the world—until a raucous pair of crows had brought him down to earth again.

By the time he had emptied the teapot, he had decided he had no choice but to take it upon himself to fly to Washington. By now Steve would surely have set off on his lecture tour. If he could get into his lab and his office, there was just a chance he would find something that would settle the matter one way or the other. The thought had terrified him, but he had known that if he didn't do it, he would regret it for the rest of his life.

His hands trembling at the prospect, he had opened one of Jane's drawers to find the Swan Vestas matchbox from his pipe-smoking days, now used as a repository for his orphaned keys. Lying under a couple of Yales from his former home near Calderstones Park were three he had unintentionally brought back from his sabbatical leave with Steve. After untying the leather shoe lace that held them together, he had placed them on the desk side by side: one to the door of the rent-free flat they had given him, another to the laboratory, and most important of all, one that until now he had never had any reason to use— to the office occupied by Steve and his PA.

"Here's hoping Steve hasn't changed the locks, Alfredo," he had sighed, waving the all important pair in the direction of the portrait.

Twenty minutes later, he had worked out his plan. He would tell Steve's staff he was on his way to the West Coast, and had dropped in to gather some information for his autobiography: details of experiments he had performed during his sabbatical, a description of the interior of the building and the lab, a few photographs, and so on. Then, left alone in the evening, he would let himself into Steve's office, and snoop around for anything to do with *Achilles* or *Deidamia*.

As he had been replacing the box, the thought of being caught red-handed by one of the cleaners, or by one Steve's staff returning to switch off a piece of equipment, had hit him like a thunderbolt. News travels fast on the academic grapevine. He had pictured the looks that would greet him on his return to the College, Sir Quentin's face as he greeted him in the entrance hall of the Lodgings, the sniggering of the students, the raised eyebrows of the other dons as they gathered before dinner. And worst of all, he had imagined how it would be reported in the newspapers. He would certainly have to resign. There was no doubt about that. But it was a risk he would have to take. It wasn't just a question of ethics, justice, and fair play. The integrity of medical science itself was at stake, to say nothing of the reputation of the Nobel Prize. As fate had put him there, he was under a moral obligation to do all he could to uncover the truth, wasn't he?

If he had had any doubts about the strength of his conviction, they would have been dispelled when the crescent of the waning moon appeared from behind a solitary cloud above the Great Tower.

"Good heavens! There it is…again," he had gasped. "So bright, just as it was last time…and the time before …and always after I've been thinking about Steve and *Achilles*, never any other time. It *has* to mean something, doesn't it?"

He had stood up to lean out of the window and get a better view, only for a gust of wind to send it crashing against his head.

"Damn! Right, that's it," he had growled, raising his fist to the sky. "You really are trying to get a message home, aren't you?"

Seeing that the watch on his outstretched arm said it was five fifty-one, he had assumed it must have stopped. But then his smartphone had told him otherwise.

"My God, it's almost 6.00 a.m.! I must have been asleep for hours. Okay, Giles, there's no time to waste."

He had crossed the Rubicon. After agonising for so many days, his decision had come with a heady cocktail of emotions. Most of all there had been a huge sense of relief. He had felt liberated, unshackled. At last he could act, plan, do something, instead of just ruminate from dawn until dusk. The prospect of the adventure to which he could now devote himself had been exhilarating, but there was also a gut-wrenching fear of the unknown. He had never been in a situation remotely like this. How many had? And what would Fiona say? Would she try to stop him? A heavy nausea had hit him in the pit of his stomach. Quivering and perspiring with the sudden rush of adrenaline, he gulped down a mouthful of cold water from the tap, and splashed more over his head and face. After pacing between the two rooms several times as he'd struggled to come to terms with his predicament, the moon's reappearance through Jane's window had had a strangely calming effect. He had settled into the sofa again, wiped his brow with his sleeve, and taken a few deep breaths.

"There's no point walking around in circles like a headless chicken for the rest of the morning, Giles. You'll have to get on with it this instant, or it'll be too late.

"So…come on! *Get moving!*"

His first job had been to gather together every item that had anything to do with the story, and cram them into his briefcase:

newspaper cuttings, photographs, the programmes of the Sorrento and Oahu meetings, journal articles, photocopies of this and that, notes and jottings on scraps of paper, pages from downloaded websites, printed emails, and any letters that were relevant. Next had been his address book, a couple of diaries, his leather-bound notebook, several flash drives of different vintages, and finally the students' essays from Fiona's latest practical class that he should have marked by now. That done, he had left a backup of his laptop running while he hurried home to pack a few essentials—socks, handkerchiefs, underwear, a few shirts, his wash bag, a travel adaptor, a dressing gown, and his old Barmah hat. Before heading back to the College, he had booked a flight for the same morning and printed his boarding pass.

"Well that should be everything," he had panted on re-entering the office. "Oh Jesus, no it isn't! A note for Jane."

After thinking hard about what explanation to invent for his sudden disappearance, he had taken a sheet of paper from the rosewood bookcase.

"Jane, have gone to USA! Fisher Center for Familial Cancer Research, Georgetown University (Washington DC) called. Invited me to collaborate in a grant application. Could mean a lot of money for Magdalen and the deadline's imminent. Too good to miss. Please let Mavis know. Will call from there. Prof."

After placing the message in the centre of her desk, he had stared at it long and hard, brimming with self-reproach.

"Now look, Giles," he had muttered wearily, "you either go on this bloody mission, or you don't. And if you do, for now the truth *has* to be a secret, doesn't it? There's no bloody choice, is there? And if there's no choice, there's no reason to feel guilty."

His conscience satisfied, he had hurriedly tidied up both rooms before pausing to brace himself for his great leap into the unknown. The sun now was up, the dust disturbed by his frantic activity swirling and glinting in the shafts of light through the curtains. Gazing at the chequered shadows cast by the leaded windows on the walls and floor, he had shuddered at their similarity to the bars of a prison cell. Is that where his reckless dash was going to take him? After all, what he had in mind was very serious, wasn't it?

He had never felt so lonely. After moving to the mirror, the sight of his face — pale, unshaven, and heavy-eyed—had shocked him. Straightening his back and running his fingers through his hair, he had addressed himself sternly once more.

"Okay, Giles, you scruffy ugly brute, let's go through it all again so there's not a single doubt in that thick head of yours. Fact number one, Steve's been under huge pressure. His career has been on the line. A man in that situation could resort to anything. Fact number two, he came up with *Deidamia* incredibly quickly. Hard to believe. Number three, some of the world's top geneticists have been unable to fathom what his computer programme might be about. Five, I mean four, Steve's been extremely secretive about it. Five, he says he can patent it, but we know he can't. He says he's applied for one, but we know he hasn't. So he's lying. And if he's lying, there's a reason. Six, in Sorrento he was extremely jittery. Normally, he's full of himself at such meetings, brimming with confidence, especially when he's top dog. So were the girls. Quite a coincidence that the latest members of his team are so gorgeous! And Fiona was right about their names. And finally, there were those moons, the symbol of Islam itself, always when Steve had been on my mind.

"None of it might mean anything. But it would be irresponsible to ignore it all. It's too important. If Steve has been up to something crooked, the world needs to know. And Giles, you're the only one who can do anything about it. So, you've got to bight the bullet and do whatever needs to be done, whatever the consequences."

He had broken off to draw back the curtains and gaze across the lawn in the direction of Mansfield Road.

"I wonder what Fiona's doing right now. As so often, she was right, wasn't she? 'Stay on your own for a while,' she said. 'Think hard about the facts. Consider the worst-case scenario. Then decide what to do. And just do it!' You've taken her advice and walked the leather off your shoes. So it's all yours now. You know what has to be done. Perhaps there's a simple explanation, and you'll make a fool of yourself in the eyes of some. But what the hell! You'll have done the right thing, the honourable thing. That's all that matters."

After stooping to pick up his bag and briefcase, he had looked at himself again, this time with a wry smile.

"And whatever happens, at the least you'll have plenty of new material for that bloody autobiography. Harry Barnes knew what he was on about!"

Returning his bags to the floor, he had felt his pockets for one final check…phone, cards, cash, keys, passport, boarding pass…before looking inside his briefcase to check that his laptop was switched off.

"Are you okay in there, Boris? All set? I've got a feeling I'm going to need you soon. So hold onto your mouse! Here we go. No time to waste. What did Henry the Fourth say? 'Let us away; advantage feeds him fat, while men delay.' Or something like."

Having closed the door behind him, very gently out of fear the room above was occupied, he had hastened to the New Building, avoiding the route through the Cloisters lest he bump into somebody. Once in the relative safety of the portico, he had written a line from Robert Burns on a scrap of paper dredged from the depths of his briefcase.

'For facts are cheels that winna ding an' downa be disputed'

"She'll know what that means, for sure," he had whispered, slipping it under the laboratory door.

And with that he had been off—across the lawn, under the boughs of the Magdalen Plane…stubbing his toe on its roots in the process…past the Auditorium, and through the gates into Longwall Street.

***

The aircraft having commenced its approach to Dulles Airport, Vicky came waltzing down the aisle with her usual broad smile.

"No more thinking, Professor. Almost there. Seat belt buckled?"

"Yes, thanks, Vicky. No more thoughts to think actually. It's all done. Perfect timing. Now it's time for some action."

Chapter Thirteen

As the cab turned into The Jefferson's small forecourt, Giles was delighted to see Virgil standing on the doorstep, as cheerful and as courteous as he remembered him. After a crushing handshake and flashing white smile, he led the way to a bright room on the third floor, overlooking Sixteenth Street.

After a shower, a change of clothes, and a trip to the bar for a coffee, Giles returned to his room to rehearse the telephone call he would make the following morning. After repeating his lines several times over, he was confident he knew exactly what to say. Words were not his problem. Sounding both surprised and disappointed at the news that Steve was already on his lecture tour was going to be the real challenge. When it came to playing a part, he was definitely not a natural.

With the advantage of jet lag, he was up early the next morning for a walk around the block, during which he did a few more rehearsals. Then it was back to his room, and straight to the telephone.

A young man answered.

"Salomon lab, NCI," he croaked. "Adnan here."

"Oh, er, yes, good morning, This is Professor Giles Butterfield, Oxford University. I'm calling from The Jefferson hotel. Would it be possible to speak to Dr Stephen Salomon?"

"Afraid not. He's on a lecture tour before he collects his Nobel. You knew he'd got it, I suppose?"

"Yes, I did. How disappointing. I'm an old friend on my way to San Francisco. I hadn't realised he'd be out of town."

"Sorry about that. Anything I can do?"

"Well, my chief reason for dropping in was to congratulate him, but there is in fact something else. A few years ago, I spent my sabbatical leave with him. Now that I'm writing my autobiography, I'd like to spend a couple of hours looking through my old lab books and taking a few photographs for the chapter on my time here. I imagine the lab books are still around. Steve was in the habit of archiving everything. Don't think you were around in those days, were you?"

"No. I'm Steve's AF from Saudi."

"His?"

"Sorry, Alhazen Fellow."

"Ah, yes, of course. So, do you think I could spend a few hours in the lab?"

"No problem, Dr Butterfield. When would it be?"

"This evening? I'm busy all day."

"Not possible, I'm afraid. We've got some heavy equipment being installed. There'll be all sorts of people here: electricians, carpenters, technicians, you name it. But tomorrow morning should be okay."

"Er…unfortunately I'm at Georgetown University all day tomorrow. How about tomorrow evening?"

"No problem. Dr Salomon's lab will be empty."

"Perfect."

"As it happens, I'm also planning to go to Georgetown tomorrow, to attend a lunchtime seminar. Can I give you a lift from your hotel?"

"Oh…thank you…but no, I've a breakfast meeting there at seven-thirty."

"Ah, yes…too early. What a pity."

"Don't worry, I'll get a cab. But thanks anyway. By the way, Adnan, do you work in the same lab as Dr Salomon?"

"No, he keeps it to himself. I use the one across the corridor. When I go home tomorrow, I'll leave the door of his unlocked, and tell the porter to expect you. You'll have to ask him to lock it again when you leave."

"Thank you very much. You've been most helpful, Adnan. Good-bye."

Giles spent the following day trying to relax by the Potomac, nipping off at lunchtime for a steak and fries at M & S Grill on Thirteenth Street. He arrived back at The Jefferson at around seven. After a meal, followed by half an hour with the Washington Post in the bar, Virgil hailed a cab to take him to Bethesda.

Upon arriving at the NCI, he found Adnan had been true to his word.

"Dr Butterfield," the porter boomed enthusiastically, offering his hand. "Welcome back. I've been expecting you. So nice to see you after all these years."

"Joe! I wondered if you'd still be around. You're looking well."

"Can't complain, sir. I've been told you need access to Dr Salomon's lab?"

"Yes, for some work on my autobiography. Shouldn't take me long."

"Autobiography? Do I get a complimentary copy?"

"Definitely, autographed."

"I'll keep you to that, sir. Can you remember your way?"

"I'm sure I can."

He took the elevator to the third floor and walked the length of the corridor to Steve's laboratory at the far end. After putting his head inside to check it was empty, he entered to take a few photographs for the record. After pausing while he reminisced about his sabbatical year, he moved to the office suite that Steve shared with his PA, and tried his key in the door.

"Damn! It doesn't work. Don't tell me he's changed it."

He started to rattle the door violently. Then, just as he was about to panic, the key turned with a reassuring click.

"Thank God for that!"

After glancing down the corridor, he closed the door behind him and passed the PA's desk to Steve's section. Standing in the doorway, he took several photographs to have a record of what everything looked like before he had gone to work.

"Still the same mess," he muttered nervously. "Papers everywhere, books on the floor, half-empty paper coffee cups, a long-forgotten cheeseburger, banana skins. Where do I begin?"

Seated behind Steve's desk, he searched carefully through its three drawers, but found nothing of interest. Next, he flicked through a couple of lab books propped against the lamp. They contained details of many experiments, but none that had anything to do with either *Achilles* or *Deidamia*. After carefully replacing them, he looked around the room. The mountains of papers visible inside half-open cupboards were a daunting prospect. Others were stacked on filing cabinets, on the coffee table, even under the easy chair and in the sink.

He recalled that Steve had been in the habit of hiding highly confidential documents, such as budgets and contracts, between reprints of scientific articles or in brown envelopes with misleading labels. There was only one thing for it. He would have to go through the whole lot methodically, step by step.

He worked his way around the room clockwise, casting his eyes over every page, flicking through every book. By the time he was back where he had started, it was almost half past twelve.

"Nothing!" he groaned. "Not a thing on *Deidamia* or a computer programme. And come to think of it, nothing on *Achilles* either. You'd think there'd be a mention of it somewhere."

As he sensed the rug under his feet was lumpy in places, he pushed the coffee table and easy chair to one side, and lifted it to see what lay underneath. Apart from a few peanuts, all he found were a teaspoon, a plastic pen, and several postcards from Barcelona signed by a Louise.

He picked up a computer mouse that had been under the chair, and tossed it disconsolately into the trash can.

Wondering if Steve's PA might have handled all the *Deidamia* work, he moved to her desk and hit the Return key of her Apple computer. To his surprise it woke up and skipped the login screen, going straight to the desktop.

"That's convenient! Now, let's see. What operating system is it? OS 9.2. That'll do."

Opening the search utility, he clicked on *File Names*, and entered "patent." The window listed three folders, all to do with different types of laboratory equipment. He looked at their dates. One had been modified within the past month, the others not for a couple of years.

Returning to the dialogue box, he entered the first few words of the title of Steve's Science paper. A message appeared saying there was nothing. When he entered "manuscripts," he was given a long list of articles Steve had written, but none had anything to with *Achilles*. Next, he tried "Achilles" and then "Deidamia," but each time there was nothing.

Realising he could be seen from the corridor through the glass pane in the door, he put the computer to sleep again. After dejectedly returning to Steve's desk, he caught sight of some papers on the windowsill, propped behind the half-drawn curtains.

"Probably nothing," he thought, "but might as well take a look."

Finding it was a printout of the *Achilles* website that had been announced in Oahu, he decided to flick through it in case Steve had added anything. But there was nothing...until he reached the last page.

"Jesus!" he gasped. "What's this?"

He closed his eyes momentarily, as if hoping he was hallucinating.

"But this is....! Oh my God, Steve, surely you didn't...?"

With his back against the wall, he slowly sank to the floor and remained there, stupefied by what was in front of him. He raised his head to gaze at Steve's desk, the same desk on which he must have penned so many seminal papers. He pictured him working late into the night. He had achieved a reputation and position most scientists could only dream of. After all that effort, and doubtless many sacrifices along the way, to have risked everything would have been an act of pure madness. And yet that's exactly what he seemed to have done. There could be no other explanation, could there?

"What a fool you are, Steve!" What a *bloody* fool!"

He looked at his watch. It would now be 6:02 a.m. in Oxford. Fiona would have just got out of bed. He took out his phone and called her flat. She answered sounding very bleary-eyed.

"Giles! What a relief. How are you? Where are you? What are you up to?"

"I'm fine, thanks. I'm at the NCI in Bethesda, sitting on the floor of Steve's office. I tried to call you several times yesterday."

"I took the day off and my mobile's battery was flat. Sorry! Went to London and got some lovely shoes."

"Did you find my note?"

"Yes, thanks. Very impressive! I didn't realise you knew any Burns. But what impressed me more was what you'd written in pencil on the other side."

"I didn't write anything on the other side."

"Not then, no, but you had done at some time in the past."

"Had I? I didn't notice. Why, what did it say?"

"How long have you been taking Viagra?"

"It said that?"

"No, I'm asking you a question."

"Pardon?"

"I asked how long you've been taking Viagra?"

"*Viagra?* What the hell are you talking about? I've never taken the stuff."

"There was a shopping list on the back. Wait a sec, I'll go and fetch it."

She returned a minute later.

"Here it is. It says, 'Notebooks, paper clips, printer cartridges, rubber gloves, Viagra.'"

"Notebooks, paper clips, cartridges…? I remember now. That wasn't Viagra! It was ViaGram."

"What's that?"

"It's a reagent kit for fluorescent staining of bacteria. I wanted to see if those cancer cells we got from Jim Jones were infected with Helicobacter. You weren't looking at a shopping list, dear. It was a list of things we needed in the lab."

"Oh! Sorry! Now I feel stupid."

"No reason. But we've got much bigger problems than anything like that, Fiona.

Listen carefully. I need to keep my voice down."

"I'll turn up the sound. Hold on."

"I've found a printout of the MECCAR website that announced the discovery of *Achilles*. On the front of it is written this: 'To Dr Stephen Salomon, Ahmad C Sharif, Sorrento.'"

"Okay."

"Now, you'll recall that the website had a picture showing the structure of *Achilles*. Well, the same picture is on the last page of this document. I'm looking at it now. And written above it are the letters CTGGTAC. Familiar?"

"Say them again."

"C...T...G...G...T...A and C."

"That's the sequence of bases in *Deidamia*, its genetic code, written in the usual shorthand— cytosine, thymine, guanine, guanine, thymine, adenine, and cytosine again."

"Exactly. And near those letters is also written: 'insert at minus 7430.'"

"Which is the position where *Deidamia* has to be put in the chromosome for it to work— a distance of exactly seven thousand four hundred and thirty bases upstream from *Achilles*."

"Correct. Now, are you sitting down?"

"Yes, as it happens."

"Good, because it looks to me as if the two sets of handwriting were done by the same person. In fact, there's no doubt about it. And what's more, they were done with the same pen, a felt tip with green ink."

"What are you saying? That I was correct? *Deidamia* is nothing more than the Bedouins' switch, and...?"

"Ahmad passed the details to Steve in Sorrento on this document. That's right. I can't think of any other explanation... can you?"

"Not off the top of my head, no. Where on earth did you find it?"

"Behind a curtain here in Steve's office."

"That was a bit sloppy on his part."

"Probably he put it there before rushing off on his lecture tour."

"This is incredible."

"The big question is where do we go from here?"

"I know where *I'm* going—to the loo. First thing Monday, you have to talk to somebody. Yes?"

"Afraid so. This is pretty devastating. But now I need to tidy up this place, take a few quick photos, and then go for a walk to think it over."

"A *walk*...where you are in the early hours? Are you mad? You'll be found dead in a gutter. Take a cab."

"I'll be careful, don't worry."

"Giles, don't be stupid. Please!"

"Okay."

"Promise?"

"I promise."

After taking a photocopy of the document, he returned it to the windowsill. Then he replaced everything else to exactly where it had been, before locking the door behind him, and making his way down the staircase.

"I'd almost forgotten about you, Dr Butterfield," a familiar voice called, as he tiptoed across the entrance hall. "Success?"

"Er...yes, thanks, Joe. Took longer than expected, but I found what I needed in the end. You'll need to lock the lab door."

"Yes, Adnan called to remind me. Let me get you a cab."

"Thanks. It'll be safer than hailing one."

"You bet! You'd get soaked too. It's pouring down."

It was well after 3.00 a.m. by the time the cab was drawing up outside The Jefferson. As Giles knew Fiona would have arrived in the lab by now for her Saturday morning review of the week's work, he raced up the staircase to call her from his room.

"Fiona, it's me again, this time from the hotel."

"Thank goodness for that. I was worried to death. Which one are you in, by the way?"

"The Jefferson in downtown DC. Sorry, I should have told you."

"Is it nice?"

"Very."

"Good food?"

"Yes."

"Comfy bed?"

"Yes, but why the questions?"

"No reason really. Just trying to picture you there. So, what have you decided to do?"

"It's a choice between talking to Hank Weinberg at the NIH, the Nobel lot in Stockholm, the local cops, or the man himself. I'm in a quandary."

"Wait while I switch off the new kettle. It's in my office."

She returned a couple of minutes later.

"Well, if *you* can't decide what to do, Giles, I'll do it for you. Definitely not Steve. What would be the point? The cops would say it's nothing to do with them. And the Swedes would say there isn't enough to go on. For all they know, you might have a chip on your shoulder, a grudge against Steve, and have forged the writing. So, as Director of the entire National Institutes of Health, of which the National Cancer Institute is a part, it has to be Hank. Yes?"

"Seems obvious, I agree. But bad news for the NCI is equally bad news for the NIH, isn't it? What if Hank would prefer to bury it?"

"I'm sure he would…and probably also a hatchet in your head while he's at it! It does worry me how he'll react. But I think it has to be him."

"I think you're right."

"But you know, Giles, there's something I don't understand."

"What's that?"

"The fact that Ahmad put his signature on it. It wasn't just pointless, it was pretty stupid, wasn't it? Why put his head on the block by leaving such irrefutable evidence of the crime?"

"Perhaps he didn't realise he was writing *Deidamia's* details on that particular copy. Steve could have duped him into believing it was a different one, so if at any time in the future he was accused of stealing the information, he could present it as evidence that Ahmad had given it to him. The signature is on the *first* page, remember, and the details on the *last* one."

"Quite possible, I suppose."

"Damn! I've just thought of something."

"What's that?"

"When I was in his office, I found a mouse under the rug, and threw it into the trash can. Then, when I was tidying up before leaving, I forgot all about it."

"Ugh! A dead mouse?"

"No, a computer mouse. One of those small ones for travelling. What if Steve sees it when he returns?"

"Presumably, he won't. The cleaners will assume it was broken and toss it out with everything else."

"Yes, I suppose so. Let's hope. So where was I? Oh yes, Hank. I'll call him first thing Monday for an appointment."

"Good. And be really careful round there, Giles. Remember, you're not in Little Compton."

"I'll look after myself, don't worry. Have a good weekend."

"Thanks, but somehow I doubt it."

Chapter Fourteen

After spending the remainder of Saturday catching up on lost sleep, Giles went to the Smithsonian Institution the next day to see an exhibition of bronzes from Benin. But no matter how magnificent the sculptures, his mind kept wandering to the unpleasant task that lay ahead. He had not spent much time with Hank Weinberg during his sabbatical in Steve's lab, but he knew him well enough to expect a very difficult time. He was smart and quick on his feet, someone who made decisions on the spot and then pushed them through no matter what. In some ways these were admirable qualities. Certainly, they were essential survival tools for someone in his position, arguably the biggest medical research job in the world. But he also had a reputation for pursuing his ambitions ruthlessly, trampling on other people in the process. He did not like having his opinion questioned or having inconvenient truths put in his way.

Come eight o'clock Monday morning, Giles was trying hard to concentrate on the Washington Post over breakfast. His eyes moved nervously between the newsprint and the telephone. He was beginning to wonder if he would ever pick up the courage to make the call, when his eyes fell on an article lauding Steve as "a modern-day Richard Coeur de Lion, who had recaptured the West's honour from the Muslim world."

"What a load of shit!" he muttered. "'Coeur de Lion' my foot, more like Cur de Lyin' from what I've seen."

Tossing the newsprint aside, he emptied his cup and picked up the phone.

Hank's PA answered to say that her boss was at a meeting in Philadelphia for the day. The best she could do would be to transfer the call to his mobile in the unlikely event it was switched on. Fortunately, it was.

"Hank, this is Giles Butterfield, calling from DC. You probably remember me. I did a sabbatical in Steve Salomon's lab a few years back."

"Er sorry…the name again?"

"Giles Butterfield."

"Er…sorry Jules…I'm pretty pooped right now. Give me a clue."

"Let me think…I know…I must be the only man who's knocked a bottle of Shiraz over one of your wife's *Chanel* dress, a white silk creation, and followed it up an hour later with a chocolate soufflé in her lap."

"Ah, Giles Butterfield? At La Chaumiere. How could I forget? How are you, Giles? Ruined any other dresses lately?"

"I'm fine, thanks. And no, I haven't. I now drink only Chardonnay and have vanilla ice cream for dessert."

"Ha, ha, very wise! What can I do for you?"

"I'd like to see you, if I may, rather urgently."

"Urgent? Sounds ominous. Can you tell me more?"

"I'd rather not, if you don't mind. Not on the blower."

"Okay, if you insist. How about tomorrow morning, eleven-fifteen?"

"Perfect. Thanks, I appreciate it. Same office as before?"

"Yeah, afraid so, same boring office."

"I'll be there."

"By the way, Giles, you do know Steve's out of town?"

"Yes, thanks. On a lecture tour before his big day. See you tomorrow."

Knowing Fiona would have spent the weekend alone worrying about his next step, he called the lab at once.

"Fiona, it's me."

"Oh, Giles! Any news?"

"I'm seeing Hank Weinberg tomorrow, in his office at eleven-fifteen."

"Did you tell him anything?"

"Only that it was urgent."

"I'm really worried about how he's going to take it."

"So am I. But I can handle him. Don't worry."

"I hope so. Well, good luck. I'll probably finish early tomorrow and do some shopping to take my mind off it. Bye for now."

The following day, Giles arrived at the NIH to find Hank at his desk studying his diary. Dropping his pen, he leant forward to offer a muscular handshake.

"Nice to see you, Giles. Come on in."

After asking his PA for a pot of coffee, he herded Giles to a low table in the centre of the room.

"My new PA," he remarked, nodding in the direction of the door. "Sacked the last one—the bitch who leaked Ted Crabb's meeting with Steve in the Oval Office to Newsweek."

Hank squeezed himself into his wingback.

"What a damn fool I was to take her along. You can imagine what Ted said when he saw that article? Anyway, water under the bridge now. Steve's done us proud since then, thank goodness. What a great guy! Saved his neck, mine *and* Ted's with one stroke of pure, unadulterated, high-octane genius. Pow!"

Hank pumped his fist in the air.

"Crisis? What crisis? Now, what can I do for an old friend?"

Giles opened his briefcase and placed his copy of Steve's Science paper on the glass tabletop. Hank beamed as he stroked it affectionately.

"And well, well, well…there it is. You won't believe this, Giles, but I keep a copy of that article under my pillow. Isn't that something? Look at it last thing every night. It's also in my smartphone. Look, I'll show you."

"Later, thanks, Hank. I'm a bit pushed right now. But there is something I would like to see."

"What's that?"

"A copy of the software Steve developed, the programme that made *Deidamia* possible. I don't suppose you've got that in there too?"

"Ha…some chance! What if my phone was hacked? Steve's had strict instructions from his attorney to keep it under wraps. Believe me, that's some hot property, boyo."

After pausing to steel himself, Giles took the bull by the horns.

"Hank, I'll get straight to the point. Steve may not have one."

"May not have one what?"

"Computer programme."

"What are you talkin' about?"

"This is difficult, Hank, but I'm beginning to suspect Steve may not have a programme at all."

Keeping his eyes fixed on the table for fear of Hank's reaction, he finished the job.

"And…not only that, I'm starting to think *Deidamia* may not be what she seems to be either."

Hank glowered at him across the table.

"What the goddamn hell are you talking about, Butterfield? What's going on?"

"Let me explain, Hank."

"Please do!"

"This is not easy for me either, Hank, so let's keep calm, shall we? On Friday evening, I was in Steve's lab going through the records of the experiments I did during my sabbatical with him. I'm writing my autobiography, and I needed to check a few facts. As I was leaving, I noticed this on the floor, under one of the benches."

He lifted the Science paper to reveal the *Achilles* website report beneath it.

"Recognise it?"

"Yeah, course I do. It's that MECCAR report, isn't it?"

"That's right, the original announcement of the discovery of *Achilles*. As you can see from the front page, it was given to Steve by the author, Ahmad Sharif, when they were in Sorrento together."

"So? Pretty common gesture, isn't it? Do it myself at meetings all the time."

"Yes, it is. We all do it. But now look at the last page."

Hank did as requested.

"What do you see?"

"A diagram of the *Achilles* gene, with the genetic code of Steve's chunk of DNA scribbled near it."

"That's right. And…?"

"And what? That's all there is."

Giles turned the report over to show the front page again.

"Notice anything about the writing?"

Hank adjusted his glasses, as he flipped the document over several times.

"Giles, this is gettin' me real confused. What's this all about?"

"I'm confused too, Hank. I don't understand either. I was hoping you might have some ideas."

As Hank was comparing the two pieces of handwriting once again, his PA entered with a tray.

"Leave it on the desk, Cybil," he snapped. "And next time, please knock!"

Giles waited for her to close the door before continuing.

"It looks very much to me, Hank, as if the base sequence of what we all know as *Deidamia* was put there by none other than Ahmad Sharif."

Hank poured the coffee, the top of the white china pot rattling as he did so.

"What are you suggesting, Giles—that *Deidamia* is nothin' but that Bedouin switch?"

"I'm not suggesting anything, Hank. I'm just asking you to draw your own conclusion."

"Sorry, Giles. I've known Steve for years. He's a straight guy. He couldn't do a thing like what you're suggestin'. It's impossible. There must be a simple explanation."

Hank pushed a cup across the table, clumsily slopping coffee into the saucer. Giles took a paper handkerchief from his pocket to mop it up.

"That's just what I thought, Hank. Steve's a straight guy, I said to myself. There has to be a simple explanation. I was hoping you might know what it is. That's all."

Hank slurped his coffee pensively.

"No, I don't. But I do know it stands to reason that *Deidamia* couldn't be that goatherds' mutation. Why? Because MECCAR's top man would have spotted it at once."

"It's not that simple, Hank. Rashid Yamani was under oath not to go public with anything unique about the tribe's DNA. He would have had no choice but to keep quiet."

"But what about Steve's computer programme? Why would he have…?"

"As I said, I have doubts about that too. Are you absolutely sure he has one?"

"Of course, I am."

"You've seen it?"

"Of course. In this very office, as it happens."

"You saw it working? Steve demonstrated it to you?"

"He didn't have time to there and then. You know how he is, always run off his feet. But he said he would. That's good enough for me."

"So what *did* you see?"

"The CD."

"Just a CD…nothing more? He didn't run any part of it?"

"Look, Giles, it was obviously the real thing. There was a fancy label on it."

"Ah, it had a label on it, and a *fancy* one at that? In that case it *must* have been genuine!"

That was too much for Hank to take.

"Look, Butterfield, I don't like your attitude. We haven't seen each other for God knows how long. Then out of the blue you arrive from nowhere without any warning. You poke around Steve's lab behind his back, think you've found some dirty washing, and then come here to rub it in my face. You're making a grave accusation about one of my most trusted colleagues on the flimsiest evidence. You push your way in here with libellous accusations. What the hell's going on? You jealous of Steve's Nobel or somethin'? I know Oxford hasn't gotten one for a while. Is that what it's all about? You were sent here by your university to do a bit of muckraking? And now you think you've found something that'll get you big promotion? Well let me warn you, Butterfield, if you go public with any insinuations, the NIH will drag you into court before…"

"Hold on, Hank, calm down! I told you what happened. I was in Steve's lab getting information for my book, and came across it by accident. That's all. Having stumbled across something very puzzling, and rather worrying, I thought I should let you know about it. In fact, I assumed you'd want me to. No?"

Hank struggled out of his chair for no apparent reason and moved to his desk, remaining on his feet, his back to his visitor. When he was ready, he turned, pale and visibly shaken.

"Yeah, of course, Giles. Gee, I'm sorry. I apologise. I've been at it too hard lately. My plate's perpetually too damn full. You know how it is. Life can get on top of you at times."

He returned to the table with the coffee pot, and placed a hand on Giles's arm before squeezing into his chair again.

"You did *exactly* the right thing, Giles. It's very confusing for both of us, but there has to be a simple explanation. Your cup's empty. Here, have some more."

As Giles took up the offer, Hank thumped his fist on the table, splashing coffee over his guest's hand.

"Gee, sorry, Giles! But I've got the answer," he exclaimed. "I bet some shithouse planted it in the lab. That must be it. Steve's got a stack of enemies. There's so much envy and jealousy around this goddamn place. Who let you into the lab?"

"A member of his team."

"Male or female?"

"A young man…why?"

"Catch his name?"

"Adnan."

"What, that Arab? He's one of those Alhazen guys from Iraq, or somewhere like that. Did he know you were coming?"

"Yes, I'd called."

"That's it, then. Simple! Must have been him. I'm sure the Arabs aren't happy about Steve usurping their guy's throne.

Obviously, he downloaded a copy of the document, forged what you've shown me, and planted it in Steve's lab, knowing you'd find it. Wait till I get the louse in here. No questions—just out, back to where he came from!"

Hank twisted his hands as if wringing a chicken's neck, before noticing that Giles was looking uncomfortable.

"Sorry, Giles, if that gesture upset you, but…"

"It's not that, Hank. It's just that what I told you before wasn't really true. I didn't find the report in the lab. I found it in Steve's office. Sorry about that. So it couldn't have been anything to do with Adnan."

"Steve's office? What the fuck were…?"

"Hank, keep calm. I can explain. I'd finished taking a few photos of the lab for my book, when I thought it would be nice to have some of Steve's office too. During my sabbatical, we had some memorable discussions about our work in there. I have really fond memories of the place. I was going to ask the porter if he could let me in, but then I noticed the door was ajar. So I went inside, assuming the cleaners were around. And while I was there, I saw the report lying on Steve's desk."

Hank crossed his arms and looked at him suspiciously.

"If that's really what happened, Giles, why didn't you say so to begin with?"

"Yes, sorry Hank. It's because I know I shouldn't have been there. I know the rules. Offices are out of bounds. But then when you said you were going to give Adnan such a hard time, I had to come clean."

Giles could see from Hank's body language he was reluctant to accept Adnan's innocence.

"You're absolutely right, Giles. You shouldn't have been in there. But what difference does it make? Why does that get that Arab off the hook? Being linked to MECCAR, he has to be the prime suspect. Can you imagine how that lot feel about Steve getting a Nobel instead of their man? Of course they want to bring him down. It stands to reason. After Steve had set off for Europe, that Adnan guy must have dropped the report on

Steve's desk, knowing his PA would see it sooner or later. But it just so happened you got to it first."

"But do you really think she would have noticed what I've shown you, Hank? And if she did, would she understand its significance? Of course not!"

"That's not the point, Giles. It's what that Adnan guy *thought* would happen that matters."

"But Hank, it's pure speculation, isn't it? You've no evidence. You can't convict him on the basis of pure speculation. If you terminate his fellowship, he could take the entire NIH to court for unfair dismissal. And he would win hands down. How do you think that would look in the newspapers?"

Hank was rubbing his chin vigorously as he took it all in.

"And the whole scenario doesn't make sense anyway, Hank. Sure, I can imagine how MECCAR might feel about Steve's Nobel, but if they tried to block it by fabricating a case against him in the way you're suggesting, the whole world would get the message that Ahmad Sharif had been a traitor. Do you think MECCAR would want everyone to believe that of their golden boy?"

Giles picked up the report and waved it in the air.

"There are obviously no grounds, Hank, for believing MECCAR would want to discredit Steve, and there's a bloody good reason why they wouldn't want to go about it in this way. Think about it, and think of the possible consequences for you and the NIH of acting rashly."

Hank got up again to pace up and down, fiddling with coins in his trouser pockets.

"Okay, you win, Giles. It's time to call it a day. I'll set up an internal inquiry tomorrow. I agree we'll have to look into this. Leave it to me. I'll keep in touch, and let you know the outcome."

As Hank moved to open the door, Giles stood his ground. For "internal inquiry" read "cover-up" he was thinking.

"Are you sure that would be the best course of action, Hank?"

"Yeah, course I am."

"I'm not, I must say. Steve might have a perfectly plausible explanation for what's on that report that hasn't occurred to either of us. He might be completely innocent of any wrongdoing. Jumping into an internal inquiry would be risky. It would be impossible to keep a lid on it. It's bound to leak out. Remember Newsweek? The press would make a meal of it. Even if Steve were cleared, that wouldn't be the end of it. They'd still accuse you of a cover-up. And before you know where you are, the rat pack would be demanding an independent inquiry, a congressional hearing…your head. Whatever the facts of the case, whatever the truth, a massive amount of damage would be done to the NIH—apart from all the hassle, stress, work, embarrassment. Why not just give Steve a call and see what he says? Perhaps there *is* a simple explanation. At least he deserves an opportunity to explain."

Hank's glasses having fallen to the floor, he stooped to pick them up.

"Er…well, I suppose that could make sense. On the other hand,…"

"Good man. Why not call him this very minute? Get it off your plate. No time like the present."

"What if he's busy or resting after the day's work? He might even be asleep for all I know."

"This is too important to worry about such things, Hank. Where is he right now?"

"I don't know."

"Got his itinerary?"

"Er…yeah, I suppose so, somewhere."

"Excellent. Let's look at it."

With obvious reluctance, Hank opened the door and gestured to Cybil.

"Cybil, find Dr Salomon's itinerary please, and send it to my printer."

After closing the door again, he stood by his desk, nervously picking his fingernails, until the pages emerged.

"He's gotten as far as Paris, Giles. Gave a lecture at the Académie des Sciences earlier today. Next stop's Berlin. Then he's off to…London, Perth, Melbourne…Tokyo."

Hank placed the first page to one side to read the second.

"After that it's Moscow, followed by Geneva, where he joins up with Marie-Claire, and from there they go to Stockholm together. What a programme! How come I only get to places like Atlantic City and Detroit?"

"Where's he staying?"

"The Plaza Athénée. Never did like slumming it."

Giles looked at his watch.

"He's six hours ahead of us in Paris. Could have his feet up now, taking a rest. Got the hotel's number?"

"Yeah, it's here. He always was a great organiser. But there's no need for you to hang around, Giles, and waste more of your precious time. There's a great exhibition of African statues at the Smithsonian. I wouldn't want you to miss it. You should spend the afternoon there. I'll give you a call this evening and get you up to date."

"Most thoughtful, Hank, but I spent the whole of yesterday there. You're right, it's fabulous, but once is enough. And anyhow, who knows, I might be useful. So, I'll hang around."

"Sure?"

"Sure."

"Okay, but first I should get rid of Cybil. These walls are not as thick as they look."

Hank found the website of the US National Library of Medicine on his computer, and searched for articles on "mitochondrial DNA," his own research specialty. After printing the list, he ringed several titles and took it next door.

"Cybil, I need to read these for the review article I'm writing. The ones I've marked aren't available to download, at least not without extortionate fees. So drop everything, please, and go get copies. It's urgent. Thanks."

After closing the door, he returned to his desk.

"That should keep her out of mischief for an hour or two. Now where's that number again?"

"Here we go: zero-one-one-three-three for France, one for Paris, then five-three- six-seven-six-five. Let's hope he's there. I'm not sure what we'll do if...oh...hold on...er...hello, I mean bonjour...Dr Stephen Salomon, please."

Steve answered almost immediately.

"Room 204, Salomon."

Giles picked up the receiver of the extension that Hank kept on the coffee table and held it to his ear, covering his mouth as a precaution.

"Steve, it's Hank."

"Hank, what a surprise!"

"How's the trip?"

"Exhausting. I'm on the bed. The French kept me at it since seven this morning. But what brings you to the phone?"

"I'll get straight to the point, Steve. It's about that symposium you went to last year in Sorrento. While you were there, did that Ahmad Sharif guy give you a signed copy of the *Achilles* website report by any chance?"

"Yeah, he did as a matter of fact. How did you know?"

"One of the cleaners found it lying around somewhere. She gave it to the porter, who sent it to me."

"Found it *lying around*? Where? And why to *you*, not my PA?"

"Pass. Does it matter?"

"Not really. It's just I'm pretty sure I left it…."

"Never mind, the point is I'm puzzled about what's on the back of it, what's written above the diagram of the gene."

"You mean my *Deidamia* base sequence?"

"That's right."

"What about it?"

"Well, er…comparing it with what's on the front page, Steve, it looks like Sharif wrote it, and that's gotten me a bit confused."

"Although it might *look* like his writing on the back, it's not. It's very definitely mine."

"Really?"

"Yeah, of course! What are you suggesting?"

"But it also looks like the same pen too, Steve."

"I know it does. And there's a very simple explanation. The bag of promotional junk from the sponsors in Sorrento contained a felt-tipped pen with green ink, a marketing gimmick from a small Italian drug company that likes to boast its green credentials. Ahmad used his to sign the report, and I used mine later on. Simple as that."

"Do you still have that pen?"

"No. Tossed it when the ink ran out. It was a cheap thing."

"So, when exactly did you write it, Steve?"

"Not long after getting back from Italy. I was at home explaining everything to Marie-Claire."

"So, when did you do the lab work on *Deidamia*?"

"Boy, this is like the Spanish Inquisition! Most of it was done before Sorrento. Did it all myself. Too important to give it to the lab techs."

"Did that Adnan guy know about it?"

"No! He's the last…"

"It's in one of your lab books then?"

"Er…no…far too hot. Couldn't risk having it lying around. Used a separate notebook."

"Is it in your office?"

"No…brought it with me in case anyone wanted any experimental details that are not in the Science paper."

"Could you scan the relevant pages and send them to me?"

"My, you're hard to convince on this one, Hank! I suppose there must be a scanner somewhere around, but goodness knows where. It might take some time."

"Anything you could show me from your laptop then, just something to back up your story?"

Giles gave Hank a nod of approval.

"Let me think. Yeah, actually there is. With the help of my computer programme, I worked out the base sequence and planned the lab work during the first day of last year's meeting of the New York Cancer Club. I remember it clearly. I was so excited about the project."

"When exactly was that Steve?"

"Er…July 28 to be precise. Then I worked on it again during the flight back to DC a couple of days later. Haven't touched it since. So, I can show you all that stuff. Can it wait until I get back?"

Giles was gesticulating to Hank to insist that Steve should email it now.

"Why not send it now, Steve? I wouldn't want any of your enemies to make trouble for you. After all, we don't know who saw it before it reached me, do we? Even someone in your own unit might have a grudge. Remember Newsweek magazine? Better safe than sorry, I always say."

"Er…right…sure thing. It's a Word file."

"Fine."

"You use a Mac like me, don't you?"

"Yeah."

"I'm still using an old operating system, OS9.2. Is that a problem?"

Hank glanced at Giles, who was shaking his head vigorously. "Nope."

"Okay, I'll send it. But you'll have to give me an hour. I'm expecting a local VIP in my suite for drinks."

"That's fine, Steve. As soon as you're ready. Bye."

Hank replaced his receiver with a deep sigh, as Giles gave him a double thumbs-up.

"He sounded okay to me, Giles. Full of confidence, I'd say. Once we've got that file, we can sleep.

About an hour later, a pink duck waddled across Hank's computer screen, laid an egg, and quacked three times.

"Isn't she cute?" he chortled. "She's telling me an email's arrived in my inbox."

After reading Steve's message, he went to the attachment, labelled "Achilles," saved it to his computer's desktop, and opened it. A description of the now famous piece of DNA, seemingly worked out by a computer programme called "Design-a-DNA", was followed by a description of experiments designed to test its ability to activate *Achilles* and kill cancer cells.

Giles ran his eye over it before taking the mouse out of

Hank's hand and closing the document. He highlighted its icon, went to the menu bar at the top of the screen, and clicked on *File, Get Info,* and *General Information* in that order. A window opened that showed the file had just been created.

"Just what I feared!" Giles said sombrely. "Sorry, Hank. It's not enough. When the file was downloaded, your Mac automatically gave it a new date and time. That's what happens. So for all we know, he could have created it while we were waiting."

Hank closed his eyes and threw himself back in his chair.

"Okay, Sherlock, so what do we do now?"

"You'll have to call him again. Sorry, Hank, but there's no choice."

With a huff, Hank picked up the phone and called the Plaza Athénée again. This time Steve took longer to answer.

"Steve, it's arrived…thanks…but there's a problem. When it was downloaded, my Mac gave it today's date. I need to know when it was created. We might as well make it watertight. You know how suspicious people can be."

"Didn't think of that, Hank. Tell you what, the file's in a folder called 'Travel Notes.' All the stuff I do on the road goes in there. As you know, if I open it in *List view*, the window will show a list of all the files it contains, along with their dates. So, I'll do that. Then I'll take a screenshot, and email it to you. Simple!"

"Hold on, Steve. I'm a computer goof. What's a screenshot?"

"A snapshot. If I take one of the open folder, you'll see the 'Achilles' file along with all the others, their dates, sizes, and so on. Can't send the folder itself, I'm afraid. It contains some confidential stuff."

"Okay then, fire away."

Hank replaced the receiver and looked towards Giles, now admiring Cybil's collection of cacti.

"He says the file's in a folder called 'Travel Notes.' He's going to open it and take a screenshot of what's inside, which will give the file's date. Okay?"

"Should be, I guess."

While they were waiting, Hank excused himself to complete some work at his desk. Giles occupied his time by going through a stack of the latest journals that Cybil had placed on a chair for her boss to read the day before.

It was well over an hour before Hank's duck laid another egg. Steve's message was brief and to the point: "Hi, Hank. Herewith screenshot of open folder. Steve."

With Giles peering over his shoulder, Hank went to the attachment. As promised, the screenshot of the open 'Travel Notes' folder showed a list of files. He scrolled down:

> Rio lecture
> Fiji workshop
> Letter to GP
> Achilles
> Notes after Singapore
> Marie-Claire
> Oncogene review
> Dave's salary
> Special budget

"Rio, Fiji…Singapore!" Hank exclaimed. "The guy needs wings."

To the right of the list was a column headed *Date Modified*, giving the most recent date on which each file had been altered in any way. The one that had most recently been changed in some way, about a lecture in Rio de Janeiro, was at the top, and the oldest at the bottom.

"Wonderful!" Hank shrieked. "His 'Achilles' file was last changed on July 30. Just as he said, see? On his way back from the Big Apple, more than one entire month before Sorrento, boyo. There's no doubt about it, Giles my good friend. Steve's as clean as a whistle, as straight as they come. I knew it."

Hank rubbed his hands with glee as he danced towards the coat stand to don his jacket.

"Now, let's eat. I'm famished. What'll it be—burger or Italian? I can tell you Le Beef does the best burgers in town, complete with pickles, French fries, slaw, their own salsa Tropicana, and a large diet Coke thrown in for good measure. How about it?"

"Sounds delicious, Hank, but I'd prefer Italian please."

"Guessed you'd say that. Antonio, here we come!"

By the time they were waiting for their meals to be served, it had become clear to Hank that all was not well. During their walk from the office, he'd assumed Giles's reluctance to chat was because he had other things on his mind—his travel plans perhaps, or his lab work in Oxford. But the fact that he had still said nothing other than to place his order was too much.

"Come on, Giles," he barked. "Spit it out!"

Giles covered his mouth with his napkin before dropping a large olive stone onto his plate as discreetly as he could manage.

"Not *that*! I meant what's on your mind, not in your chops. You look as if you've got the third-world debt on your shoulders."

"Do I?"

"Yep."

"Well, it's because something's bugging me, Hank. I'm sorry to ruin the party, but I'm uncomfortable that it took Steve so long to send that email. I'm wondering why. After all, he must have known where everything was in his laptop. And he didn't have much to do, did he? A double click to open the folder, a key press or two, and he'd got what he needed— a thirty seconds job. But for some reason it took him an hour and twelve minutes. I timed him. It's suspicious, Hank, very suspicious."

"Oh come on, Giles! They're could have been a ton of reasons. He's a very busy guy. He's a Nobel Prize winner for God's sake! He could be inundated with stuff. Anything could have happened. He might have gotten a bunch of unexpected phone calls, or visitors knocking on his door."

"For seventy-two minutes?"

"Yeah. Maybe he also went for a shower, or just needed to lie down and rest. He's only human."

"When he knew you were waiting?"

"Why not? Hell, Giles, what's got into you over this goddamn business? We've got all the evidence we need, haven't we? What more do you want? We've seen that date with our very own eyes. And I know Steve's a straight guy anyhow, straight as an arrow. So why don't you just drop it?"

With Hank glaring at him menacingly, Giles decided to do just that, for now.

"Okay, Hank, perhaps you're right."

"Phew! Glad you're seeing sense. So, let's enjoy our food. It's not every day I have an excuse to eat here. And as a matter of fact, here it comes, boyo."

Antonio's son arrived, followed closely by his younger sister.

"Can't wait to get started. Antonio's 'Super-Lasagne De Luxe' is out of this world. Just look at that masterpiece: six layers, two of pepperoni, four Italian cheeses, lashings of sauce. He's a genius!"

Tucking his napkin into his shirt, Hank watched as Giles's soup was ladled into his bowl.

"You on a diet or somethin', Giles?"

"No. It's just that I'm not a lover of rich fancy foods, Hank. One of the things I acquired during my time in Liverpool was an appreciation of the simple traditional recipes of northern England, their origins the spartan kitchens of country cottages and working class housewives, not the palaces of gleaming steel and hi-tech gadgetry of Michelin starred chefs. This acquacotta is in the same category. It's a peasant soup from Tuscany."

Giles fished around with his spoon.

"See, it's got onions, celery, tomatoes, chard, red pepper… some stale ciabatta…and a poached egg to finish it off. Simple, but nourishing and beautiful."

Hank peered at it over his glasses and gave it a sniff.

"Tuscan peasants, you say? I can believe that! Bon appetito!"

It was almost three o'clock by the time they were finishing their coffee in the lounge that doubled up as Antonio's indoor herb garden. Giles handed Hank one of the restaurant's business cards he had collected on his way through the entrance hall.

"Before we part, Hank, why don't you put your home telephone number on this, in case something occurs to me? You never know."

"Sure thing, Giles, my cell phone too…there we go. And have a good trip, by the way. I just love that city of yours— all those cute villages, the quaint churches, cream teas on the lawn…"

"The rain, the fog, the traffic jams. You should drop in some time. During the summer I could book you a room in Magdalen."

Hank offered his hand. "It's a deal!

During the journey from Antonio's, Giles asked the cabby to drop him off near the Lincoln Memorial. Now the ordeal was over, he needed time to consider the outcome of the meeting before getting Fiona up to date. The unexplained delay before Steve had sent his email had never left his mind, and with the big day in Sweden now only four weeks away, the prospect of returning to Oxford empty handed was worrying. But what could he do?

Taking the long way around to Lafayette Square on his way to the hotel, he skirted the Tidal Basin through West Potomac Park to take in the memorial to Thomas Jefferson, a man he had always admired as much for his contributions to science as his achievements as a statesman. After reaching the top of the steps, he stood alone before the imposing bronze statue.

"In matters of principle, stand firm like a rock. That's what he said, didn't he, or something pretty close to it?"

He decided there and then he was not going to let Hank bully him off the case. It might have worked on many in the past, but it was not going to work this time. Come hell or high water, he would get to the bottom of it.

As he crossed the marble floor, a strong November wind arrived from across the river, sweeping cold rain through the portico. Regretting his decision to decline Virgil's offer of an umbrella in the morning, he paused between the white columns overlooking the water. Should he wait for the weather to improve, or button up and carry on regardless?

"What would Jefferson have done?" he asked.

Turning up his collar and digging his hands deep into his pockets, he stepped out to continue on his way.

Upon arriving at the hotel, Giles was taken aback by an apparent change in Virgil's demeanour. Instead of radiating his usual warmth and cheerfulness, he was strangely diffident.

"Good evening, sir. I hope you had a good day."

"Yes, thanks Virgil. Is everything okay with you?"

"Yes sir."

"Sure?"

"Yes sir."

Moving a little closer, he whispered in Giles's ear.

"Your guest arrived a few minutes ago, sir."

"Guest?"

"In the lobby, sir."

"Er…thank you, Virgil."

Puzzled as to who it could be, Giles scanned the lobby, trying not to make it obvious he was searching for someone. He could see several couples with children gathering for a birthday party, but only one person on his own. A blond, bearded man in his late twenties, wearing a green tea shirt, ragged jeans, and a black leather coat, was nodding off on a sofa, his feet resting on a couple of well-travelled leather suitcases. Who on earth could it be?

As Giles was about to introduce himself, a young woman in a russet woollen suit and suede boots caught his eye on the far side of the room. Seated in a high-backed chair with her head in a magazine, he couldn't see her face, but her flowing red hair, tam o'shanter bonnet, and tartan scarf left him with no doubt about her identity.

As he approached, she interrupted her reading to take a mirror from her handbag. On seeing Giles's reflection, she jumped up and dropped everything.

"Giles!"

"Fiona! Good heavens! What on earth…? How…? Why…?"

"I couldn't bear it any longer," she gasped, throwing her arms around him. "I was worrying non-stop. On top of which I desperately wanted to help. I'm sure it hasn't finished today, has it? It couldn't have done. You've walked into a lion's den. The NIH will fight tooth and nail to protect its precious Nobel Prize winner.

"After your call yesterday, I did nothing but fret for the rest of the day. The evening was even worse, until at bedtime I decided to join you. I wanted to be here when you'd finished with Hank. I didn't know what the result was going to be, of course, but whatever it was I knew it wouldn't be the end, and I wanted to take some of the strain. So I was up before dawn, flew with BA to Newark, and from there to Dulles with United, arriving a couple of hours ago. And here I am!"

She planted a kiss on his forehead.

"You never cease to amaze me, Fiona. But why didn't you tell me?"

"Because you'd try to stop me, of course."

"What about Jane?"

"I left her behind in Oxford."

"Ha! What did you tell her?"

Fiona blushed.

"I'm supposed to be at home with the flu. I sent her a text. Talking of which, you'll get more than influenza if you don't get out of those wet clothes."

"Blame it on Thomas Jefferson."

"Why?"

"I'll tell you later. Is that your luggage, just one small suitcase?"

"Yes, it's all I need."

Once they were upstairs, Fiona was eager to get up to date. Stretched on the bed, her hair wrapped in a towel, she waited for Giles to complete his account of the meeting before breaking her silence.

"What happened then?"

"He took me to an Italian restaurant, where I told him I was worried about why Steve had taken more than an hour to send the screenshot. But he simply made excuses for him, and then refused to talk about it."

"Was he upset?"

Giles nodded.

"Not a good sign. And there's something else I don't like, Giles—that screenshot. It showed when the 'Achilles' file had last been worked on, but not when it had been created, yes?"

"That's right."

"That's a bit odd, isn't it? With the folder's window open, he could have shown that as well. All it needed was a click or two."

"But what's the problem? If his 'Achilles' file was last altered on July 30, it must have been created before then, yes? You don't need Einstein to work that one out."

Fiona closed her eyes while she thought about it.

"Can I use Boris later...after we've eaten? I didn't bring my laptop along."

"Of course, as soon as I've done my emails. What do you have in mind?"

"Something. Let's wait and see."

By the time they had returned from the restaurant on the ground floor, Giles was no longer in the mood for his emails.

"You can have Boris now," he sighed, pushing his laptop in Fiona's direction. "That bottle of Shiraz has knocked me out. I'm going to lie down, close my eyes, and listen to some music. Are you sure you won't join me?"

"I can't, Giles. Something is bugging me, and I have to look into it. Don't worry, I slept all the way to New York."

"And I can't help?"

"Not just now, thanks, Giles. I have an idea about Steve. Have a good sleep. You've earned it."

"Okay, give me a prod, if you find anything exciting."

Fiona opened the laptop on the writing desk, connected it to the Internet, and made herself comfortable. Despite her assertion to the contrary, she was travel weary and jet lagged. It was certainly not the best time for what she had in mind. But if she succumbed to the temptation to lie down, she would inevitably fall asleep too, and then lie awake in the early hours with the same questions running through her head.

After collecting a pen and notebook from her suitcase to keep a record of every key stroke and mouse click, she got to work.

It was more than two hours later when the excitement of her discovery dispelled any reluctance to disturb Giles.

"Giles, Giles, wake up!" she whispered in his ear, tweaking his chin. "Sorry, but I've found something *really* important. I knew it was the right decision to come here. You'll be amazed."

Wiping his eyes, Giles raised himself to see Fiona seated on the bed holding his laptop on her lap.

"What's it all about?"

"Watch."

By the time she had finished demonstrating her discovery, Giles was convinced she had made the breakthrough they needed.

"Fiona, that's amazing! How long did it take you to work that lot out?"

"I've lost count of the number of trials and errors it took. But it's all written down here in case I forget."

She fanned the pages of her notebook before tossing it on the floor.

"You're a genius, Fiona. You know the feeling I have right now? It's like when sunbeams suddenly break through a dark storm cloud. In a second, the world looks so much better, the future so much brighter, the horizons so much nearer. I feel energized again. I could kiss you…there, I've done it."

He looked at his watch—almost one o'clock.

"Is it too late? Oh, what the hell!"

When the phone rang in the living room of Hank Weinberg's colonial style mansion in Northwest Washington's Highland Place, a twenty-minute drive from the NIH, he was waiting for a call from his sister in Portland. He dropped his newspaper with a groan of apprehension, and switched off the television.

"Hi, Betty, how did it go? Give me the worst."

"It's not one of your girlfriends, Hank, it's me...Giles."

"Giles! Sorry, Betty's my..."

"Only joking. Sorry to disturb you."

"That's nice to know. What is it this time?" "

I know you're not going to like this, Hank...but do you think we could meet again?"

"Again?"

"Yes. I've discovered something that could be important."

"To do with Steve?"

"Yes."

"I thought he was in the clear. What's the problem now?"

"It's too complicated to explain on the phone, Hank."

"Too complicated?"

"Yes. Could we meet tomorrow?"

"It'll have to be early."

"That's okay."

"Very early."

"Okay. Let me have it."

"Seven-thirty."

"No problem."

"Don't be late, Giles. I've got a heavy programme tomorrow. And you're damn right about me not being happy. It'd better be real important."

"It is, Hank. See you tomorrow. And thanks. Good night.

***

The following morning, Giles and Fiona were up early to rehearse a demonstration of everything she had learnt. While she played the role of Hank, Giles explained what they feared

196

Steve may have been up to during those seventy-two minutes of silence in Paris. Once they were happy with his performance, Fiona slipped the laptop into Giles's briefcase with an affectionate pat, and wished him the best of luck as she opened the bedroom door.

"Sock it to him, Giles! I'll be with you every second."

Hank was at his desk, red-eyed and grumpy, surrounded by open books and papers, when Cybil showed Giles into his office.

"Giles…come in. Take the seat over there again."

Giles shook his hand with a nervous smile, before moving to the coffee table.

"Sorry about this, Hank. You look as if you're already buried in work."

"You can say that again! I'm doing a thing for Scientific American on the contribution of mitochondrial DNA to our understanding of evolution. Wish I'd never accepted the damn invitation. As you'll know all too well, it's so easy to say 'yes' when the deadline's nine months away. Then you keep putting it off and putting it off, until eventually, when you do get round to it, you don't have enough time to do the job properly."

"I don't do review articles anymore, Hank. I just reply very politely: 'Dear so and so, thank you very much. It's a great honour to be asked, but regrettably I don't have the time to do justice to such an important subject. Perhaps Professor so-and-so could do it instead. Yours sincerely…' And that's that—straight to the point, over and done with. You should try it. You can't imagine how good it feels afterwards."

Giles took his laptop out of his case, and placed it on the table.

"You'd better come over here, Hank," he said solemnly. "Last night, I played around with Boris here. And I need to show you something."

Seeing Hank was confused, Giles tapped the screen of his laptop.

"Ah! Okay, if you insist."

"It's like this. I've found that Steve could have created a new Word document on the spot, in the hotel while we were waiting, and made it look as if he'd been working on it months ago."

"Say that again."

"I've discovered that it's possible to have a Word file in a Mac like Steve's that the computer says had been altered in some way—edited, revised, whatever—before the file ever existed, or for that matter before computers ever existed."

Hank shook his head in disbelief.

"Giles, it can't be true. Computers are smarter than that."

"I don't know about Windows or more recent Macs, Hank, but the aging operating system Steve's using is definitely not 'smarter than that'. By chance, Boris here is running the same one."

"Let me get this straight, Giles. You're saying it's possible to produce a Word document in a computer, which the very same computer 'thinks' was worked on *before* the computer itself even existed?"

"To be precise, Hank, which the computer *says* was modified on a date before the date on which it *says* the document was created."

Hank shook his head vigorously.

"Can't be true, boyo! I'm sure if you tried to fool a Mac into something as stupid as that, it would give you a message, or freeze, or crash…*something*."

"No, it wouldn't, Hank, at least not with this operating system. Sorry to bring such bad news, but it's true. For which reason we can't be sure on present evidence that Steve's 'Achilles' file was created when he says it was."

Hank held his head in his hands.

"What did I do to deserve this? Okay, Giles, prove it."

"Watch the screen."

Hank adjusted his glasses as he leant forward.

"Last night, I created a Word document, which I called 'Demo'. All it contained was my first name. I saved it at 12:32 a.m., closed it, and had a glass of orange juice. When I'd finished it, I opened it, added 'Butterfield' after 'Giles,' saved it again, and closed it…by which time it was 12:47 a.m. Then I created a folder on the desktop, which I labelled 'Demonstration,' and dragged the Word file into it. Okay?"

Hank nodded.

"So…I had a folder called 'Demonstration' that contained a Word doc called 'Demo,' which had been created at 12:32 a.m. and altered at 12:47 a.m. Now, watch closely."

Giles pointed to the screen with his pen.

"Here, in the centre of the screen is the icon of the 'Demonstration' folder. When I double-click on it, a window opens listing its contents, as you'd expect, and you can see the icon of the 'Demo' file is here in the left-hand column. The column to the right of that shows when the document was last modified, namely today at 12:47 a.m. And the column to the right of that one tells us when it was created, today at 12:32 a.m.

"Now, hold onto your hat. I double-click the 'Demo' icon to open the Word doc, and then add my middle initial between 'Giles' and 'Butterfield.' Don't ask me what the M stands for. I'll tell you one day over a large drink. Next, I open the *Date and Time* control panel in the *Apple* menu, turn the clock back by one year, and close the panel. Then, I return to the still open 'Demo' file…save it…and close it. Finally, I go back to the *Date and Time* control panel, and turn the year forward by one year…in other words back to where it was originally. Then, I close the panel.

"Now…look at the open window of the 'Demonstration' folder again. What do you see?"

Hank adjusted his glasses again.

"Er…the date on which the file was 'created' is the same it was before, but the date on which it was 'last modified' is now today's date, but one year ago."

"Precisely. Our ever-so-smart computer is telling us that somebody altered the Word doc a year before it existed. And it's very happy with that—no messages, no crashes, no quacking ducks laying eggs.

"Now, if I wanted to fool you into believing that my 'Demo' Word doc had been created a year or more ago, I could adjust the settings of the 'Demonstration' folder's window so that it shows only when it was last altered, and *not* when it was created."

He moved the cursor to the menu bar, and went to *Edit*, then to *Preferences*, and then to *Views*. Under the *Show Columns* heading in the dialogue box that appeared, he unchecked the *Date Created* box and left the *Date Modified* box checked.

"Now, if you look at the folder's open window again, you'll see that all it tells us is that the 'Demo' file was last modified one year ago. Nothing about when it was created. And most people, even some very smart NIH Directors, would assume that the document must also have been created more than twelve months ago. But it wasn't. It was created last night, while you were waiting for Betty's telephone call.

"And I could have done the same sort of thing with any date or clock time, if I'd wanted."

Hank stared at the screen aghast.

"Quite frankly, Giles, I'm stunned. But if you're suggesting Steve would know that bag of tricks, you can forget it. He's definitely not a computer geek. He wouldn't know any of that stuff. Not a chance!"

"Nor did I, Hank, until shortly before I called you. This time yesterday, I didn't know any of this stuff either. It was only when I put my mind to it last night and played around with Boris that I discovered what's possible. Steve could have done the same. It took him more than an hour to get back to you, remember."

Hank stood up with a sigh, taking the chair with him as he fought to release himself from between its padded arms. Returning to his desk, he buried his head in his hands as he resigned himself to the inevitable.

"You want me to call him again, don't you?"

Giles nodded.

"Is it *really* necessary, Giles? Can't we leave it where it is? It's very difficult to quiz one of my closest and most senior colleagues like this, you know. And I simply don't believe Steve would do anything crooked…period."

"Hank, there's no choice. You have to finish the job. It's too important."

Hank's scowl was impossible to read. Was it just out of frustration, stress, determination to get his own way? Or was it menacing? Having heard stories about his temper, Giles feared he may have pushed too hard. Perhaps a gentle hand on his shoulder would calm him down?

"I don't need that, thanks, Giles," he resumed, turning away, his eyes fixed on the carpet. "I'm getting worried that one of us could get hurt in this business. We don't know what we're getting into, do we? If your suspicions are unfounded, which I'm sure they are, there could be serious repercussions. Steve can get very nasty. I've seen him explode under pressure. He doesn't have a safety valve. He soaks it up, and then *bang*, like a faulty pressure cooker. And he can be very vindictive. As a Nobel Laureate, he'd have no difficulty at all ousting me as Director if he claimed I'd been harassing him. Times have changed since Oahu. He's Ted Crabb's blue-eyed boy these days. I love this job. I want to keep it."

"But nobody will ever criticise you for doing the right thing, Hank. On the other hand, if Steve has been up to something, you would get a lot of credit for weeding it out. The sky would be the limit from then on."

"I'm not sure about that. And anyway, you have to think about your position too, Giles. No matter how hard I tried to keep it under wraps, eventually it's bound to leak out it was you who set the ball rolling. It wouldn't be the first time I've accidentally let the cat out of the bag when I've been overworked or preoccupied with something. And then who knows what would happen next? People can do crazy things in this country when they get mad. In some ways it's still the Wild West."

"I think I understand where you're coming from, Hank, but who'd…?"

"Steve's relatives, for example. They stand to lose a lot. Not many families can boast a Nobel. I always think it's wise to avoid confrontation whenever possible."

Giles raised his eyebrows.

"That's not the impression I got a few years back, Hank. In those days, you seemed very happy to take on a fight."

"That was then. I'm older and wiser now, Giles. It hasn't made my life any easier, but at least I haven't had a bomb under my car, like Tony Cefalu."

"Who's he?"

"He worked on liver disease in monkeys, giving them transplants. Animal rights people don't like that sort of thing. Now he's in a wheelchair for the rest of his life."

"If I didn't know you better, Hank, I'd think you were trying to scare me off."

Hank put his arm around Giles in a caring gesture of protection.

"Just being realistic, Giles. I don't want one of my most valued friends and colleagues to get hurt. This is the real world. And this is the bit of it called the US of A, where at the last count there were three hundred million guns. When some people get nasty here, they can also get trigger happy. I'm real sorry to talk like this, Giles, but you have to think about the worst-case scenario. The stakes are high. No prize is more prestigious than the Nobel. It's almost priceless."

"Well, if I'm destined to be a martyr, Hank, so be it. St Giles of Magdalen. I can see my statue now in the centre of the Cloister Quad, draped in ivy and honeysuckle, with pigeons crapping on my head.

"But to be serious, we have no choice. If there are risks, we have to accept them."

"Okay, okay, it's up to you, Giles. But if this comes back to haunt you, don't say I didn't warn you. I'll tell Steve to send another screenshot of the open folder, but this time showing when the files were created."

"I've got an even better suggestion. Why not just ask him to send the folder itself? When you save it to your hard disk, all the files inside will retain their original dates. That's something else I discovered last night."

"But some of the files inside are personal. He'll want to take them out first. Is that okay?"

"No, because it would alter the date on which the folder's contents were changed. And I don't want that. Tell him you'll trash them."

"Okay, I'll do my best, but he may not like it."

Reaching for Steve's itinerary, Hank glanced at his watch.

"It's 7:50 a.m., which means where he is it's 1:50 p.m. According to his itinerary, he flew to Berlin today to stay at the Hotel Concorde. Presumably, he's checked in by now.

"Okay, first let me get rid of Cybil. There's a doughnut joint across the road. I'll go and tell her to get some. Wait here."

After returning, Hank waited until Cybil's footsteps were at the far end of the corridor before picking up the phone. Steve answered at once.

"Ah, meine liebling! Zimmer nummer ein hundert drei und vierzig. Du…"

"Oh…er…sorry, wrong number," Hank replied.

"Hank! Is that you?"

"Yeah, is that you, Steve?"

"Sorry, Hank. I was expecting a call from…er…Meinhard Libblink at the Free University. My German's a bit rusty, but might as well use it, eh? Did that screenshot reach you?"

"Yeah, thanks, but it didn't show when the files were created, Steve, only when you last worked on them."

"But they must have been created *before* then, right?"

"I know that, of course, Steve, but some people may think it looks fishy. You know how they can be. There's a whole army of envious geneticists out there. I don't want any accusations of a cover-up. While you're running around, I'd be here holding the baby. I need a watertight defence."

"Ha…that's one thing you sure need holding a baby, Hank—a watertight defence. I know from soggy personal experience! But I'm real busy right now. Hold on, someone's at the door."

After a couple of minutes, Steve returned.

"It was the maid to change the flowers. The problem is those confidential files, Hank. I tell you what, I'll…"

"Don't worry about them, Steve. Just send the whole damn folder. I'm the Director, right? Nothing about the NCI is confidential from me. And I won't open the personal ones. I promise. You can trust me. I won't open any file but 'Achilles'. I'll trash everything else. Okay?"

"Okay, you're the boss. But I'll need some time. There's a reception for me in the town hall soon. You won't find it in my itinerary. It's an extra they've thrown in. So I'll send it this evening, probably around eight my time, that's two o'clock yours."

Hank glanced at Giles, who was holding the extension to his ear.

"You can't squeeze it in before you go?"

"Sorry, Hank, don't have the time. You can't imagine how busy this trip is. Everyone wants to shake my hand, invite me to their lab, arrange visits. It's totally crazy. The only break I get is when I go to the washroom!"

"Okay, Steve. I'll hold tight."

Hank replaced the receiver, and wiped his brow.

"Okay, job done. I told you how busy he is. Now I need to get back to this damn article. Sorry to seem so inhospitable, Giles, but how about you go for walkies and get back around two."

"Message received. Know of a good bookshop? It's my nephew's birthday in Cape Town soon. I need to send him a gift."

"Sanderson's Bookshelf. Fifteen minutes by foot. Turn left when you leave the building, take a right after two hundred yards, left at the lights, then keep going till you see a big red sign on the left. Great place, big selection, organic coffee and scrumptious muffins in the basement. Enjoy."

Giles was back at the NIH a little after the agreed time. Clearly very happy, Hank greeted him enthusiastically and hustled him to his computer.

"Sorry, I'm late, Hank."

"Get your book?"

"No, too many choices."

"Sanderson's is that sort of place. I have the same problem with their muffins. Well, I've got great news, Giles. Take a seat. Steve's folder arrived a few minutes ago. Let me show you. As I'd promised to trash his other files, I dragged his 'Achilles' one into a new folder that I'd already created on my desktop for this stuff and labelled 'Salomon'. Then I dragged his folder into the trash can, as promised, and emptied it.

"So, here's my 'Salomon' folder. Okay?"

"No, actually it's not okay, Hank."

"Why? What's wrong now?"

"When you moved his file into your new 'Salomon' folder, your Mac will have replaced the 'date modified' of Steve's folder with today's date. As I said earlier, I didn't want the dates of his folder to change. I'd been hoping to check when he last altered its contents to be sure he hadn't removed or added anything since your first call."

"Sorry! But if I'd..."

"Is your Outlook Express configured to leave copies on the server?"

"Nope."

"Pity."

"But as I said, Giles, we don't have a problem. Let me open that folder...there...now, you'll see that his 'Achilles' file was created on July 28 last year, and he last worked on it two days later...just as he said."

Giles peered at the screen to check it was true.

"Well, that is good news."

"You can say that again, boyo! Now I'm feeling real guilty I ever went along with you. I hope Steve's not too offended by all this suspicion. I knew he wasn't the sort of guy to cook the books. But you left me no choice, did you?"

"Neither of us had any choice, Hank."

"If you insist. Anyhow that's that. Now I must go, if you'll excuse me. Yet another committee meeting. Then I'm out of here. Wednesday evenings, Mary and I do a pizza and a movie."

"Do you mind if I hang around for a while? I see you've got a book of old Italian prints in the bookcase over there. I'd love to go through them."

"Sure thing, Giles, no problem. As Cybil will be going with me to take the minutes of this damn meeting, I'll give you the keys. You'll need to lock both doors on the way out, please, this one and hers."

"How can I return them?"

"You could hand them to the porter, although come to think of it, then he'd know I'd left them with a visitor, which is highly irregular. Wait a minute, I've another idea. There'll be nobody here for the next two days. I'm off to Dallas to give a lecture. How about you hang onto them and have lunch at my place Saturday? You could bring them with you. Or are you in a rush to get back to Oxford?"

"No, I'm not actually. This is just a stopover. I'm en route to the West Coast. So I'd love to. Many thanks. I'll give the people over there a call and rearrange the flight. It's a date."

"Great! We've moved since you were in Steve's lab, by the way. Gone up market. Very posh, as you Brits say."

Hank took a sheet of paper from his printer and wrote down his new address.

"There you are. Twelve-thirty, okay?"

"Perfect."

"Do you like Chinese?"

"Except when playing table tennis."

"Ha, ha…got ya! Enjoy the pics."

As Hank was leaving, he stopped, his back to Giles, and scratched his head.

"By the way, Giles, what's all that Boris business about? You in the habit of givin' your computers pet names?"

"Yes, I am actually."

"Bit odd, if you don't mind me sayin' so."

"It's because I never throw an old laptop away, Hank. I keep them all in case I want to look for an old file at a future date. Instead of giving them numbers, I use names. The last one was Cardew."

"*Cardew?*"

"That's right."

"Boy! I've heard of eccentric English academics. Now I know one! See you Saturday. Bye."

Chapter Fifteen

As soon as Hank and Cybil had left for the committee, Giles was on the phone to The Jefferson.

"Fiona, it's me. Are you okay?"

"Yes, thanks, I'm fine. Have you finished?"

"Yes."

"Why did it take so long? Did Hank give you problems?"

"No, Steve did. Said he had to go to a reception and couldn't send anything until around eight his time."

"Always an excuse for a delay! Okay, so tell me what happened."

"After I'd shown him your routine with Boris, Hank accepted its implications, albeit reluctantly. He called Steve, and got him to send his folder containing the 'Achilles' file. And from what I saw, it certainly does look as if the file was created on July 28, as Steve claimed, and that he worked on it two days later."

"Can you tell me exactly what Hank did? Last night I learnt so much about files and folders that I need a step-by-step account to be sure everything's okay."

"Certainly. As I said, Steve sent Hank the entire folder containing his 'Achilles' file. Hank opened the folder and dragged the file into a folder of his own called 'Salomon'. Then he deleted Steve's folder, as he'd promised to do as it contained some personal files. Finally, he opened his 'Salomon' folder in *List* view to check the dates of the 'Achilles' file. Simple as that."

"I see. Can you tell me more about the 'Salomon' folder? Where did it come from?"

"While he was waiting for Steve's email to arrive, Hank created it on his desktop, and put the first copy of the 'Achilles' file from Steve into it. He likes to be organised that way. Then, as I said, when Steve's folder arrived, he dragged the second copy of the 'Achilles' file into the 'Salomon' folder. Simple as that. Nothing more to it."

"Let me make sure I've got this right. You're saying that Hank's 'Salomon' folder already contained the first copy of the 'Achilles' file when he dragged the second copy into it from Steve's folder. Yes?"

"Yes."

"But that's not possible, Giles. You can't do that, can you? You can't put a file into a folder that already contains a file of the *same type* and has the *same name*. When Hank tried to do so, a message should have appeared, asking if he wanted to replace the one that was already there with the one he was trying to add."

"Jesus, of course! You're right. How stupid of me. And yet they *did* have the same name, Fiona, exactly the same. I can picture them now. How do you explain that?"

"I can't. There must have been a difference in their labels, which you didn't spot. That's the only possible explanation."

"There wasn't. I'm certain. Both said 'Achilles' and nothing else."

"There has to have been a difference, Giles. Could you see him again tomorrow, and somehow take another look?"

"I don't need to. I'm still in his office. He and his PA have gone to a committee meeting. After that, they go straight home. Hank's away for the next two days. He gave me his keys to lock up, and asked me to return them on Saturday. He's invited me to his place for lunch."

"Brilliant! So go and have a look. And don't turn your phone off."

To his relief, Giles found that Hank's computer hadn't yet gone to sleep. After tapping the space bar in case it was about to, he sat down and made himself comfortable.

"Right, Fiona, I'm looking at Hank's screen now. I've opened the 'Salomon' folder, and I'm looking at the two files inside. And I was right. The labels are *exactly* the same."

"Impossible."

"I'm looking at them, dear. They're staring me in the face, the icons of two Word docs are called 'Achilles', and there's no difference between the labels, none at all."

"Try this, Giles. Drag both files out of the folder onto the desktop."

Giles did as instructed.

"Okay?"

"Okay, done."

"Do the labels still look the same?"

"Yes."

"Are you sure? Look very closely."

Giles removed his glasses and got closer to the screen.

"Yes, they're still the…oh my God, no they're not! You're right. There is a difference. It's small, very small, but it's there."

"What is it?"

"The label on the one from Berlin has a space after 'Achilles', whereas the first one from Paris doesn't."

"There you are!"

"I couldn't see it before. But now the icons are out of the folder, their labels have backgrounds of a different colour to the screen, and I can see the space clearly."

"And that space is extremely unlikely to have got there by accident. Steve had to click on the label, put the cursor in exactly the right place, and then hit the space bar— three very different actions. He must have done that for a reason, Giles. All we have to do is find out what it was. Why did he go to all that trouble?"

"Why indeed! See you soon."

Before leaving Hank's office, Giles copied the 'Salomon' folder into the memory stick he always kept on his key ring, and took a photo of Steve's itinerary.

After arriving at The Jefferson, Fiona spotted him from the bar as he was making his way from the lobby to the staircase.

"Giles, I'm here," she called. "Join me for a drink."

Taking one of the many leather chairs on offer, he lifted her glass to take a sip."

"Ugh, Campari and soda! Mistook it for pink champagne. Let me get rid of it."

After ordering a large Dark 'n' Stormy from the barman, he returned rubbing his hands with satisfaction.

"Thanks to you, Fiona, we're now making real progress. If you hadn't taken the bull by the horns and got on that flight, I might have been on the way home by now. Actually, I don't know why I didn't invite you along in the first place. There would have been another benefit too."

"Don't count your chickens, partner! I'm still jet lagged, remember."

"As a matter of fact, I was thinking about during the flight…"

"Ha! Sorry, I've never had any ambition to join the mile-high club!"

"If you'd let me finish, I was going to say that your presence would have protected me from the attentions of a certain Canadian lady. But more on that later."

"Oh yes? Which young lady was that?"

"The air stewardess."

"Oh, is that all. In First Class, they assume all the passengers are super rich. So don't be too flattered. Here comes your drink."

Giles waited for the waitress to depart.

"Do you know, this is the very bar in which I first met Steve. Isn't that something? Little did I realise."

Fiona looked at him admiringly.

"You and I make a great team, you know, Giles. I think we're going to crack this business. I can feel it in my bones."

"Let's drink to that. Cheers!"

"Bottoms up! This evening, why don't we take the opportunity to relax, and do something really nice—a concert or a cabaret, even a jazz club, something different. It doesn't matter what it is. We've earned it. And then we can devote tomorrow to sorting out why Steve went to the trouble of doing what he did."

"It's a deal."

Chapter Sixteen

Reinvigorated by an evening in the Kennedy Centre, but conscious of the calories they'd consumed in a local Greek restaurant, Fiona had insisted that they limit breakfast to black coffee in their room. When a heavy knock on the door announced its arrival while Giles was shaving, she jumped out of bed wrapped in a towel to find Virgil with two cups and a china coffee pot on a silver tray.

Recognising the voice that greeted her, Giles hastily turned off the tap and called through the bathroom door.

"This is an unexpected privilege, Virgil. Hold on. I'll be with you in a tick."

Pulling on a bathrobe, he rushed out to join them, his face still dripping with soapy water.

"Allow me. I'm afraid Mrs Butterfield has a sore hand, Virgil," he explained, taking the tray from Fiona.

Clearly surprised, Virgil gave a deferential nod in Fiona's direction.

"Pleased to meet you, ma'am. I hadn't realised you were…"

"Changed your job, Virgil?" Giles enquired hastily.

"No sir, it's just that the usual boy is not in this morning. His mother has been taken ill."

"I see. I hope it's nothing serious."

"I don't think so. It's not the first time. Well, I must go. More trays are waiting. Have a nice day, Professor, ma'am. I truly hope that your hand gets better soon, ma'am."

After closing the door, Fiona dropped onto the bed and tossed a pillow in Giles's direction.

"Well! What was that all about? Embarrassed to be seen with me?"

Giles was already kicking himself for what he knew had been a stupid impulse. His mind went back to the crisis he'd had in the laboratory after reading Steve's Science paper for the first time. Would he never learn?

"You need to get yourself up to date, Giles. The world has changed a lot since you were in short trousers. These days, we females are permitted to do things like open doors and take trays off hotel staff. And when it comes to unmarried persons sharing bedrooms, nobody cares a toss about that either. Bizarre as it may seem, most people regard sex between consenting adults as normal nowadays. Peculiar isn't it?"

Knowing the anguish h'd be suffering, Fiona beckoned him to sit on the bed.

"I can tell you off like that for one simple reason, Giles."

"Which is?"

She kissed his cheek, and snuggled up to him.

"Does it frighten you?"

"You mean, you and me?"

"Yes. You know…Jane…Sir Quentin…the students… that lot?"

"It's not easy, I have to admit. And you?"

"Same."

"Perhaps we should change our attitude, Fiona. You know what John Milton said. 'The mind is its own place, and in itself can make a heaven of hell, a hell of heaven.' And he was absolutely right. When we get back, let's keep that in mind. But for the present, let's turn our minds to Steve, and that mysterious little space."

Giles collected his laptop from the dressing table and placed it on her lap.

"There you are. Over to you. You're the expert. While you're at it, I'll record your every action in my notebook. If you haven't succeeded in an hour or so, I'll give it a go. But not before. Okay?"

"Agreed."

Once they'd dressed and poured the coffee, they sat at the desk together, she on the chair, he on a bedroom stool.

"As a starting point," she began, "let's assume Steve *did* get the information from Ahmad in Sorrento, and then imagine how he might have reacted to Hank's calls.

"So, here we go. When Hank calls him in Paris, he invents the story that he started an 'Achilles' file on July 28, about six weeks before the Sorrento symposium; that he worked on it again a couple of days later; and that he hadn't touched it since, because from then on he wrote all his notes in a lab book. To back up his story, he creates a bogus 'Achilles' file on the spot to send to Hank. For the present purpose, let's call it 'Achilles 1'. He knows that when Hank receives it and saves it in his Outlook Express, it will be given a new date and there'll be no way of him knowing when it was created. He gambles that Hank will be content just to know the file exists. But he's wrong.

"When Hank calls again, Steve does what we've guessed. He makes it look as if the last time he worked on the file was July 30. He alters the text slightly, and then turns back his laptop's clock to that date before saving the file. He then returns the clock to the correct date, and sends Hank the screenshot of the open folder in *List* view, which shows when the files inside it were last modified but *not* when they were created.

"Okay, having done all of that while talking…there it is. I'll call this version of the file 'Achilles 2'. So far, so good?"

Giles nodded.

"Fine. Now, when Hank calls for the third time, Steve's cornered. As there's now no way he can avoid sending the entire 'Travel Notes' folder, it needs to contain an 'Achilles' file that looks not only as if it had been last altered on July 30, but also as if it had been created on July 28. As he needs time to think up a solution, he invents a reason for being unable to send it straight away. The solution he comes up with, while you and Hank are waiting, involves adding a space at the end of the file's label, more correctly its icon's label, immediately after the word 'Achilles'.

"The big questions is: Why was that? Why did he have to put that space there to achieve his objective? That tiny little teeny-weeny space is the key to everything.

"So, now I'll have to start playing around and see where it takes me, while you keep scribbling. Please don't ask any questions or make any suggestions while I'm at it. Just let me do it by trial and error, experimenting with files, folders, icons, and labels, like I did last night. Okay?"

"Yes. Good luck!"

It was barely fifteen minutes later when Fiona believed she had found a way in which Steve could have solved his problem.

"Did you get that down, Giles, what I did just then?"

"Yes, every step."

"Could you run through it, exactly like I did it?"

"It went like this. There were three steps. One, you prepared a new file identical to the first one, just by copying it. Two, you made a small addition to its text, turned the clock back to July 28 last year, and saved the file. Three, you turned the clock forward two days, deleted the addition you'd just made, and saved the file again."

"Yes, that was it. If he had done that, he would have ended up with *exactly* what he needed, namely an 'Achilles' file that appeared to have been started on the twenty-eighth and last modified on the thirtieth. But for some reason, he *didn't* do that, did he?"

"No…because it wouldn't explain that extra space in the label."

"Absolutely! So, he did something else instead. In a state of panic, as he sweated over the keyboard with the world crashing around him, he didn't work that one out. Instead, he stumbled on a routine that involved adding that space to the file's label. And then when he'd finished, he forgot to delete that space, because as you discovered in Hank's office…"

"As long as the file was in the 'Travel Notes' folder, it wasn't visible."

"Correct! So, the big question still remains…"

"What *did* he do?"

"Precisely."

Fiona continued to play around with files and folders using different routines— opening and closing them at different times, altering the text and later deleting the changes, adding and taking away spaces in the icon's label, using *Save* or *Save As* to save files, altering the computer's clock at different points in the sequence, and an assortment of other manoeuvres. When she hit upon a promising routine, she would attach the result to an email addressed to Giles, and then go to his inbox to see what happened at the receiving end. There was no science to it. There couldn't be.

When she had still not cracked it by eleven o'clock, they agreed it was time to take a break. Over the years, when struggling to solve a problem in his research, Giles had learnt that an interruption for an hour or two could make all the difference. His theory was that during prolonged intense activity, his brain cells gradually slowed down like tired muscles due to the build-up or depletion of an unknown chemical. Then after a rest, the cells would have a burst of renewed activity, analogous to withdrawal symptoms but with the difference of being only beneficial. During such periods, he'd found that the toughest of problems had sometimes been solved in a flash. Fiona had never been convinced about his theory, for whenever she'd tried the same routine, she had only fallen asleep and then forgotten where she was up to. Her approach had always been to keep plodding on. But on this occasion she was persuaded.

After wrapping themselves up and collecting the laptop, they set off down Sixteenth Street arm in arm with no particular destination in mind. Having skipped breakfast, it was not long before Fiona drew Giles into the first coffee shop that appealed to her. It was the kind of place she had never imagined existed in Washington. With three large tinted windows in carved wooden frames, each etched with ornate patterns, it had an unexpected Victorian charm about it. A welcoming fire, whose flickering flames were reflected in a long mahogany counter bedecked with crystal glasses and antique bottles of various shapes and colours, was irresistible. Upon entering, a brass chandelier with twelve candles swayed in the draft, its chains creaking above the whistle of the wind.

Seated snugly at a table near a window, where they could enjoy the view of Meridian Hill Park, their snow-dusted coats and scarves tossed onto nearby chairs, Giles gestured his approval with a wink.

"Good choice!"

"Thanks. Normally, I love being in a new environment, away from the familiar sights and sounds. But having dashed here the way I did, and now under so much pressure, I feel the need to wind down a bit in a place that feels like home. Whatever happens from now on, I'll remember this trip for the rest of my life. The tickets were worth every penny."

Giles had reached for his inside pocket and was about to pull out his cheque book, when the morning's incident with Virgil came to mind.

"Which reminds me, I need to…er…give you some suggestions for your next session with the students. It'll be on top of you when you get back, won't it?"

Fiona shrugged her shoulders and stared at him inquisitively.

"But what's that got to do with money?"

"Well, it does cost us something, doesn't it? I often tell Sir Quentin the expense of teaching shouldn't come out of our research budget. I'm sure the Marchese wouldn't be too happy."

"Interesting how the human brain works, isn't it? At the mention of my tickets, yours jumped to the fact that our grants are subsidising the university."

"Yes, quite."

"Obviously, parts of our brains are continuously monitoring what's going on in other parts, and prompting yet others to respond. And we know nothing about it. It just happens. We have no control over our brains, do we? The truth is they're in control of us. In a sense, they are us. The rest of us is just a brain support system."

She clasped her head in her hands.

"I sometimes marvel at what's going on in there after waking up from a dream. Somehow while we're sleeping our brains create all those pictures and sounds and emotions, mixing past experiences with fantasies, and while it's happening another part is recording it like a movie camera, which we can replay later. Extraordinary!"

She prodded her temples with her fingers.

"You know, the other day I read that inside here there are two hundred billion nerve cells, each of which communicates on average with ten thousand others firing up to fifty electrical impulses a second. That adds up to a total of ten trillion impulses every second! Perhaps you're right about those poor wee cells needing a good rest when we get stuck on a problem!"

"Excuse me, guys," a bearded waiter in green jeans and leather suspenders interrupted, offering the menu as he pulled a Stetson over one eye. "Overheard what you were saying. When I'm not here, I'm a psychology postgrad. Agree with you about those dreams. And I can say a few other things about sleep that might interest you."

"Yes?"

"Yep! Did you know only half a dolphin's brain sleeps at a time, and that some birds sleep while they're flying? Isn't that cute? Give me a wave when you're ready."

"So much for the Victorian ambiance!" Fiona whispered in Giles's ear.

As she ran her eyes over the menu, her mind returned to the students' practical class. Normally, it was something she looked forward to. But not this time. The idea of returning to Oxford on her own was too painful.

It was the first time she'd felt so deeply about leaving anyone. Ten months had passed since he had returned from Majorca, ten months during which her feelings had grown stronger by the day, until the point had been reached at which she felt naked without him. And now the wonderful experience of being together so far from home, and working as partners on something so exciting and yet unrelated to their regular work, had forged a bond the like of which she had never experienced.

Conscious that Giles was waiting for the menu, she flicked through the pages aimlessly as if undecided about what to choose.

The only downside of getting emotionally attached was the risk of losing some of her freedom. In fact, it wasn't just a risk. It had already happened. Would she be able cope with that? From an early age, she had always been independent, living a life with no strings, nobody to answer to. During a rather lonely childhood in the Highlands with no brother or sister, she had grown accustomed to being self-sufficient in every way. She loved Scotland, especially the west coast, and she loved the people there. They were down to earth with no frills, genuine and generous. But she had never asked much of them.

After moving to Aberdeen, there had been several boyfriends, but none to whom she had become very attached. In Oxford her interest in socialising had waned, finding many of the males "a bit posh" for her liking. Giles was different. Although he'd started life in a relatively affluent family, it hadn't affected him in a way she considered negative.

As she glanced furtively over the top of the menu to see him patiently unfolding a napkin, she wondered what was going through his mind. She reminded herself of how tricky their relationship had been for him. It was impossible to imagine a more difficult workplace in which to get involved with a colleague. Perhaps that's why…

"Taking a while, dear," he interrupted. "Difficult choice?"

"Yes, I am, aren't I…sorry. I've decided all I'm going to have is a coffee. But the problem is I've never seen so many flavours in my life. Very straightforward if you're into a 'cinnamon coconut fantasy' or looking for a 'Brazilian bananarama', but if all you want is coffee-flavoured coffee made from coffee beans, it takes time to find it. Ah, there it is! Bottom right, in small print. Okay, I'll take a black Americano. Over to you."

"I thought you were hungry. No?"

"I was, but it's worn off now I've warmed up."

"Okay, I'll do the same. But I'll make mine a double espresso."

Fiona waved the Texan student over and placed their order.

"Do you think I'll have to return ahead of you, Giles, just to teach the students?"

Giles mulled it over, as he poured her a glass of water.

"I hope not. If it does turn out Steve's been up to no good, I'd certainly need you for the next stage, whatever it might be. But somehow we'd have to keep Sir Quentin and Jane in the dark, wouldn't we? Let's not fret about it yet. We have a job to do. The important thing is to get it done—whatever it takes."

"Whatever it takes?"

"Whatever it takes."

Fiona reached across the table to shake his hand.

"Put it there, partner. Now let's enjoy our coffee. And while we're waiting for it, I think I'm ready for another session."

Giles looked at his watch as he reached for his laptop.

"By all means. According to my theory, your brain cells should be just about ready to burst into action. It's important to catch them at the right moment."

Fiona smirked.

"We'll see!"

Two refills later, Giles was in danger of losing faith in his method. The secret of why Steve had put the space in the 'Achilles' label continued to be a mystery in spite of Fiona's imaginative efforts. Perhaps it had been a typo after all, he thought. What other explanation could there be? Fiona was just about to let him have a go, when she stumbled on the solution.

"Of course! What else?" she screamed, thumping the table. "And about time too you numbskull!"

A startled waitress, who had just enquired in Giles's ear if they would like a basket of freshly baked muffins, made a hasty retreat. By the time the waiter had arrived at Fiona's shoulder with a selection, she was gazing serenely at the screen as if entranced.

"Thank you, Boris," she purred. "I could kiss you."

There was no doubt in her mind she had discovered the answer. Giles smiled to himself with a knowing nod, before checking he'd recorded everything clearly.

"You didn't believe me, did you, Fiona? But there we are. The proof is in the pudding."

He read out the sequence of key strokes and clicks for Fiona to do a repeat performance, which to their excitement worked again.

"That's what he must have done, Giles. It has to be the explanation! Somehow you have to show this to Hank, don't you?"

"I'm afraid so."

"Poor you! What will you do, call him?"

"Not necessary. Remember, I told you he'd invited me around for lunch on Saturday?"

"Oh yes…perfect!"

"Not quite perfect, I'm afraid. When Hank's in a sticky situation, he can be extremely difficult. On top of which, his wife is his biggest ally. It's not that she's aggressive. It's worse than that. She's smart and as crafty as a fox, scheming and manipulative. She's notorious throughout the NIH. Many believe it was she who got Hank to where he is. But at least we have the advantage of surprise, and as every general knows, that can be critical. Shall we drink up and go?"

"What about the muffins?"

"We can take a couple in a bag. Wait here while I pay the cashier."

On their way out, as she was putting on her coat while Giles went ahead, Fiona caught sight of the waiter and waitress glancing at her and giggling in the doorway of the kitchen. Once on the sidewalk, she turned to look at them again through the windows before giving Giles a nudge.

"Did you see those two sniggering at me?"

"Yes, I did actually."

"What's got into them, do you think?"

"Perhaps you said something that amused them."

"Can't imagine what."

On reaching The Jefferson, they dropped into the bar to consider their plan of action for the next thirty-six hours. The priority would be to spend the rest of the day rehearsing Giles's presentation. It would have to be near perfect, and he'd have to be ready for every possible eventuality. Hank's reputation was at its most fearsome when threatened by a colleague. His response would always follow the same pattern. First, he would stonewall, try to make out he didn't understand, or claim the subject was overblown or trivial—anything to convince them they were not going to get anywhere. He wanted them to understand they were dealing with a powerful man who was not easily persuaded, and they should think carefully before wasting everyone's time. If that didn't work, he would become broody, a signal that if the nonsense didn't stop soon, he would get angry. Every trick in the book would then be used to intimidate his adversary, for that's how he viewed anyone who had unwelcome news or a different point of view. He might even start using veiled threats. If his wife happened to be around, she would keep out of it until she thought he was losing, at which point she would go on the offensive in her own special way. Yes, Giles knew he was in for a very difficult time.

Back in their room, once the presentation was as good as they could make it, they went through it again, this time with Fiona assuming the role of Hank—interrupting Giles to upset his flow, arguing the point, raising irrelevant issues, and generally being difficult and obnoxious. Although not something for which she had a natural bent, she also did her best to be sweetly manipulative. It couldn't be like the real thing, but at least it gave Giles a chance to prepare for different types of attack. Their guiding principle was that whatever happened, he mustn't lose his cool. For in reality, they were the ones in the driving seat, not Hank.

"Talking about driving seats," Fiona concluded, "tomorrow we should give ourselves a complete rest. We should rent a car, and go for a drive. Set off for the countryside, get some fresh air, try and relax. So that when you do see the fat toad and his slippery snake, you'll be ready for them."

"Great idea. Why don't you take charge of the project?"

"I already have!"

"So where do we go?"

"It's all worked out. It might be a little late in the season, we'll see, but how about the Shenandoah National Park? It's only about three hours from here. Yes?"

"Splendid."

Although Fiona had been right about the park not being at its best, it lived up to her expectations nevertheless. As they cruised along the Skyline Drive, neither she nor Giles had ever seen leaf colours of such variety, intensity, and richness—oak, birch, chestnut, poplar, sumac, maple, and more. Even the fallen leaves looked beautiful, as they scattered in the wind and formed an ever-changing mantel on the forest's undergrowth. The general lie of the terrain, the rocks and the waterfalls, reminded her of her beloved Scotland. She had read about the Shenandoah River many times, but never imagined it was quite so graceful.

"Oh Giles!" she gasped, as they opened the car doors at Hogback Overlook. "Just look at that view. Imagine what it must have been like for Native Americans and those immigrants in their log cabins living in such isolation—in the spring multitudes of flowers, in the autumn all these leaves, in the summer the sounds of insects and birds, and all year round the freshness of the air, the smells, and the animals—deer, raccoons, opossums, foxes. For someone like me, brought up in the Highlands and Islands, this is a paradise. Even this granite beneath my feet reminds me of the Cairngorms. At times like this, you can keep your Washington and your Oxford."

Not wanting to travel in the dark, they limited themselves to one more stop, this time at Elkwallow Wayside, where they finished the remains of the packed meal that Virgil had arranged. Three hours later, as they passed the Manassas National Battlefield Park, Giles instinctively slowed down out of respect for those who had died in the American Civil War.

"Tomorrow's going to be *our* big battle, isn't it," Fiona sighed as she admired the equestrian statue, "the one that will make or break this mission. And 'Stonewall Weinberg' will be waiting for you."

"And his missus! You can bet that while Hank is standing his ground, ducking the bullets, she'll be working on me with every ploy in the war psychologists' handbook. But I'll be up to it, don't worry. Thanks to you, we're well prepared. And if 'Stonewall Weinberg' doesn't see the light, I have a feeling that, like the famous general, at the end of the day he might be shot down by his own man."

Chapter Seventeen

"Hi, Giles!" Hank shouted as he heard the gate squeaking from behind the old maple tree that overhung his front drive.

"Morning, Hank. How was the movie?"

Hank appeared in muddy overalls with a pair of rusty secateurs in one hand and a soil-laden trowel in the other.

"So-so. Mary insisted on a thing set in a village in eighteenth-century Japan. Apparently, it won the Palm d'Or last year in Cannes. But as you'd say, it wasn't exactly my cup of tea, old boy."

"Sorry about that, Hank. The smell from the kitchen's wonderful. Hope she isn't working too hard."

"She loves it, believe me. I'm under orders not to disturb her. The kids are with friends, thank goodness. Come inside and have a drink."

Hank took off his muddy boots at the doorstep before leading his guest into the vast reception room that overlooked the rear garden.

"Ain't this new home of ours great? Just look at that view. We bought some Scotch in your honour. On the rocks?"

"Very kind of you, Hank, but I'd prefer to stay with my usual, if you happen to have the ingredients."

"Which are?"

"Gosling's Black Seal rum, ginger beer, a slice of lime, and a few ice cubes — the recipe for Dark 'n' Stormy."

"Never heard of that one before. You could have it with pleasure, if it wasn't that we ain't got no rum, or ginger beer, or limes. But we do have some delicious ice cubes from the local gas station."

"Toss a few into some of that Scotch then, thanks. And before I forget, here's the keys to your office."

After doing the honours, Hank made himself as comfortable as possible cross-legged on the parquet floor.

"If you're thinking that movie's made me go all Jap, Giles, you're wrong!" he laughed. "Mary's highly protective of those chairs. If I got dirt on that velvet, I'd be in the doghouse. Cheers!"

He pointed towards the plastic shopping bag Giles had placed on the sideboard.

"Bought your nephew's book on the way over?"

"No, Boris is hiding in there."

Hank furrowed his brow in apprehension.

"Sounds ominous. He's not going ruin my lunch, I hope?"

"Let's leave it for later, Hank. It can wait. I learnt on CNN this morning, by the way, that Congress has increased your budget."

"Yeah, great news. Ted did a real good job. He's a great guy. There'll be some new money for US-UK collabs too. You and Steve could do some nice stuff together. The three of us should talk. But let's get back to business. If you've got something on your mind, Giles, spit it out. There's no time like the present."

"As I said, Hank, it can wait until…"

"No, it can't! Fire away, boyo."

"If you insist."

Giles got up to retrieve his laptop.

"It's like this, Hank. After you left your office the other day, it dawned on me that when you put Steve's second 'Achilles' file into your folder, your computer should have refused…because the first one was already in there, and you can't put two Word files that have exactly the same label into the same folder."

"You sure about that?"

"Yes. You must have come across that before?"

"Must I? Perhaps so. Can't remember. So how come?"

"You were able to do so because the labels were in fact not identical. The label of the one from Berlin had a space at the end, whereas the one from Paris didn't. I spent much of yesterday…"

"How do you know that…about the spaces?"

"Because when the thought occurred to me, I looked very closely at the labels."

"What are you saying? You used my computer?

"Yes. Sorry, Hank."

"What! If you weren't such a good friend, Giles, I'd be extremely upset about that. What about the password?"

"You hadn't switched it off, and it hadn't gone to sleep by then. Nevertheless, I should apologise. The problem was I couldn't call you because of your committee meeting. And I didn't want to call you later, knowing you and Mary don't get much quality time together."

Hank smirked.

"Thanks. Yeah, I had some real quality time, screwing up my eyes at subtitles under pictures of Japs eating bowls of rice in the rain! But you still should have called, Giles. That was a serious invasion of privacy. Okay, carry on."

"Well, since then I've spent a lot of time trying to fathom why Steve did that…added the space to the label, that is."

"And your conclusion?"

"That he might have done it when falsifying the date on which he claimed the file was created. You remember how long he took to send it?"

Hank looked unimpressed, casually picking his nose as he gazed at the floor.

"I'll show you what he *could* have done."

Giles knelt on the floor beside Hank, taking his glass with him.

"Ouch! My knees are not what they used to be."

Placing the computer between them, he switched it on and attached the mouse.

"Now, watch. I'll create a new file and call it 'Achilles'… there it is. Now let's imagine Steve fabricated it to send to you after your first call. He knows your Mac will give it a new date when you save it, but he thinks 'So what? Hank trusts me. Just the sight of the document will keep the old fool happy.'"

"Steady on, Giles!"

"No offence meant. When he gets your second call, he goes through the routine I showed in the office, so as to make it look as if he'd been working on it on the thirtieth of July last year. He pops the file into his 'Travel Notes' folder, like so…opens the folder in the *List* view…configures it so that it shows only the *Date Modified* and not the *Date Created*…takes a screenshot…and sends it to you. That's that, he thinks. But it isn't. When he's in Berlin, he gets your next call. To give himself time, he says he's busy but will send it soon. While we're waiting, he does this. Watch.

"He reopens the 'Achilles' file…turns the clock back to the twenty-eighth of July…and clicks *Save As*. A window opens…of the options he clicks *Save*. The next window asks if he wants to replace the existing 'Achilles' file with this one, his Mac having recognised that the two Word files have identical labels. He's stressed and in a hurry. As he's not sure what he's doing or where it's leading, he doesn't want to lose the first file in case he needs to go back to it. So, he plays safe. He clicks *Cancel*, and when prompted with *Save Current Document as…*, he adds a space after the word 'Achilles' in the dialogue box…like so…then clicks *Save*. That small addition is enough for the computer to treat the two files as having different labels, and accept them in the same folder. So now his 'Travel Notes' folder contains both his original 'Achilles' file and the new one with the false *Date Created*. Next, he drags the original file into *Trash*…like so…and changes the *Date Modified* of the new one to the thirtieth of July by performing the routine I showed you in the office……like this. Now he's got what he needs, an 'Achilles' file that's identical to the first one he sent, except that it now has both a false *Date Modified* and a false *Date Created*. The only problem…for him…is that he forgets to delete that extra space in the label before attaching the file to an email and sending it you. Why? Probably because as long as the file was in the folder, the space wasn't visible…as you can see. However, the space becomes very visible when the file is moved to the desktop… like so."

"Okay, okay! I get the point. My head feels like it's just gotten out of a spin drier. Can you go through that again, this time more slowly?"

"I thought you might say that. Fair enough, I'll…"

"On second thoughts, don't bother! I believe you. I mean I believe that that's what you think Steve could have done. Is that the only way he could have done it?"

"No. There was at least one other way, a much simpler way, but presumably it didn't occur to him."

Hank started to pick his nose again.

"Well, that's your theory, Giles. But it's only a theory, or to be correct, since we're both scientists, your hypothesis. I've another one. That space is a typo, pure and simple. Cybil does 'em all day long. It got there by accident…period."

"Very unlikely, Hank. Adding a space there requires three separate actions. Watch. One, I need to click on the label to highlight it. Two, I need to place the cursor in just the right place after 'Achilles'. Three, I type the space. All that couldn't happen by accident; impossible. Try for yourself."

He pushed the laptop towards Hank, who repeated the procedure twice.

"Okay, it takes a bit of care, I suppose. But you haven't proven that what you showed me is actually what he did, have you? In my book, there are still at least two possible explanations, yours and mine. What do you expect me to do now, call the FBI and tell them there's a fifty-fifty chance that the top man at the NCI is a crook? Get real, Giles! They need much better odds than that."

Hank finished his Scotch and struggled to his feet crunching a mouthful of ice cubes.

"I need time to mull this over, Giles. It's a lot to take in."

"Of course, Hank, and while you're at it, I'll use your washroom, if I may."

"Off the entrance hall."

When Giles came back, he found Mary returning to the kitchen with a bundle of clothes under her arm, and Hank in one of the easy chairs wearing nothing but his boxer shorts and socks. Mary reappeared after a few seconds.

"Sorry, I haven't said hello yet, Giles, but I couldn't leave the kitchen. It's wonderful to see you again after all these years."

She squeezed his hands and kissed him lightly on the cheek.

"It's nice to see you too, Mary. I hope you're not working too hard."

"I don't mind working hard for good friends…of course not. And it's a special pleasure in your case, Giles. I'll be out again soon."

As she left the room with a sweet smile, Giles turned towards Hank.

"Too hot in here, Hank?"

"No. My butt was killing me on the floor, despite its ample padding, but Mary insisted I strip off before sitting in her sacred chairs."

"I see. So, have you had any thoughts?"

"Yep! If I remember correctly from what you showed me during the week, for Steve to have given his original 'Achilles' file July 30 last year as the last time he changed it, the procedure would have involved changing the file's text in some way. That was an essential ingredient, right?"

"Right."

"Well, later on, when he was in Berlin, if he'd used the same file to do what you've just suggested, that change will have been copied, along with everything else, when he did the *Save As…* routine, yes?"

"Yes."

"And then later on he made a second change to the text, when falsifying the *Date Created*, right?"

"Yes. I'm impressed. So, you *did* follow it, after all?"

"That bit, just about. All of which would mean that the text of what he sent to me from Berlin would have differed from the one he sent from Paris in two ways, right?"

"Right."

"Good! Because what you don't know, Giles, is that while you were returning to the office from Sanderson's, I ran my eyes over both docs. And they're *exactly* the same. There's absolutely no difference between 'em. So clearly, he couldn't have done what you said. Sorry to disappoint, boyo, but as I always say, hypotheses are made to be broken!"

As Hank licked his teeth in self-satisfaction, Giles shook his head.

"Sorry, Hank, but they're not. I don't mean hypotheses are not made to be broken, but that those two documents are not the same. What you mean is they *look* the same...which under some circumstances they do...but in fact they're very different. Watch this."

After checking the kitchen door was closed, Giles put Boris onto Hank's lap, and sat on the arm of the chair with the mouse on his knee. Plugging in his memory stick, he opened the two files he had copied from Hank's office computer.

"Okay, Hank, look at the last line of text in each of these documents. What do you see?"

"They both end with '...epithelial cells, liver cells, and fibroblasts.'"

"That's right, the three types of cell he was supposedly going to use for his lab experiments with *Deidamia*. Now see what happens when I click the *Show/Hide* button in the menu bar."

With the Paris version of the file active, Giles clicked the button. Two symbols appeared below the line of text, in the left margin, one above the other.

"Now what do you see, Hank?"

Hank moved closer to the screen, screwing up his eyes.

"Two squiggles have appeared."

"That's right, paragraph breaks to be precise. And what they show is that at some stage Steve hit the return key twice after that line. A rather unusual thing to do, I'd say."

Hank silently shrugged his shoulders and picked his teeth.

"Keep watching."

Giles made the Berlin version active, and then clicked on the *Show/Hide* button again.

"Now what do you see?"

"This time there are four of those break things, one above the other."

"Correct. So, for some reason, before sending the file to you from Berlin, Steve decided to hit the return key again…and again. He couldn't see those paragraph breaks…but we can."

Giles clicked the *Show/Hide* button repeatedly.

"Now we see them, now we don't; now we see them, now …"

"Okay, okay, okay, I'm not blind!" Hank blurted. "It makes a nice story, Giles, I'll give you that. But none of that stuff proves anything. Think about it. All you have is an extra space in a label, and now…lo and behold…a few paragraph squiggles too. Wow, big deal! So what? Maybe he was fiddling with his fingers while thinking. I do it all the time. You'll need more than that, Giles, to cancel Steve's ticket to Stockholm."

"It's not enough to hang him, Hank, I agree. Perhaps there's an innocent explanation, but the point is…"

"That we have to keep an open mind. That's the real point, Giles. Don't forget we're scientists. Being objective is a big part of our job. As you said, perhaps there's a simple explanation. And as time's short, very short, I don't see we have any option but to give him the benefit of the doubt. Ain't that right?"

"I think what's right, Hank, is that we have to continue to work on it. Time's short, yes, but it's not zero. I don't have any big ideas at this moment, but something might occur to me… or to you. In the meantime, why don't you call him again to tell him you're happy with what he sent? As he hasn't heard from you since, he might be wondering what's going on. I wouldn't like him to read anything into your silence."

"What d'you mean?"

"I wouldn't like him to misunderstand and do anything rash."

"Like what?"

"Something careless."

"Careless?"

"Yes."

"Boy, you Brits can take a hell of a time spitting it out! Like what?"

"Like accidentally erasing his hard disk, for example, or accidentally knocking his laptop out of the hotel window, or accidentally getting it stolen."

"Here, take this!" Hank snapped as he grasped the laptop. It's getting me overheated, like its owner. You know, you'd better be careful, Giles. If this goes too far, and you've got it wrong, all hell will break loose between here and the White House. I'll call Steve now and then get dressed for lunch. Mary should be just about ready."

"Wonderful! I could eat a horse."

"Ha! Not in the good old USA, Giles," Mary quipped as she reappeared with some fresh clothes for Hank. "Slaughtering horses for consumption is illegal here. I discovered that when I wanted to cook picula ad caval for an Italian professor who was visiting the NIH from the university in Piacenza. Charming man, a lot like you actually, Giles. It's a traditional dish there, you see. Had to use beef instead."

As always, Mary had prepared an ambitious meal. The table was laid with her best china and silver, crystal glassware, antique hand-carved ivory chopsticks from Hong Kong, genuine Chinese silk napkins, and three mini-menus in wooden stands handwritten in Chinese, one of which she took pleasure in translating.

"We're going to start with Chicken ginseng soup," she announced with a tense smile, "after which there'll be catfish in garlic sauce, stir-fried abalone with Chinese cabbage, crab wonton in blackberry Szechuan sauce, and gingko nuts with black mushrooms—all served with Hank's favourite fried rice, Yong Chow. As the desserts are a secret, they're going to stay in Chinese, assuming you don't speak that along with all your other languages, Giles. To drink there's Tsing Tao beer. So… why don't you both sit down, and let's enjoy!"

As she'd been reading, Giles had thrown his mind back to his sabbatical year in the NCI. He had met Mary on only two occasions, the ill-fated dinner party when he'd ruined her dress, and during a barbecue at Steve's home on Thanksgiving Day. He hadn't got to know her very well during either event, but the impression gained had been of an ambitious wife devoted to husband's career. Not satisfied with his being Director of the NIH, in those days rumour had it she was pushing him to run for a seat in the Senate. In retrospect, that now seemed unlikely, but the manner in which she'd flitted around Steve's rose garden, confidently interrupting one conversation after another with Hank in tow, had left Giles in no doubt about where her priorities lay.

Her mood was now very different—tense, less self-assured, a little withdrawn. Was she steeling herself for something to come, he wondered, or merely struggling to cope with the demands of preparing such a feast?

"Delicious soup, Mary!" he remarked to test the water. "Must be exhausting putting a meal like this together. Don't know how manage."

"Thank you, Giles," she answered quietly, her mind clearly elsewhere, before fixing her gaze on her husband. "Actually, I enjoy every minute of it. I find cooking quite therapeutic. I'd love to tell you something about Chinese cuisine. But I'm sure we…I mean, you… have more pressing things to talk about… don't you, Hank?"

Guessing from her tone that she'd been earlier listening to the two of them through the kitchen door, Giles readied himself for the opening salvo of what he feared would be a long and bloody battle. Sure enough, as soon as she'd collected the empty bowls, she launched into a sermon about Steve's many good qualities—how reliable he was, how honest and trustworthy, garnished with flattering anecdotes about his professional and private life. Continuing well into the next course, the monologue tested even Giles's patience. He thought it wise to say nothing, at least for a while, limiting himself to the occasional nod, his eyes fixed on his plate while Hank remained silent throughout.

As he suffered the barrage, Giles began to wonder if his hosts might suspect there was more to his interest in Steve's behaviour than the pursuit of truth and justice. After all, they had seen little of him during his sabbatical. For all Hank knew, he and Steve might have had a tiff that had left a deep and festering wound.

As soon as Mary returned to the kitchen to collect the dessert, he took his opportunity to allay any such misunderstanding.

"Excuse me, Hank."

Gazing vacantly at the tablecloth, flicking his fingernails, Hank gave little more than a grunt in reply.

"I thought it might be worth reassuring you that although Steve and I didn't always see eye to eye…"

"CIA!" Mary shrieked as the kitchen door flew open. "We've never had anything to do with those people, have we, honey?"

Giles looked at her bewildered as she placed a large bowl of Peking Dust in the centre of the table.

"I didn't say anything about the CIA, Mary. Why should I?"

"Er…oh, no reason at all, Giles. But I thought you did, just then…didn't you?" "

"You misheard me. I was telling Hank that, although Steve and I didn't see eye to eye…"

"Oh…ha, ha! See eye to eye! It's that delightful English accent of yours. Sorry, do go on."

Giles's mind flashed back to Fiona's conspiracy theories involving the CIA, payoffs to Ahmad for the secret of the Bedouins' switch, and even Ahmad's death. Was any of it possible?

"I said go on, Giles. Are you in a dream?"

"Sorry, Mary. The thing is I'd simply been reassuring Hank that Steve and I were on good terms after my sabbatical, and have been that way ever since."

"That's what I thought," Hank grunted. "Why are you telling me?"

"It's just that I wouldn't want you to imagine I'm doing all this for the wrong reasons."

"A kind of feud or vendetta, you mean?"

"That's it. And while on the subject of friendships, I'll also say I don't want this unpleasant business to cause any problems between you and me, Hank. I understand you're in a difficult position, and I'm really sorry about that. But all I'm after is the truth."

"The truth, the whole truth, and nothing but the truth, eh?"

"Exactly. Basically, I share Mary's opinion of Steve. But don't forget he was under huge pressure after meeting Ted Crabb in the Oval Office. And he got some really awful press. His reputation, his career, everything that matters most to him was on the line. Even Crabb's extra funding was a mixed blessing. No excuses for failure after that! And it must have made him many enemies. You've said so yourself. He wouldn't be the first upright man to break down under such circumstances. He's only human, after all."

Hank said nothing until he'd cleaned his bowl and pushed it towards Mary.

"So, what's next then?"

"Isn't that enough, honey?" she said, laughing. "I thought you were trying to lose that paunch."

"Mary," he exploded, "I'm talking to Giles! There are more important things right now than your dessert, or my…paunch!"

Jumping up, Hank strode to the fireplace, hastily returning on seeing Mary's tearful reflection in the mirror.

"I'm sorry, Mary. All this business and Chinese beer don't mix right now."

He gave her a hug and offered his handkerchief before returning to the table.

"Y'know, Giles, Mary and I were saying only last night how Steve's been a real valuable colleague to you over the years. Those papers you did together must have done your career a power of good. Do you think you would have gotten where you…"

"Yes, okay, Hank, I know what you're going to say. I agree I'm indebted to Steve in many ways. But I can't let that cloud my judgment, can I?"

Flushed and visibly trembling, Mary about-turned and disappeared into the kitchen. Upon re-emerging with a tray of Longjing tea and two silver bowls of cakes, she herded the men into the conservatory.

Hank put on some Debussy and adjusted the volume carefully, while Mary poured the tea and arranged the chairs.

"I hope there's not too much sun for you there, Giles?" she enquired caringly. "I know it's quite weak this time of the year, but if it gets in your eyes, let me know, and I'll draw the blinds. And that Norfolk Island pine is not too close, I hope?"

Reassured that everything was perfect, she leaned forward and put her hand lightly on his.

"Giles, listen to a friend. I'm very, very fond of you. I include you among a small group of very special people. And quite frankly, I'm worried about you. You don't look at all well. Henry said the same this morning. You're looking pale, drawn, worn out—not the jolly Giles Butterfield we used to know. That's why we invited you here today for some good food, fresh air, and relaxation, away from that stuffy hotel room all on your own, buried in your thoughts. There's no point worrying yourself sick about what Steve might or might not have done. Hank thinks he was in line for a Nobel anyway for his work on leukemia years ago. But they gave it to those two Japanese professors, one of whom was later found to be a crook, remember? So, in a sense it's only fair Steve should get it this year. Perhaps that's God's way of restoring justice."

"Mary's made a good point there, Giles," Hank followed up, "about your health, I mean. Don't forget your father had a heart attack about your age."

"Have one of these cakes," Mary resumed. "I was up ever so early making them. They're hard on the outside, but soft and sweet on the inside—just like you!"

She laughed heartily as she patted him on the arm.

"The ones in the blue bowl are 'tau sah pneah' — stuffed with mung bean paste and fried onions. The others are 'beh the saw' and contain molasses and sesame seeds. Enjoy!"

Giles helped himself while she arranged a napkin on his knee.

"You know, Giles," she continued, brushing a few crumbs off his sleeve, "I think it will help you to cope, if you can keep this Steve business in perspective. When I was working in the Dibner Library, you know the one on science history here, I learnt that quite a few Nobels have been shrouded in intrigue, suspicion, and controversy. It's nothing new at all. In medicine in particular, there's been lots of disagreement about who deserved the credit for this or that. Some even think Florey and Fleming didn't deserve it for penicillin."

Hank tossed a pastry into the air and caught it like a baseball.

"And I agree. You know, Giles, when the Chinks invented these muffins thousands of years ago, they were already rubbing mouldy beans into their cuts to treat infections."

"That's very true, Hank," Mary responded, discreetly raising her hand to subdue him, "but what's more to the point, Giles, is that four years before Fleming published his article on how the Penicillium mould could kill Staphylococci growing in a Petri dish, two bacteriologists in Belgium had already published a paper showing *exactly* the same thing, except in their case it wasn't due to a sloppy accident, it was the result of real scientific experiments.

"And it gets worse. Years before that, a young Frenchman called Ernest Duchesne had already shown that an extract of the same sort of mould could prevent guinea pigs from dying after injections of bacteria. He was in the army, and his Arab stable boys had put him onto it, after noticing that the horses didn't get festering sores if the saddles were allowed go mouldy. He submitted a dissertation on his work to the Pasteur Institute, but they completely ignored it. Then fifty years later, Florey does the very same thing with a bunch of mice, and gets the Nobel Prize. What a joke!"

"Yes, I've heard those stories, Mary, but…"

"You could also take the one that was awarded for diabetes research," Hank added enthusiastically, as Mary took a rest. "Why was Charlie Best ignored and Macleod included, when Best did all the early work with Banting, and Macleod wasn't even a co-author on those papers?"

"In fact, Giles," Mary added, "some think none of those Canadians should have gotten it, as several men had already shown that extracts of the pancreas could cure animals of diabetes. A German by the name of Georg Zülzer had even treated a comatose patient with the stuff. And he would probably have saved his life if the supplies hadn't run out.

"And while Hank refills the pot—will you, please, honey? — I'll tell you something you may not know about the 1962 Prize for the structure of DNA. Watson and Crick got the credit, of course, along with that Englishman whose name I always forget, but apparently it was an Austrian called Chargaff who put them onto the fact that thymine would attach to adenine and guanine to cytosine, the entire basis of the genetic code. But did they make that clear in their famous Nature paper?

"So, you see, Giles dear, there have probably been many, many times when all those kronors went into the wrong pockets."

Hank chuckled as he emerged from the kitchen, nursing the warm teapot between his hands.

"I think you mean euros, honey. Kronors are what the Poles use."

"I knew about those stories too, Mary," Giles returned, resisting the temptation to correct Hank, "and I could tell you some others. But there's a big difference. All those winners deserved some kind of reward. Perhaps they got more credit than was due, but in Steve's case we might be talking about fraud and intellectual property theft. Sorry to be so blunt. And that's completely different, isn't it?"

"No, Giles, it really isn't! That's the point. Do you really think that Fleming was unaware of the Belgian work, or that two highly intelligent men simply forgot about what Chargaff had said?"

"Oh, come on, Mary, there's no comparison! When scientists write a paper they can't mention every single conversation they've had or every article they've read on the subject. Be realistic. And as for that Belgian paper, It's very likely Fleming simply didn't know about it. If I remember correctly, it was in French, wasn't it?"

"Yes. Even so, that doesn't let the Nobel people off the hook, does it? They have a responsibility to be familiar with the literature in all languages. What's so special about the ones in English?"

"You're expecting too much, Mary."

Mary held her head in despair.

"I don't think I am, Giles. All I'm saying is the history of science is littered with people whose contributions have been overlooked or ignored, and with others who've taken advantage of other people's ideas, and so on. It's inevitable, and just something we have to live with."

"Don't be too hard on him, Mary," Hank said, smirking. "Don't forget Crick,

Florey, and the rest were Oxbridge types. Giles wouldn't be human if that didn't cloud his judgment."

Before Giles could protest at the accusation, Mary had paced to the bookcase to pick up a dog-eared paperback.

"Listen, Giles. Let's see if you can tell me who said this."

She found a page and cleared her throat.

"'Nature revolves'…I mean…'*resolves*…everything into its component atoms. Material objects are of two kinds, atoms and compounds of atoms.'

"Can you guess who said that?"

Giles rubbed his chin thoughtfully, trying not to look irritated.

"Must have been Dalton I suppose, talking about his atomic theory."

"*His* atomic theory?"

"That's right."

"*Dalton's* atomic theory?"

"Yes."

"And when would that have been?"

"Early nineteenth century."

Mary smiled smugly as she found another page.

"How about this one then? 'Through an undisturbed vacuum all bodies must travel at equal speed though impelled by unequal weights.' No problems with that one, I imagine?"

Mary winked at Hank as she waited for Giles to answer.

"Every English schoolboy knows that one, Mary. Galileo, describing the gravity experiments he did in Pisa. But what's the…?"

"Hold on, Giles! Last one, I promise. Let me find it. Ah, here it is on page one fifty-six…with a bit of paraphrasing, if you don't mind, as it's rather long. 'No part of our bodies was created so we could use it. The thing having been born created its use. The ears developed before a sound was heard. The limbs existed before they had a use. They cannot have grown for the purpose…'"

"Has to be Darwin, Mary, explaining evolution by natural selection. Now, if you could tell me what this is…"

Mary raised her hand to silence him as she slowly approached, holding the book to her chest.

"Sorry, Giles, dunce's corner for you. Zero out of three. The same man said them all, and what's more, did so more than one thousand years before Galileo, Dalton, and Darwin were born."

Mary exposed the front cover of Latham's translation of "De Rerum Natura" to reveal the beguiling face of a pensive Pompeian lady, wax tablets and stylus in hand.

"So that's what you're getting at! Mary, Lucretius was a very clever man. No doubt about that. But what he was describing was philosophy, not experimental observations. It was pure speculation."

"Ha!" she hooted, dropping the book onto the dining table. "Pure speculation that just happened to be right every time. Giles, isn't it just possible that some of those ancient people were smarter than we give them credit for; that they could work some things out from basic principles without doing fancy experiments?

"The point is this, Giles. Think about it. Try to get things in perspective. Given the long and varied history of science, does it really make sense to put so much time and energy into Steve? *Deidamia* is already history even now. Science and medicine have moved on. We shouldn't keep looking back. It's what lies ahead that matters. Who gets the gongs isn't very important."

"Mary's talking sense, Giles," Hank added in support. "I couldn't have said it better myself."

Giles could see there was no chance of getting Hank to accept his point of view. He and Mary had tried every trick in the book to try to persuade him to back off. The more he allowed them to continue, the more difficult the situation would become. If he started to push too hard in return, undoubtedly Hank would become aggressive. And who knows where that would lead? It was time to call it a day.

After expressing alarm upon checking the time, he apologised for needing to rush back to Sanderson's to buy his nephew's book before it closed. After hastily gathering his laptop, he thanked Mary for all her work, kissed her on the cheek, and followed Hank to his Mercedes.

They cruised to Bethesda in silence, until Hank stopped the car outside the bookstore.

"Bon voyage, Giles," he said with a tight-lipped smile. "As you said, we won't let this come between us, eh? We just look at life differently, that's all. You've got your point of view. I've got mine. Perhaps it's something to do with you being a Brit and me a Yank. You do whatever you think is right. But think about it carefully. Don't rush into anything. Think about the possible consequences…all of them."

Giles offered his hand through the open window.

"What sort of conseque…?"

"Whoops! There's a truck behind. Must go! Ciao."

Chapter Eighteen

Not fully satisfied with his shortlist of books for his nephew, Giles paused at the foot of Sanderson's staircase in the hope of getting some inspiration from the directory. He scanned down the alphabetical list.

"A computer book?" he thought. "No, Guy must get more than enough of them from Conrad. Geography…history… something about the United States perhaps? Mythology? Now, there's an interesting idea. Greek mythology would make a nice change."

He followed a group of students to the third floor and found the section he was looking for. To his delight, an entire shelf was devoted to books of that genre for young people. In an instant, his eyes fell upon a picture of a large wooden horse with soldiers emerging from its belly against a backdrop of the moonlit walls of an ancient city.

"The Tale of Troy by Roger Lancelyn Green," he murmured. "Brilliant! With all this *Achilles* business, what could be more appropriate?"

After flicking through a few pages, he decided to take a closer look over a cup of coffee in the basement. After skipping half way down the spiral staircase, he stopped in his tracks.

"Wait a minute!" he thought. "The Trojan horse—that rings a bell. Didn't Conrad tell me about computer viruses of that name, which crooks use to snoop inside computers? Now there's an idea!"

Excited by the possibilities, he dropped onto the steps unmindful of the bottleneck he was causing as others struggled to pass.

"Steve's hard disk should contain a record of everything he's done, shouldn't it? If he has been up to something, all the evidence should be sitting there. And if Conrad could send him one of those spy viruses, who knows what…?"

"Are you okay down there?" a lady enquired, stooping to get a better look at his face, as she nudged his arm with her handbag. "Shall I call an ambulance?"

"No thanks," he said with a chuckle, rubbing his hands together, "never felt better in my life. But thank you all the same."

He jumped up and continued on his way to the coffee shop. The idea was exhilarating. But it was also terrifying. As he felt himself marching inexorably towards something about which he had grave misgivings, but also feared might be too tempting to resist, his pulse began to race. He preferred not to dwell on the last time he'd felt that way, and all the problems it had caused. But that was irrelevant, wasn't it? Sex is sex. This was different.

After half-filling a large paper cup with black coffee, he made his way to a table well away from the crowd. Taking off his glasses, he slipped them into his top pocket, then removed his bow tie and dropped it to one side.

Of course, he might be getting excited about nothing, he cautioned himself. Perhaps he'd misunderstood his brother on that sultry summer evening on Table Mountain. After all, they were on their second bottle of chardonnay by then, weren't they? Also, even if it were possible, would Conrad know how to create one of those spy viruses? And would he agree to it?

He took out a pencil and jotted down a list of questions on the back of a menu in his usual methodical way, his fingers trembling with the rush of adrenaline.

1) Would it be legal?
2) Would it be morally right?
3) What would we be looking for?
4) Could Conrad do it?
5) Would he do it?
6) Would there be enough time?

He put a large cross against the first one. No doubt the police were allowed to do this sort of thing, but a private individual? Not much chance!

"So, should I go to the police and ask them to do it instead?" he thought. "No. What did Hank say? 'All you have is an extra space and a few paragraph breaks,' something like that. The boys in blue would say the same.

"But would it be morally right? That's what really matters, isn't it? After all, there are times when the law should take second place to morality. Contrary to what Mary said, the issue of whether a Nobel is about to be given to a crook is important, very important. Committing a small crime to uncover such a big one would be justified. It would be on a par with parking your car on the pavement to help someone who had just been mugged, or forging your wife's signature to buy urgent medicine for a sick child with her credit card. Both would be illegal technically, but they'd be the right things to do. Looking into Steve's laptop wouldn't be any different…would it? As Gloria Steinem once put it, 'The law and justice are not always the same.' Even Magdalen's Alfred Denning thought the law and morality had grown too far apart. So, if some nitwit of a lawyer wants to make an issue of it, and tries to put me behind bars, let him!"

He put an emphatic tick next to number two on his list, breaking the lead of his pencil in the process.

"Damn! Okay, number three. What would we be looking for? Goodness knows, but leaving Fiona for a few hours with Boris might be all it takes to sort that one out.

"Number four. Could he do it? Conrad's brilliant at his job, but is that enough? An IT security expert and a hacker might be two different species for all I know. Not many car mechanics could design and build a gearbox.

"Would he agree? Who knows? There'd be a lot at stake: his reputation, his job, his company…even his conscience.

"Last one…enough time? Again, who knows? The ceremony's less than four weeks away now. If Conrad's got a business trip lined up, that might put an end to it."

Recognising he'd gone as far as he could, he dropped his coffee cup with its untouched contents into the rubbish bin by his table. As he replaced his glasses, the face of a giggling little girl of about seven, now clearly visible on the far side of the room, caught his attention. On his way out, he stopped to squat beside her, and gave her mother a wink.

"Hi there, sweetie!" he said softly, tweaking her chin. "I know why you're laughing. Like a silly old fool, I've been mumbling to myself, haven't I? Well, you see, it's like this. When I take off my glasses, I can't see anything properly unless it's very close. It's all fuzzy, a bit like looking through fog. And because I can't see anybody's face very clearly, I sometimes forget they can see me! Funny, isn't it?"

She continued to giggle, gripping her mother's hand tightly, as he offered her his glasses.

"Hopefully you'll never have to wear anything like these, but if you do, I'm sure you'll look just as pretty as you are now. Bye!"

As he patted her on the head and got up to go, her mother broke her silence.

"It ain't nothing to do with that, sir," she said, laughing. "It was that cute spotted necktie you was wearing. When you took it off, you dropped it in your coffee cup."

Giles felt his collar.

"My God, you're right!"

Chapter Nineteen

When Giles arrived at The Jefferson, he found Fiona in her favourite seat in the corner of the bar looking distressed.

"Thank goodness you're back," she sighed, jumping up to greet him. "I've been worried about you."

"Sorry, dear, couldn't call. After Hank dropped me off, I found the battery in my phone was flat. Forgot to plug it in last night after our trip."

"Never mind, the important thing's you're here. Sit down and tell me all about it. Drink?"

"Yes thanks, my usual."

Fiona signalled to the waitress, who promptly tossed a lime in the air and gave a thumbs up.

"All that rehearsing certainly paid off. The demonstration went without a hitch. But of course, Hank refused to take it seriously, or at least to accept we should carry on. I think Mary must have been listening from the kitchen. Once we were into the meal, she really worked hard on me, while Hank remained quiet in the background. She tried every trick in the book, but I didn't budge. Eventually, I decided to bail out before Hank got too upset."

"So how did you leave things?"

"Basically, we agreed to disagree. He drove me to a local bookstore, where I bought a book for my nephew in Cape Town. And that was that."

"So, no progress?"

"Except Hank knows that, whatever he might think about it, we haven't finished, which is important. And we're in the clear, because we've told the NIH all we know."

"But what do we do next? Is that it...end of story?"

Giles raised his finger and winked with a cheeky smile.

"Watch this space. The most important thing happened afterwards. Look here."

He unwrapped the book and passed it to her.

"This is for your nephew?"

"Yes."

"Looks interesting, Giles, but what's so special about it?"

"See the picture? It reminded me of those viruses called Trojan horses, which can spy inside computers."

"And…?"

"I started wondering if my brother in Cape Town, who as you know is an IT security geek, might be able to send one to Steve's laptop. If Steve did what we think he did, there might be a smoking gun lurking inside."

Fiona's eyes lit up as she clasped her head in delight.

"What a fantastic idea!" she gasped, looking around to see if anyone was in earshot. "Would there still be something in there, do you think? What if he's deleted those files?"

"I don't know much about computers, but there might be, I suppose."

"Aren't you naughty? But I like it! It's brilliant."

She leant forward to squeeze his hands and look into his eyes.

"I'm beginning to enjoy this in more ways than one," she said, grinning. "All of a sudden, medical science seems boring. No wonder Arthur Conan Doyle invented Sherlock Holmes. We need to do some more work with Boris, don't we— to see what might be tucked away?"

Giles nodded.

"When can you start?"

"After dinner?"

Giles raised his glass.

"Cheers!"

It was almost three-thirty on Sunday morning before Fiona was ready to switch off the laptop. She had been at it solidly for almost five hours. It had been demanding, tedious, and at times frustrating. But it had been worth it, every minute of it. As she threw her arms in the air in quiet celebration, her only emotion now was one of exhilaration. She stood up to stretch her legs and looked around the room. She wanted to remember it just as it was. Time would tell, she thought, but this might be history in the making.

She looked at Giles. This was not the time to awaken him. There was too much to show, too much to explain. It could wait. It was time to sleep.

After a quick shower, she joined him under the sheets. As she snuggled into the blankets, she relived the steps that had led to her success. Working on the assumption they'd been correct about the sequences Steve had followed in Paris and Berlin, she'd gone through them repeatedly, each time searching the hard disk for footprints it may have left behind. On several occasions, she had lost track of the web of links she had followed. But through dogged persistence, she had got there in the end, and then rounded it off by recording what she had found, exactly where it would be on Steve's hard disk, and how to get there. As she closed her eyes, she had every reason to be very pleased with herself.

When Giles woke up at five past seven, he was disappointed to find Fiona asleep beside him. Certain she would have disturbed him if the news had been good, his mood went into freefall. Dropping onto his pillow, he gazed at the sun's sliver of light from the space between the curtains, reflected by the chandelier onto the wall, likening it to a laser beam that had severed his hopes from painful reality.

It was only after several minutes that he noticed a yellow Post-It Note stuck to his bedside table. Reaching across, he peeled it off and brought it to his eyes, leaving his glasses where they were. There were just four words: "Next stop Cape Town." It could only mean one thing!

Putting on his glasses, he looked at the clock on the desk and then at Fiona's forehead and red locks, all that was visible between the sheets and her pillow. He was longing to learn the details, but she had let him sleep, hadn't she? And there was no rush anyhow, was there? After all, with Cape Town being six hours ahead of DC, he had until the middle of the afternoon to call Conrad. Better get up quietly and sneak downstairs for breakfast, and wait for her there.

Giles was struggling to spread chunky marmalade onto a floppy slice of toast, when Fiona appeared at the restaurant's doorway earlier than expected. Jumping to his feet, he gave her a hug and a kiss.

"Fiona! I didn't expect you for a couple of hours. I saw your note, thanks. Sounds like success, yes?"

Fiona nodded with a broad grin and sleepy eyes.

"Yes, a really big one too. Although I must admit, at one stage I thought I might be on a wild goose chase."

"Ha! I like it—on a wild goose chase after a smoking gun. Makes a change from the other way around!"

"Well, Steve's goose will certainly be cooked, if we can show his laptop's home to what's inside Boris right now. Wait a tick, while I'll go to the buffet."

"A warning about the toast. They insist on buttering it in the kitchen while it's still warm, an unfortunate American habit. So instead of nice crisp slices with crunchy crusts, you end up with something resembling a wet Echo."

"A wet what?"

"Sorry, scouse expression. That's the local newspaper in Liverpool. Like this."

Giles took his toast by a corner, and waved it limply in the air.

"Ugh! I'll take some rolls instead."

Fiona returned with a selection of rolls and croissants, and several small pots of different types of jam.

"I brought some for you too."

"Thanks."

"There's no doubt about it, Giles. If Steve did what we think he did, he'll have left a clear trail of evidence. I'll show you after this. The big question is whether we'll get the opportunity to dig for it?"

Fiona looked at him apprehensively.

"Everything depends on Conrad, Fiona. It'll be entirely up to him. He's not going to jump at it, that's for sure. His company's employed to stop this sort of caper, not perpetrate it. It'll be tricky."

"What are the chances, do you think?"

"Fifty-fifty."

"Is that all?"

Giles nodded glumly.

"Okay, so be it. So what's the next step?"

"I've been thinking about that. Later today, I'll call him to say I'm on my way to visit him for a short break. There'll be nothing new about that. His door's always open. He'll be delighted. He's a great host. Then when I'm there, I'll take my opportunity. I'll give it to him straight, argue the case. But not too forcibly. He doesn't like that. It annoys him. With Conrad you have to work slowly, give him plenty of time. Even then he might not agree. He'll have to think of his company's reputation, his future, all sorts of things. If it turned out to be a great success, he'd be a local hero. But if it all went wrong, he could lose his job. Perhaps worse."

Fiona did little more than stare at the table, before blowing her nose on her napkin and throwing herself against him.

Giles put his arm around her.

"I know exactly what you're thinking, dear. But have no fear. You're coming with me. Your contribution to all this has been too important. Anything else would be unthinkable. Besides that, Conrad adores you. It was obvious when the two of you met a couple of years ago. He often asks about you. So, having you around will be useful in more ways than one."

"That's made me so happy, Giles," she whispered, raising her head from his shoulder to kiss him lightly on the check. "But what will you say about you and me?"

"What would you like me to say?"

"Whatever you like."

Giles gave her a hug and tweaked her nose playfully.

"In that case, that's exactly what I'll do!"

She snuggled into him, drying her eyes on the napkin.

"And what about Magdalen? Will you call Sir Quentin and tell him what's going on?"

"I wish we could. The problem is what we've got in mind is probably illegal, isn't it? In which case, even if the old shrew were on our side, as the College's President there's no way he could condone our plan. If I came clean, he'd inevitably demand we return to Oxford immediately. He'd have no choice but to say it's a job for the NIH. And we all know where that would lead. No, unfortunately we can't tell him or anyone else the truth, apart from Conrad when we get there. It has to be our secret, and ours alone.

"You said you told Jane you had the flu, right?"

"Yes…and you?"

"That I had to rush to Georgetown University, a couple of miles from here, to help with a grant application."

"So we could leave it at that, couldn't we, for the moment anyhow?"

"Yes, why not? Let's do that."

Fiona sat up to pull herself together.

"I feel so much better now. After breakfast, I'll go back to bed."

While Fiona was resting, Giles got ahead with changing their tickets to a United Airlines flight, departing from JFK the next day at 10:40 a.m. and arriving at Johannesburg a day later at 8:30 a.m. After a fifteen-hour flight, preceded by one from Dulles to JFK, he reckoned they should then rest for twenty-fours before the final leg. They would need to have clear heads by the time they reached Cape Town. Overnight they'd stay at the Birchwood, a stone's throw from Tambo airport. A late morning would be followed by some relaxation in the hotel's gardens before catching a South African Airlines flight at 3:40 p.m. This would get them to Cape Town at 5:50 p.m., hopefully late enough for Conrad to meet them at the airport.

That done, he looked at his watch—11:10 a.m., 5:10 p.m. in Cape Town. Perhaps he should call Conrad now and get it over with? After all, being a Sunday he might be at home all day.

Giles took the telephone into the bathroom, closed the door quietly, and called Conrad's landline. After getting only the answering machine, he tried his brother's mobile—but again no reply.

Frustrated and worried that Conrad might be on a business trip, he called his home again to leave a message.

"Conrad, it's Giles. I'm in the States. Fiona and I have been visiting the NIH. We're both pooped, and as there's not much happening in Oxford, I thought it would be nice to take the long way round and spend a few days with you and Helen. I've booked a flight to Jo'burg, leaving tomorrow. We'll stay overnight at the Birchwood, and continue to Cape Town next day, arriving Wednesday at around ten to six. If you're away on business, don't worry. I'll let myself in. Your key's always on my ring. If you get this message before—"

Conrad picked up the phone.

"Giles! I heard every word from the loo. I've been trying to call you for days. I've had some good news. I've been promoted to Vice-President for R and D."

"Well done! You deserve it, the hours you put in."

"Thanks. It'll be even more work and greater responsibility, of course, but also more money, which will be great. Anyhow, to get back to you, I'd love you to come, naturally. Did you say you've got Fiona with you?"

"Yes."

"Interesting...very interesting! So, you've taken my advice at last? About time too.

I'm thrilled. She's a delightful girl."

"Isn't she? Anyhow, more when we meet. Mustn't chat too long. These hotels charge the earth. Any chance of a lift from the airport?"

"Try and stop me! I can show off my new BMW."

"Thanks. See you soon, brother dear. And by the way, I've bought Guy a nice book for his birthday."

"He'll be pleased. Veilige reis!"

"What?"

"I've been learning Afrikaans. It means 'safe journey.'"

"Thanks."

Chapter Twenty

With his tall athletic physique, mutton chop sideburns, and straw boater, Conrad would have been unmistakable even if the arrivals lounge of Cape Town's airport had been overflowing. As it happened, it was pleasantly quiet as Giles entered with Fiona a step behind at his shoulder. In his typically enthusiastic manner, Conrad waved to them with both hands and raced to take their bags.

"Giles, what a nice surprise! This is really fantastic. And how wonderful to see you too, Fiona. Welcome to South Africa. Welcome to Cape Town."

Conrad was one of those people who had the gift of putting people at ease, at once making them feel more than welcome. It was never contrived, always genuine and spontaneous, a natural warmth that emanated from his heart. He loved people, and he loved looking after them and entertaining them. Fiona smiled in appreciation, and squeezed Giles's hand. They were off to a good start.

Conrad's new car was soon speeding down the N2 towards Camps Bay, where his comfortable villa was nestled below the Twelve Apostles. Having agreed with Fiona to wait at least a day before revealing the true purpose of their visit, Giles limited his conversation on the road to Conrad's recent promotion. The unexpected news had put him in high spirits, and he was more than happy to do most of the talking. Although the job had put him under a lot of pressure, it had also given him greater freedom to organise his work and life in general as he wished.

"That's how I could pick you up today," he explained with a wink. "Wouldn't have been possible before. It's fantastic. This time last week, I was able to take Guy to Arrowe Park for some camping with the Scouts. Which reminds me, he'll still be there on his birthday. Sorry about that."

By the time they had reached the villa's tall wrought-iron gates, Giles was feeling a surge of optimism about the outcome of their venture. However, as soon as the car reached the end of the drive, Conrad announced some unwelcome news. Helen was in Durban, he said, visiting her brother in Edward VII Hospital after a car accident. As they collected their bags from the back of the car, Fiona could tell from Giles's expression that this was a big blow. As she would later learn, Helen was someone whose support Giles could usually rely upon, whenever he and Conrad had a serious difference of opinion. On more than a few occasions, her persuasive skills and debating talents, honed during her days as a political science student, had been crucial to winning him over. She knew exactly how to get the most out of her husband.

After a chat on the terrace over a jug of iced tea, a blood red sunset told them it would soon be time for dinner. As Conrad never missed an opportunity to show off the good life he was enjoying in his adopted country, it came as no surprise to learn that his daily had prepared a gourmet meal. Salmon and caviar from Kamchatka, homemade tagliatelle with Italian truffles, roasted Scottish venison with vegetables from a local market, a perfect Grand Marnier soufflé, and a bottle of L'Avenir Cabernet Sauvignon were impeccably served by a white-jacketed waiter hired for the occasion. Then it was back to the terrace to relax over a pot Conrad's favourite coffee, Beaver Creek Estate Reserve.

Giles loosened his belt and patted his paunch.

"I hope you don't dine like that every day, Conrad. Perhaps your cook could do us a small Lancashire hotpot tomorrow?"

"Ha! Giles, as you know all too well, our tastes in food have gone separate ways over the years. Don't expect me to change direction now. You can have your hotpot, potato and onion pie, and potted shrimps when you get back to Mavis. Meanwhile, my Malika will carry on as normal."

Conrad raised his arms, as if to embrace the wonderful view that lay before them.

"Ah, this is the life! But whatever you eat or don't eat, Giles, there's everything you could possibly want around here. I know I keep saying it, but why don't you pull up the anchor and move in with us? The bungalow at the end of the garden has just been refurbished. It's got everything you'd need, even a study. It's sitting there, empty, waiting for you. You could always get your own place after a year or two. What do you think, Fiona? It's very cosy in there."

Conrad threw a mischievous grin across the table towards Giles.

"I don't suppose I could have a D 'n' S, could I, Conrad? I'm not up to the Courvoisier I can see you've lined up."

"Help yourself, old boy. Everything's in the cabinet. What would you like, Fiona?"

"Nothing for me, thanks, Conrad. Could I use the washroom?"

"First right in the lobby."

Conrad poured himself a cognac and gazed into its vortex as he swirled it under his nose. He looked at Giles out of the corner of his eye.

"Sorry about that comment before, Giles. It was inappropriate, in fact more than that, inexcusable. Put it down to the wine. I know you're not here to seek my advice on your private life. It's none of my business. But I will reiterate that I think she's a wonderful girl. On your own admission, you were always pretty inept with women. If she's fond of you, and she obviously is, don't miss the opportunity. She's a jewel. Go for it! That's that. Promise to say no more.

"Now to change the subject, I've got a sneaky feeling you're not here for a vacation, are you?"

By now Giles had prepared his drink and was back in the rattan chair.

"Why do you say that?"

"Well for one thing, you don't normally have one in November, do you? Although you said there's nothing happening in the university, I know for a fact it's always a pretty busy time. Michelmas term doesn't finish for another two weeks or so. And apart from that, I can sense you're edgy, not your usual self. I'm pretty sure you're here for another reason, aren't you? Come on, out with it. What's it all about?"

Fiona reappeared at the doorway.

"Would either of you mind if I had a bath and went to bed? I shouldn't be tired really, looking at the clock, but I guess I'm not used to long-haul travel."

Conrad jumped up.

"Of course, no problem, Fiona. Malika's prepared the bedroom at the far end of the hallway, and you'll find plenty of towels in the en suite bathroom. There's also a cotton dressing gown hanging behind the door."

Conrad's eyes flashed uncomfortably between his guests.

"You are…er…sort of…travelling together…yes? If not, I can…"

"Thanks, Conrad," Giles interrupted. "I can put your mind at rest. We're travelling *together*, yes."

"Splendid! I mean, fine."

Feeling much more relaxed now the arrangements had been settled, Fiona turned to leave.

"Good night, Conrad. Thanks for a wonderful evening. I'm sure I'm going to enjoy the visit enormously."

As she made her way up the broad staircase, Giles rose to lean against one of the terrace's columns, balancing his glass on the balustrade.

"Okay, back to where we were. Never could fool you, could I, Conrad, even as a kid? I was going to wait until tomorrow, so we could enjoy the evening celebrating your promotion. But now that you've given me no choice, here it comes."

Sipping his cognac, Conrad listened attentively to the entire story, from the day of MECCAR's opening to Giles's uninvited visit to the National Cancer Institute, and all that had happened since. Only when it was clear Giles had completely finished did he comment.

"My goodness! That's quite a saga. If it hadn't come from the horse's mouth, I wouldn't have believed it. And how about Fiona! The way she followed you to Washington, and then did all that computer stuff. Very impressive!"

He poured himself some coffee from the Mbunda earthenware pot that Malika always used for the purpose.

"And now you're faced with to do next? From what you've said, you're not going to get any help from that Hank Weinberg man."

"No."

"Coffee?"

"Thanks."

For several tense minutes the two of them sat in silence, Conrad stroking his bushy sideburns, Giles fixing his eyes on the Zulu beadwork tapestry that hung behind him, barely able to look his brother in the eye. Conrad had sensed Giles was about to break the silence when he got in first.

"I suppose you realise that what you want to ask of me is illegal, don't you?"

A broad smile broke across Giles's face.

"You always could read me like a book, couldn't you? I haven't sought legal counsel, but I've assumed it probably is."

"Well, it is, definitely. You can take my word for it. There's no 'probably' about it. Any unauthorised intrusion into someone else's computer is illegal. There's no doubt it would be possible to see what he's got in there. That sort of thing is happening all the time in spite of the best efforts of companies like mine. Furthermore, if you know what you're doing, writing that kind of code isn't usually very difficult, though it can take time. Computers simply do what you tell them to do. Whatever you can do with a keyboard and a mouse, you can also do with a set of instructions over the Internet. No, the question isn't whether it could be done. It's whether it should be done. Would it be worth the risk?"

Conrad stood up to share the moonlit scene with Giles: the dramatic silhouette of Lion's Head, the Twelve Apostles, the broad sweep of Camps Bay with the twinkling lights of Victoria Road. He listened to the distant rumble of surf pounding against Whale Rocks, and the rustle of the palm trees in the sea breeze. He inhaled the fresh, slightly salty air, mingled with the delicate aromas from his garden's flowers and the neighbouring eucalyptus trees.

"I've got a lot to lose, Giles. It hasn't been easy to achieve all this. And I'm not at a stage in life when I could recover from losing my job and reputation. If it turns out he's innocent, and later on it's discovered we'd infected his laptop with spyware, the powers that be might not be interested in the fact we were trying to do the right thing. And even if your suspicions are correct and he's guilty, I still don't know how the company would react. It's the kind of crime Southern Securi-Systems was created to prevent. The fact that I'd helped uncover an important piece of scientific fraud would be a plus, of course, but the fact I'd done it illegally would not. For the company, it would be a mixture of good and bad news. And whatever happens in the boardroom, there might be litigation from Dr Salomon."

By now, Giles was preparing himself for the worse.

"But if we found nothing incriminating, Conrad, nobody would know what we'd been up to, would they?"

"It's not so simple, Giles. There are many ways of hiding malicious code from the average person, but dealing with a specialist is a different matter. If your American friend noticed his laptop had slowed down and took it to a technician, it might not take him too long to uncover it."

"Could he tell where it had come from?"

"Not necessarily, you can route malicious code via websites that make it anonymous. It's as if the post office removed the sender's address from an envelope before giving it to the postman. But I'd rather not involve third parties. You never know where it might lead.

But we're going too fast. I haven't made up my mind yet. I'm not going to say 'no' right now, Giles, but I'm not going to say 'yes' either. You'll have to give me some time. I'm sorry, but I need to think about it.

"I tell you what. Tomorrow morning, you and Fiona take Helen's car, the Saab. It's an automatic, very easy to drive. You'll find a map of the region in the glove box. Cruise around, the two of you. Take in the scenery. As you know, it's gorgeous around here. And it'll all be new to Fiona. She'll love it: the flowers, the coastal scenery, the animals. Have a picnic. I'll ask Malika to rustle up something for you. Do whatever you want, but don't get back until the evening. Then, I'll give you my answer. That's a promise. Not what you wanted, I know, but the best I can do on the spot.

"Now, when we've finished our drinks, how about we follow Fiona's example and get some kip?

Chapter Twenty-One

Conrad was busy in the bathroom when Giles and Fiona made their way downstairs, looking forward to their day trip. Malika had prepared the table the night before and left a message to say she had put a packed lunch in the fridge. The keys to the Saab were on the bookcase in the entrance hall.

After Giles had collected the map, they planned their route over a breakfast of coffee, freshly baked croissants, and raw fynbos honey, several pots of which Fiona vowed to take back with her to Oxford. Ever since a lecture on the subject at university, she'd been fascinated by the floral diversity of South Africa's Fynbos region.

"I've always wanted to taste this stuff, Giles," she said, licking her sticky fingers with evident satisfaction, "and I'm pleased to say it's lived up to expectations. You see, this is a special part of the world when it comes to flowers. In an area not much bigger than Wales, there are more than six thousand species of flowering plants that are found nowhere else? And this honey was made by bees that live in the middle of it all. They must be the happiest in the world!"

"Not from what I've heard. African bees are pretty aggressive, aren't they?"

"Some, yes, but not the ones that created this honey. They're called Cape bees, much more docile."

Giles dipped a spoon into the pot, and gave it a try.

"You're right. You should try it in your raspberry cranachan when we get back."

"Good idea!"

After some discussion about the relative merits of different routes, they agreed to take the coastal road through Llandudno and Hout Bay, then the M65 to the Cape, where they would have their snack and go for a walk. The return journey would be via the east coast, through Simon's Town and Fish Hoek, before cutting inland through the Tokai Forest and the vineyards of Constantia.

Arriving at the villa at around seven o'clock, Giles parked the Saab in the forecourt and walked the length of the drive to close the gates. As Fiona had spotted Conrad through the bay window asleep on the sofa, they avoided the front door and entered quietly through the kitchen, stopping to brew a pot of tea. While the kettle was boiling, Conrad entered, rubbing his eyes.

"Giles, Fiona, welcome back! Good trip?"

"Wonderful thanks, brother. It's like heaven down there."

"Well, you know what I keep saying. Any wildlife?"

"Plenty!" Fiona replied eagerly. "Baboons, ostriches, antelopes, tiny striped mice scuttling around the rocks. We even saw what we think was an eagle high in the sky."

"Glad you enjoyed it. Pour me a cuppa too, Giles, while you're at it, please. No milk, slice of lemon."

Giles studied Conrad's body language in the hope of guessing his answer to the big question. But he was giving nothing away.

"I won't keep the two of you in suspense," he declared wearily.

"I've agonised about it all day. As you know, my pockets were empty when I came here. Now, after working my guts out, I've got all I could ever want. I live in a beautiful part of the world. I've got cash in the bank. I love this house. I love my work. And I've just been promoted. So, I asked myself time and again: does it really matter if the Nobel Prize goes to the wrong person? Is it important enough for me to risk all I've achieved?"

Conrad broke off while he tried to make himself comfortable on one of his new barstools.

"It may surprise you, Giles, but I've never been enthusiastic about the Nobel Prize, at least not the one for medicine."

"Why's that?"

"Because as far as I can tell, the winners aren't selected purely for the intrinsic merit of their work, are they? It's more for its eventual value to medicine, which is often totally out of their control and not clear until many years later. I don't think that makes sense. Scientists can determine how many hours they put in, the originality of their research, its ingenuity, its thoroughness, complexity, accuracy, and so on, but they have little or no control over *what* they discover, or its eventual *value* to humankind. To be frank, the whole business strikes me as a bit crazy."

He paused to adjust his bottom on the stool, while searching for an example to illustrate his point.

"Imagine that a chap in your university does an experiment to see if a new chemical he's produced kills the bacteria that cause malaria."

"Malaria's caused by a protozoan parasite, Conrad," Giles interjected, "not bacteria. That's the...."

Giles stopped in midstream, as he caught sight of Fiona's frown of disapproval.

"Thank you, Herr Professor," Conrad returned with a deferential nod. "Let's say the chemical kills those creatures in the lab, and he publishes his results. Meanwhile, a chap in Cambridge does the same sort of work with a different chemical he's invented. This one also works in the lab. Pharmaceutical companies compete with each other to develop two new drugs based on these molecules. Both are found to cure malaria in clinical trials, but the Cambridge one also produces some nasty side effects that could not have been predicted...on the heart or kidney, for example. So only the other one goes to market. It saves millions of lives. The Oxford man gets the Nobel Prize. The other one's forgotten.

"Where's the sense? There was nothing to choose between their work. The Oxford man just got lucky. The other man's work might even have been of a higher standard, but it just so happened that the side-effects let him down. So I asked myself today: if the Nobel Prize depends as much on luck as on merit, is it important enough for me to risk everything?"

Giles knew from past experience this was not the time to dive headlong into a heated disagreement. Nothing was guaranteed more to push Conrad in the wrong direction. If there was to be any chance of winning him over, he would have to go about it slowly.

"You're absolutely right, of course, Conrad. It's undeniable that luck plays a part. You conjured up a hypothetical scenario. I could give you some real ones. Ever heard of prions?"

"Something to do with mad cow disease, aren't they?"

"Full marks. They're the infectious agents that cause it. And yet they're not bacteria, or fungi, or viruses, or protozoa, or worms. In fact, they're not any type of organism at all. There not alive. There's no genes or DNA. They're simply misshapen molecules of a protein that's a normal component of our brain cells."

"What do you mean by misshapen? I thought proteins were just long chains of…what are they called?"

"Amino acids."

"That's it."

"They are. But the chains are folded and coiled on themselves, each in its own specific way, and fixed like that by chemical bonds where they cross. The resulting three-dimensional structure is critical in determining a protein's properties, whether it's an enzyme, an antibody, whatever. In the case of the prion protein, the function of the normal version in our brains is not known. But if just one molecule gets incorrectly folded for some reason, it causes other prion molecules nearby to become misfolded in just the same way. They in turn cause others to misfold, and so it goes on in a kind of domino effect. Then, when there are enough of them, these misshapen molecules start sticking to each other in a way that clogs up the brain. And to make matters worse, they're infectious. They can be transferred from one animal to another to start the same process all over again. Am I boring you?"

Conrad covered his mouth, and feigned a deep yawn.

"I'm sure you'll get to the point, if I wait long enough."

"Good. Okay, now you know about prions, we can get to the nitty-gritty, namely how they were discovered. Before mad cow disease existed, a rare disease called scrapie had been affecting sheep for centuries. It was a puzzle. Although it behaved like an infectious disease, no organism could be found. Then a couple of vets came up with the idea it might be due to an infectious protein. Understandably, most people thought they were bonkers. But not a British chemist called John Griffith, who soon published a theoretical mechanism by which conformational changes in a protein could be propagated auto-catalytically."

"Christ! Slow down, Giles. What does that mouthful mean in English?"

"Sorry, just a fancy way of saying what I've already said—a process in which one misshapen molecule causes others to become misshapen. After that, not much happened until the 1980s, when an American called Stanley Prusiner isolated the agent that causes scrapie, and showed that the two vets and Griffith had been right. A few years later, mad cow disease arrived, and was found to be a variant of scrapie. Then, when a few people seemed to have caught it from eating infected beef, the experts were predicting an epidemic of brain disease was on the horizon. Politicians were panicking. Prions were all over the newspapers. And in next to no time, Prusiner got the Nobel Prize. Now, the big question is…"

"Would he have got it if mad cow disease had not been passed on to a few humans?"

Giles shrugged his shoulders.

"Precisely. A Nobel Prize for discovering the cause of a rare disease of sheep?"

"Presumably the other scientists you mentioned shared it?" Conrad continued.

"No, they didn't. Griffith, for one, was dead by then."

"So there you are, Giles. It proves my point. Presumably, Prusiner's work was brilliant, but some might say he also got lucky."

"Yes…but not as lucky as a chap called Gajdusek."

"Why?"

"He'd already won a Nobel twenty years earlier for supposedly showing that scrapie and a rare brain disease in humans called kuru are caused by an unusual kind of virus. However, it turned out he was wrong. We now know both are caused by prions."

"At least in his case he had to give it back, I presume?"

"No, he didn't. Nor did Heinrich Wieland, when he got a Nobel in the 1920s for getting the chemical structure of cholesterol wrong. You see, once you've got one, you've got it for good, and all that goes with it. That's why it's so important to make sure they don't get into the wrong hands."

"So…the whole business is a bit of joke, isn't it? That's my…"

"No, it isn't. It's inevitable that luck comes into it to some extent, and that every now and then an error is made. That's life. Stories like those don't lower the status of the Prize at all. There's no doubt the life blood of science comes from new ideas, hypotheses and so on, but it can also take brilliance to prove which ones are right and wrong. Although Gajdusek and Wieland made mistakes, their work was pioneering and took us closer to the truth. Gajdusek's work also took enormous courage."

"Why."

"Would you have moved in with a bunch of cannibals in a jungle in New Guinea just to prove they were getting a brain disease from eating their grannies?"

Conrad gulped down his tea.

"Is that true?"

"Absolutely."

"Jesus! But I do know there have been times when luck was the *only* factor, Giles. According to The Argus, some Nobel discoveries were entirely the result of accidents. You have to admit that's crazy."

"No, I don't. The problem is you've never done experimental research, Conrad. It can take an exceptional mind to spot the unexpected, especially a small detail; to grasp its significance; and then drop everything to go after it, especially if it means dumping an idea of your own you've cherished for years. There are two quotations I give to my students about that. The Greek philosopher Heraklietos said, 'In searching for the truth, be ready for the unexpected.' More than two thousand years later, France's greatest scientist, Claude Bernard, wrote, 'The true worth of an experimenter consists in his pursuing not only what he seeks, but also what he did not seek.'"

Conrad poured himself another cup.

"Well, I'm certainly not going to argue with those two. Okay, you win that one...I suppose...just about. But there's something else to get off my chest. Alfred Nobel made a fortune from two inventions because they were extremely at killing people: dynamite and gelignite. The French rightly called him 'le marchand de la mort.' When dying in his home on the Italian Riviera, after a lifetime of cosseted luxury financed by the misery and pain of others, he came up with the big idea of his prizes. Why? So the world would remember him as something he was not: a Mr Nice Guy. He wanted his bread buttered on both sides. And every time one of you lot accepts some of his blood money, you're spreading it on thick."

"That's a bit over the top, Conrad."

"I don't think so. Take an analogy. Mikhail Kalashnikov, inventor of the AK-47, the best-selling gun in the world, didn't make a rouble out of it in the USSR. But if he'd been an American and got ten dollars a shot—no pun intended—he would have been in the same league as the Russian oligarchs. What if he'd used some of that money to create, let's say, the 'Kalashnikov Prize for Trauma Surgery'. How would you feel about it?"

"Come on, Conrad, get serious!"

"I am. Or how about the 'Henry Shrapnel Prize for Plastic Surgery'?

"Ha, ha! Conrad, I said get serious."

"You jest, Giles, because such cases would be so flagrant as to be offensive. But Nobel's awards are no different. It's just that their association with death, pain, untold misery, amputations, septicaemia, gangrene, tetanus, blindness, fatherless children, widows, depression, and destroyed lives is not so conspicuous. Most people don't know how Nobel got his wealth. If he'd called his gelignite 'Nobel-ignite,' for example, he wouldn't have got away with it."

"But you may be wrong about his motives, Conrad. It may not have been to salvage his reputation. As death approached, he may have felt genuine remorse, and have wanted to do some good before he left this world."

"Poppycock! For one thing, his prizes don't actually do any good. In what way do they benefit mankind? I can't imagine any scientist works harder for the one in a zillion chance it might lead to a Nobel. Nor do they speed up progress by giving scientists more of what they need for their work. If Alfred wanted to do some good, why didn't he create a charitable foundation or a medical research centre like Rockefeller, Howard Hughes, Henry Wellcome, the Mayo brothers, and others did?"

"So that's it, is it, Conrad? End of story? Fiona and I have been wasting our time and yours? Sorry."

Giles winked at Fiona.

"Not necessarily, Giles. I just needed to explain why I've had such a difficult day. Is the Nobel Prize important enough for me—and you, and Fiona—to risk everything? What do you think, Fiona? You've come a long way with Giles. I suppose you must agree with him, do you?"

Fiona nodded, reluctant to get drawn into a difficult conversation she had not prepared for.

"Of course, you're both medical scientists."

Conrad grimaced as he prised himself off his stool and wandered into the living room to flop onto the sofa.

"Ugh…that's more like it! You two did the right thing not to sit on those new stools of mine. I must get some extra cushions for them. Can you believe the mail order company is called www.soft-stools-4u.com? They should give up on furniture and sell laxatives instead. Come in here, and make yourself comfortable.

"Where was I? Oh yes…I do understand where you're coming from, and why it's so important to you. Inevitably dyed-in-the-wool academics like you look at it differently. The Nobel Prize is a big thing for you lot. The prestige of universities depends on them. So you have to preserve their gloss."

Fiona decided it was time to say something.

"Protecting the award is not what we're about, Conrad. It's something we think we should try to preserve, yes, but our real concern is about more important things— honesty, truth, fair play, justice. That's really what brought us here."

Conrad looked at her with eyes that spoke of acceptance of the inevitable before responding in a more muted tone.

"And so, knowing what you do know, you feel you have a moral obligation to do something, I suppose?"

"Yes, we do, Conrad, to do all we can. Giles and I are completely at one on that.

Going to Washington was a big step for both us. By letting himself into Steve Salomon's office and making off with that report, Giles committed acts of burglary and theft. That's not something you do lightly. When I followed him, I lied to the college. I'm away from one the most famous universities in the world, the kind of job many would give their back teeth for, without leave of absence. The air fares cost us thousands. Giles has made an enemy of the Director of the National Institutes of Health, one of the most powerful figures in medical science. Coming here to ask you this favour was also very difficult."

"And you did all that because morally you felt you had no choice?"

Fiona nodded.

"You knew you'd never be able to rest, unless you did what was right, even if it meant risking your job, your reputation, even a criminal record?"

Fiona nodded again.

Giles could see the clouds were clearing. It was classic Conrad. Hopefully, all that was needed now were a few gentle nudges.

"Remember what Mum used to say to us as kids," Giles said with a smile, "about peace of mind being more important than pieces of eight?"

Conrad chuckled as he reminisced.

"Yes, I can hear her now, when an ice cream vendor accidentally gave me too much change one wet and windy day in Scarborough."

He looked up mournfully and invited the two them to join him, patting the sofa's soft leather cushions.

"At around two o'clock, while you were enjoying yourselves, I was here, where I am now, struggling with my decision. I got up, looked at myself in that mirror over there, and said aloud— we both have that peculiarity, Fiona; he's not the only one who's mad— 'Forget it, Conrad. It doesn't make sense. Give Giles and Fiona a damn good holiday, then pack them off to Oxford a few shades darker and a few pounds heavier. Eventually, they'll forget all about it.' Then I poured myself a scotch and nodded off.

"About an hour later, I woke up, and my brain started surfing again. But this time it took a different tack. Part of it reminded me how important it is in life that we adhere to standards, all of us, because that's what civilised society is all about. If we throw out honesty, integrity, fair play, and respect for our fellow beings, what are we left with?"

"A professional soccer match!" Giles quipped, feeling it was time to lighten the mood.

"Ha! A few years ago, I would have said the jungle. But you're right. The jungle's more civilised…and safer."

It was time to gently turn the screws.

"So shall we get it over with, Conrad?"

Fiona glanced at Giles for a nod of affirmation before turning to Conrad with a diffident smile.

"Giles and I appreciate this is a huge decision for you, Conrad. We knew it would be when we got on the flight in

New York. In fact, we wondered if it was fair to drop it on you like this. But we really had no choice. Time is short. Steve Salomon is already on his triumphal lecture tour before the ceremony on December 10. The countdown has started. The world needs to know the truth about *Deidamia*. Did he really invent it, as he claims, or is it actually nothing more than the Bedouin's switch, whose details he got from Ahmad Sharif?"

She paused to let it sink in before resuming.

"So, are you ready?"

Conrad closed his eyes and nodded.

"I think so."

"And is it no…or yes?"

"It's……yes. I'll do it, or at least I'll give it a bloody good try!"

Thinking it inappropriate to show too much emotion, Fiona moved to squeeze his hand and kiss him lightly on the cheek.

Giles took his turn to give him a hug.

"I'm proud of you, brother."

Conrad raised both hands.

"Hold it! First, I need to come clean about something else in the equation."

"What was that?"

"I know MECCAR's top man."

"What!" Giles gasped. "You know Rashid Yamani?".

"Yes."

"How on earth?"

"When they were planning MECCAR, my company won the contract to set up its IT system. I didn't mention it before, as it's supposed to be confidential. Even I don't know all the details, and what I do know I can't say much about…sorry. Since then, we've been helping them with a couple of other institutes in the pipeline."

"Why on earth did they choose a South African outfit?"

"They were afraid countries big in medical research, like the USA, EU, Japan, and so on, would plant spyware. It's easily done."

"What is there you *can* tell me?"

"No expense was spared. Basically, they were obsessed with security. One was to develop an unbreakable encryption system for a new VPN system we set up."

"VPN?"

"Virtual private network. They're used for Internet security. Everything is encrypted to and from your computer. It prevents anyone from listening in. They're already quite common, but they wanted their very own, one that was more secure than any other. There was also software to run an iris recognition system for laptops they issued to all those research fellows they sent around the world. This was in addition to fingerprint and voice recognition systems. Extraordinary!"

Fiona looked at Giles.

"I told you Aram is obsessed with security, Giles. He's terrified to let me near his laptop. I can understand why they want to make MECCAR's servers secure, but why so much security for people like him? Sorry to interrupt, Conrad."

"That's okay, Fiona. To get back to Rashid, I grew to like him and developed a great admiration for his commitment to the cause. He's just the guy MECCAR needs, I thought— totally dedicated to returning the Arab world to the forefront of medical science. And a man of impeccable character too, I would say. So, if your suspicions about Steve Salomon are right, I'd like Rashid to know about it. He deserves to know the truth, and I'd like to play my part…... even though the prospect is pretty scary."

Conrad broke off to wring his hands, clicking his fingers audibly, as he lent on his elbows to gaze pensively at the rug beneath his feet. Almost a minute had passed before he spoke again, his visitors eying each other anxiously for fear of what might be coming next. During their trip to the Cape, Giles had warned Fiona it was not unknown for his brother to pull back at the last second.

"I won't deny I'm worried," he resumed. "In fact, to tell the truth, I'm shit scared. But… there's no going back, not this time. I've made my decision, and that's that."

Fiona gave Giles a discreet thumbs up.

"I'll do the work here. Tomorrow, I'll go the office to collect a few things. After that, I'd better keep away from there. Did you say he uses a Mac?"

Giles nodded.

"I don't have one here. I'll pick one up over the weekend."

"Any idea how you'll go about it?"

"Too soon to say. There are many types of code you can write to attack another person's computer. Everyone's heard of viruses and worms, but we won't be using either. One option would be what we simply call malicious mobile code, which can do many things. Another would be one of several types of backdoor, which let you look inside and even control someone's entire computer remotely. They're made up of two parts. One is sent to the victim; the other stays with the attacker. Then, the two parts talk to each other over the Internet, sending and receiving instructions and information. Different types of backdoors provide different levels of control. They're used quite legitimately for some purposes, but of course we'll need to conceal ours."

Giles raised his eyebrows.

"You mean a Trojan horse?"

"You could say that. A Trojan's just any piece of code that's disguised to evade detection. But if you don't mind, that's as far as I'll go for the moment. How about we get ready for dinner?"

"I'll second that," Fiona said, laughing. "I'm famished. A baboon grabbed our sandwiches at the Cape. So, let's eat, drink, and be merry, for tomorrow we may spy!"

Chapter Twenty-Two

By seven the following morning, Giles, Fiona and Conrad, all eager to make an early start, were admiring the garden from the terrace, while Malika prepared a pot of coffee. Conrad was keen to get more information before going to the office.

"Okay, Giles, let's start. Tell me what you know about Steve's equipment."

"Not a lot, I'm afraid. He's using the Mac OS9.2 operating system, I do know that, and for emails Outlook Express."

"OS9.2? Bit slow to change, isn't he?"

"He's an academic, don't forget. We're not like you business types, flush with cash. We have tight budgets. If it works, why change?"

"Fair enough. But it'll test me. I'll need to brush up on Macs, and get a second-hand Powerbook or iBook from somewhere. Do you happen to know if he uses anything to protect against spyware?"

Giles shrugged his shoulders.

"No idea, possibly not. The NIH has its own IT security, and he reckons Macs are safer than PCs anyhow. That's one reason he uses them. So, he might not do so."

"Okay, let's hope for the best. Another thing is we'd better check his hotels have broadband, at least the ones that matter."

Giles smiled reassuringly as he took Steve's itinerary from his back pocket.

"As you'll see here, five-star luxury is an essential for Steve. In Stockholm he'll be at the Grand, of course, where all the Laureates rest their brainy heads."

He passed it to Conrad.

"My, quite a trip! Let me see. His last hotel before Stockholm is the D'Angleterre in Geneva. He gets there on the second, is joined by his wife the next day, and they go to Sweden three days later, a Monday. Next morning there's a press conference. Wednesday afternoon he gives a lecture in the Adam Lecture Hall of the Berzelius something or other…can't pronounce the Swedish…at the Karolinska Institute. Next day seems to be free. Then Friday the tenth is the big one—the ceremony in the Concert Hall at four-thirty, followed by the banquet in City Hall.

"Okay, that's enough for now. As soon as we've finished breakfast, I'll be on my way. Expect me back around five. Between now and then, why don't the two of you look at this? It's the best there is."

Conrad handed Fiona a copy of 'Malware: Fighting Malicious Code' by Ed Skoudis.

"Then we'll all be on the same wavelength. Closer to it anyhow."

***

When Conrad returned from his office a little earlier than expected, Giles was on the terrace making notes from Ed Skoudis's book, while Fiona was inside flicking through the latest issue of Africa Geographic magazine and listening to music on Conrad's earphones.

"Hi, Giles, Fiona," he called cheerily. "I'm back. How did you get on with the book?"

"Very well, thanks," Giles answered.

Conrad joined Giles, kissing Fiona lightly on the forehead as he passed.

"Good stuff, isn't it? Welcome to my world!"

"All very interesting, I must say. But also pretty terrifying. I never imagined so much could be going on inside my laptop without my knowing it: viruses infecting, worms multiplying, backdoors opening and closing, Trojan horses galloping, root-kits burrowing. From now on, every time I'm online I'll be wondering if someone in Hong Kong's recording my keystrokes, or if Boris is a global distribution centre for child pornography. It's horrifying."

Conrad chuckled.

"Now you know why, after a brief chat with me in Amman's Le Royal, Rashid Yamani decided to splash out. There's a whole army of hackers out there. They're very bright, and they're coming up with new tricks all the time. It won't be long before one of them brings down the entire Internet, or crashes every computer in NATO. Some of those guys are so good they're headhunted by the Pentagon before they're even out of prison. One day, wars will be declared with a salvo of worms. The first side to cripple the other's command and control system, broadband, and mobile phones will win. It'll all be over in hours, minutes even."

"The First Worm War! Sounds like good news to me. Better dead computers than dead humans."

"Definitely. But it's a nightmare for banks, industry, governments, you name it. I saw it coming years ago. That's why I'm in this beautiful villa, while you're in a draughty little flat with a leaking roof and creaky floorboards."

"It's not a flat. It's a draughty little house with a leaking roof and creaky floorboards. And I like it that way. It makes me feel close to nature. And talking about nature, after reading a few chapters of this book, something that fascinates me is how similar malicious computer codes can be to biological systems. They multiply like real viruses. They can change their appearance while keeping their harmful properties, like HIV and flu viruses. And it says here that two different pieces of malicious software can even combine inside a computer to produce a hybrid, just like lengths of DNA can recombine to form new genes. And if that's not enough, they can lie dormant for months, like hibernating bears, and then wake up when the time is right."

"I can see my brother's realising there's more to life than genes."

Giles laughed.

"Until today, I'd always believed there's no life without them."

Conrad stretched his arms and inhaled the fresh sea breeze.

"Ah, that's good! But when you think about it, Giles, perhaps the similarities between computers and biology are not so surprising. After all, silicon chips and biochemical reactions both depend on the movement of electrons, don't they?"

"True, but you could say that sort of thing about more or less everything, Conrad. Just think, every single object we're looking at—the trees, birds, the rocks, the beach—is composed of the same tiny building blocks. The only difference between your nose and that mountain is the precise arrangement of billions of electrons, neutrons, and protons. We're all parts of one immense Lego set."

Giles waved his pen in the air.

"And yet this is a pen, and you eat, and drink…"

"Which is exactly what we should be doing now," Conrad roared, "instead of prattling on like two ancient Greek philosophers. Can I smell curry?"

"Malika prepared it this morning. It's in the oven. She's a gem. Where did you find her?"

"She's from Mauritius. Married to a nightclub bouncer from Jo'burg. Two children, a boy and a girl."

Malika's cooking was as good as its promise. Only when every morsel had been consumed did they move into the library. Conrad rolled up his sleeves and poured himself a glass of cognac.

"I suppose you'll have your usual too, will you, Giles?"

Giles nodded.

"A double please."

"Sure? You drank most of the wine, you know."

"I'm thirsty after that curry."

"If you insist."

"And you, Fiona?"

"Mineral water, please."

Conrad gave his cigar a few deep puffs before blowing the smoke out of the open window.

"That feels better! Nothing like a good dose of nicotine to get the brain cells working. So, let's consider how best to attack Steve's laptop. Sorry about the aggressive language, but that's how hackers talk. And I'm afraid that's what we're about to become. I've thought about it a lot today. Ideally, I'd like to do it in two stages. Whether that will be possible depends on whether there would be two different pieces of evidence in his laptop, or just one."

Conrad's eyes flicked apprehensively between the two of them.

"You need a double-barrelled smoking gun?" Giles quipped. "Over to you, Fiona."

Pleased to be getting down to business at last, Fiona moved her chair closer to the others.

"If our suspicions are correct, the answer is yes. There would be two, definitely."

"Great! In that case, I suggest we kick off by getting a copy of one of them from his laptop for you to take to Stockholm. It won't be necessary for that bit to prove your suspicions are correct, only to provide the Swedes with sufficient evidence to take you seriously and ask for more. Then in front of their noses, we'd collect the second piece of evidence, the killer blow. We won't look for that yet. We won't even go near it. It will stay right where it is, unseen and untouched, until the right moment arrives. All I need is your assurance that, if he's guilty, both pieces will be there."

Giles frowned.

"Why not collect both in one go, straight away?"

"Put yourself in their shoes, Giles. Somebody they might never have heard of, with all respects to you, turns up out of the blue claiming this year's Nobel Laureate in medicine is a fraudster and a plagiariser. What do you expect them to do? Take your word for it, and cancel the biggest show in Sweden's national calendar at the last minute? For all they know, you might be a nutcase, who's fabricated the lot. If they've any sense, and I suspect they've got plenty, they'll want more evidence than what's just arrived on their doorstep from darkest Africa. They're going to want to see some hard evidence collected in front of their own eyes. And it should be untouched, unopened. Otherwise, later on there might be accusations in the courts we could have tampered with it. Better play safe and keep well away. And when they ask for it, assuming it's there, we'll give it to 'em. Zap!"

Giles emptied his glass.

"Makes sense, of course. Sounds a bit hairy though, Conrad. Can't we take a quick peek to confirm that the second lot is actually there before setting off to Sweden?"

"Definitely not! Macs are not my usual playground, don't forget. I'm in unfamiliar territory. If we left a footprint, Steve's attorney would have a field day accusing us of planting the evidence."

"But presumably collecting the first lot will leave a footprint, won't it?"

"Hopefully not. You'll understand why in a tick."

Giles mixed himself another double D 'n' S.

"A top up for you too, Conrad?"

"No thanks."

"Fiona?"

"No thanks, Giles."

Conrad scribbled a diagram on a legal notepad he had taken from his office.

"Take a look at this. We'll start by you sending Steve an email with two Word files attached. It doesn't matter what they're about, but it's essential he opens them there and then. This won't work if he leaves them for later. Any ideas, either of you?"

Fiona and Giles looked at each other nervously.

"Something he feels he must look at straight away?" Giles asked. "I can think of a few snaps of you on the beach he'd appreciate, Fiona."

"Giles!"

"Sorry, brother. How about something with a really tight deadline?"

Giles wandered off to walk around in circles, glass in hand, while he struggled for inspiration.

"I've got it!" he yelped. "Yes, that'll work. He knows about my autobiography. I could ask him to look through a last-minute addition about his Nobel Prize–winning work. One of the attachments could be a page or two describing his achievement, and the other a photo of his lab. I'll beg him to take a quick look at them, on the basis that I need to get them to the publisher urgently."

"Is that plausible?" Fiona rejoined. "Why on earth would it be urgent?"

"Because they want to get it into the shops before Christmas."

Conrad doubled up with laughter.

"For Christmas? Your autobiography? You've definitely had too much booze, Giles."

"He'd fall for it, Conrad. I'm sure he would. I know him inside out. It would flatter him, boost his ego. I'll tell him Steve Salomon and *Deidamia* are household names in the UK, and the publisher wants to cash in on it."

Conrad wiped the tears from his cheeks.

"But is it realistic to say they can print a book in a few weeks?"

"I'll tell him the rest's already done, and now they're just waiting for this bit."

"It's still not credible, Giles," Fiona added. "There's much more to it than printing. There's the binding, marketing, distribution, and so on. It's a big job. Conrad's right, there's not enough time for that. I think you'd have to say it'll be print-on-demand or an e-book, something like that. Or alternatively they want to get it out in the spring."

"Good ideas, Fiona," Conrad resumed. "And you have a photo of his lab, Giles?"

"Yep. As it happens, I took some a few days ago."

"Excellent! So let's follow one of Fiona's suggestions. Now, each of the attachments will have a piece of mobile code hidden inside it. Since we're already into Greek mythology, I'm going to call one *Adonis* and the other *Aphrodite*. The instant Steve opens the attachments, those two will jump onto his hard disk. Then *Aphrodite* will go to sleep."

"Fall asleep, all alone with *Adonis*? Won't he be offended?" Giles joked, his speech now slightly slurred.

"I'll ignore that, Giles. Meanwhile, while she's asleep, *Adonis* will poke around."

"*Poke around?* Ha, ha, ha! Then she *would* get offended! I always imagined Greek deities were more sophisticated than that."

"Jesus, Giles, this is not the time to fool around! I don't think you should drink any more of that Bermudan concoction. Obviously, it doesn't go very well with red wine."

"Sorry, old boy."

"Fiona, can you tell me what it is that *Adonis* should look for?"

"That's easy. Steve has a folder called 'Travel Notes'. The evidence would be in there. So he should look for that."

Conrad jotted it down on his notepad.

"Okay, so when *Adonis* finds that folder, he will email a copy of it to Giles. Then he'll self-destruct."

"What do you mean?" Giles asked, looking confused.

"He'll disappear, hopefully without a trace."

"Is that possible?"

"Should be in his case."

"Poor *Aphrodite*," Giles joked, slopping his drink onto his shirt. "She'll be so disappointed when she wakes up."

"Giles, I think you're drunk, aren't you?"

"Course not! And to prove it, here's something you might not have thought of.

What if Steve switches his laptop off before *Adonis* has sent us the gods, I mean the goods?"

"That's very unlikely. As he'll know what to look for, finding it and sending you a copy will only take a few seconds."

"And you're sure this is all possible, Conrad?"

"You read the book, didn't you?"

"It still seems too fantastic to be true."

"Don't worry, Giles, it isn't."

"Don't you want to know why the 'Travel Notes' folder is so

important, Conrad?" Fiona asked, wanting to be sure nothing had been overlooked.

"Eventually, but not just now, Fiona. It's not necessary. As long as you're sure about it, that's all that matters. You can explain everything, when it's safely tucked inside Giles's inbox. But that does remind me of something. We need to agree on what to tell the Swedes when they ask how we got our hands on it. We obviously can't tell them the truth."

"We could tell them it's the folder Steve sent to Hank, couldn't we?" Giles suggested.

"Brilliant! Perhaps you're not so drunk after all, Giles. Next question. Everything depends on Steve checking his email regularly. Does he, Giles?"

"I don't know, but there's a good chance. He's what psychologists call a type-A personality. Always wants everything yesterday. But how he'll behave under these circumstances is anyone's guess. He'll be excited, nervous, busy meeting people, giving lectures, and so on. The sooner we get it to him, the better."

"Right. Okay, fingers crossed."

"So finally, Conrad, what about the fair *Aphrodite*? What will she do?

More than snooze, I assume?"

"You bet. She'll be the star. When I get your telephone call from Stockholm to say the Swedes want more evidence, I'll give her a prod over the Internet. She'll wake up and get to work."

"You mean she'll look for the second lot of evidence?"

Conrad nodded.

"How?"

"You'll see."

"Is that all you're going to say?"

"For now, yes. No point filling your head with unnecessary details. Something I learnt in the army."

"Oh, I get it. You're the five-star general now, and we're Corporal Butterfield and Private Cameron. Ours is not to reason why…"

"Rubbish, Giles! It just makes good sense, that's all. One thing we must talk about, though, is the question of timing. We must be sure that when *Aphrodite* wakes up, there'll be nobody around. We don't want Steve or his wife anywhere near. Any suggestions?"

Giles unfolded Steve's itinerary and looked at it apprehensively.

"That's a tough one. I think there's only one choice—when they're on their way to the ceremony."

"So late?"

"How else could be we be sure both of them are not there?"

"What time will that be?"

"About three forty-five. Any earlier and Marie-Claire might still be powdering her nose."

"And the ceremony starts when?"

"Four-thirty."

"Jesus! Forty-five minutes to connect with his laptop, find the evidence, show it to the Swedes, and stop the ceremony—if that's what it comes to."

"Oops!" Fiona gasped. "I've just thought of a problem. What if Steve has switched off his laptop before they depart? That's more than likely, isn't it?"

"Good point, Fiona. Why didn't you think of that, Giles? But no problem. I'll include some script that would automatically switch it on and open the programmes we need at exactly the right time."

"Brilliant! I'm in awe, Conrad. So, is that it for today?"

"It is indeed, Giles, and a damn good day it's been."

Long after Fiona had excused herself to retire for the night, the two brothers were still in the library.

"It's been so good to catch up with all your news, Giles," Conrad said wistfully. "Whenever I listen to your anecdotes about life in Magdalen, I almost wonder if I should have tried academia myself. But I know the reality is it would have driven me bonkers. I don't have the right type of brain."

Giles nodded in affirmation.

"I'm sure you're right, Conrad. You made the right choice, no doubt about it. University life can sound idyllic at times, I know. But there's as much stress, frustration, and disappointment as in any other walk of life. More cognac?"

"No thanks, I need to work tomorrow. And with that in mind, if you can give me those attachments in the morning, I'll start on the scripts straight away. I've told Christine—that's my PA—not to expect me for a few days. And oh yes, another point. Make a note that when I wake up *Aphrodite* in Steve's computer, your Mac must already be online in Stockholm. Okay?"

Giles gave a salute and clicked his heels

"Yesss-sir! Now, shall we follow Fiona's example?"

"Agreed."

Upon reaching the minstrel gallery at the top of the broad curved staircase, Giles paused to admire Conrad's collection of antiques in the entrance hall below—the Thomas Wagstaffe grandfather clock, still ticking in its third century; the George III inlaid mahogany bookcase, its shelves stacked with rare brooks bought in London auction houses; the eighteenth-century mirror from Italy with its open-scroll Baroque frame; and above them all a magnificent Murano glass chandelier.

"You've certainly got a lot to lose, Conrad. No qualms?"

"No qualms, Giles. And you?"

"Not a qualm in sight. Plenty of butterflies, but no qualms, because I know we're doing what's right."

"Here, here!"

Chapter Twenty-Three

Giles wasted no time putting together the bogus document that would hopefully grab Steve's attention despite the excitement of the occasion. After copying it together with a photograph of Steve's lab onto a CD, he had just dropped it onto the study desk when Conrad entered from breakfast, cup of coffee in hand.

"Morning, Giles. Done your stuff already in spite of a hangover? Good man. I've just told Malika I'll have all my meals up here until I've finished. When that's happened, I'll let you and Fiona know. But you can assume, I'll be here the entire weekend."

Conrad offered his hand for a parting handshake.

"That's when I'll emerge, Giles...and not before. So, see you then. Ciao."

That was the last they saw of each other until midday on Monday, when the telephone rang. As it stopped before he could get to it, Giles assumed Conrad had answered it upstairs in the study. He was right. A few minutes later, his brother came galloping down and stormed into the kitchen.

"Damn!" he exclaimed. "I thought it was going too smoothly, Giles. Believe it or not, I have to go to Durban immediately."

Giles dropped the shoes he was polishing and slumped onto a stool, assuming it was bad news about Helen's brother, still in hospital there.

"What's happened?"

"It was Christine, from the office. A hacker broke into our biggest client's server last night. The bank's top man insists I go there personally to sort it out. Unfortunately, I have no choice.

As our contract is up for renewal pretty soon, I need to keep him sweet…if it's not already a lost cause."

"When do you leave?"

"At once, I'm afraid. Malika, please don't touch anything in the study until I get back. Let the dust collect. Okay?"

Conrad was away for three precious days. When he arrived back, it was to everyone's enormous relief to learn that the problem had been fixed.

"So much for promotion letting me organise my own time!" he groaned wearily, hanging up his jacket in the entrance hall. "And it still hasn't finished. Today's Thursday, isn't it? Between now and Monday I need to write a damn report, and then on Tuesday I'll have to brief the CEO. What's the date today?"

"Twenty-fifth, Mr Conrad," Malika called from the laundry.

"And Steve's big day is the tenth," Giles added. "Just fifteen days away."

"Jesus! It's going to be touch and go, Giles. Let's hope there are no more surprises."

The following days were long and anxious ones for Giles and Fiona. On the few occasions Conrad emerged from his study, to go to the washroom or take a walk in the garden, he was lost in thought. Trying to read his body language became such a tormenting obsession that they started taking refuge in the library every time they heard him coming down the stairs. There was always the nagging worry that he would come up against an unexpected obstacle, or wouldn't be able to get it finished in time.

As a diversion, they immersed themselves in reading—newspapers, magazines, professional journals, books from the library, anything. But it was no good. Neither of them could concentrate on anything for very long. Next on Giles's list of panaceas was gardening. Even in Oxford this would have been a challenge, but in Camps Bay their lack of familiarity with the local plants risked a disaster. Eventually, they found that helping Malika with the household chores was the only activity that worked.

It was not until the following Sunday afternoon, December 5, as Giles was nodding off over several pairs of shoes he was supposed to be polishing, that Conrad leapt joyfully onto the terrace.

"Giles, watch out!" he yelled, as he frisbeed a CD in his direction. "The bugger's done at last. That's your copy."

Giles opened his eyes to see Conrad holding a bottle of champagne.

"It's wonderful to be out here after being locked up for so long. I'm sick of the sight of computer screens, code, books, and paper."

Giles collected the CD from the marble tiles.

"Is this it?"

"Yes, and I've even done a rehearsal. On Friday, while you and Fiona were cleaning the windows, I went to a second-hand store to get myself an iMac and an iBook. I gave each an email account and installed all the software we need. I set up the iBook to play the part of Steve's laptop, complete with a folder called 'Travel Notes' on the hard disk, and the iMac to take the part of my computer, which I'll continue to use from now on. Using your laptop, I then invented an email from you to Steve, hid *Adonis* and *Aphrodite* in the attachments you'd prepared, attached them to the email, and sent the lot to the iBook's address. A few minutes later, I pretended I was Steve and checked the inbox. The message from you was there. I opened it and had a quick look at the attachments. After a trip to the loo, I returned to your laptop, and to my relief found an email from *Adonis* in the inbox, complete with a copy of the 'Travel Notes' folder copied from the iBook. Then I went back to the iBook, looked for *Adonis*, and couldn't find him. Just as instructed, as soon as he'd done his job, he'd self-destructed. Next, I switched off the iBook and waited until three o'clock, which is when I'd set the script to switch the computer on again for this dummy run. Sure enough, right on time, the iBook lit up. Then, I woke up *Aphrodite* from my iMac over the Internet, and we were ready for the second stage."

"Conrad, you're a genius! If you weren't such an ugly brute, I'd kiss you."

"I'll do it instead," Fiona announced, cheerfully skipping onto the terrace. "No, on second thoughts, to be merciful, I shouldn't. I've been eating raw garlic while helping Malika with the pasta sauce. I overheard everything, Conrad. How wonderful! Congratulations!"

"Thanks, Fiona."

Conrad opened the bottle and filled three Champagne flutes. "To *Aphrodite* and *Adonis*!"

It was not long before Giles's delight at Conrad's progress was dampened by the thought of the ominous task that lay ahead. It was as if they had struggled up a mountainside, and now, having neared the summit, were faced with the prospect of jumping across a deep ravine for the final stage of their journey—without being certain they could make the distance.

"So, now we've got everything we need?" he asked, his face noticeably paler.

"That's right, Giles."

"And you're sure *Aphrodite* and *Adonis* can do their stuff?"

"That's right."

"All we have to do now is to send the of two of them on their way?"

"That's right."

"And we're definitely doing the right thing?"

"Correct."

"And…right now we're all shitting in our pants?"

"Ha! You can only speak for yourself there, Giles. Does he often use that sort of language in front of you, Fiona?"

"No, he doesn't actually," she replied, looking a little shocked. "I think it must be your bad influence, Conrad. To punish him, I'm going to give him that garlicky kiss, the one you were spared. Giles, come here and take your punishment."

She grabbed him by the collar and planted a wet one on his nose.

"He hasn't liked garlic since his time in Liverpool, have you, Giles? It doesn't go too well with Blind Scouse, Finny Addy, or Wet Nelly."

"Is that supposed to be food?" Conrad scoffed. "Sounds more like a gang of Aussie bushrangers!"

"Now listen here, you two," Giles retorted, "you never hear me slanging the food of Scotland, do you? But since you've provoked me, if you think a haggis…"

"Only teasing, Giles," Fiona giggled, tweaking him on the chin.

The merriment continued until Malika arrived from the kitchen pushing a silver trolley bearing a lemon cheesecake.

"I've been waiting for this moment," she said with a twinkle in her eyes. "I prepared it yesterday, when everyone was busy, and left it in the fridge. I'll go and get some napkins and the rest."

"And while you're at it, get yourself a glass, Malika," Conrad called after her. "The rules about not drinking on the job don't apply at times like this."

It was almost an hour before Malika wheeled the trolley away with the empty serving dish and bottle to continue with her sauces. The others had now settled down, sitting side by side on the tiles with their backs against the balustrade.

Conrad emptied his glass, leisurely savouring the last drop.

"Ah, nectar! Okay, well now we've got the celebrations out of our system, it's back to reality, I'm afraid. There's still a bit to do. We should resist the temptation to rush into action. As there are still five days to go, let's give ourselves tomorrow to make sure we haven't forgotten anything. Spend the day just thinking, and rethinking, and re-rethinking again. And no taking it easy! No magazines, no music, no books, no TV, nothing but cogitation about what could go wrong, even the most unlikely scenarios. We can't afford to overlook a single detail. We each need to go through the entire sequence of events time and again. Imagine we're in Steve's position, put ourselves in the shoes of the Nobel people, speculate about what might happen that we haven't prepared for, what might go wrong, even a one-in-a-million chance. Because once I've sent *Adonis* and *Aphrodite* on their way, we've reached the point of no return. There'll be no going back for them, or for us."

Giles and Fiona looked at each other uneasily.

"And when do you plan to send them off?" Fiona asked.

"It seems Steve has a press conference in Stockholm at 11:00 a.m. on Tuesday. So I'll send the email to him at around twelve-thirty our time. If he goes back to the hotel after lunch and checks his emails that afternoon, with any luck we should have his 'Travel Notes' folder before sunset."

Chapter Twenty-Four

By late afternoon the following day, everything seemed to be going to plan. To be on the safe side, Conrad had done two further cold runs, both of which had gone without a hitch. While he had been doing so, Giles and Fiona had re-examined the route in Steve's computer that *Aphrodite* would need to follow to uncover the incriminating evidence in Stockholm. To their relief, no unexpected problems were encountered. If their theory was correct, she should find it exactly where Fiona had reckoned.

After that, they did their best to think of other potential problems. They had been at it for almost an hour—Fiona stretched out on the sofa, Conrad in his easy chair by the fireplace, Giles alternating between walking around the garden and sitting on the kitchen doorstep—when Giles came running through the kitchen howling in despair. As he stumbled into the living room, his face was drawn with anguish.

"Conrad, Fiona, I've had a ghastly thought!" he panted. "When *Adonis* makes a copy of Steve's 'Travel Notes' folder to send to me, what if his laptop gives it a new date? If that happens, it won't be any use to us. What we receive *must* have the same dates as the original. They're absolutely crucial."

Fiona opened her eyes to see Conrad with his head in his hands.

"It's only just occurred to me," Giles continued. "We know, thanks to Fiona, that when a folder is sent as an email attachment, it keeps the original dates. At least it does with the operating system in these Apple computers. We don't know about PCs. But what about this situation? Do you know, Conrad?"

Conrad parted his fingers to stare between them into the fireplace.

"I don't think there's a problem, Giles. But I have to admit I'm a bit out of my depth. Never had reason to think about it. But let's not panic. Go and take a look at what *Adonis* emailed to you in my dummy runs. That'll give us the answer."

Giles stood his ground, looking uncomfortable.

"Is there another problem?"

"Sort of, Conrad. Well, more than sort of. You see, after I'd opened those emails, I trashed them."

"And I you emptied the trash too, I suppose?"

Giles nodded sheepishly.

"Jesus, Giles! You always were obsessional about cleaning up after yourself. I've never understood…."

"Sorry, but I always do, ever since being told the trash can takes up memory."

"So it does, but not…okay let's keep cool. Duplicate a folder in your laptop, any folder that's already there, and see what happens. That should be enough. After all, that's exactly what *Adonis* will do. Go and grab your laptop, while I go for a pee."

Having returned to find the room empty, Conrad was pouring himself a drink when Giles lurched in again, this time looking more distraught than ever.

"It's not there! Can you believe it? It's gone! I left it by the front door, and it's disappeared."

"WHAT!"

"I was sitting on the front doorstep before, writing a few letters while chatting to Malika. She was taking the shirts off the line. When she'd finished, I got up to help her take them into the kitchen. From there, I wandered into the back garden to feed the goldfish. Ten minutes later, I suddenly thought about that folder and came dashing in here."

Conrad closed his eyes.

"Giles! You left your laptop on the front doorstep? I can't believe this. Your email with the attachments containing *Adonis* and *Aphrodite* is in there…two very illegal pieces of malicious code addressed to one of this year's Nobel Laureates. A highly respected Oxford don and the Vice President of an IT security firm are just about to join the criminal class, and lo and behold one of them leaves his laptop containing all the evidence on the front doorstep. Brilliant! See you in Pollsmoor!"

"Where's that?"

"Never mind. Was anyone around—the neighbour's gardener, children, a delivery van, the postman?"

"There were a few lads in the road, kicking a ball around."

"Still there?"

"No."

"Jesus Christ! How could you be so stupid, Giles? Was it switched on?"

"Asleep."

"Just like bloody you!"

Giles nodded in silence, prompting Conrad to swill down his whisky and toss the tumbler into the fireplace in a rare display of real anger.

"Where's Malika?" he thundered. "Perhaps she saw somebody. If not, we'll have to call the police. Think of that—asking the cops to search for the evidence of your own crime! Malika! Malika!"

"I'll go and look for her," Fiona offered, having returned from the terrace.

As it happened, Malika was already on her way. She skipped into the room with a broad smile on her handsome chubby face, carrying Giles's laptop before her like a tray prepared for afternoon tea.

"Here's your little Boris, Mr Giles, and he's got some very good news for you. Haven't you, Boris?"

The three of them looked at each other aghast.

Malika propped the laptop against her bosom, and gave the top of the screen an affectionate pat.

"Can I sit down?"

"Of course!" Conrad urged, patting a cushion.

"Thank you, Mr Conrad. When I heard what Mr Giles was saying about the dates and so on, I collected Boris from the front door and took him to the kitchen. I put him on the ironing board, woke him up, made a new folder on the desktop, waiting a short while, and then made a copy of it. And here they are...the two of them. And as you can see, if you come closer, the second one is exactly the same as the first. Each one says it was made today at 16:17 hours and 26 seconds. So you see, everything's okay. When you copy a folder in one of these computers, it keeps its dates. So you can all relax!"

Giles dropped onto the sofa in relief, while Conrad and Fiona looked at her dumbfounded.

"How on earth did you know how to do that, Malika?" Conrad asked.

"My little Jabu's got a computer. It's very old, always stopping and giving him problems. Makes him cry a lot, you know. But he's learning. He's very proud of what he can do and likes to show me. He's taught me how to make folders and do some other things. So, there you are. I'll leave Boris with you now, and get on with those shirts."

Giles sprang up.

"Oh no you won't, Malika, not a chance! If we jump into the Saab, there's enough time to buy your little Jabu a brand-new laptop before the store closes—one of the very latest, complete with a mouse and a printer. You can help me choose, Fiona. Come on, let's go!

"Conrad, you can finish the ironing. It'll be good for you... occupational therapy."

Chapter Twenty-Five

Conrad did not appear the following day until the aroma from Malika's stir-fry and the clattering of china had left him in no doubt that lunch was ready. The meal was a subdued occasion, very different from the usual lively chatter. Sensing the tenseness of the atmosphere, Malika kept out of the way, tidying up the kitchen before moving into the garden to cut some flowers. Giles tried some light conversation to try and take their minds off his laptop, waiting in the library with *Adonis* and *Aphrodite* on the launching pad.

"Heard from Helen again, Conrad?" he uttered almost inaudibly.

"Yes, got an email. Said she'll be another two weeks. Tony's developed a complication of some sort."

"Sorry. Difficult time for her."

"Yes. They're very close."

"Pity I can't see her."

"Yes."

"Or Guy, for that matter."

"Yes. Sorry about that. But you know how much he loves camping. Wants to be an Eagle Scout."

"Once an Eagle, always an Eagle. Isn't that what they say?" Fiona managed, feeling obliged to contribute.

"That's it, Fiona. Once an Eagle."

"I'm sure he'll get there," Giles added. "He's a real high-flyer."

"Clever."

"Yes, that too. I agree."

"No, I meant you, Giles. Eagle scout…high-flyer. Very clever!"

"Ah, so I was! Must come naturally. Hope he likes the book."

"I'm sure he will."

"Not too serious?"

"No…he'll love it, Giles. Good choice."

"Is everything okay now with the bank in Durban, Conrad?" Fiona enquired.

"Yes, thanks. All sorted."

A long silence followed while Fiona replenished their glasses with mineral water, all alcoholic drinks having been forbidden by Conrad until the ordeal was over.

"Jesus!" he gasped after emptying his glass in one go. "I don't know about you two, but I'm getting more neurotic by the minute. As no more glitches in the software have occurred to us, why don't we just send the two buggers off now and have done with?"

After agreeing there was no point in dragging out the agony, they moved to the library and closed the door so as not to be disturbed. Fiona rested against a bookcase with her fingers crossed behind her back, trying to look calm. Giles, hands in pockets juggling keys and coins, stared out of the window at nothing in particular. Conrad sat on the corner of the mahogany table and laid his hand gently on the laptop's mouse.

"Okay, Giles?"

"Okay."

"Okay, Fiona?"

"Yes."

"Both ready to cross the line to become hackers?"

"Come on, get on with it," Giles urged.

Conrad clicked the mouse.

"Off you go, my beauties. Bon voyage! Now it's in the hands of the gods—a god and a goddess, to be precise."

Conrad jumped off the table and opened the door.

"Okay, let's have some coffee. Better be decaf in my case. I've had enough palpitations to last a lifetime…in fact, almost to finish one!"

Most of the afternoon was spent on Conrad's new tennis court. After losing three straight sets to Fiona, Giles suggested they should switch to chess on the terrace, believing his chances would be better. He was wrong.

"Checkmate!" she cried triumphantly less than twenty minutes later, after losing only two pawns and a bishop.

"Well done, Fiona!" Conrad roared from the library, busy rearranging his books. "I'll not forget this afternoon's pleasures. So pleased you could accompany Giles. Could you put the kettle on now, dear? And while she's doing that, Giles, why don't you put the pieces back—the chess pieces, that is, not what's left of your ego—and then take a look in your inbox. *Adonis* might have sent you something by now."

Giles returned looking glum, his trouser pockets turned inside out.

"Nothing but spam," he groaned.

From then on, Fiona checked his inbox on the hour. By the time the grandfather clock in the entrance hall was chiming midnight, Conrad's nerves had reached breaking point.

"Jesus!" he screeched. "Here's something none of us thought of. I didn't programme *Adonis* to let us know if he couldn't find the folder. What if Steve's deleted it by now or changed its name for some reason? If nothing's arrived by the morning, that'll be that, I'm afraid. We'll never know. And I'm beginning to think I don't bloody care! Let's get some kip."

After a restless night, Giles was up before the others. He crept downstairs, trying unsuccessfully to avoid a couple of creaky floorboards, and went straight into the library to check his inbox. To his great relief, he found that *Adonis* had done his job. The email was there, complete with a copy of Steve's 'Travel Notes' folder. He opened it at once to look for the evidence he'd been expecting, and had only just closed it again, when Conrad called from the minstrel gallery.

"Is that you down there, Giles?"

"Er…yes, it is, Conrad. Good morning. Sorry, tried not to disturb you."

"No problem. Any news?"

"Er…yes. It's here, complete with what we've been waiting for. Good old *Adonis*."

"Thank God for that. Were your predictions correct?"

"Fiona's really, but…yes."

"You've got the evidence we need then?"

"That's right."

"Wonderful! You don't sound very excited. Is there a problem?"

"No…nothing."

"Sure?"

"Yes. No problem at all. I guess it's because I'll soon be on my way. Bit nervous. It's starting to hit me."

"Stop worrying. You'll be fine. The evidence will speak for itself, won't it?"

"Yes, that's right. It will, won't it?"

As Malika was not expected until seven o'clock, they rustled up some scrambled eggs, smoked salmon, toast, and a pot of tea.

"Are you all right, Giles?" Fiona asked across the kitchen table. "You're extremely quiet this morning."

Giles looked at his watch.

"Yes, I am, thanks. It's just that if *Aphrodite* proves us right, in about 60 hours from now one of the biggest shows on earth will be thrown into an unimaginable crisis, with the news reverberating around the world, and us at the epicentre. It's a bit terrifying, isn't it?"

"I think it's important not to look too far ahead," Fiona suggested, offering the toast rack. "Take one step at a time. And for the first one, why don't you show us the 'Travel Notes' folder *Adonis* sent? I'm sure Conrad's as keen as I am to see it, aren't you, Conrad?"

"You bet!"

"I'll go and fetch Boris then, while you sweep the table. Mice don't like toast crumbs, at least not this type of mouse."

When Fiona returned, she rearranged the chairs so as to sit between the two men.

"Okay, here's the folder *Adonis* sent," she started eagerly. "I'll open it to show you the list of files inside…like so. As you can see, one of them is a Word document called 'Achilles'. You can also see it says it was created on July 28, when Steve says he was at a meeting in New York. You can also see that there are several other files in the folder. Some of them were created before July 28, and others were created more recently. Now, I'll close the folder, highlight it with a click, go to *File* in the menu bar at the top, then to *Get Info* in the dropdown menu, and select *General Information*. There you are. Now, what does it say about when the 'Travel Notes' folder was last altered in any way?"

Conrad leaned forward. "It says it was on the twenty-eighth of July."

"Correct. So…that's supposed to be the most recent date on which anything was added to the folder, taken out of it, or deleted. And it's the same date as the one on which the 'Achilles' file was supposed to have been created. But if July 28 is the most recent date on which anything was added to the folder, how did the files that were created since then get in there?"

Conrad stared at the screen.

"Bloody good point! You tell me."

"The only way that could have happened is like this. The other files were already in the folder when Steve created a bogus 'Achilles' file describing fictitious work on *Deidamia* to send to Hank Weinberg. To make it look as if he'd created it before he went to the Sorrento symposium, he had to get his laptop to give it a phony date. There was only way of doing that, which was to turn the computer's clock back to the twenty-eighth of July last year before saving the file. Next, he put the file into his 'Travel Notes' folder, closed the folder, and restored the computer's clock to the correct date and time—all in that order. The result was that the computer recorded the twenty-eighth of July for both the 'Achilles' file's *Date Created* and the 'Travel Notes' folder's *Date Modified*. But all the files that were already in the folder before he started kept their original dates and times, because they hadn't been changed."

Conrad looked at her in utter admiration.

"Hence, the seemingly impossible situation of a folder containing files that were created more recently than the last occasion on which the folder's contents were changed."

"Fiona, that's brilliant. Fantastic! We've got the bastard. We have got him by the nuts."

Conrad jumped up to dance the conga, singing as he went.

"We've got him by the nuts-nuts! We've got him by the nuts-nuts! Dadaah-dah-da…dadaah-dah-da. We've got him by the nuts-nuts! We've…"

At that moment Malika entered through the front door, earlier than usual, stopping in the entrance hall to put on the white canvas plimsolls she always wore in the house.

"Morning, Mr Conrad, Mr Giles, Miss Fiona," she called cheerily. "You're up early too, I see. My little Jabu couldn't sleep. Insisted on showing me how his new computer works. I've never seen him happier. Thank you so much, Mr Giles."

Conrad danced towards her without the lyrics to plant a kiss on her cheek.

"Mr Conrad!" she shrieked, dusting herself down. "What were you saying in the kitchen about nuts? I got some lovely Brazils in the market yesterday, if you'd like some."

"Forget about computers and nuts for now, Malika. We've reason to celebrate again. Today is a very special occasion. A champagne breakfast awaits you. Off to the cellar! The choice is yours."

A few minutes later, Malika reappeared decked in a crisp floral housecoat and flame-coloured head-wrap, soapstone earrings, and matching necklace. Conrad rubbed his hands in appreciation.

"Wow! You look splendid Malika. And what a choice!"

He caressed the bottle in the silver ice bucket she'd presented to him.

"J.C. Le Roux Scintilla! My, you must have been reading my latest copy of Decanter."

"Well, you did say it was very special day, Mr Conrad."

"And so it is, Malika."

After filling four glasses, Conrad raised his for a toast.

"Here's to a successful trip, Giles. Jesus, that reminds me! I almost forgot. Malika, sorry, take a sip then get the travel agent on the blower. Their out-of-hours number's in the book. Giles is off to the frozen north tomorrow. We need to book his flight. But hold on. That raises a point. Will you be going to Sweden too, Fiona?"

"Of course, she will," Giles answered. "She's more than earned it. And besides, I couldn't…"

"No, Giles, I don't agree," Fiona interrupted. "Thank you, but I don't need a reward. I joined you in Washington because I wanted to help, for no other reason. Now that I've done my bit, it would be a mistake to take me along. I really appreciate the gesture, but I'd get in the way, cramp your style. You should go on your own."

"Well said, Fiona," Conrad followed, clapping enthusiastically. "She's absolutely right, Giles. She's done a magnificent job, but as always what she says makes good sense. As there are no direct flights from here to Stockholm, however, why don't you do the first leg together? Then Fiona can catch a connection to London, while you take one to Stockholm.

"Malika, they'll need the earliest SAA flight tomorrow morning, probably to Frankfurt would be my guess. Business class, or if it's not available, make it First. Giles will need to arrive in good shape. And he'll need a hotel in Stockholm. Make it the Sheraton. That's where I always stay, and it's in an ideal position for this job. If Fiona's flight gets into London late at night, book a room for her in Heathrow. Everything goes on my account. The lot. Here, I'll give you the details."

After Conrad had found a pen and scribbled his account number on Malika's sleeve, they took their glasses into the library.

"Would you believe it?" Giles exclaimed, walking towards the bookcase on the far wall. "The first book I set my eyes on is Dad's copy of the original Cranwell edition of Lawrence's

'Seven Pillars of Wisdom'—the same Seven Pillars that are now just a stone's throw from MECCAR in Wadi Rum. Isn't that amazing! I haven't looked at it in years."

He prized the book from between its much heavier neighbours and pensively flicked through its yellowing pages.

"You know, if I were religious, I'd think somebody up there was sending me messages."

"What do you mean?" Fiona asked.

"This may sound crazy, but I feel as if I've been given a special mission in life, a mission on behalf of the great scholars of the ancient Islamic world—men like Ibrahim al-Fazari, Thabit ibn Qurra, and Abul Wafa. You and Conrad have never heard of them, but they were centuries ahead of Europe. We were illiterate and ignorant, when they were studying astronomy, mathematics, medicine, physics, and much more. We owe so much to them. But now their huge contribution to human progress is known only to historians. They're not getting the credit they deserve. Effectively, we've stolen their achievements.

"Exactly the same thing is happening with MECCAR. Ahmad Sharif's brilliant work, the discovery of *Achilles*, is being buried by the falsehood that it took Western genius and technology to unlock the gene's potential by inventing *Deidamia*. Poor Ahmad is dead and Steve's about to get the Nobel Prize. If we don't put a stop to it, before we know where we are, the Americans will be claiming they've ridded mankind of the scourge of cancer despite the best efforts of a bunch of Arab goatherds. But not if I have my way!"

"It's certainly a good cause," Conrad replied. "I'm with you there. But I'm not a believer in the idea that some of us are somehow chosen for a grand mission in life. What did T.E. Lawrence say? 'All men dream, but not equally. Those who dream by night in the rusty recesses of their minds wake in the day to find it was vanity. But the dreamers of the day are dangerous men, for they may act their dreams with open eyes.'"

"Very impressive, Conrad, except I think they were 'dusty' recesses, not 'rusty' ones. I don't think I am dreaming. I think it all started when you chose to remain in Slindon with your rugby chums, leaving me to go off to Cairo with Mum and Dad. Perhaps there was a reason for that."

"Ha! As the Irish chiropodist said to the young lady, 'Your fate was in me hands.' Sorry, Giles, I find that a bit hard to swallow. And as for that book of Dad's being an omen of some sort, I recall the last time you thought you were getting messages. Do you remember? It was when I was trying to talk you out of moving south. Magdalen had to be your destiny, you said. 'I'll be among buildings designed by Giles Gilbert Scott and George Bodley,' you said, 'the two that created Liverpool's Anglican Cathedral, whose great tower I can see, and whose bells I can hear, through the window of my office. It couldn't be a coincidence,' you said. And we all know what happened. By your own admission, you're a a bit of a square peg in a round hole in Oxford."

"But he wouldn't have met me, would he?" Fiona added with a smile.

"I can't deny that, Fiona. He was certainly a lucky man there. But have you had any other supposed omens, Giles, or is spotting Dad's book on the shelf the only one?"

Conrad smirked in Fiona's direction with a wink, only to receive a disapproving frown in return. She had believed in premonitions ever since her gran had claimed to have seen the face of a snarling Scottish wildcat in the waters of Loch Insh in the Cairngorms, and then again in her bedroom window in nearby Kingussie after being woken up by thunder in the early hours. Everyone had poked fun at her, until a few days later Fiona's young cousin was attacked by a large cat in the local Kinveachy Forest. The police thought it was a domestic cat, but she was adamant it was too big for that.

While the incident was running through Fiona's mind, Giles moved to the window to gaze at the stars, still visible in the early-morning sky, before answering Conrad's question.

"Yes, as a matter of fact there have. I was about to tell you. Listen to this. On three occasions during this saga, I've found myself mesmerised by the waning moon, which is as near as you can get to the ancient symbol of Islam. On the first occasion, I was on Christ Church Meadow after a sleepless night, during which I'd been tormented by my doubts about Steve and his computer programme. On the second, it was just after reading in my newspaper over breakfast that Steve was to be given a Nobel. And then it was there again, bigger than ever, when I departed from Magdalen to catch the flight to Washington. Three times, and on each one I'd been thinking about Steve. Now, if that's not very odd, I'm a bloody…"

"Lunatic!" Conrad scoffed. "But you've seen a waning moon many times in your life. We all have. So what?"

"But it was the timing, Conrad, always after being preoccupied with Steve or something to do with him. And what's more, on those occasions it was so bright that my eyes were glued to it. It was as if it was trying to speak to me. It was weird, eerie. Each time it felt as if ice-cold water was trickling down my spine."

"Well, when you put it like that, it does sound a bit strange, I must admit."

"On top of which, the very place where MECCAR was built in Jordan, Wadi Rum, is known locally as the Valley of the Moon."

"Really?"

"Yes. And now I'll tell you the best part. Do you know what day it is today?"

"Of course, I do. The eighth of December, two days before Stockholm's Nobel Day. How could I not?"

"And to the likes of you, that's all it is, yes?"

Conrad nodded.

"Well, to about one and half billion people on this planet, today is a very important day, a very important day indeed."

"In what way?"

"It's Al Hijrah."

Conrad looked mystified.

"What on earth's…?"

"It's the first day of the first month of the Islamic calendar. It marks the day, corresponding to the sixteenth of July in AD 622 in ours, when Mohammad made his historic journey from Mecca to Medina. All Islamic dates are expressed relative to that day, the birth of Islam, just like ours are expressed relative to the birth of…"

"*J-e-e-sus Christ!!*"

Chapter Twenty-Six

Once the SAA flight to Frankfurt was on its way, Fiona started to prepare mentally for the meeting with Sir Quentin that would likely follow her return to the College. Partly out of a genuine concern for the well-being of his colleagues, but also to ensure everything was above board, he was in the habit of inviting anyone who'd been absent for more than a week to his spacious office in the Lodgings for a chat over a cup of tea by the fireplace. It was now four weeks since she'd dropped everything to fly to Washington, during which she'd called Jane only once, from her mobile phone, when Conrad was in Durban, to say that her influenza had been complicated by bronchitis and the GP had prescribed penicillin. The day after Conrad's return, she had emailed Jane to say she'd had to stop the tablets on account of a rash, further delaying her return, and then again to decline her offer to deliver some shopping to the flat, explaining that a neighbour had already done so. She abhorred this sort of dishonesty, and could feel herself blushing at the mere thought of it. But Giles had agreed there had been no alternative. For his part, he had kept to the story that he was at Georgetown University working on an NIH grant application at the Fisher Center. As some of the budget from such a grant would normally go to the College, he'd been confident of Sir Quentin's continued support. The prospect of having to pretend that the application had failed in five or six months did not concern him.

Feeling weary after all the excitement and effort in Cape town, Fiona had already decided she would text Conrad from Frankfurt to accept his offer of a night at Heathrow, from where she would travel by train via Paddington station in the morning. Upon arriving at Oxford, she would buy some sandwiches, a bottle of milk, and a box of Sir Quentin's favourite biscuits from the Covered Market, before walking to Longwall Street, taking the quiet route via Brasenose Lane and Cattle Street in the hope of avoiding any familiar faces. Upon entering the College grounds, she'd follow the path past the Grove Building and the Deer Park to her office in the New Building. In that way she would avoid both the Porters' Lodge and the St Swithun's Quad, where Jane might be at her window. For the rest of the day, she would lie low in her office, going through her mail, before sneaking out after sunset. The weekend would be spent at home, living on frozen food and occupying herself with housework, listening to music, and reading Umberto Eco's 'Il Nome della Rosa' in preparation for her next Italian lesson.

Her biggest worry was whether Aram would be in the lab. If so, she would gesture that she had laryngitis and lost her voice, followed by a bout of coughing to make sure he kept his distance.

While she had been working all this out, Giles had been trying to take his mind off Stockholm by preparing for the students' next practical class on DNA fingerprinting. It was too late to fit it into the Michelmas term, but he was sure there would be another opportunity in January. This time, Fiona would show them how the technique can be used to solve paternity disputes.

As soon as he had drafted something for Jane to print as a hand-out, he read it to her.

"Okay, Fiona, is this a good time?"

"Yes, thanks. I've got that other business off my mind now. Fire ahead."

"Here goes. 'You have been given nine drops of blood. Number one is from the mother of twin boys. Numbers two and three are from the twins. Number four is from the lady's husband. Numbers five, six, seven, eight, and nine are from her known lovers during the month of conception. Isolate DNA from each sample and determine which of the men is the father of the twins, and whether the twins are identical or non-identical.'"

Fiona looked through her diary to find a convenient slot after Christmas. She would need a full day to organise the equipment and select the frozen blood samples from the freezer, a couple of hours the next day for the class itself, and finally another hour or two to go through the students' reports.

Once that had been sorted out, they ran through Giles's plans for Stockholm. Having done her usual research in the villa, Fiona knew that the Chairman of the Nobel Committee was a Professor Gunnar Eriksson, an elderly cardiovascular physiologist of formidable intelligence and critical powers. Having stood his ground successfully during several protracted disputes among the Karolinska Institute's hierarchy, he was clearly also a man not easily persuaded. His attitude towards Giles would be very different from Hank Weinberg's, but no less daunting nevertheless.

What a pity they hadn't been able to leave Cape Town a few days earlier, Fiona lamented. If it hadn't been for Conrad having to go to Durban, Giles would have had more time to prepare for the ordeal. But there was no point complaining. Tomorrow was Nobel Day. And that was that. Nothing could change it.

They agreed that first thing in the morning Giles would telephone Gunnar Eriksson from the Sheraton to request an urgent meeting. As the top man in the day's event apart from the royals, he would have such a busy schedule ahead of him that Giles knew he would have little chance of success unless his introduction was spot on. His mind drifted back to the other important calls he had made in Washington. He had done pretty well then, hadn't he? So why not now? But despite many attempts to reassure himself, he had been worrying relentlessly since bidding Conrad farewell.

After prompting Fiona for her views on the matter, she did her best to lighten his mood, fearing it was getting on top of him.

"Let me mull that one over," she said, burying her head in her hands. "I think a profoundly solemn tone will be essential, like a vicar giving a sermon. At the same time, you'll need to sound very professional, totally trustworthy, and of course super-confident with not the faintest hint of uncertainty or edginess, like a prominent prosecuting barrister summing up a case that's cut and dried. A subtle overtone of confidentiality would also be appropriate, not forgetting a touch of empathy, recognising the difficult position you'll be putting the poor man in."

"Are you…?"

"Hold on, I haven't finished yet. Moreover, you should start slowly, I would advise, gently and rather quietly, almost stealthily, and then progressively raise the tenor and pace of your diction, until it has metamorphosed into what will sound to his subconscious like a command he cannot refuse."

"Finished now?"

"Almost. And keep in mind he's not English. So, pronounce your words carefully, without overdoing it of course, and avoid fancy words he may not be familiar with. How does that sound?"

"Like something that would have given Sir Lawrence Olivier stage fright!"

"Sorry, but you asked for my advice," she giggled. "So, I gave it to you."

"Thanks very much! I know, why don't you do the intro instead? As he wouldn't know where you're calling from, you could say you're my PA, and you're with me. Might impress him. No hold on, that wouldn't work! This is supposed to be secret, isn't it?"

Fiona turned to look at him sympathetically.

"Sorry, Giles. There's no way out of this one."

"Afraid so."

"Why don't you try and forget about it, until you wake up in the morning. Then do a few quick rehearsals in your usual way, and get it over with."

"Good idea."

"So, assuming he does agree to see this strange English professor who's just arrived from nowhere, let's consider what will happen next."

They agreed that Giles should take his laptop to the meeting to show Gunnar Eriksson how the copy of the 'Travel Notes' folder from Steve's laptop had the impossibility of containing files that had been created more recently than the latest date on which anything had been added to or removed from the folder. If Gunnar Eriksson didn't want to take the matter further, out of suspicion of Giles's motives, practical considerations, national prestige, or whatever, it would be the end of the story. There would be nothing they could do about it. But if he took it seriously enough to ask for more evidence, Giles would give Conrad a call and find some way of connecting the laptop to the Internet.

As the aircraft descended through the northern darkness, they could feel the tension rising as never before. The sight of so much snow after the warmth and sunshine of Cape Town, broken only by the crystal twinkling of lights along the roads, brought home to them how much the world they were about to enter differed from the one they'd left behind. Tucked away in Conrad's comfortable villa, they had been in a sanctuary, isolated, protected, undisturbed, pampered by Malika's cooking and attention. Only they had known their whereabouts. But very soon they would be exposed and unprotected, among other people once again, and all the work of the past few days would be put to a brutal test on an international stage. The biggest theatre in Sweden's year was just hours away, and Giles was about to create mayhem under its floodlights. It was terrifying.

Sitting by the aircraft's window, Fiona's eyes were fixed ahead as her mind moved to the prospect of their parting in Frankfurt. Deep down, she longed to remain by Giles's side. But she knew she had made the right decision. Conrad's immediate acceptance of her argument had been proof of that, hadn't it?

Turning towards the window to wipe a tear, she caught sight of the moon high in the sky.

"Giles," she whispered, finding his hand under the newspaper and squeezing it tightly, "look outside. Is that how bright it was on those other occasions? Do you think it can mean anything, the fact that it's waxing this time, not waning? That it's sort of turned its back on us? Or am I being stupid?"

For the rest of the flight, their minds pulsated with the same question. Was it possible something had happened that they didn't know about, something that could ruin their plans? Could they even be heading for a tragedy?

Chapter Twenty-Seven

Having received the pre-arranged text from Fiona to say she had arrived safely at Heathrow, Giles finished his second slice of kanelbullar in Arlanda airport's coffee bar and donned the woollen sweater and scarf that Malika had added to his suitcase at Conrad's suggestion. The short walk from the aircraft had been enough to tell him how much he was going to need them in the coming days.

As he collected some bank notes from a cash machine and stuffed them into his top pocket, not bothering to count them or collect the receipt, he felt strangely alone, much more so than after his arrival in Washington. How would he fare without Fiona's companionship, ideas, and support? How would she manage, wondering what was happening to him in Stockholm? Would she bump into Sir Quentin or Jane upon arriving in the College and be faced with the task of describing her supposed illness, or of coping with Jane's suspicions about the real reason for their sudden disappearance?

Checking into the Sheraton after the thirty-minute taxi drive down the E4 highway, he learnt that Conrad, true to form, had instructed Malika to reserve a room overlooking Lake Mälaren, the fresh water lake that sojourns through the city on its way to the Baltic Sea. After a brief text to express his gratitude, he joined a group of businessmen in the elevator as far as the fourth floor. The view of the Old Town across the water, its glassy surface broken only by the gentle wake of a solitary slow-moving ferry, was just what he needed to settle his nerves. The simple but elegant tower of Östberg's iconic City Hall, in which Steve's banquet and ball were soon to be held, seemed almost within touching distance. He raised his eyes to address at the moon defiantly as it traversed the three golden crowns.

"Whatever you're telling me this time, I don't care!" he whispered, conscious of a maid in the corridor outside. "I might make a damn fool of himself, walk into trouble, disgrace the College, whatever. Who knows? But what the hell! I haven't come this far to turn back."

Charged with energy, and for once not bothering to unpack, he buttoned up his jacket with Malika's scarf tied tightly around his neck, and set off to get some Baltic air into his lungs.

Pausing for a moment outside the hotel's entrance, he compared the panorama with the view from Conrad's terrace. There was no doubt his villa was in a wonderful spot. To listen to the sea crashing against the distant rocks at night and watch the trees swaying in the salty breeze could be exhilarating. But the clean lines of Stockholm's simple buildings, its clearly marked cycle lanes, its tidy windows, its uncluttered pavements, and the pervading sense of calm and civil order were just what he needed right now. Nordic architecture didn't move him like a Gothic church or Venetian piazza, but it did have a beauty of its own—sober, solid, sensible, reassuring.

His hands deep in his jacket pockets, he made his way at a steady pace towards the nearby Vasa bridge. As he walked its length, disturbing a cormorant from one of the lamp posts on the way, he stopped to admire the City Hall once again, and tried to picture the preparations he assumed would still be in progress. Upon reaching the Old Town, he headed along Slottskajen to look at the Royal Palace, wondering how the king was going respond if Gunnar Eriksson was moved to stop the ceremony. From there, it was the long route back over the Strömbron to get a good view of the Grand Hotel, where Steve and Marie-Claire were staying. He wondered if they were still awake, unaware of *Aphrodite* sleeping in their midst. And how would Steve be feeling? Conrad had been right when he'd said no right-minded scientist has the Nobel Prize as an ambition. It wasn't something you could aim for. You didn't get one because you'd published the most papers, or even for doing the best experimental research. No, usually, it was for a single idea or discovery that after many years had changed medical practice forever. Whatever had been behind it—a flash of inspiration, dogged perseverance, an insightful interpretation of someone else's data, or just good fortune—it had been the foundation upon which everything else had been built, the apex of an inverted pyramid, one that had grown by a slow process of accretion to which hundreds, sometimes thousands, of other scientists had contributed. For this reason, by the time they received their call from Stockholm, most Laureates had long suspected they were in line for the honour. But for Steve it had been very different. Whether or not *Deidamia* was truly his invention, it had all happened so suddenly he must have been struggling to cope with the reality.

Rubbing his hands in the cold air, he saw it was already half an hour past midnight. Just enough time to call Fiona before she retired. But this was not the place to do it. He'd been dreading this moment ever since she'd disappeared from view in Frankfurt airport. For throughout the long journey from Cape Town, a dark secret had been tormenting him. There had been no possibility of revealing it in the villa, but he had known he'd have to do so pretty soon. More than once during the flight, he'd almost picked up the courage, only to pull out at the last second. But now he had no choice. He had to get on with it.

He returned to the Sheraton dragging his feet via Strömgatan along the waterfront. After pausing in the lobby with the idea of giving himself some Dutch courage in the bar, he decided against it. Better get it over with, he thought.

Once in the bedroom, he readied himself for what might be in store.

"Fiona, it's me," he said meekly. "Good flight?"

"Yes thanks. And you?"

"Yes. How's the hotel?"

"Very nice. You have a wonderful brother."

"You can say that again. You should see the view from my window."

"You sound a wee bit quiet, Giles Are you okay?"

"Probably because I've just returned from stretching my legs. It's cold out there after Cape town. Fiona…there's something I need to tell you, something to get off my chest."

"Oh! Fire away, then."

"Do you remember in the villa, how I crept downstairs in the morning to see if *Adonis* had sent me the 'Travel Notes' folder?"

"Of course."

"And you know how later on you collected Boris to show Conrad how the dates were impossible, how there were files that had been…"

"Yes."

"Well, you see…it wasn't exactly like that."

"What do you mean?"

"Are you sitting down?"

"On the loo, actually."

"That may well turn out to be the best place."

"What on earth are you…?"

"Well, you see, dear, what you showed Conrad wasn't exactly what *Adonis* sent."

"In what way?"

"The truth is that when I checked the 'Travel Notes' folder, while you and he were still upstairs, I got a surprise. I found that the last time it had been altered was not given as the twenty-eighth of July last year at all, as we expected, but as the thirtieth of November this year, just over a week ago."

"What! But…"

"By a stroke of bad luck, Steve had put a Word document called 'Nobel lectures' into the folder during his recent lecture tour. According to his itinerary, he would have been in Moscow at the time. It was the day after Conrad had returned from Durban; the day you emailed Jane about your problem with penicillin. And in so doing, of course, he destroyed the evidence we were assuming would be there, so to speak."

"Sorry, I don't understand. If that was the case, how…?"

"Before Conrad came down, with the folder still open I went to the Control Panel and turned the computer's date to the twenty-eighth of July last year. Then I dragged the 'Nobel lectures' document into the trash, emptied the trash, closed the folder, and returned the computer's date to the correct one."

"What! You mean you fabricated the evidence?"

"More like resurrected it, I'd say, or replenished it. Otherwise the whole plan would have gone down the chute. Without that critical piece of evidence, of course, there wouldn't have been a cat in hell's chance of Conrad's continued support. Nor would there have been any point in my being here. As we'd agreed, coming empty-handed would have been a complete waste of time."

"There's no doubt about that. But what if we got it wrong? What if the evidence had not been there in the first place? We can't be *absolutely* certain, can we?"

"No, but we're pretty sure, aren't we?"

"Pretty sure is different kettle of fish from being certain though, isn't it? What if *Aphrodite* finds zilch tomorrow… assuming you get that far? What happens then?"

"I'll be up to my eyes in you know what, I suppose. But I thought it was a risk I had to take. Otherwise we'd never know. Did I do the right thing?"

Fiona was silent for several long seconds. The truth was she didn't know how she felt. But now was not the time to consider the pros and cons, or even to show a glimmer of uncertainty. After all, there was no going back, was there? And the last thing he needed right now was a dent in his self-confidence.

"Of course, you did the right thing!" she enthused. "I would have done exactly the same myself, if I'd been able to think as quickly as you did, which I very much doubt. You did brilliantly! You saved the entire project. You showed courage and decisiveness. It was nothing short of heroic."

"I needed that, thanks, Fiona. It's like a shot in the arm."

"And there's something else. Whatever happens, disaster or triumph, it'll make a great addition to your autobiography!

You can now say you've not only become a burglar, thief, and computer hacker, but also a fraudster. Not many Oxford dons can claim that. It'll sell like hot cakes."

"Ha! You may jest, but now I've reached the final scene of the final act, it feels very strange. It's like I've been dropped into a bog, quite honestly. With each step it gets deeper and more difficult to manoeuvre. Soon it'll be impossible to escape, even if I wanted to. One slip tomorrow and it would be good-bye.

"I was thinking about all the things that could go wrong—Gunnar Eriksson not being in his office when I call; refusing to see me because he doesn't have time; refusing to accept the evidence in the 'Travel Notes' folder; a problem with the broadband in Steve's hotel; Steve leaving his laptop somewhere…the battery being flat…and so it went on… and on."

"Giles, there's no point thinking about those things. They're all unlikely, and you can't do anything about them anyway. Don't get stressed over things that are not under your control. Just focus on the plan, and block everything else out of your mind. I've got a feeling it's going to be your finest hour.

"But if things do go wrong, if something unexpected happens, if disaster looms, remember you're a Brit— chest out, chin up, grit your teeth, stiff upper lip."

"All at once? They'll think I'm having a fit!"

Chapter Twenty-Eight

Despite many rehearsals over breakfast, Giles was resigned to the fact that his introduction to the Karolinska Institute's man of the hour was going to sound painfully stilted. Over the years, he had developed a routine to help him prepare for this sort of situation. Basically, it was an adaptation of the method he used for public speaking and important lectures. He would go through all the ways in which he could make a mess of it, and then consider the consequences of each. Invariably, it had led to the same conclusion: that it would not be a disaster, and what's more, it would quickly be forgotten anyhow. Although it had always served him well, on this occasion it had failed miserably for the simple reason that he knew it *would* matter. Unfortunately, there was no alternative but to pick up the phone, launch himself into it, and keep going. If he paused for a second, he was sure to lose his way.

After checking that the "Behaga stör ej" sign was hanging outside his door, to be sure he wouldn't be interrupted, he lubricated his mouth with a glass of water, made himself as comfortable as he could, and picked up the telephone.

"Good morning, Professor Eriksson," he boomed with the contrived self-assurance of a City estate agent. "I am Professor Giles Butterfield of Oxford University. I am terribly sorry to have to trouble you on such an important day, but I travelled a great distance yesterday in the hope of having an urgent meeting with you about something of extreme importance to do with Dr Stephen Salomon. I cannot divulge any details over the telephone as it is highly confidential, and am hoping it will be possible to meet you today as a matter of urgency."

"Gunnar's PA here, Professor," a young man replied. "I'll put you through."

Gunnar Eriksson listened quietly while Giles completed a much better rerun. Without pressing for more information, he suggested they should talk at one o'clock on one of the benches near the quay of Södra Riddarholmshamnen overlooking the lake. Although it was just a short walk from the Sheraton, he was sure they would be completely alone this time of the year.

While waiting for the right time to set off, not wanting to arrive too early or a minute late, Giles wandered into the hotel's lobby to try and relax with an anthology of Seamus Heaney's short poems. He'd been intending to read one ever since meeting the author during one of the College's garden parties, and had spotted it in the airport after waving goodbye to Fiona. Soon after making a start on The Skunk, however, he realised it was not the right moment for straying into such unfamiliar territory. Slipping the volume into his inside pocket for another day, he tucked Boris under his arm, and set off to brave the cold.

After stopping to buy a newspaper, he arrived at the quay several minutes ahead of time. As Gunnar Eriksson had predicted, apart from a few birds fighting over a crust of bread, the spot was completely deserted. Pulling up his collar, he strolled to the water's edge to contemplate the view of the City Hall again, but now from a different perspective. It was no longer its architecture that interested him, but its place in his life. For whatever the outcome of the day's events—triumph or disaster, pleasure or pain—it was destined to leave an indelible image in his mind.

Turning his back on the lake as a strong gust pelted his face with an ice-cold spray, he contemplated the row of empty benches before him, in the warmer months no doubt occupied by lunching office workers and tourists at this time of the day. His mind likened them to those of a courtroom awaiting the return of a jury. But in this case, the jury was to be just one person—astute, meticulous, analytical, critical, and no doubt very circumspect. Gunnar Eriksson would also be anxious, under pressure, and short of time. How was he going to react to what he was about to learn from an uninvited stranger—denial, ridicule, anger, suspicion…?

To take his mind off the prospect, he approached a small group of well-tended trees to get a closer look at a bird flitting among its branches. But as soon as he was within a few feet, it flew off to perch on the hat of the nearby statue of Evert Taube. Curious that a jovial balladeer, lute in hand, should have been placed in such a position, with no audience but the occasional distant ferry or lonely seagull, he wondered what had been in the mind of those who put it there. What did it say about the Swedish character? At a time when he needed a source of reassurance, the realisation that he didn't know the Swedes very well only heightened his anxieties about the coming exchange.

Moving to one of the benches, he dusted off its light covering of snow with his Herald Tribune, only to expose the lumpy sheet of ice that was yesterday's frozen slush. Unable to chip it off with a broken cobblestone, he resigned himself to sitting on the newspaper. As he folded it clumsily with stiff fingers, another arctic blast penetrated his clothing. He pulled his hat over his ears and tried not to think of Conrad in his rose garden.

Each minute seemed like an hour, until a tall, grey-haired man with gold-rimmed spectacles, clad in a Swedish military-style greatcoat and brown fur ushanka, approached from the direction of the bridge.

"Professor Butterfield, I presume?" he enquired sternly as he offered a hand, his equine face showing not a glimmer of a smile. "Sorry about the weather. It can be bitter here in December. But as I said, that's why I chose it. As you can see, there's not a soul in sight."

Seated side by side, Giles gave his account as quickly as his chilled facial muscles would permit. Listening to every word, Gunnar Eriksson said nothing, constantly staring at the snow between his heavy boots, his hands planted in his coat's deep pockets. Every now and then would nod or make a soft grunt, as if to provide reassurance that he was still awake. Only after learning about Stephen Salomon's 'Travel Notes' folder did he speak.

"You can show me that, I suppose?" he asked sombrely.

Giles patted his laptop.

"Yes, of course. It's in here. But I wonder if we could go indoors first. I'm worried my Boris is about to freeze."

Gunnar Eriksson looked up and tugged the corner of the Herald Tribune that was protruding from under Giles's jacket.

"You should have brought a few more of these with you."

"Ha…ha! No, you misunderstood, Professor," Giles replied, more than a little embarrassed. "Boris is my pet name for my laptop."

"That's what I assumed. I call mine Sven. In the middle of winter, I sometimes wrap it in several layers of newsprint. What did you think I meant?"

They made their way to a small but blissfully warm coffee bar, the "Toppen av isberget", and found a table behind a stack of cardboard boxes that once held bottles of Ramlösa mineral water. Gunnar Eriksson watched attentively, as he was shown how the most recent date on which the 'Travel Notes' folder was supposed to have been changed preceded the dates on which some of the files it contained had been created.

"You say you noticed this impossible situation, Professor Butterfield, when you were with Dr Weinberg?" he enquired, rubbing his chin thoughtfully.

"Yes."

"What did he say?

"Er…that he needed to talk to his computer people."

"Did he?"

"No."

"Why not?"

"I…er…told him we should keep it confidential for a while."

"Good! Quite right. And what did you do?"

"I got on a plane to Cape Town to visit my brother. He's an IT security expert. I thought I should talk to him in case I'd got something wrong."

Gunnar Eriksson raised his eyebrows.

"All the way from the United States to South Africa! Couldn't you have telephoned?"

"I'd been planning to visit him anyway. I go every year."

"I see. And what did he say?"

"He agreed with my interpretation."

"From what you said, you must have gone there about three weeks ago. Yes?"

"Yes."

"Why so long coming here?"

"I'm embarrassed to admit it, Professor Eriksson, but it took me a while to pick up the courage."

"I see. Understandable, I suppose, but regrettable nevertheless. All this puts me in an extremely difficult position. The ceremony is at four-thirty. I know less about computers than most children. What you've shown me is very worrying, of course, but it's not enough to call off the ceremony. Don't take it the wrong way, but for all I know this could be a hoax, or you might have got it wrong. I'm afraid I need much more than what you've shown me."

"Exactly what I thought you'd say, Professor. And as it happens, I do have more, or at least I'm sure I will very soon. Something that will make this smoking gun look like a kid's water pistol, and prove beyond a shadow of doubt that Dr Salomon is a fraudster."

Gunnar Eriksson went from grey to white.

"Well, if that's true, we chose a very appropriate place for our cup of coffee."

"Why is that?"

"'Toppen av isberget' means 'Tip of the iceberg.' So, where is the rest of this particular iceberg? And when can I see it?"

"To show you that, I need to get Boris online, and make a call to Cape Town."

Gunnar Eriksson removed his steamed-up spectacles, and wiped his watch with his sleeve.

"Ten past two already. Oh, dear! I need to get ready. We'll go to my flat. I'll ask Dr Henrik Olsson, one of my faculty, to join us. He knows a lot about computers."

After calling his colleague, Gunnar Eriksson hailed a taxi for the short journey to his apartment near Kronobergsparken in Kungsholmen.

When they arrived, Elsa Eriksson was getting ready for the ceremony. After apologising for answering the door in her nightdress and slippers, she led them to the living room.

"Henrik has just called," she said, combing her short blond hair in the framed Gustavian mirror that hung over the fireplace. "Said he'll be here in ten minutes. I've made a pot of coffee to warm you both up. Now I'll go and finish my face, if you don't mind."

Without visibly acknowledging her, Gunnar marched down the long hallway that led to his study, beckoning Giles to follow in haste. Upon entering, he swept the papers from his desk onto the floor, and offered Giles his chair.

"You can set up your laptop here, Professor. There's a broadband cable in the bottom drawer, and that's the outlet under the window. Give me a shout when you're ready. By all means use the phone too, of course."

When Giles called Camps Bay, Malika answered sounding very distressed.

"Malika, what's the matter? Are you sobbing? Why on earth…?"

"I'll hand you to Mr Conrad, Mr Giles. He'll explain."

After a worrying pause, Conrad took the phone, sounding tired and frail.

"Hi Giles. How are you getting on?"

"It sounds as if 'How are *you* getting on?' would be more to the point. You sound awful. And what's up with Malika? Are you both all right?"

"Just about surviving," Conrad groaned. "But everything will be okay, don't worry. I'll explain in a tick. Where are you?"

"In the flat of the Nobel Committee's chairman. He and his wife are getting ready for the ceremony. So far so good, but we don't have much time. What do I do?"

"Is Boris ready?"

"Yes."

"Good. So let me explain. *Aphrodite*, still snoozing in Steve's laptop, is a special type of Trojan backdoor, what's known as a netcat listener. She has a sister in my iMac, *Athena*—what we call a netcat client. When I wake up *Aphrodite*, the two of them will talk to each other over the Internet. This will enable me to send commands to Steve's computer and get information back. It's what's called remote command-line access."

"Will *Aphrodite* send the evidence to you or me?"

"Neither. It'll stay where it is. For this to be credible, the Swedes will need to see it all happening. My iMac also contains a GUI remote control package. With the help of *Aphrodite* and *Athena*, I'll install one part of it into Steve's machine. From then on, if all goes well, I'll have total control of his laptop. I'll be able to use my mouse and keyboard as if they were his, and my screen will show exactly what's on his screen. That's why I needed to be sure he wouldn't be around. It'll look as if his laptop's acquired a life of its own."

"Strewth! But how does that let the Swedes…?"

"I haven't finished. When your back was turned, I installed a VNC viewer in Boris. Everything on Steve's screen won't just appear on mine; it'll also appear on yours."

"Brilliant!"

After a few instructions about what Giles needed to do, Conrad dropped a bombshell.

"And there's something else."

"What's that?"

"I'm in hospital. Your call was redirected to my mobile. Malika's with me."

"What! Which one? Why?"

"An hour so after you and Fiona left for the airport, I started with bellyache. The GP sent me to Groote Schuur. They think it's my appendix. I'm waiting to go to theatre."

"This very minute?"

"Afraid so. I'm already on a trolley."

"Bloody hell! Conrad, you idiot! How many times have I've told you to have that damn thing taken out? But you never took my advice, did you? Rather listen to that useless GP. Irritable bowel syndrome, he said. Then it was a food allergy, then adhesions from your other job, then a virus, then stress—everything but the bleeding obvious. A third-year medical student could have…"

"Giles, calm down! I can cope, don't worry. I refused sedation. They're going to do it under local. So I can do everything. But we'll have to work quickly. They've moved me down the list twice already, and the surgeon's refused to do so again."

"Where's the iMac?"

"On my desk at home."

"At home? But what…?"

"I installed a remote-control package in my laptop, which I brought with me in the ambulance. And as the ward has wi-fi, there's no problem."

"Okay, Conrad, so let me get this right. You're going to use your laptop from a theatre trolley in the Groote Schuur Hospital to direct *Athena*…who is in your iMac on your desk at home…to communicate with *Aphrodite*, who is in Steve's laptop, currently presumed to be sitting in the Grand Hotel here in Stockholm, to set up a GUI remote control system, which will then enable you to control Steve's keyboard and mouse to search for the evidence we think will be on his hard disk? And we'll be able to watch everything as it happens right here in Professor Eriksson's study?"

"That's it. A kind of computer daisy-chain."

"What if they drag you off to theatre before we're finished?"

"I'd refuse, or take my laptop with me."

"They'd take it off you."

"They couldn't. Malika also fetched a pair of her hubby's handcuffs, and my laptop's got a security cable."

"You mean it's attached to you?"

"That's right."

"To your wrist?"

"That's right."

"Simple then…quite straightforward…nothing to worry about!"

"More or less. So, I'd better get on with it. As soon as it's up and running, I'll call your mobile."

At that moment, Henrik Olsson's red face and tousled mop of ginger hair appeared from behind the door.

"Professor Butterfield, isn't it? Sorry, I should have knocked. I'm Henrik."

"Delighted, Henrik. Fetch the Professor, will you? We're ready to go."

Gunnar Eriksson came running down the hallway in his shirt and socks.

"Sorry, but I'm getting late. The limousine will be here any minute."

Giles got him up to date before looking at the cuckoo clock on the wall. Almost three-twenty.

Gunnar grabbed Henrik's arm.

"I'll have to leave it to you, Henrik. But before I go, Giles, if I may, one question: how will Henrik know it's Dr Salomon's computer on your screen and not someone else's?"

Suddenly Giles could see the entire edifice crumbling before his eyes. Why hadn't that occurred to them in Cape Town? All those hours spent thinking about potential glitches, checking and double-checking. Even little Jabu could have thought of that one.

"Ha!" Henrik scoffed. "That'll be a snip, won't it, Professor Butterfield?"

"Er…absolutely, Henrik, a snip."

"Good! Skip the details. How will you get the answer to me, Henrik? I'll be in the Concert Hall by then."

"I'll send you a text message."

"But my mobile will be off."

"Leave it on. Set it to 'silent' for incoming calls and to 'vibration' for text."

"Yes, okay. Now I must get dressed."

He returned a few minutes later, grasping Elsa's hand.

"We're off! The limousine's here."

After hearing the vehicle move away, Giles took Henrik into the living room to give him the background to the drama—what he had found in Steve's office; the way Steve might have falsified his 'Achilles' file; how *Adonis* and *Aphrodite* had been planted in Steve's laptop; and what he had shown to Gunnar in the coffee bar.

No sooner had he finished than his mobile sprang into life. It was now exactly four o'clock. Conrad's voice was a little stronger.

"Everything's going to plan, Giles," he said calmly. "We're in good shape. Where are you?"

"In the study again."

"Okay, do what I say—nothing more, nothing less."

Within a few seconds of following Conrad's instructions, an image of Steve's computer desktop appeared on Boris's screen.

"Just look at that! Conrad, you're a genius."

"You can see Steve's screen?"

"You bet. But before doing anything more at your end, you'll need to show that it really is Steve's we're looking at."

"Of course. I'd assumed that."

Steve's cursor moved as if on a magic carpet to open the *Apple* menu and click on *About Microsoft Word*. A window opened:

> *"This product is licensed to: Stephen Salomon MD, PhD National Cancer Institute*
> Product ID: 82979-040-0046477-19146"

"That'll do nicely, thanks," Giles said, sighing with relief. "Now listen carefully, Conrad. Go to the *Apple* menu and open the 'Recent Documents' folder, then to the *View* menu at the top of the screen, and click on *As List*."

The pointer remained motionless.

"Well go on!"

Nothing happened.

"Conrad, can you hear me?"

No reply.

"Conrad, are you there?"

Still no reply.

"C-O-N-R-A-D......WHERE THE HELL ARE YOU?"

After a few seconds of continued silence, a weak voiced answered.

"Sorry, Giles. Doubled up with the most terrible colic and nausea. Thought I was about to throw up."

"Is that all? Thank God for that! I'll repeat what I said. Go to the *Apple* menu and open the 'Recent Documents' folder; then to the *View* menu and select *As List*.

"Okay, now we've got this far, my eyes will be closed from now on. The suspense is too much. Henrik, you keep watching the screen, please."

Giles rested his elbows on the desk, covered his eyes, and thought hard, knowing he needed to get it right without a single glitch in the short time available. The ticking of the clock overhead seemed to get louder with each second.

"The first column in the window will be a list of aliases," he resumed, "shortcuts if you're a PC person, Henrik, to all the files Steve has worked on recently. The next column will be headed *Date Modified*, and the one next to that *Date Created*. Each column will give the clock times as well as the dates. Now, if our theory is wrong, I repeat *wrong*, there will be only one alias there, called 'Achilles'. But if we're right, there will be two with that name. So how many are there?"

"Two," Henrik answered. "Wait a minute, two aliases with exactly the same name? I'm not a Mac expert, but is that possible?"

"Well spotted, Henrik! No, it isn't. Watch carefully. Conrad, drag both of them onto Steve's desktop, and look at their labels again. You'll now be able to see that one of them has a space after the word 'Achilles', whereas the other one does not. Right?"

"Right," Henrik echoed.

"Keep watching. According to our theory, the one without a space used to belong to an old 'Achilles' file that Steve later destroyed. If that's correct, when you double-click on it, Conrad, a message will appear saying that the file can't be found. Yes?"

"YES!" Henrik screeched.

"This is because once an alias has been created in the 'Recent Documents' folder, it stays there even when the file to which it is linked has been trashed. If you now put both aliases back into the folder, Conrad, you'll see that they have the same *Date Modified*, namely November 10—the date on which Steve did the dirty deed in his hotel, exactly one month ago today. You'll also see that the clock times of the aliases differ by a minute or two. Right?"

"Right!"

"So far, so good. Now let's turn our attention to the other 'Achilles' alias. This one should be linked to the 'Achilles' file that's still in Steve's 'Travel Notes' folder.

Don't double-click on it. Instead, just highlight it, then press the *Apple* and *R* keys together. The 'Travel Notes' folder should open with the icon of the 'Achilles' file already highlighted inside. If you now press the *Apple* key and the *I* key together, another window will open saying that the last time the file was modified was on July 30 last year. Right?"

"RIGHT!" Henrik and Conrad cried in unison.

"Got that? It says the file was last modified on July 30 last year. But as we've already seen, the last *Date Modified* of that file's alias is given as November 10 this year."

Giles opened his eyes to see Henrik's perplexed expression.

"The explanation of this anomaly, Henrik—are you listening too, Conrad?—lies in the fact that Macs with the operating system Steve is using update the *Date Modified* of an alias in the 'Recent Documents' folder whenever the file to which it is linked is opened, and do so at that instant…but the computer doesn't update the *Date Modified* of the file itself until the file has been altered and saved again. So if someone who wants to make a file look as if it was last changed on a bogus date opens the file, turns the computer's clock back, alters the text in some way, saves the file, and then returns the clock to the correct time, all in that order…"

"Although the file will have the desired false *Date Modified*," Henrik interrupted, "the file's alias will not. It will tell the truth. Wow! So he did exactly what you suspected, Professor. He tried to fool Dr Weinberg into believing he'd been working on *Deidamia* before his trip to Sorrento. But the truth is he hadn't. He'd learnt the details of the Bedouin's DNA switch from that website report, the one he'd obtained during the symposium, thanks to Dr Sharif's note on the back. Professor Butterfield, Conrad, you're geniuses."

"Conrad perhaps, Henrik. But me? No. All you've just seen was discovered by my wonderful assistant, Dr Fiona Cameron, late at night in The Jefferson hotel in Washington."

"Well, tell her from me I'm very impressed," Henrik enthused. "I hope poor Professor Eriksson will have the guts to go through with this. The king should be at the ceremony by now. Here goes."

Henrik grabbed his mobile. As his simple message in Swedish, "SKYLDIG," was already set up, he placed a trembling finger on the green button. He knew he was about to detonate the biggest explosion in the history of the Nobel Prize. Within hours, minutes even, its blast would shake the entire world, its fallout contaminate the scientific world for years to come.

He glanced at Giles for a nod of approval, took a deep breath…and then the phone rang.

"FAN!" he exclaimed, peering at the screen.

"Who the hell's that?" Giles screeched.

"Eir."

"Come on, man!"

"Eir."

"Er, er! For Christ's sake, out with it. Have you gone dumb?"

"It's my girlfriend. That's her name, Eir. She's Norwegian."

"Christ! Ignore it then."

"I can't."

"Why?"

"It'll be the result of her pregnancy test."

"Fucking…! Okay, leave it to me, Conrad. Must go. Call you later."

After finding Gunnar's number in his own phone, he fired off his message.

"GUILTY!"

It was out of his hands at last.

Chapter Twenty-Nine

It was the third time Henrik had looked at his watch since dropping into one of the velvet wingback armchairs that stood in front of the Erikssons' fireplace.

"Poor man!" he sighed. "I wouldn't like to be in his shoes right now."

"Misplaced sympathy, Henrik," Giles asserted from the far end of the room, where, too fidgety to sit down, he was perusing the bookshelf that lined the wall. "The man's a fool. He's only got himself to blame, and he knows it."

"Not Dr Salomon, sir…Professor Eriksson. I'm wondering how he'll handle it. What a nightmare! And this year of all years, the Karolinska Institute's bicentennial."

"He'll be fine. He's the strong and silent type. That's one thing you don't have to worry about. Your girlfriend's condition is another matter."

Henrik ignored the comment and kept his eyes on the ornate hand-painted Mora clock that stood beside the mantelpiece.

"He's just the man for the job, Henrik. Sober as a judge, cool as a cucumber, sharp as a needle, and steady as a rock. Totally unflappable. It would take a lot more than this to upset him."

"What do you think he'll do?"

"Stop the show, I suppose, call the police, and let them get on with it. Simple as that."

"The *police*! I hadn't thought of that. Of course, there's money involved, isn't there, apart from everything else."

Giles nodded sternly.

"Afraid so. It's not just a question of stealing intellectual property. We're also talking about fraudulently pocketing more than a million dollars. If you or I stole a small fraction of that from the Nordea Bank, we'd go behind bars for a long time."

"What a disaster!"

"For him, yes, Henrik. But for the rest of the world, a triumph. Not only will justice have been done, it will be seen to have been done in a glare of publicity. And you'll have played your part. Now, why don't you get on your bike, go home, and wait to read about it in the papers tomorrow?"

"And you?"

"I'll take a cab to the Sheraton, pour myself a strong drink, tune into CNN, and hold my breath."

"Not a chance! You can jump on my crossbar. We can be at the Konserthuset in fifteen minutes. You wouldn't find a cab this evening anyhow."

It was the most hair-raising and coldest journey Giles had endured since being persuaded against his better judgement to climb Mount Snowdon via Crib Goch one December day as a student. As they neared the Concert Hall, the howling sirens of police cars left no doubt that Gunnar had acted swiftly and with effect.

Giles pointed to a bus stop on Hötorget.

"Drop me off there, Henrik. I'll sit in that bus shelter and watch. Don't want to get too close to the action. Couldn't bear to watch him being carted off with his wife in tears."

Henrik did as requested before shaking Giles's hand.

"I need to go and see Eir now, Professor. Hope you understand."

"Of course, Henrik. Give her my best wishes."

"I shall. Thank you. You're an extraordinary man. I'm proud to have met you. See you tomorrow, I expect, somewhere."

After pushing his bike a few metres along the pavement, Henrik stopped to take a small camera from his pocket and swivel on his heels.

"Got you! You'll be famous tomorrow," he said, laughing. "This moment will go down in history."

Left alone at the bus stop, Giles raised his collar and tried to make himself inconspicuous, as he prepared to watch the dreadful scene unfold. Of the many people milling around the entrance of the building, he was unable to recognise any, even though he knew several colleagues must have been invited. After a few minutes, he spotted a man of Steve's height and build get into one of the police cars, before it sped off at high speed up Slöjdgatan. Several other cars followed in quick succession, leaving a small group of men in evening suits on the steps. They remained there until a black Daimler bearing two flags of the Swedish royal household arrived. Once that had departed at a sedate speed, everyone went inside again. A few of the lights went out, only to come on again when a white Volvo arrived to collect a lady and two young women, each wearing an ankle-length fur coat and stiletto heels. And that was it, at least from where Giles was sitting.

The dark empty silence that followed was a sickening experience for Giles. While his eyes remained fixed on the building's windows, hoping for a clue as to what might be going on, all that had happened since his hurried departure from Magdalen sped through his mind: the flight to Washington; reading the website report in Steve's office; his difficult meetings in Hank's office; Fiona's unexpected presence in The Jefferson's lobby; her brilliant work with Boris; lunch with the Weinbergs; the dash to Cape Town; and all that had happened in Conrad's villa. It was as difficult to believe it had happened as it was to accept that it was now all over.

After rubbing his numb hands together and stamping his feet back to life, he picked up the canvas bag Henrik had provided for Boris, and hung it over his shoulder. It was time to leave. As he had a pretty good idea of the route back to the Sheraton, he ignored an approaching bus and set off in the general direction of the water.

Upon arriving at the hotel, he went directly to the long gas fire in the bar to thaw himself out, inadvertently disturbing a young Japanese couple drinking tea. After warming his hands, he resisted the temptation to have a coffee, and instead made his way upstairs to get Fiona up to date.

"Hello, dear, it's me," he said, dropping onto the bed fully clothed. "You can relax. It's all over. Everything went according to plan, thank goodness. Your work was spot on. *Aphrodite* found exactly what you predicted. You're a hero. The ceremony was stopped, and a bunch of police cars arrived in next to no time. I saw it all happen from a bus stop."

"Was it difficult?"

"Not really. Pretty nerve-wracking, of course, after what happened in the villa. But the Swedes were fantastic."

"No problems?"

"Not here, but after you and I left Conrad, he went down with appendicitis. Poor chap had to do the whole thing lying on a theatre trolley, using his laptop to control the computer in his study."

"Oh, my God!"

"Exactly what I thought at first, but it went without a hitch."

"Did you see Steve leave?"

"I think so, from a distance, getting into a police car. But I'm not sure. I couldn't see much from where I was. I saw the royals leave, and also three women who could have been Marie-Claire with her daughters. No doubt the gory details will be in the newspapers tomorrow. Is everything okay in the College?"

"More or less."

"What does that mean?"

"It's to do with Aram, but I shouldn't worry you with it now. I'll leave it until you're here."

"No, if it's troubling you, fire away."

"Are you sure?"

"Yes."

"Well, the day before I left to join you in Washington, I asked him for a copy of an article by an Italian called Tommaso Fionda on gene expression in white blood cells. I wanted to read it for a review I'm writing. He emailed it to me the next day, but as I didn't need it in the States, I didn't look at it until I got here.

"Now, listen to this. What was attached to his email was a file called 'FIONDAT', which turned out to be his shorthand for 'Fiona's data,' which lo and behold contained all the results from my last five experiments. When I demanded an explanation, he said he'd meant to send me a file called 'FIONDA T'. The one he'd sent in error contained results he'd copied from my laptop when I was at one of those evening lectures on statistics. It seems in my rush to leave the lab, I'd left it switched on. He apologised and said he'd been so curious to see how his lab results compared with mine that he couldn't resist copying them. Even if I believed him, it would be inexcusable. But I don't."

"Why not?"

"Because when I asked him to show me his own results, he said he hadn't had time to do the experiments yet. No time in four weeks with the lab all to himself! And why did he need the results from my last *five* experiments? Surely, one at a time should have been enough. So out of interest, I called Sue Braithwaite in Cambridge, to see if she'd had any problems with their Alhazen fellow."

"And…?"

"She had. A while ago, he was caught listening to a secret recording he'd made of a confidential internal presentation of her work. So, I then called Abe Samuels in Birmingham, and learnt that a few weeks back, his fellow was caught photographing one of the pages of a PhD student's lab book."

"Sounds like a pattern."

"You can say that again. As you know, I've always had my suspicions about Aram. But now it's looking as if it's not just him. It's the whole lot."

Giles paused while he took it in.

"You know, now you've told me this, Fiona, I'm beginning to wonder about a comment Hank made about not trusting Steve's Alhazen fellow. I put it down to simple bigotry at the time, but perhaps there was more to it than that. Those chaps don't seem to recognise the sanctity of their colleagues' intellectual property. Perhaps it's a cultural thing."

"Or something else."

"What do you mean?"

"Perhaps the entire MECCAR organization is up to something?"

"Such as?"

"I don't know. But it seems very odd to me."

"Okay, let's not get carried away. Leave it with me, and I'll have a word with Aram as soon as I get back."

"Please do."

"I promise. Okay, now I'm going downstairs for a large D 'n' S. And then I'll get some kip, if you don't mind."

"Of course, see you soon. And well done! Kiss."

By nine o'clock the following morning, a crowd of excited journalists had gathered for a press conference in the lecture theatre of Gunnar Eriksson's department in the Karolinska Institute. Thanks to a text message from Elsa, Giles had got there in plenty of time. He tried to make himself small on the back row, huddled behind a copy of the morning's Svenska Dagbladet that he had collected on his way through the hotel lobby.

He had been there for only a few minutes, when Henrik's unmistakable mop and blue eyes appeared over the top of the newspaper.

"Didn't know you could read Swedish, Professor."

"Shh! I can't. I'm hiding."

"Who from?"

"Everyone. Publicity makes me nervous. If there's one thing I've never had any ambition for, it's celebrity status."

Henrik climbed over from the row in front and sat beside him.

"In that case, I won't…oh, never mind."

"You won't what, Henrik?"

"I'll tell you later."

"No, you won't. What is it?"

"I've just sold that photo, the one of you at the bus stop."

"To whom?"

"That newspaper."

"This one here?"

Henrik nodded.

"Can you make me out?"

"Quite clearly. Otherwise they wouldn't have bought it. Are you upset?"

Giles recalled Hank Weinberg's comments outside Sanderson's Bookshelf.

"Of course, I am. If it gets around that I'm the culprit, who knows what'll happen."

"The culprit? What are you talking about? You're a hero. Not a culprit."

"To you, Henrik, yes. To Professor Eriksson, possibly. But to Dr Salomon, his family, and his staff who are about to lose their jobs, to the top man in the NIH…and to a certain US president? What about them?"

Henrick shrugged his shoulders.

"I think you're overreacting, sir. And anyhow, there's no way you can hide from this, is there? It's far too big. My picture was only the first. There'll be many more."

"What a ghastly thought!"

Giles raised the newspaper to see if Gunnar Eriksson was in sight anywhere.

"I hope your boss doesn't see me. How's Eir, by the way?"

"Don't mention it. I've been up all night."

"No comment."

Henrik ignored the jibe as he read the newspaper.

"Wow!" he gasped. "Apparently, when Prof Eriksson got your text, he screamed 'stop everything!'—in Swedish, of course—just as the king was about to present the gold medal. It caused so much confusion he was almost knocked over. Apparently, when Dr Salomon got to the police station, he claimed the information had fallen into his hands by accident. Ahmad Sharif had given him the signed website report as a gift, he said, and it wasn't until he was on the flight home that he saw what was written on the back. From then on, he had an ethical responsibility, he claimed, to do the lab work and publish the results as quickly as possible, as it might save the lives of millions of people with cancer. He had no alternative but to pretend it was his invention, he said, as otherwise the Bedouins would have assumed MECCAR had broken its word. When he learnt about his Nobel Prize, he had no choice but to accept it, and his plan had been to create a new charitable foundation with the money.

"Do you believe him?"

Before Giles could answer, the chatter of the packed auditorium suddenly dropped, heralding the arrival of Gunnar Eriksson and his secretary.

"Okay, here goes!" Giles sighed, handing the newspaper to Henrick.

After introducing himself, Gunnar scanned the many rows of faces purposefully.

"Ah...wonderful!" he boomed. "There he is, everyone...on the back row...the hero of the hour. Ladies and gentlemen, it is my great honour to introduce you to Professor Giles Butterfield of Oxford University, to whom goes the credit for the extraordinary events that have brought you here this morning.

"Giles, Giles, come and join me! Tell us your story. It's only right that you should take centre stage."

As a barrage of camera flashes lit up the room, Gunnar raised both hands above his head and began clapping loudly, prompting the rest to do likewise in a tumultuous standing ovation.

The next hour of tributes, questions, and photographs, while sitting on a rather uncomfortable wicker chair, was an ordeal Giles would never forget. At the end of it all, as the reporters slowly made their way out, the occasional one stopping to pat him on the back, Gunnar approached with a broad smile and held out his hand.

"Well done, Giles!" he said with feeling. "It must come as a shock at first, I suppose. You crawl out of academic anonymity, like a snail emerging from its shell, to be tossed into a maelstrom. Battered on all sides by waves of questions, you feel yourself being drawn deeper and deeper into the depths of hell. You're not the type for this sort of caper, I know. Neither am I. But I'm sorry, there's no escape. You'll just have to face up to the fact that you're an overnight…"

"Celebrity!" Giles anticipated. "God, how I hate that bloody word!"

"Sorry, but that's what you are. So, you'd better get used to it. I've never been one, thank goodness, but I have learnt how to handle publicity, bad as well as good. As Chairman of the Nobel Committee, I've had a few ups and downs. As you may know, the Assembly's voting hasn't always been greeted with universal approval.

"If you want my advice, the best thing you could do is to get the next round of interviews behind you as quickly as possible, and then take a few days away from it all to recover."

He took a small diary from his waistcoat and fanned its congested pages.

"By the time you're back in your hotel, your voicemail will be full of invitations. I'll get Ebba here to extend your stay at our expense, to be sure you can fit everything in. Then on Thursday, Elsa and I will take you to our cottage on the island of Fjäderholmarna for a long weekend. How does that sound?"

"Wonderful, thank you."

Chapter Thirty

It was a week later, the nightmarish experience of seemingly endless interviews, press conferences, photo shoots, and receptions behind him, when Giles was relaxing in the dining room of the Erikssons' cosy cottage. As he enjoyed the warmth and crackle of the log fire, he watched the snowflakes settle on the conifers through the window, while his host set the table with his now familiar attention to detail.

"Gunnar," he opened hesitantly, "perhaps it's out of place for me to say this, but I've been wondering if it might be appropriate to give next year's Prize to Rashid Yamani, MECCAR's top man. What do you think? Somebody should get it for *Achilles*. I imagine Ahmad Sharif would have done so, if it hadn't been for his death...yes?"

Gunnar remained silent and expressionless as he carefully positioned a small bowl of African violets in the centre of the table.

"I'm sure you're right about Sharif," he said, stroking the velvet texture of the leaves with his fingertips. "Yes, he would certainly have been there the other day. What a tragedy his death was, a real tragedy."

The renewed silence that followed as Gunnar toured the room at a leisurely pace, drawing the curtains and adjusting the lighting, was not unexpected. Giles had learnt that one of the reasons why he was such a good committee chairman was that he never rushed into a decision or an opinion. But it was unnerving nevertheless. Was he angered by the presumptuousness of the proposal? Perhaps he should have kept his mouth shut?

"Have you thought about MECCAR much?" Giles followed up timidly.

"Many times," Gunnar mumbled almost inaudibly before turning towards him, "and quite frankly it worries me a little."

"Worries you? Why?"

"You were there, weren't you?"

"Pardon?"

"In Sorrento, when Ahmad Sharif was found dead in the pool."

"Oh…that? Yes, I was."

"It may surprise you, Giles, but when I first heard about it on the radio behind you, I wondered if he'd been murdered by a jealous scientist or for political reasons. What with all the venom between the United States and the Middle East these past years, and the embarrassment the White House had suffered, I didn't think it such a crazy idea at the time. I even wondered if Mossad could have been involved, given all those offensive things MECCAR had said about Israel's nuclear reactor in the Negev and its alleged effects on the local Bedouins."

Giles's mind jumped to Fiona's conspiracy theory back in October, to Mary's odd remark over lunch in Chevy Chase, and Hank's ominous warnings outside the bookstore in Bethesda. Was it possible the CIA was behind it after all?

"Were you still at the hotel," Gunnar continued, "when the maid found him?"

"Yes."

"Did the police question you?"

"It was the Carabinieri. No, they didn't."

Gunnar raised his bushy eyebrows.

"Rather odd, don't you think?"

"I'm not sure about that. They knew from his wife, who was in Lugano during the symposium, that he'd been complaining of jet-lag. He'd flown to Italy from Indonesia, you see. And there was an empty beer bottle on the table when the maid found him. So the Carabinieri assumed he'd had a drink to help him to get to sleep. Later, he went on to the terrace and caught his toe on the tiles around the edge of the pool. And as he was a non-swimmer, that was that."

"Rather clumsy, wasn't it?"

"They reckoned he wouldn't have noticed the tiles were raised, owing to the glare of the underwater lights."

"I see. But Muslims don't touch alcohol, do they?"

"They're not supposed to. But I know for a fact some do. Mind you, I wouldn't have thought Ahmad was one of them. That did surprise me. He seemed pretty devout. Earlier in the day, he'd been a little late for his lecture because of his prayers. And shortly after that, he'd refused a glass of wine in the bar. He even declined some olives because it was Ramadan. But there's no doubt he had been drinking."

"Why?"

"They found alcohol in his blood."

"I see. I suppose that clinches it then."

The two of them gazed pensively into the fire for several minutes. The first to break the silence was Giles.

"Actually, Gunnar, there's also something else that surprised me."

"Yes?"

"Yes. Apparently there was no drinking glass anywhere. Not even a used plastic cup, for that matter."

"That doesn't surprise me, Giles. You're old fashioned. Around here, lots of folk drink from the bottle these days. My Agata does it all the time. It's trendy, cool."

"The problem is I don't think you could say Ahmad was cool by any stretch of the imagination. How old is your daughter?"

"Twenty-eight."

"What does she do?"

"A banker. Anyhow, Giles, I don't suppose you and I should be worrying about these things, should we? It's not our job. We both have enough on our plates. But to return to your suggestion...yes, I do think it would be appropriate for MECCAR's Director to be honoured. But I couldn't nominate him. Someone else would have to do it, and pretty soon too. The deadline's just a few weeks away. Are you on our list of nominators?"

"No, but I know some who are."

"Splendid. When you get back to Oxford, round them up. That's your next assignment—although I can't make any guarantees, of course. At the end of the day, it'll be up to the Committee to decide whether to put him forward, and then up to the members of the Assembly how they vote.

"Ah, here comes Elsa with the meal. Let's prepare ourselves for tomorrow's hike around the island. You'll need some fuel inside you. Elsa thought she'd give you a local treat you won't have come across before. It used to be popular with the sailors around here. We call it 'lappskoj', the Germans 'labskaus.' You've probably never heard of it."

"Never heard of it? Ha! If I'm not mistaken, it's the original 'scouse', Liverpool's favourite dish. Wonderful stuff!"

***

A couple of days later, as his SAS flight made its way to London, it was with a renewed sense of optimism that Giles contemplated the coming days. After the ordeal of Stockholm, the long weekend with the Erikssons had done him a power of good. Refreshed and eager to return to his normal routine, there was much to look forward to: a quiet evening with Fiona recounting their adventure over dinner in a local gastropub; discussing her lab work in the morning; coffee in the Smoking Room with the newspapers; an afternoon with the students. Then, for the rest of the week, the pleasant process of rounding up support for Rashid Yamani's nomination. What an occasion it would be in Stockholm next year if everything went to plan. It would be more like the Mirbad Festival than Nobel week! How would the Swedes cope with that one?

He relished the thought of doing so many positive things again—his research, his seminars, the occasional lecture, entertaining foreign visitors—instead of constantly looking for evidence of skulduggery and trickery, lies, and deception. He couldn't imagine how detectives lived with it day in and day out.

And how did they cope when they were in the middle of one pressing case and another one arrived from nowhere…and then a third? No wonder Sherlock Holmes sought refuge in cocaine.

The only job he wasn't looking forward to was that of reprimanding Aram about copying data from Fiona's computer. Seeking a distraction from the prospect, he looked at the white fields below and contrasted them with the warm colours of the wine estates they'd viewed from the air during their ascent from Cape Town. Perhaps Conrad had been right about moving there. It wouldn't be too long before the Oxford dampness gnawed into his joints, would it? But would Fiona like it? Italy was much more her kettle of fish…and his too, for that matter. For both, nothing compared with the pleasures of a stroll down the cobbled high street of an old Italian town of a summer's eve, the swallows twittering overhead, the smell of espresso emanating from the bars, the pastry shops and restaurants tempting you every step of the way.

As he rested his head and pictured the scene, he felt an unwelcome tap on his shoulder.

"Would you like a drink, sir," a soft Nordic voice enquired, "beer, wine, coffee?"

He opened his eyes to see a tall blonde girl holding a bottle of beer in one hand and a small bottle of red wine in the other. As the beer was not one he immediately recognised, he took it from her to read its distinctive green label.

"It's Danish," she explained. "It's pronounced Svaneke Session."

His mind flashed back to the report in Il Mattino the morning after Ahmad's death. The very beer he had been drinking! Giles remembered it, as it reminded him of his first PhD student, Anneke Svensson.

"So, this is the stuff?" he murmured.

"Pardon, sir?"

"Sorry, dear. A friend of mine recommended this to me a few weeks ago, and I've never got around to trying it. So yes, I will, please."

As she continued on her away, his mind was transported back to Sorrento. Pushing aside the paper cup and napkin she'd provided, he took the bottle to his lips as if to re-enact Ahmad's last moments. A deep uneasiness gripped his stomach as he struggled to picture the scene.

"No," he thought, "Ahmad of all people wouldn't have done this, would he? Swigging it down like a city slicker or a soccer fan? Not a chance! Even in the privacy of his own room, he was too refined for that, wasn't he? He wouldn't have put a bottle to his mouth any more than he would have chewing gum.

He felt the same uncomfortable sensation welling up inside him that had become so irrepressible when his doubts about Steve had first taken root. It was if he had climbed out of a dark gorge into glorious sunlight only to put his foot on a pebble, and was now wobbling with nothing to grasp to prevent him from falling headlong into the next one.

His mouth drying, he took another sip before placing the bottle in front of him and addressing it in silence.

"Tell me…bottle…did one of your cousins have a story to tell before being crushed in a recycling plant somewhere near Sorrento? As it stood alone in the centre of that ebony table while poor Ahmad was in the pool, had it witnessed an event of which we know nothing, a dreadful horrible event?"

He knew exactly where it was leading. He'd been there before, hadn't he? The mystery that was tormenting his mind, the suspicions and speculations that were gathering like mists on a summer morn, the soul searching. He closed his eyes as he slid into the awesome reality.

. "It's happening again, Giles, isn't it? But you owe it to Ahmad, don't you? The facts just don't add up. And if you don't look into it, nobody will. As far as the rest are concerned, it's all over. To them it's history. But what *is* the history?"

As the stewardess passed again, he opened his eyes and turned his face towards the window. The clouds below, so white and appealing a few minutes ago, now seemed only dark and threatening.